The
Controller

J. Michael Aiken

www.thecontrollerbook.com

The official website of

The

Controller

The
Controller

This is a work of fiction. Names, characters, places, and incidents either are the product of the author's imagination or are used fictitiously. Any resemblance to actual persons, living or dead, events, or locales is entirely coincidental.

PUBLISHING HISTORY
First published August 2005

Published by
J. Michael Aiken
El Paso, Texas, U.S.A.

ISBN: 0-9771966-0-7

Manufactured in the United States of America

ACKNOWLEDGMENTS

It is with great satisfaction that the dream of publishing *The Controller* has finally become a reality. My hope is that the reader will find this book very entertaining and at the same time will understand the underlying message about the importance of honor in the midst of the ferocious warfare of global business. Laughter is such wonderful medicine for the heart, and I have endeavored to provide the reader with an abundant dosage in the pages of this thriller.

I would like to express my gratitude to the following individuals. First and foremost, I would like to thank my precious wife of 15 years, Belem, for her steadfast support in writing this novel. *Tú eres la mujer perfecta para mi. Te amo con todo mi corazón.*

I would also like to thank my children, Ana Michelle and J. Michael II, for their understanding during all the times when Daddy was in his home office working so diligently on this book. I love you both more than life itself.

A big tip of the hat goes to my editor, who also happens to be my mother, Betty Aiken. It seems like only yesterday, Mom, when I was a youngster sitting in front of the typewriter in the dining room working on newspaper articles for my column in the local paper, yet that was 30 years ago. Thank you for your encouragement, support, and technical advice throughout the years.

A special thank you is due to Jason Bonham, a young man of many talents and a fellow black belt in Hapkido. Jason, you did an excellent job of taking the image of the book cover pictured in my mind's eye and converting it

into graphical form. Thank you, as well, for the great work you did with the 𝕿𝖍𝖊 𝕮𝖔𝖓𝖙𝖗𝖔𝖑𝖑𝖊𝖗 website.

The following reviewers of 𝕿𝖍𝖊 𝕮𝖔𝖓𝖙𝖗𝖔𝖑𝖑𝖊𝖗 provided important feedback on the novel. Thank you to Belem Aiken, Christa Bonham, Jason Bonham, Justo Flores, Armando Granados, Enrique Pineda, Manny Rodriguez, Gus Sapien, Arvind Singh, Kim Steiner, Tim Vida, and Norma Vlieger.

In addition, the expertise of Randy Drake helped to bring more realism to the action scenes of the novel.

Finally, I would like to thank God for giving me the strength, courage and tenacity to finish this project in spite of the many obstacles I encountered.

J. Michael Aiken
July 25, 2005
El Paso, Texas
United States of America

The Controller

Chapter 1

The Door to Monterrey

"Final boarding call for flight 864 bound for Monterrey, Mexico," called the flight announcer in a rich, flowing Mexican accent so pleasing to the ear. "All passengers please board now."

The passengers flocked to the gate to present their passports and board the Boeing 737 departing from Houston, Texas, bound for the industrial city of Monterrey, Mexico. The announcer repeated the message in Spanish: *"Esta es la última llamada. Pasajeros con destino a la ciudad de Monterrey, México favor de abordar el vuelo 864."*

William Bradford Jenkins, or "Brad" as he was known to his family and friends, boarded the plane and took his seat in the economy section. Brad's youthful face and tall, athletic, body deceptively hid his forty-two years. Traces of grey, which highlighted all sides of his full head of brown hair, were the only clue that this financial executive might not be the young man he appeared to be at first glance.

There was a classic quality about Brad that seemed to transcend time. It was reflected in his refined manners, in his attire, and in his speech. He was a man *chapado a la antigua* whose traditional values were reminiscent of a time long ago when honor and virtue dictated one's actions. While there were those who spent a lifetime trying to acquire wealth, Brad had spent his life searching for wisdom. He was also a compassionate man who cared about others. This patriotic American had a steadfast belief in the importance of individual liberties. At the same time, he was ever mindful that individual interests were inextricably bound together and should be compatible with the greater good of mankind. Everyone who knew Brad Jenkins simply described him as a man of honor.

* * * * * * * * * * * *

This new job in Monterrey with AMA Electric International was the opportunity for which Brad had been waiting many years. He had been preparing himself for an expatriate assignment in Latin America since graduate school back in the late 1980s. Brad studied for his Master of Accountancy degree at a top university in Georgia. During that period, the mild-mannered accountant took some Spanish courses on the side in the university's language department.

Undaunted by the fact that he had never studied a foreign language before and that his Spanish classes did not even count toward his master's degree, he flung himself headlong into his Spanish studies. At the age of 25, he had discovered a love of learning foreign languages. Of all the languages he most wanted to learn, Spanish topped the list. Whenever he heard Spanish being spoken, Brad marveled at the beauty and richness of this romantic language.

After graduate school, Brad went to work as an auditor at the El Paso, Texas office of a major accounting firm. He immediately was assigned to audits in Mexico because of his Spanish-speaking ability. However, Brad tired of auditing after two years and went back to Atlanta to work for a manufacturing company. After six years with the same company in various domestic locations, he returned to El Paso to work for a company with several *maquiladora* manufacturing plants across the border in Ciudad Juárez, México.

A *maquiladora* was a Mexican company which enjoyed special customs and tax privileges. The *maquiladora* program allowed U.S. and other multinational companies to export machinery and equipment into Mexico without having to pay import duties. The machinery and equipment were exported temporarily but could reside in Mexico for a substantial period of time. *Maquiladoras* could also import most raw materials duty-free as long as the final product was exported from Mexico back to the U.S. or to some other country outside of Mexico.

The Mexican government began the *maquiladora* program in 1965 as a vehicle to create more jobs for Mexican workers. However, over the years it had developed into a huge component of the Mexican economy, with literally thousands of Mexican *maquiladora* factories located primarily in the northern part of Mexico along the U.S. - Mexican border. *Maquiladoras* provided manufacturing jobs to over one million Mexicans.

The building of these Mexican manufacturing plants also created secondary jobs in the companies that supplied goods and services to these *maquiladoras*. In effect, the emergence of this type of manufacturing had created a sub-culture within Mexico: the world of the *maquiladoras*. That was the world in which Brad Jenkins worked.

* * * * * * * * * * * *

That evening Brad arrived in the industrial powerhouse of Monterrey, Mexico. As he made the 45-minute taxi ride from the airport to downtown Monterrey, he took in the sights of this magnificent city. Monterrey had a rich history dating back to the sixteenth century. Located about 150 miles south of Laredo, Texas, and sitting in a valley surrounded by mountains, it was the third largest city in Mexico and the capital of the state of Nuevo León. Monterrey's climate was hot, dry, and desert-like except for certain areas such as the green municipality of Garza García, where much of Monterrey's wealthy resided.

Brad's taxi pulled into the Hotel *Regiomontano* around 8:00 p.m. The Controller checked in and had a quick, light dinner. Then he called his family back in El Paso, Texas.

"Hello," answered a little voice on the other end.

"Hey, Love. How are you?"

"Daddy!" his seven-year-old daughter Liliana exclaimed enthusiastically. "Where are you, in Mexico?"

"Yes, Sweetie. I just arrived in Monterrey, where your Mommy grew up."

"Yeah, I know. We are going to move there next week, aren't we Daddy?"

"We certainly are," Brad said in his warm, reassuring, fatherly voice. "By the way, Sweetie, remember that you are in charge of watering the trees this week while I am gone. You need to take extra care with the Italian cypress trees in the back yard. Being in a desert, they do not get enough water, so I am counting on you to make sure that they do not get thirsty."

"Oh, Daddy, I watered them today, all twenty-one of them. I counted them. It was easy!"

"That's great, Sweetie. Did you use the special nozzle that I use to ensure that you soak the ground with lots of water?"

"No, sir, I used something even better: my squirt gun!" Liliana said proudly. "I filled up my yellow squirt gun and then squirted each tree one time really well."

Brad chuckled to himself. "Sweetie, I'm afraid that one squirt from your squirt gun is not going to be enough. You need to use that special nozzle and hose the area around each tree with lots of water for about one minute, just like I showed you before I left. Do you remember?"

"Why can't I use my squirt gun, Daddy? It gets little Michael real wet when I squirt him!"

"I know, Love, but you need to give those trees a lot of water. They are very thirsty out there in the desert, O.K.?"

"Yes sir."

"Thanks, Love. I appreciate your handling that for me in my absence. You are getting to be such a big girl. I'm proud of you. May I speak with your mother?"

"O.K." Liliana turned her head to the back of the house where her mother was watching TV in an adjacent room. "Mommy, Daddy *quiere hablar contigo*," she yelled.

Unfortunately, Brad did not move the phone away from his ear in time to mitigate the boisterous sound of Liliana's exuberant call to her mother.

Within a few seconds, Brad's wife Sofía picked up the phone. She had tan, *morena,* skin, and her gorgeous, naturally curly brown hair fell onto a small, athletic frame. "*Mi amor, ¿cómo estás?*"

"Apart from the ringing in my left ear, I am doing great, Baby. How are you?"

"I miss you already. I can't wait until Friday so that you will be back with us."

"Friday will be here before you know it, *mi vida*. I plan on taking the early flight out…"

"Dad-dy?" said an innocent little voice on the other end. Two-year-old little Michael had picked up one of the other phones.

"Son! How are you, Big Guy?"

"Fine. Dad-dy, where are you?"

"I'm in Monterrey, Mexico, son."

"Oh," said the toddler. "Dad-dy, do you know what dis is?" Little Michael reached over and put the phone in front of his black Stetson cowboy hat. "See?"

Brad remained quiet on the other end of the line, trying to imagine what Michael was doing.

Little Michael put the phone back to his mouth. "Do you see, Dad-dy? What is dat?"

"I don't know, son," Brad said with a playful tone in his voice. "What is it, Big Guy?"

"My cowboy hat! Yook at it, Dad-dy! Yook at it!" Once again Michael held the phone up to his hat. "Do you see, Dad-dy?"

"I can see it, son, in my mind's eye. I can see a super cool, black cowboy hat. I like that hat."

"Yeah, I like dat hat, too. It's my hat, Dad-dy."

"It's a good hat, too, son. Why don't you put it on and go play cowboy with Liliana?"

"Yeah! O.K. Daddy," said the toddler as he scurried off to play with his big sister.

Brad continued chatting with his wife. As he listened to her talk, he closed his eyes and lay back on the bed. "I love to hear your sweet voice," he said out of the blue, catching Sofía by surprise. "Did I tell you how beautiful you look tonight?"

"Silly, you can't see me," Sofía said as she giggled like a teen-ager.

"I beg to differ, *señora*, and there is a two-year-old who will corroborate my position fully," Brad said teasingly. "Hmmm…I can see a beautiful, radiant smile, eyes that sparkle like diamonds, and skin that is as soft and smooth as silk. Wow…you are truly a sight to behold."

"Mi vida," Sofía said lovingly, basking in the warmth of Brad's romantic conversation. *"Te amo mucho."*

After a few more minutes on the phone, Brad said good-night to his wife. The well-seasoned accountant felt excited about the promise of things to come in his new job. He wanted to retire early that night so that he would be rested tomorrow and ready to start a wonderful new chapter in his life.

Brad had no idea what fate had in store for him as the door to Monterrey was opening.

Chapter 2

Meeting the Flamboyant Victor Reyes

The next day Brad arose at 5:30 a.m. and hustled down to the hotel gym, where he spent thirty minutes on the stationary bike. Even though there were several TVs turned on from which the morning news was blasting away at annoyingly loud volumes, Brad's mind was elsewhere. He was reflecting upon the challenges ahead as he embarked upon his two-year assignment in Monterrey as the Controller for the five manufacturing plants of AMA Electric International Corporation.

AMA was a fast-growing manufacturer of electrical products based out of Atlanta, Georgia. It had a relatively new management team in place, headed by Chief Executive Officer Rick Less. Under Rick's leadership, over the last two years AMA had grown dramatically through an aggressive strategy of acquisitions of other companies. During that time, AMA had established a reputation as a consistent performer with an uncanny knack for meeting Wall Street analysts' predictions for revenues and earnings quarter after quarter. While other companies in the electrical products industry were reporting either flat earnings or modest growth, "The Street" could always count on AMA to be leading the pack in growth and profitability.

Rick Less had become the talk of the electrical products industry. Industry publications hailed him as a superstar CEO able to carve out profitable growth in a mature industry through good, fundamental business execution coupled with brilliant management at the business strategy level. Rick had the demeanor to be a superstar CEO as well. He was a relatively young Anglo-American in his late 40s who boasted a slim and fit physique and boundless energy. His oral communication skills were on a par with those of a senator, a benefit of a strong liberal arts undergraduate education. Propelled by his articulate nature, street smarts, and an Ivy League MBA in accounting, the fast tracker had moved up quickly through the ranks in the finance area at another company before coming to AMA.

When the charismatic CEO first seized the helm of the company, AMA had sales revenue of $4 billion per year with only modest profits. The 75-year-old company was nearly debt-free, the result of many years of ultra-conservative management by prior administrations. Over the years AMA had accumulated $800 million in cash. Contrary to his predecessors, Rick had converted this $800 million into a war chest to support his strategy of growth through acquisitions. This strategy hinged upon successfully completing acquisitions of privately-held companies that were competitors or that offered a good fit with AMA's primary business of electrical products. Rick Less called these companies "bolt on" acquisitions. This strategy required utilizing the $800 million in cash as well as new capital from the issuance of stock to finance AMA's assault on the competition.

From the beginning, Rick's plan had worked brilliantly. As the AMA stock price moved up, management was able to make larger acquisitions by financing them in part with stock valued much higher than the $22 per share when Rick had begun his administration two years ago. Currently, the AMA stock was trading at $47 per share and moving up steadily. Internally, Rick had convinced all the executives that it was feasible to drive the value of AMA stock to $60 per share.

* * * * * * * * * * * *

Thirty intense minutes on the bicycle had left Brad feeling invigorated. The Controller hastened back to his room and showered, after which he ate a breakfast consisting of *huevos a la mexicana* and some fruit on the side. He then waited in the hotel lobby for Victor Reyes Cardoso, the *Director General* of AMA Electric International's manufacturing operations in Mexico. Victor had founded these manufacturing operations ten years ago. Then, under a directive of CEO Rick Less, AMA purchased the Monterrey facilities two years ago in an acquisition valued at USD $28 million.

"*¡Buenos días*, Brad!" Victor graciously greeted his new Controller. "I am so happy that you are going to be part of our team in Monterrey. *¡Bienvenido a México! ¿Hablas español, verdad?*"

"*Sí. Gracias*, Victor, I know enough Spanish to be dangerous," responded Brad jokingly, not knowing that one day those very words would come back to haunt Victor. "It is great to be here. I appreciate your coming to pick me up this morning."

Victor Reyes appeared to be in his early 50s. He was of short stature, around five feet six, and he was completely bald on his crown. Brad was surprised to see that Victor was bald, because most Latin men were blessed with a thick head of hair. Black hair did, however, cover the lower part of his head. His lack of hair on top was nicely balanced by a thick, black macho moustache. Victor was well-built for a man his age. He looked as solid as an oak tree with broad shoulders that tapered down to a small waist. Brad was sure that Victor lifted weights. *It takes a lot of hard work in the gym to be in that good a shape at his age*, Brad thought to himself.

There was no denying that Victor Reyes dressed to impress. That morning he had on a charcoal gray, expensive Italian-made suit. The amount of gold and diamond jewelry that Victor was wearing caught Brad's eye immediately. On his left hand he had a large, gold wedding ring with several diamonds set within the ring. There was another gold ring on his right hand. In addition, his starched and pressed, all-cotton, white shirt was highlighted by gold cuff links, also embellished with diamonds. As Victor gestured with his hands, his left sleeve crept up his arm just enough to reveal a stunning jeweled watch. Having witnessed Victor's stylish flair in his attire, it was no surprise to Brad when the valet pulled up in Victor's new luxury sedan.

"Company car!" said Victor proudly as they drove off toward the industrial sector of Monterrey located off Romero Highway close to the Monterrey airport. "You will get a company car, too, although it will probably not be as snazzy as mine. I have arranged for you to meet with the Director of Human Resources, Carmen Silva, to order your vehicle. Carmen is very good. She has worked for me for 10 years. In fact, all the managers and directors at the Monterrey facilities worked for me when I owned the company. They were all such good managers that Atlanta accepted my recommendation not to make any changes after I sold my manufacturing facilities to AMA."

That comment surprised Brad. *There were no changes in personnel in Monterrey after this became a public company? That is unheard of,* he thought to himself.

After a 30-minute drive, they arrived at the five-plant manufacturing complex. Victor explained that these plants formed a legal entity called AMA Monterrey. As was the custom with multi-plant facilities in Mexico, the administrative services were centralized in a shared services organization. That shared services group provided Mexican payroll, legal, customs, treasury, accounting, tax, information systems, human resources, and purchasing services to all the plants.

They made their way to Victor's office so that they could get to know each other better and discuss Brad's assignment in further detail. Victor's office décor was just as luxurious as his clothing and his car. As Brad entered the office, the commercial-grade carpet outside Victor's office gave way to a beautiful black, marble floor. All the wood in the office was exquisite, reddish-brown West Indian mahogany. Lining the left side of the office and running down about half the length of the room were book shelves and cabinetry, all hand-crafted with astounding detail. Off to one side Victor had a rather large, round conference table surrounded by four black, leather wing chairs.

Victor's desk was situated in the middle of his office. It was simple but elegant. He did not have a computer, which Brad noted right off the bat. When Victor saw Brad noticing his desk, he commented that he did not like computers and left the details to others. That's why he hired good people like Brad, he said, while patting Brad on the back. At the end of the office there was a large bathroom. The light was still on inside. The counter tops were granite and the faucets were brass-plated. In the corner of the bathroom mirror, Brad could see the reflection of a tall glass shower stall, also outlined in brass, and a mini-fridge. *This office must have cost a fortune to furnish*, he thought.

A tall, slim young woman with silky black hair and slightly tan *aperlada* skin entered Victor's office. She had on a light blue dress by Ann Taylor that subtly outlined her slim figure.

"Brad, I would like to introduce you to my executive assistant, *la señorita Lupita Anaya.*"

"*Mucho gusto, señorita.*"

"*Mucho gusto, Señor Jenkins*," she said with a pleasant smile. "I am happy that you will be working with us here in Monterrey."

"Please have a seat, Brad," Victor instructed graciously. "Would you like a cup of coffee?"

"Yes, that would be nice. I like it hot and black, if that would not be too much trouble."

"Lupita, *¿nos traes dos cafés, por favor?*" requested Victor.

"*Sí, como no, Ingeniero.*"

As they sipped their coffee from cups made of fine china, Victor opened the conversation. "Even though you did not interview with me in Monterrey, I reviewed your résumé and gave Atlanta my feedback. I was favorably impressed by your education and your work experience in Ciudad Juárez. You have a good understanding of the Mexican *maquiladora* manufacturing industry which I am sure we can put to good use here in Monterrey. I also understand that your wife is *regiomontana*—she is from Monterrey, right?"

"That's right, Victor. She was born and raised in this great city. That is one of the main reasons we are so happy to have this work assignment. Working in Monterrey will afford us the opportunity to spend a lot of time with her parents, and that is important to us."

"Ah, a family man. That's good, Brad. I'm glad to hear that. *La familia es lo más importante en la vida.*"

"That is certainly the way I feel, Victor."

"Brad, I would like to hear about your impressions of Juárez. You have worked there for many years. Believe it or not, I have never been to Juárez. I am curious to hear your feedback, as an American businessman, on Juárez as a Mexican site in which to locate manufacturing facilities. Monterrey competes vigorously with Juárez for foreign investment in the *maquiladora* sector, and I would like to know what we are up against."

"Well, Victor, I truly enjoyed working in Juárez during the years that I was there," the Controller remarked with conviction. "The people are warm, friendly and hard-working. As far as a place in which to do business, I consider Juárez to be an amazing city which is supremely dedicated to manufacturing."

"What do you mean by that, Bradley?"

"Juárez boasts mile after mile after mile of industrial parks and manufacturing facilities, including the largest industrial park in the world. People migrate from all over the Republic of México and from as far south as Central America to work in the famed *maquiladoras* of Juárez. Many of the engineers in Juárez are world-class, and some have even obtained patents on their manufacturing process designs for the U.S. parent company."

"*Ya, ya, ya,*" Victor said with a playful laugh. "You sound like a commercial for the Juárez Chamber of Commerce."

Brad smiled.

"What about the crime in Juárez? You know, the gunfights of the *narcotraficantes* in broad daylight and the murders of the young women."

"In my opinion *muy personal*, as a city of almost two million residents, Juárez does indeed have problems with violence, but so do all large cities all over the world. That includes cities in my own country such as New York, Chicago, Atlanta, and Los Angeles. I worked in Juárez for many years, and I always felt safe."

"You never were assaulted?" Victor asked.

"No. I never had any trouble because I stayed away from the drug world and avoided bad neighborhoods. That is the same thing I would do in Atlanta or any other large city anywhere in the world. It's just common sense, Victor. Look, Juárez governmental officials take the issue of safety very seriously. The livelihood of the Juárez manufacturing community depends on adequate security to be able to attract and retain foreign direct investment. For instance, the Juárez city government, in conjunction with the Juárez *maquiladora* association, has actually started a force of 50 industrial police officers that focus exclusively on policing the *maquiladora* factories to mitigate any crime there."

"That's interesting," Victor agreed. "Perhaps Monterrey should consider doing the same. But you still have not completely answered my question about the issue of the deaths of those 300-plus women in Juárez over the last 10 or 12 years."

"I am not trying to belittle the tragic deaths that do occur in Juárez. The murder of women in Juárez is a terrible situation. Quite frankly, I feel that there have not been enough resources and energy focused on stopping that problem. Some of my friends in Juárez are fed up with the government's inability to stop those murders and are demanding a more concentrated effort at the local, state, and federal level to stop these horrible crimes. The people in Juárez are tired of the finger-pointing between the levels of government. They want results now.

However, if you look at the statistics, you will see that there are far more deaths of women in other areas of Mexico, such as in Mexico City, than in Juárez. Also, of the 364 deaths that I have read about in the press, two-thirds of them have been solved and the criminals are in jail paying for their crimes."

"I understand how your friends feel," Victor said. "Unfortunately, those sick murderers are preying on women who come from very poor families, and so the repercussions are not as great as if they had killed a girl who came from money or killed a girl from across the border in El Paso. In business, if you have a major problem, you assign resources to that problem and you fix it, or you may go out of business. That is the beauty of free markets."

"That is a good comparison," Brad elaborated. "However, to be able to completely understand the crime in Juárez, one must recognize that most of the murders there occur between the *narcotraficantes* who are settling scores among themselves."

"Yes. They call that *ajustes de cuenta*," Victor added. "They are happening all up and down the border right now as the *narcos* are battling for power. I have read that there is a gap in power since some of the powerful leaders have been killed or jailed."

"That's right. It has nothing to do with the normal population and much less with the hundreds, perhaps thousands, of American *maquiladora* workers that go back and forth from El Paso to Juárez every day. My experience simply has been that the notoriety of Juárez for being such a dangerous place is exaggerated, and it is not fair to the *juarenses* to characterize their town as such. I am much more concerned about being assaulted or kidnapped in Mexico City than I am in Juárez. The lack of security in Mexico City is absolutely ridiculous."

"Yes, I see your point," Victor said. He was impressed by Brad's well-spoken and insightful comments. "Perhaps that notoriety has been unfair to Juárez, especially compared to the intolerable levels of crime in Mexico City. *Bueno,* if you don't mind, Brad, I would like to change the subject and ask a personal question."

"Go right ahead, Victor."

"I was just wondering, Brad, as to how a *muchacho* like you from Georgia ended up working in Mexico. What got you interested in this type of a career? When you were in school, did you study international business? I did not see that on your résumé."

Brad laughed softly to himself and looked down at his cup of coffee, almost embarrassed to answer. After a few seconds, he looked back at Victor. "I would like to be able to say that it was because I had a burning interest in foreign affairs or because I wanted to improve bilateral relations between our two great nations," he said with a chuckle. "However, if you want to know the real reason…."

Victor was smiling and leaned forward in his chair closer to Brad's face. "Yes I do, Brad," he said, intrigued by Brad's hesitation. The suspense was killing him.

"Well, the real reason, or as you say here in Mexico '*la neta,*' why I became interested in Mexico was because as a young man I was very attracted to Mexican women. I think that they are gorgeous. I was mesmerized by the beauty of the Mexican *morenas.* After I traveled to Mexico a few times in my early 20s, I decided that I was going to marry a beautiful, Mexican *señorita.* However, that was hard to do in Georgia, especially back in the mid-1980s. So, I came to the conclusion that the best way for me to accomplish that goal was to live and work in Mexico. That is what brought me to Mexico…originally."

"Hah-hah-hah-hah!" exclaimed Victor with joy as he slapped his desk. "Brad, you are a man after my own heart! So you came to Mexico to get yourself *una mexicana*. *¡Órale!*" Victor continued to laugh heartily. He could barely contain himself. This revelation warmed up the relationship more than Brad would ever know.

"That's right, Victor. I met Sofía while I was on an audit in Monterrey in 1990, and within 10 months we were married. That was 14 years ago, and I have been very happy ever since sharing my life with her. She is the perfect woman for me."

"Of course she is a great wife! She is *mexicana!* Mexican women understand what true love is, Brad. You chose well, *amigo mío,*" Victor said, thrilled with what he had just heard. He patted Brad on the shoulder. "I like you already, Brad!"

They continued talking about family. Victor also spoke highly of his wife of 31 years, Montserrat. She had come from an humble family, but through hard work she earned scholarships and obtained a master's degree in romance languages. Her native language was Spanish, but she also spoke fluent English and French. She had studied for two years in a private university in Paris.

"Not only is she multi-lingual, but she is also a gifted painter. She painted that picture behind you," Victor said proudly as he pointed to a warm, touching scene of an old man in dark clothes and a *sombrero* leaning on his cane while he walked along the side of a house. His faithful dog was walking alongside him. The house was an enormous Mexican *hacienda* with white walls and a reddish-orange tiled ceramic roof. The *hacienda* was surrounded by vegetation on all sides: bushes and trees, flower beds, and green grass. Brad nodded his head to indicate that he was impressed. It was indeed a beautiful work of art.

In typical Mexican fashion, Victor had covered the family first and now was ready to discuss business. "Bradley, as you know, Atlanta wants to move four more plants from the U.S. to Monterrey over the next two years. It took us ten years to get the existing five plants up and running efficiently. *¡Híjole!* Atlanta is expecting a lot, but I know we can do it!"

"Exactly, Victor, and that is why AMA hired me—to help with not only the transfer of the production lines but also with the business controls that accompany an effective production line transfer."

"Remember that this business had been a family-run business until AMA bought it two years ago. As such, we have done things *a la mexicana*," Victor laughingly exclaimed as he patted Brad on the back. "You realize that, except for the gringos…you don't mind if I say gringos, do you?"

"No, not at all."

"*Bueno*, except for the gringos that come here for a limited time with the production line transfers, you are the only gringo in the operations. Currently, we have 2,400 employees working in the five plants. With the transfers scheduled to occur over the next two years, the number will go to 5,000 employees. I am counting on you to do your part to fit in, to be a part of the team."

Victor paused and looked at Brad with earnest eyes. "Bradley, I cannot over-emphasize how important it is for you to be a team player. Your actions can help or harm the attainment of our goals in México. You realize that, don't you?"

"*Sí, señor*. I am very conscious of how important working as a team will be. I will do my utmost to be a team player."

"*¡Qué bueno, Brad!*" Victor exclaimed with great joy. He appeared relieved to hear Brad's comments. "That is exactly what I wanted to hear. Your wife is *regiomontana*, so I know you will fit in here. As I told you earlier, I have known the directors and plant managers here in Monterrey for many years. They are not just my teammates, they are also my *compadres*. With all the pressure we have and the work that is scheduled to be transferred to us, it is essential that we all work as a team!"

* * * * * * * * * * * *

Around noon, Brad's phone rang. "BRADLEY! How is your first day going, *amigo mío*?" shouted the voice on the other end.

Brad moved the receiver away from his ear a bit due to the shouting. It was Francisco Delgado, the Director of Purchasing. During the course of the day, Brad had also learned that Francisco was Victor Reyes' nephew. He was a relatively young man, in his early 30s, around five feet four inches tall with a robust waistline. The most striking features about Francisco were the utmost confidence he seemed to possess in himself and his wonderful sense of humor.

"*Oye*, Brad, the *compadres* and I are going to go out tonight to a topless bar to drink some *cheves*. Why don't you come with us?"

"I appreciate it, Francisco, but...."

"Paco, all my *compadres* call me Paco, Brad."

"OK, Paco" said Brad smiling. "Thank you for the offer, but I am not much of a fan of topless bars."

"*¿Cómo?* Brad, Victor tells me you like Mexican women, so come on and go with us."

"Paco, I have been off the market for over 14 years."

"Bradley, you are *never* off the market, *carnal*. Anyway, forget about the topless women. Just come with us to get to know the other *muchachos* on Victor's team."

Victor's team. There was that phrase again. "Paco, generally every night I work out at the gym. Why don't you come to the gym with me tonight? You may enjoy it, and we can chat there."

"What…are you saying that I am a *panzón*, Bradley? A fatty?"

"No, I was just wondering if you wanted to join me …."

"Don't worry, Bradley, I was just messing with you. As a matter of fact, I am a *panzón*," said the pudgy Paco, laughing heartily at the fact that he had put Brad on the defensive so easily. "Tonight I will add a little more to this big belly of mine drinking my *cervezas*. Why don't you forget about the bench press for one night and join us?"

"Thanks for the offer, Paco, but I really need to get to the gym and work out some stress."

"OK, Bradley. You work out stress *your* way, and I'll work out stress *my* way! Hah-hah-hah."

Brad smiled, hung up the phone, and went back to work.

Chapter 3

Who is this Gringo?

That night, while Paco and his *compadres* were having a rowdy time at one of Monterrey's topless bars, Brad took a cab to a local gym called "*El Cuerpazo*." He had seen the gym advertised in the business section of the phone book in his hotel. *El Cuerpazo*, loosely translated as "The Great Body" or "The Bod," was not one of those chic, upscale fitness centers that the yuppies frequented to socialize as much as to exercise. This gym was for the hard-core bodybuilders and other athletes who were interested in building their bodies into lean, muscular examples of what most people wished they could look like if they only had the time...or the drive...or the genetics.

These dedicated souls were the low-profile elite of the exercise world. They did not wear cute little outfits like those patrons of the upscale gyms. Instead, they chose to adorn themselves with loose-fitting garments that would accommodate their task at hand: to sculpt their bodies into the best that they could be.

Brad entered the gym and was greeted by a smiling man with a friendly voice. He was of medium stature, in his early 30s, and wore a short-sleeved shirt and shorts that revealed his well-developed musculature. Brad introduced himself and explained that he was here on business this week and wanted to get in a few good work-outs. The man said his name was Rogelio and he was the owner/manager of *El Cuerpazo*. Rogelio complemented Brad on his good Spanish.

Normally Rogelio charged 50 pesos for non-members to work out, but he would let Brad work-out for 35 pesos. "You are the only *norteamericano* I know that speaks Spanish," he joked. "So, I'll give you a discount for that. *¿Te parece?*"

Brad thanked him and asked where he could sign in. Rogelio grabbed the pen, and Brad noticed the formidable trapezius muscles that flowed from the top of Rogelio's neck down to his broad back and cantaloupe-sized shoulders. Brad took the pen from Rogelio and caught a glimpse of his well-defined, massive arms.

"Are you a professional bodybuilder?" Brad asked in his easy-going nature.

"I used to compete back in the '90s," Rogelio said. He pointed behind the counter to a cement wall with several pictures of himself posing for the judges in various bodybuilding tournaments in Mexico. "I won Mr. Nuevo León in 1997 and '98," he said proudly. "Then, I got married, had kids, and wanted to do something that would allow me to spend more time with my family. So, I opened a gym. I won't get rich, but I am happy and so is my family."

Brad smiled. He knew exactly what Rogelio was talking about, and he was uplifted to hear such a macho-looking guy talk about how important his family was to him. "It seems to me that you already are rich, Rogelio," Brad said matter-of-factly. "You have your health, a family that loves you, and you are your own boss. You are rich in the things in life that really matter."

"*Gracias, Brad*. Have a good work-out," Rogelio said as he rang up the sale on his electronic cash register.

"*Muchas, gracias, Rogelio. Con permiso.*"

Brad had already changed into his work-out clothes back at the hotel, so he was ready to hit the weights. He saw a bench press available and made his way toward the exercise floor to begin his work-out. The Controller was on a push-pull-legs routine, which was a weight-lifting routine that grouped the exercises by movement. Today he was working the "push" muscles which included the chest, shoulders, and triceps.

After spending a generous amount of time stretching, he began with a warm-up set of 135 pounds on the bench press. Brad moved up progressively in weight on each set, topping out at 315 pounds. He struggled and grunted to get that up five times. He had to be careful because, unlike the guys next to him, he had no partner. From the bench press, he moved to dumbbell presses, and then to dumbbell flyes. He worked his chest vigorously, not like a 42-year-old executive but rather more like a young boxer training for a championship fight with a hunger to get stronger. As a middle-aged man, Brad knew he could not beat the clock, but he could certainly slow it down by taking care of himself.

By the time he reached the incline bench press, his body heat had gone up and he had broken a sweat. He took off the baseball shirt which had been covering his tank-top shirt. Now more of his body was exposed. His well-chiseled, youthful-looking body and handsome American face caught the eyes of a couple of nice-looking, well-endowed, athletic women in the gym. They began gazing at him flirtatiously.

"*¿Quién es este gringo?*" they wondered to themselves, smiling and gawking at Brad with inviting eyes. They were wasting their time, however. Brad was oblivious to their stares. He only wanted to please one woman—his loving wife of 14 years—Sofía. All other female eyes, however beautiful and tempting they might be, were simply irrelevant to him.

Brad completed his routine with cable crossovers and dips. The Controller then walked over to the desk where Rogelio was making a protein shake for another one of his customers. "*Oye*, Brad, would you like to try a protein shake? It's only 20 pesos, and it's made with 100% whey protein. That's a high-quality protein source. I'll throw a banana in there to give it more taste and add some carbs. *¿Te gustaría?*"

"That's sounds great, Rogelio." Brad gulped down the nutritious protein shake, relishing the satisfaction of having pushed himself so hard during his exercise. His body was drenched in sweat and he was tired, but it was a good kind of tired. He smiled to himself. *No, you can't beat the clock, Brad my boy, but you can certainly slow it down.*

* * * * * * * * * * * *

Rogelio had been nice enough to call a taxi for Brad. On his way out to the parking lot to wait for the taxi, Brad heard someone off in the distance. He walked a little further, and heard the voice again. It was a woman screaming!

"*¡Auxilio!* Help me!" she cried out.

Brad ran around the corner to the back of the gym where he heard the screaming, and he saw an older woman on the ground being kicked by two young Mexican men. He yelled at them as he raced over to help the poor woman: "Hey! *¡Déjenla en paz!* Leave her alone!"

As he came closer, he saw that the two men were actually teen-agers. One was well over six feet tall and of medium build while the other was around Brad's height and rather thin. They had various tattoos on their bodies and looked like gang members.

Brad approached them cautiously, not knowing if they had guns. "Why are you beating up this lady? Are you out of your mind? Leave her alone and get out of here!" Brad chastised them.

"*Mira, gringo,*" the shorter one said, "why don't you get out of here before you get hurt?"

"Yeah, scram!" yelled the tall one.

By now Brad could see that neither of the two punks had a gun. The short one was carrying a knife and the taller one was carrying a Japanese nunchaka composed of two sticks joined by a chain. "*Por favor, señor, ¡ayúdeme!*" cried out the desperate older Mexican woman, still lying on the ground.

"Grab his bag, Marco!" the shorter one ordered. The taller punk, Marco, began swinging his nunchakas back and forth. He was trying to scare Brad and set himself up to strike him in the head. Brad, a black belt in the deadly martial art of Hapkido, immediately shifted into a fighting stance and began moving around to make himself a more difficult target.

"Oh, a tough guy, eh?" said the tall punk Marco. "Do you want some of me, gringo? Well, I hope you have medical insurance!" Both thugs laughed heartily at Brad.

Unknown to them, Brad worked out frequently with nunchakas. He knew how the nunchakas moved and he knew how to move them. Marco advanced toward Brad and swung the nunchaka at his head. Brad quickly side-stepped the nunchaka and delivered a crushing side kick into Marco's ribs after the nunchaka went by his head. Brad followed up with another side kick to the side of Marco's right knee, fracturing his leg just below the knee cap. Marco fell down on his right knee and dropped the nunchakas as he screamed in pain with a flurry of vulgarities directed toward Brad.

With lightning reflexes, Brad moved in to grab the nunchakas. However, the other gangbanger with the knife moved in quickly.

"*¡Cuidado, señor!*" warned the *señora*, terrified by what was happening.

The smaller punk was coming at Brad with the knife, so Brad jumped at the nunchakas, grabbing them as he did a forward roll. His momentum carried him back up to his feet, and he quickly turned around and held the nunchakas straight out in front of him. The thug advanced toward Brad, preparing to stab him in the chest with an overhead knife strike. As the attacker's knife moved down toward Brad's chest, Brad blocked the knife with the chain part of the nunchakas and kicked the punk in the abdomen, knocking the wind out of him. Then, with his right hand he whipped the nunchakas around to the right and struck the young hoodlum in the head with great speed, rendering him unconscious. The hood fell to the ground.

"Look out!" screamed the older lady again. Marco, the tall gangbanger whose right leg was broken, had managed to pull a knife out and was crawling over to stab Brad. Brad spun around and gave Marco a swift roundhouse kick to the head, knocking him unconscious.

Suddenly, out of nowhere, a stocky Mexican man rushed Brad from behind. This man was several years older than the first two, perhaps the leader of the gang. No sooner had Brad turned around than the stocky man grabbed Brad in a ferocious bear hug. He lifted Brad up off the ground and squeezed Brad with the crushing strength of a python. Brad was in trouble. He could not expand his lungs to breathe.

Instinctively, Brad slapped both ears of his stocky attacker with the palms of his hands, stunning his strong attacker. The *bandido* loosened his grip on Brad somewhat, but not completely. Brad hit him again even harder with the same double-palm strike to the ears. The blow was so hard that he burst the eardrums of both ears of his attacker. Blood began to trickle out of the stocky *bandido*'s ears.

Brad followed that second palm strike by raking his fingers down across the face of the stocky attacker, scratching his eyes. The *bandido* let go of Brad, and Brad landed on his feet. Like greased lightning, Brad then kicked his stocky attacker in the groin with a front snap kick. The stocky guy bent over with his hands over his groin, moaning in tremendous pain. To finish off the *bandido*, Brad drove his knee into the man's face, breaking his jaw and sending him flying backward to the ground. Brad looked around, surveying the situation. All scumbags were accounted for and rendered helpless.

The Controller picked up the lady's purse and walked over to her. When Brad came close to her, he was astonished by how strikingly attractive this older woman was.

"*Muchas gracias, señor. Que Dios lo bendiga,*" she said gratefully as Brad helped her to her feet.

The poor victim appeared to be in her mid to late fifties, but the years had been kind to her. She was tall for a Mexican woman, and she had obviously taken good care of herself. Her clothing suggested that she was a woman of meager means, yet her simplicity could not hide her abundant beauty. She wore very little make-up on her *morena* skin. Her smooth and youthful complexion needed little else. Nature had done the rest. She had a figure of which many girls half her age would have been envious. Brad thought to himself that in her day she must have been a real knockout.

"What is your name?" she inquired, revealing a lovely smile.

"Brad Jenkins," he replied, still trying to catch his breath from the rigor of the fight.

"Brad Jenkins," she repeated his name. She glanced at Brad's shoulders, arms and chest and saw that he was solid as a rock. *"Mucho gusto, Señor Jenkins.* I am Aurora Loya."

"Mucho gusto, Señora Loya."

They made their way toward the front entrance of the gym, leaving the thugs lying lifelessly on the pavement.

Rogelio was at the front desk when they walked into the gym. Brad explained what had happened, and immediately Rogelio instructed several big bodybuilders to go out to the parking lot to take care of the three ruffians while he called the police. Within minutes police arrived on the scene.

Señora Loya was a kind lady who had been walking home from the bus stop after visiting her daughter-in-law in the hospital. She explained to the police that her daughter-in-law had just given birth to a baby boy. The hoodlums had followed her from the bus and attacked her behind the gymnasium building, and then this nice American came to her rescue. Brad gave his statement to the police. Then the police carried the *bandidos* off to jail.

While she was lying down on the ambulance stretcher, *Señora* Loya turned to thank Brad for his bravery. Fortunately, she had only suffered a couple of scrapes and bruises. *"Señor* Jenkins, thank you again for rescuing me. You were my guardian angel tonight. I will not forget you."

"Any gentleman would have done the same, *Señora*," Brad said modestly. "Do you need me to call anyone for you?"

"*Muchas gracias*. They are taking me to Santa Cruz Hospital, the same hospital where my daughter-in-law is. There are family members there already. Besides, I just have some minor cuts and bruises. I really should not even go to the hospital. It's a lot of fuss for nothing."

"Very well, *Señora*. I shall retire to my hotel. I hope that you recover quickly," he said with a warm smile.

Señora Loya, with tears in her eyes, smiled as she was loaded into the ambulance. Rogelio looked at Brad. "Brad, did you take out those three gang bangers all by yourself?" he inquired.

Brad, always humble, just smiled and modestly nodded his head. "You would have done the same thing, Rogelio."

"You're a good guy, Brad. Most people wouldn't have stuck their neck out like that, even for an older lady like this *señora*."

"Yeah, well, it looks like my workout tonight was more than I bargained for," Brad said with a wink and a smile.

"That's right, Bradley. You came here to work your chest, shoulders and triceps, but you ended up with a full body workout. We always give you your money's worth at *El Cuerpazo!*" Rogelio said jokingly.

Just then, Brad's taxi arrived. "We'll see you tomorrow, Rogelio. It will be back and biceps night," Brad said as he boarded his taxi.

"*Sí*, Brad, *hasta luego*."

* * * * * * * * * * * *

The following day Brad asked all of the members of the finance team to meet with him in the second floor conference room so that he could properly introduce himself. As Controller of AMA Monterrey, S.A. de C.V., he was responsible for the cost accounting which was performed at the plants and for most of the Mexican shared services center which was located in the primary building of the AMA Monterrey campus. A total of 33 people reported to him.

Me da mucho gusto tener la oportunidad de trabajar con ustedes," he told his staff. He continued in his best Spanish: "I believe that as accountants our most important job is to tell the truth. Always."

He stopped speaking so that the gravity of his admonition could sink in. Silence seized the room. As he looked at his group, he saw puzzled looks on some faces, blank stares on others, and a few people who were nodding and smiling. Many of them were unnerved by the fact that the corporate office had sent an American to Monterrey rather than hire a Mexican national.

"How do we do that?" Brad asked.

Finally, a man in the back of the room raised his hand. "We need to make sure that our accounting records are correct and that they report what is really happening in our business," he said with confidence.

"That's right," Brad replied approvingly. "What is your name?"

"Javier Peralta. I am a cost accountant."

"Very good, Javier. That is exactly what I was driving at with my question." Brad continued. "Financial reporting and capitalism itself depend on trust. Think about it for a moment. Our neighbors, our parents and grandparents, members of our armed forces—people from all walks of life invest in the stock market to help provide for their financial future. Some of them invest in

AMA Electric International stock. These same people that invest their hard-earned money in the stock market are counting on us, the accountants, to report the truth in the financial statements. That means that a spirit of transparency should guide every journal entry that we make in the accounting records and every line and footnote that we prepare in the financial statements. The American public trusts us, and we must never violate that trust. *Gracias*."

A look of pleasant surprise overtook the finance team as they heard the message. They were caught off guard by Brad's forthrightness. "Who is this gringo?" a couple of them whispered. It was not what they were accustomed to in Mexico. Nor was this *norteamericano* the stereotypical American whom they had read about in the Mexican press and seen in American movies. As they made their way out of the second floor conference room and went back to their desks, a renewed spirit of optimism permeated the office. There was a promise in the air that business would be different at AMA Monterrey beginning that day.

* * * * * * * * * * *

Later that day Brad decided to walk downstairs to meet with Carmen Silva, the Director of Human Resources, about his company car. Carmen was in her late 40s, although she made it a point to tell everyone that she was in her late 30s. She did not fool anyone, however. Over time her exaggerated use of facial expressions and years of exposure to the sun had taken a heavy toll on what was once a youthful, attractive, *morena* face. She tried to compensate for her faded beauty by applying an excessive amount of expensive make-up that mercifully began to fade as the day wore on.

Perhaps her most notable feature was her hypnotic snake eyes. They were dark and full of evil, with an almost elliptical pupil, just like the eyes of a pit viper.

Carmen was well-endowed and liked to flaunt what she had with low-cut blouses. She was very proud of this feature and loved to get close when talking with others to give them a full view of her décolletage. As time passed, however, she had added several pounds each year so that now she carried about 30 pounds of excess weight for her five-foot six-inch frame. The tight skirts she wore only accentuated her excess weight and tasteless image.

From the start, there was something about Carmen Silva's nature that made Brad feel uncomfortable. She was pushy and controlling. Her smile looked forced and unnatural, somewhat like the smiles of most politicians. She would produce that smile whenever she felt like she needed to make a point or convince someone of her position.

Carmen showed Brad brochures of the company cars from which he could choose. She showed him several nice, sporty-looking foreign luxury coupes. Brad shook his head at each one. He indicated instead that he would prefer a less-elegant, mid-sized car as his company car, something that was economical yet reliable. The Controller chose a gold-colored, four-door American sedan with a six-cylinder, 3.6 liter engine. The vehicle had a spacious interior and offered good value without sacrificing performance. By choosing this as his company car, the value-conscious executive would be making the right statement to the rest of the directors and the employees: we operate a lean, tight ship here. We want good value for our shareholders' money, and luxury items are not a part of that equation.

"Why do you want a car like that, Brad?" Carmen asked, clearly puzzled and noticeably irritated. "You can have a much nicer car than what you selected. You are the top finance person here. Get something really nice for yourself. You know that status is very important in Mexico."

Brad was slightly perturbed at Carmen's insistence. "Carmen, I just think that there are better uses of the company's money than to spend it on a fancy car for me," Brad said diplomatically. "Besides, you are defined by your actions, not by your car."

Carmen looked at Brad, surprised by his response and once again manufacturing her trademark fake smile. She tried relentlessly to convince him to select a certain expensive make and model which she felt went well with his sporty, athletic nature.

Brad was beginning to lose patience with her. *Man, she is pushy*, he thought. "Please, Carmen, let us not quarrel on such short acquaintance. I ask that you respect my decision. Now if you don't mind, I shall return to my work."

"*Muy bien*, Brad. If this is what you want, I will order it for you," she said with a frustrated voice. She was not used to losing arguments.

After his meeting with Carmen, Brad walked back upstairs to his office and began going through old files to acclimate himself to all the issues left pending by his predecessor. Brad later learned from Javier Peralta, the cost accountant, that Carmen Silva had a terrible reputation within the company. "Be careful with her," he warned. "None of her people can stand her. She is not the kind of woman that you would want to take home to meet your mother."

"Do you mean to say that she is a woman of unchaste character?"

"Well, yes, that, too," Javier said with a laugh, "although that was not the word I was thinking of. A very descriptive word for her comes to mind, but I try to refrain from using it unless I am in a kennel."

Brad nodded his head. He understood the message perfectly.

Chapter 4

The Lovely Lolita Loya

At 3:00 p.m. Wednesday of his first week Brad walked down to the first floor to meet with the *Director General*, Victor Reyes. Lupita Anaya, Victor's assistant, greeted Brad with an energetic and cheerful "*¡Hola!*" and asked him to wait. She always brightened up when Brad was around. You could see the enthusiasm in her eyes. About five minutes later, Victor came walking out.

"Bradley. Please, come on in," he beckoned.

After they had been comfortably seated, Victor opened up the dialogue: "Bradley, I wanted to talk with you briefly about our forecasting accuracy. My boss is Harry Allen, the Chief Operating Officer in Atlanta. Well, Harry has been on my case about the lack of accuracy in our monthly forecasts. Apparently, we can never seem to come close to our monthly forecasted numbers. Sometimes we do much better, and sometimes we do much worse. However, we seldom approach what we say we are going to do. Harry says that if we cannot accurately forecast our operations then we are not in control of the operations. Would you work with your people so that they can get it right for once? They are making me look bad."

"Sure, Victor. I will put that at the top of my list. I would like to add that…"

Victor's cellular phone rang.

"*Perdón*, Bradley. *Bueno*. No, I cannot talk right now. I'll call you back. Where are you? OK. *Adiós*." Victor returned his attention to Brad. "I am sorry, Bradley, what were you saying?"

"I was just saying that my experience with improving the accuracy of our forecasts and budgets has been to first reach an understanding with the plant manager that the forecast is a commitment from that plant manager. In order to prevent the forecast from being 'accounting's numbers' rather than a commitment from the entire plant, the plant manager and his staff must be intimately involved with its preparation and review."

"Yes, that sounds reasonable. You should get the plant managers involved, too."

Once again the cellular phone rang. This time Victor appeared to be talking to his wife, but the voice sounded very young. Brad detected a flirtatious overtone in Victor's voice as he chatted with the mysterious caller. Victor quickly terminated the phone call, this time a little embarrassed.

"*Muy bien*, Brad. I am counting on your help. Remember, be a team player," Victor emphasized with conviction as he placed his arm on Brad's shoulder. "That is the most important thing that I ask of you—to be a team player. Right now I have to visit one of our vendors, so please excuse me."

Victor left the office hastily, leaving Brad sitting there. Brad stood up and headed for his office. As he passed by Lupita's desk, she could not hide the fact that she felt uncomfortable about the impolite gesture of her boss. She had an idea where Victor was headed, but she kept quiet as usual. Lupita needed her job.

* * * * * * * * * * * *

After the meeting with Victor Reyes, Brad was making his way through the office to his door when his secretary Leticia stopped him.

"You have a telephone call from the United States, *Señor* Jenkins," she informed.

"*Gracias*, Leticia. Who is it?"

"It is your daughter."

"Please, transfer the call to me. I hope nothing is wrong." Brad scrambled into his office, his heartbeat increasing rapidly. *Why is Liliana calling me? What has happened?* He breathed deeply, trying to calm himself.

The phone rang in his office, and he picked it up quickly.

"Brad Jenkins." The concern in his voice was quite noticeable. On the other end of the phone all he heard was giggling. "Liliana, is that you?"

"Yes, Daddy," she said, trying to recover from her silly laughter. "You sound so funny. Why did you answer the phone that way? Why don't you just say 'this is Daddy'."

"Sweetie, that is just the way I answer the phone at work," he replied, still worried about the nature of the call. "Is everything all right, Love?"

"Yes, sir. Why?"

"Sweetie, this is an international call, so I was worried that something was wrong. Where is Mommy?"

"She is looking for Michael. But I know where he is. He is hiding behind the sofa so he can do pooh-pooh without anybody seeing him. You know that he does not like people to know that he is doing pooh-pooh in his diapers."

"OK, Love," Brad replied, unable to fight back a smile. "Sweetie, why did you call me?"

"I saw your telephone number on the refrigerator. It was on a piece of paper with the telephone number of

Abuelita, Prima Donna Pizza Palace, Dr. Branagan's office, and the video store. Your number was last. That is why I am calling you last."

"Liliana, did you call all of those numbers?"

"Of course."

"Why?"

"Because I wanted to talk!"

Brad smiled from ear to ear. He glanced lovingly at Liliana's picture on his desk and tried to think of the right words to say to his seven-year-old daughter. "Love, all those people you called today are busy trying to help others. So, you should not call them unless you need them to help you. All righty?"

"All righty."

"I will see you Friday night. Remember that you, Mommy, and your brother are coming to live here with me next week."

"Goody! I get to ride on an airplane! Bye-bye. I love you, Daddy."

* * * * * * * * * * * *

Back in El Paso, Sofía was busy attending to the details of the upcoming move to Monterrey. They had decided to keep their house in El Paso and rent a furnished house in Monterrey, but Sofía still had to contend with what they would need to bring in terms of clothes, toys, and personal items. Definitely, Brad's weights and martial arts equipment would go with them. She also had to get Gino ready for the trip.

Gino was a beautiful, solid black Holland shepherd that Brad had imported a few years ago when Gino was just a puppy. Gino's father had been a police dog in Holland. As Gino grew up, he received obedience and protection training. Brad had actually participated as the dog handler in the training. As Gino had grown older, the faithful canine had become more of a playmate for Liliana and little Michael than an attack dog.

Since he was a shepherd, Gino had a very high level of discretion, which made him a very patient dog. That patience was indeed a virtue, especially when little Michael pulled on Gino's tail. Unfortunately for Gino, the tail pulling was a daily event. However, over time Gino had perfected an evasive technique which was as good as any boxer's and which made it exceedingly difficult for little Michael to actually grab Gino's tail in spite of his incessant attempts to do so.

Little Michael would be outside playing with his sister and would see Gino's tail wagging. His eyes would brighten, and he would get a big, mischievous smile on his face. Then, to the extent that a two-year-old could, he would advance toward Gino's tail slowly and quietly so as to be able to take the tail by surprise. Then, he would leap for the tail. Just as he was about to have Gino's tail in his hands, Gino would suddenly shift his posterior to the side, just out of Michael's reach. This would go on and on until one of two things would happen: either Michael would become frustrated and give up, thereby leaving Gino in peace, or Gino would tire of moving his rear-end to the left and to the right, and would trot over to the other side of the back yard away from his two-year-old companion.

To Brad and the children, Gino was more than just a dog. He was a member of the family. However, to Sofía, Gino was merely an animal with fleas and nasty habits. To her the black shepherd certainly was not a creature worthy of being inside their home. It was the only point of friction that existed between Brad and Sofía.

* * * * * * * * * * *

Victor Reyes was curled up on the leather sofa in the luxurious apartment of his number one *muchacha* on the side, the lovely Lolita Loya. They had been together since noon. While Victor's wife Montserrat was attending evening mass with her daughters, Victor was up to his old "tomcat" tricks with Lolita.

Lolita looked at Victor with adoring eyes. *"Mi amor, te quiero mucho,"* she whispered into his ears as he watched television.

"Yo también," Victor said with a comfortable smile as he turned toward her, marveling at her beauty and savoring every minute of his time with her.

Lolita was breathtaking. This incredibly gorgeous young woman was bountiful in all the gifts that a woman needed to captivate a man. She had long, wavy, black hair. Her pearly-white teeth were picture perfect, and her bright, innocent smile was an eye-catching contrast to her *morena* skin. The tight, cream-colored dress she was wearing that day hugged every luscious inch of her and highlighted all the flowing, tantalizing curves of her voluptuous body. Lolita's dress was cut low at the top, revealing her natural endowments, and it ran about half-way down her thighs. Victor had bought her this particular dress as a gift for their second anniversary. There was no doubt about it. Lolita was one fine *mamacita*.

Oddly enough, Lolita really did love Victor. To understand her love for Victor, one must understand the history behind their relationship. Two years ago, when she was just nineteen years old, Victor spotted her working at the front desk in one of Monterrey's large hotels. Unbeknownst to Lolita, Victor had spent the night at that hotel with another one of his young *muchachas*, Zulema Palma. While Zulema was in the hotel room getting ready to leave, Victor befriended Lolita. Later, he bribed another front desk clerk to get Lolita's phone number and address. Armed with that information, he went about his pursuit and conquest of the Latin beauty.

At that time Lolita was living at home with her parents. Her father, who had labored as a construction worker for 30 years, had recently fallen off of a platform at work and had injured his back. The small, struggling construction company which had employed him had refused to offer him any financial assistance, alleging that he had shown up for work drunk and had fallen off the platform due to his own drunken negligence. This accusation was totally without merit and was made only in an attempt to relieve the employer of any liability toward Lolita's father.

Following the accident, the inability of her father to work had put an almost unbearable strain on the family economically. Putting food on the table became a challenge. Lolita had to abandon her high school studies and find work to compensate for her father's lack of income. To compound their problems even further, Lolita's older sister was a diabetic. However, due to their financial situation, she was unable to afford the necessary medical treatment to keep her condition under control. Lolita had two older brothers who were unemployed. The older of the two was a drug addict.

Victor arrived on the scene like a knight in shining armor to save the day. He began sending the family generous sums of money every month that not only met their meager needs but also enabled them to splurge on a few luxuries such as cable T.V. and a family car. Victor paid for a series of back operations and subsequent physical therapy that literally put Lolita's father back on his feet. He personally accompanied Lolita's sister to the finest diabetic treatment center in Monterrey and met with the doctor during the first few visits to ensure that her sister received all the attention she needed. Of course, Victor covered all her medical expenses.

Victor also encouraged the family to have faith in the reformation of Lolita's oldest brother Pablo. Victor had seen others overcome various drug dependencies, and there was no reason why Pablo could not do the same, with the proper support. With the family's consent, Victor enrolled Pablo in the finest detoxification program in Monterrey to get him off drugs. Within six months, Pablo had defeated the devils that had tormented him for so long. The family could not find the words to express their gratitude to Victor.

Lolita was overwhelmed by Victor's kind, generous nature. She greatly admired his drive and economic success in life. Their age difference of over 30 years was of no consequence to her. On the contrary, it actually made Victor all the more attractive in her eyes. She was completely enchanted by Victor's charming personality. As a result of Victor's benevolent acts and his showering of Lolita with attention, she had fallen deeply in love with him.

As time progressed, Victor established a cafeteria company with Lolita as the principal stockholder. Victor removed the current cafeteria company at AMA Monterrey and replaced it with Lolita's company. Lolita's father managed the cafeteria company and her brothers worked there as well, all of them earning very good salaries for that type of work.

Victor also paid for the spacious, 3,000 square foot luxury apartment in which Lolita resided. Lolita was unaware, however, that Victor was also the owner of the entire apartment complex and that his apartment manager had been charged with the responsibility of keeping an eye on Victor's number one *muchacha*. The lovely Lolita Loya was always being watched.

The other members of the Loya family overlooked the fact that Victor was married when the master of deception explained to them that the relationship between him and his wife had been over for years. According to Victor, they no longer lived together as husband and wife but had remained married only for financial and political reasons. This was a shameless lie, of course, but Victor was a man without honor whose only loyalty was to his unmitigated lust for women and money. None of the members of the Loya family were aware of the other women with whom Victor was involved romantically. The entire family believed that their beloved Lolita was the sole recipient of Victor's amorous affection.

* * * * * * * * * * *

That afternoon Lolita had prepared a special lunch to celebrate their second anniversary. While they were still on the couch, Lolita revealed an interesting incident that had occurred the night before. "*Mi amor*, last night *mi mamá* went to visit my brother and sister-in-law and their newborn *bebé* in the Santa Cruz Hospital. Then, she took a bus home while I stayed there with my new nephew. I pleaded with her to take a taxi, but she would not listen to me. You know how stubborn she can be at times. She told me that she had been riding on buses all her life, and there was no sense in spending good money on a taxi."

Victor was looking up at Lolita and smiling as she chatted with him, but his thoughts were not on what she was saying. She was so young and so beautiful. Just to gaze upon her was enough to arouse him. He could hardly contain himself. *Ay-ay-ay. Qué hermosa mujer*, he thought to himself.

Lolita continued, "After she got off the bus, she was walking around the back of that gym which is close to our house. I think it is called *El Cuerpazo*. Anyway, out of nowhere three men jumped her and tried to take her purse."

Victor's smile disappeared in an instant. "*¿Qué?* She was attacked?"

"*Sí,* Victor, but she…"

"Is she all right?" Victor interrupted as he sat up.

"*Sí, mi amor, gracias a Dios.* She fought back, but they knocked her to the ground. The ambulance brought her back to the Santa Cruz Hospital and they treated her for some minor cuts and bruises, nothing serious, and then the hospital released her. I took her home in my car late last night. It was so funny to see her in that red sports car."

"Who are the *desgraciados* that did this? I'll have them taken care of…permanently!" Victor said with anger in his voice.

"Victor, *mi amor*, I have never heard you talk like that before. You are scaring me."

"No, Lolita, *esto no se vale.* Beating up a *señora* like your mother and stealing from her—that's despicable. They've got it coming to them. Who did this?"

"There were three of them, and they were all arrested by the police. If it had not been for a brave American who stepped in and defended *mi mamá*, who knows what would have happened to her."

"An American? What are you talking about?"

"*Mi mamá* said that some *norteamericano* named *Señor* Jenkins heard her screaming and …"

"Jenkins? Brad Jenkins?"

"*Sí, mi amor*, that was his name," Lolita said with a surprised look on her beautiful, *morena* face. "Brad Jenkins. How did you know? Do you know him?"

Victor sat there on the leather couch, stunned. He did not know what to say. The thought of Brad having contact with someone in Victor's secret life was discomforting to say the least. "What was Brad doing there?" he finally asked.

"I think that he had just finished lifting weights at that gym and was walking out to the parking lot. Why, *mi amor*? How do you know him?"

"He works for me. Brad is the new Controller for AMA Monterrey."

Although Victor was caught completely off guard by the situation, he was, nonetheless, a master of deception. He kept his cool and played it off as if it were nothing. "That's right, *preciosa,* he and his lovely wife and two children still live in El Paso," Victor clarified, with an emphasis on "lovely wife." "They will be moving here for two years while Brad helps us grow the Monterey operations."

Lolita giggled when she realized that she had inadvertently made Victor jealous. "Victor, *mi amor,* you are the only man for me. You know that, silly."

Victor smiled, relieved to hear Lolita say that.

"Victor, are you not pleased that he saved my mother from those bad men?"

"Of course I am, *preciosa*. I am just a little surprised. It just does not fit the mold I had for him. He is an accountant. Accountants are a bunch of wimps. I am having a hard time picturing him kicking the tar out of three street fighters, that's all."

"According to *mi mamá*, he used some martial art that she had never seen before. She said *Señor* Jenkins handled himself really well," the Latin beauty said with a smile, her eyes lighting up as she recalled the vivid detail in which her mother explained how heroically Brad had fought. "They had knives and those nunchaka things with chains, but he still took care of them with no problem. He is my mother's hero! Wait until I tell her that he works for you!"

There was a long silence as Victor pondered the situation. *I have to think of something to say so that Brad never makes the connection between the lady he had helped and Lolita. That would be disastrous!*

"*Hola,* Earth to Victor. Come in, Victor," Lolita teased, flashing her beautiful smile and bright eyes inches from his face.

Victor grabbed Lolita gently on her shoulders and looked directly into her eyes. His face turned very serious. "*Mira,* Lolita, you know how important my privacy is to me. I do not want Brad interfering in my private life, so let's keep this between you and me, OK?"

"You don't even want me to tell *mi mamá*?"

"No, I don't want you to tell anyone. I need you to promise me that. Would you do that for me?"

Lolita's look of confusion and uncertainty articulated nonverbally how she felt inside. Nevertheless, she would do anything that Victor asked of her. He was the kindest, most gallant man she had ever met. "*Sí, mi amor.* I promise."

Victor gave her a big smile and kissed her on her lips. "*Gracias, preciosa.* I appreciate your understanding this. It is important to me."

"That is what love is all about, *mi amor*," Lolita said softly. "Thinking of others instead of yourself."

That comment glanced off Victor like a raindrop falling from the sky. He would never be able to understand the simple wisdom in what Lolita had just said. All he cared about was the fact that she was going to keep a lid on this. Nevertheless, he was surprised to learn that Brad was a force to be reckoned with in the street. That was not a comforting thought. All of sudden, his stomach grumbled loudly.

"Your body is talking to you," Lolita said, laughing as Victor's stomach growled once more. "You need to put some food in that stomach."

The two of them sat down at the dining room table. Victor surveyed the food set before him. "This looks delicious, Lolita. Thank you for going to the trouble of preparing this meal."

They proceeded to eat at a relaxed pace, forgetting about the incident with Lolita's mother and her American hero. Victor eased into some romantic conversation as he dined with this gorgeous young woman. He looked across the table at her and uttered, "*¡Qué chulada de mujer!*", the equivalent of "What a foxy babe!" in English. After Victor had cleaned his plate, he looked at his voluptuous *morena* and inquired: "What's for dessert, *preciosa*?"

Lolita looked back at Victor and made an inviting gesture with her hands. "You're looking at dessert," she announced with a seductive smile.

"*¡Ándale!*" Victor remarked. "Bring on the dessert!"

Chapter 5

Café, Anyone?

That first week at AMA Monterrey had been a full week. Brad felt encouraged by the way things were going. He sensed that he would truly be able to make a positive impact on the Monterrey organization. It was important to him to make a difference with his work.

Now, Friday was upon him. Within a few hours he would be reunited with his family in El Paso. That was a comforting thought. Since he had left them on Monday, he had felt a deep sense of separation. He needed to be with them again as much as he needed the air he breathed.

Friday was also payday for the Monterrey operations. Although Article 101 of the Mexican Federal Labor Law required that Mexican companies pay their workers in cash, it was an antiquated regulation dating back decades that had not been changed to accommodate advances in technology. To legally circumvent this stipulation, most Mexican *maquiladora* plants had included verbiage in their labor contracts that each employee signed when they were hired which indicated that payment in cash could be accomplished via an electronic transfer, similar to payroll direct deposit in the U.S. Generally, for the workers to accept direct deposit, the *maquiladora* plant would have to install an ATM machine within the facility that was easily accessible by the employees during breaks and before and after work.

It had struck Brad as quite odd that AMA Monterrey had not yet implemented direct deposit for its labor force. In Ciudad Juárez all major *maquiladora* plants that he knew had converted to direct deposit years ago for all employees, including the hourly workers who made up the majority of the payroll. It was much more convenient for the workers.

In addition, because the companies paid the costs, the workers actually enjoyed the privilege of having a bank account in their name and a debit card in their wallet. This provided them with a sense that they were improving their status socio-economically because, in many cases, it was the first time that they or anyone in their family had ever had a bank account. It was a sign that they were moving up in the world. Perhaps the most important reason most *maquiladoras* had switched to direct deposit was because it substantially reduced the risk of theft. Stealing the fat cash payrolls of *maquiladora* plants along the border had developed into a big business for Mexican crime syndicates in the late 1990s.

For all those reasons, it just made good sense to Brad for AMA Monterrey to switch from paying the workers in cash to paying via direct deposit. Thus, on Thursday of that first week Brad had made a comment to Carmen Silva, the Director of Human Resources, that he wanted to implement electronic payroll as soon as possible. Brad did not understand why Carmen received his suggestion with little enthusiasm. Only the directors enjoyed this benefit, she said, and it had worked fine so far. She saw no reason to change the status quo.

Brad explained the benefits to her of direct deposit, but she was unimpressed and unmotivated to act. Her mind was already made up. Brad walked away from her office feeling less enthused than ever about her competence level. Regardless of Carmen's reaction, however, payroll reported to him and he intended to move ahead with direct deposit. He had discussed this with her as a professional courtesy before proceeding with his plan. His low opinion of the HR director went down another notch. Something about Snake Eyes was just not right.

* * * * * * * * * * * *

On this particular Friday morning, just like every Friday morning, a large, bullet-proof truck from the Nompago company arrived around 8:00 a.m. at the AMA Monterrey headquarters office. Five armed security personnel who looked like members of a S.W.A.T team marched up the stairs, down the hall of the accounting area and into the payroll room. In this 14' x 20' room, the guards delivered the payroll in six large, heavy-duty plastic bags containing 2,400 individual envelopes filled with pesos.

This week's payroll was the equivalent in pesos of US $1,000,000 dollars. It included $400,000 in cash for the regular salaries, overtime, and other benefits such as food coupons and attendance bonuses. It also included an additional $600,000 in profit sharing, which represented 10% of the *maquiladora's* profits. This annual pay-out was obligatory under the Mexican federal labor law. The timing of the pay-out of the profit-sharing was a closely guarded secret. Only Brad, the payroll supervisor Consuelo Mateos, and Victor Reyes knew the exact day in which it would be paid.

The Nompago armed personnel excused themselves after receiving the sign-off from Consuelo, indicating that they had, in fact, delivered the correct number of envelopes. Consuelo was a rather plump lady in her late

20s with short hair and wire-rimmed glasses. The degreed accountant had a beautiful complexion and a friendly smile that complemented her pleasant personality. She was a conscientious worker who was adept at resolving the myriad of problems which inevitably surfaced within the payroll function.

After the Nompago guards had left the payroll office, Consuelo along with her clerk Severo Gutiérrez went about their business of sorting the envelopes by shift by manager. Severo was surprised to see that the profit-sharing was being paid. Consuelo herself had processed that portion of the payroll to maintain the confidential nature of the pay-out. After they sorted the payroll envelopes, they would then proceed to the production floor and distribute the pay envelopes to all the eagerly awaiting workers who had done their part that week to advance the interests of the shareholders of AMA Electric International.

Consuelo was very encouraged when Brad had mentioned to her that the company would soon convert to direct deposit payroll. She took advantage of that occasion to convey to Brad explicitly that she was uncomfortable with the current pay procedure. According to Consuelo, the payroll procedure was a lousy one because it left her and Severo alone with a lot of cash from the time that the Nompago security guards left until the time that she and Severo gave the workers their pay envelopes. The first shift was paid around 11:00 a.m. and the second shift was paid around 6:00 p.m. Brad told her to have patience. He intended to address this risk immediately. Consuelo would serve on the project team along with IT, or information technology, to implement direct deposit.

This Friday was just like any other Friday, at least that was the perception in the office. No one had seemed to notice the four new faces which had entered along with all the other operators at 6:45 a.m that morning. These four strangers arrived in one of the many buses that brought the workers to the five *maquiladora* plants every morning. They stepped off their bus nonchalantly that morning with Brazilian-made .38-caliber Rossi revolvers tucked under their shirts. With 2,400 employees, it was hard to keep track of who was who. New employees were entering the work force every week. They meshed with the other workers as they entered the plants.

Before the alarm sounded for the 7:00 a.m. shift to begin, they all quietly slipped into the men's bathroom and hid in the stalls, waiting patiently. There were 10 stalls in the bathroom, so there would be no logistical problem with others having to wait. They knew that the bathrooms had been cleaned by the night shift and that the day-shift janitor would not make his next round until 10:30 a.m. They were ready and waiting for their next move. These *bandidos* had done their homework.

Two months ago one of their associates, a tall, lanky 23-year-old, originally from the Mexican port city of Veracruz, had applied for and received a position as a level one operator in the electronics plant that was adjacent to the main office. He did so with the specific intention of learning as much as he could about the inner workings of the payroll function. Over the following two months he had paid close attention to the arrival times of Nompago and provided that intelligence to his villainous associates as they plotted how they would walk out of the plant that day unnoticed with a booty of $1,000,000 dollars. They knew that the Nompago guards never were present in the building for more than 10 minutes. Most surprisingly of all, they knew that today was the day that the profit-sharing would be paid. Not even the payroll clerk Severo had known that.

When the security guards left, they knew that the cash would be alone in the payroll office while Consuelo and Severo organized the cash into stacks by shift by manager. They knew that all the other administrative personnel ate breakfast in the cafeteria when the payroll arrived. These *bandidos* even knew exactly where the security camera monitors were in the main office so that they could spray them with black paint just as they made their way up to the second floor.

The tall, lanky infiltrator had conveniently resigned on Monday of that week, citing a sign-on bonus of $300 pesos at a *maquiladora* plant closer to his home as the reason for leaving AMA Monterrey. No one was the wiser. The *maquiladora* industry was plagued by high turnover as workers moved from manufacturing plant to plant. This high turnover rate was an unfortunate cost of doing business in the *maquiladora* plants of northern Mexico.

To help stack the odds in favor of this band of thieves, they would also have help from the inside. One of the security guards, Misael López, who worked for the outside security company providing guard services to AMA Monterrey, would collaborate in orchestrating this robbery. The leader of the band of thieves, negotiating through a third party, was able to buy off Misael. For the sum of US $5,000 dollars, which represented a year's pay for Misael, this unscrupulous security guard had agreed to help ensure that the thieves would have clear passage after the robbery and that no one would raise a red flag when the security cameras were taken out. He was paid $2,000 up front and the balance would be paid upon successful completion of the job.

It was a clever move, because Misael was a long-time employee of the security company and was the group leader assigned to the security guard crew working that morning. Not even he would know the identity of the thieves until they he saw the red bandanas around their heads. That was the signal. To make it look proper and not incriminate him, they would point their guns at him and tie him up as they left.

These four *bandidos* had the entire payroll operation down to a science. They had carefully developed a solid plan which took into account all contingencies. All contingencies, that is, except for one—the Controller.

* * * * * * * * * * * *

Brad had met earlier that morning with Victor on the goals and objectives for the upcoming year. As usual, Lupita had filled his coffee cup to the brim with boiling hot coffee as he walked out of Victor's office. She always went out of her way to do nice things for Brad. Her morning coffee was not the only thing that perked her up when Brad was around.

Brad watched his coffee as he carefully took each step up in the stairwell, hoping not to spill any on his hand during his ascension to the second floor. He dared not take his eyes off his cup lest he surely spill the piping hot beverage on himself. As he completed the first 15 steps and arrived at the midpoint leading up to the second series of 15 steps, he looked up and saw two men coming down the stairs.

The Controller did not recognize their faces, but these two *muchachos* were dressed as operators. One was a burly and robust man about six feet six inches tall who was carrying a large, red duffle bag over his shoulder.

The burly fellow must have weighed close to 300 pounds.

Is it Christmas already? Brad jokingly thought. *Santa is already here.* He looked at the other scruffy-looking man, who by now was on his last step down before he reached the half-way point in the stairwell. Brad greeted them both in his typical friendly and unassuming manner. Always the gentleman, Brad was waiting off to one side so that the two strangers could pass. The scruffy-looking man was of medium height and build but had not shaved for a couple of weeks. He did not have enough facial hair to really grow a thick beard, but he had apparently persisted in spite of a lack of cooperation from Mother Nature. His patchy beard did not become him.

The scruffy-looking fellow was keeping his right hand hidden behind his back, a detail that did not escape the Controller. As they passed Brad got a good look at what he was carrying: it was a pistol! Brad's eyes opened wide and he looked into Scruffy's face. At that instant, the friendly look on Scruffy disappeared and was replaced by a nervous look, which quickly transformed itself into an angry scowl. He began to raise his pistol.

Almost without thinking Brad quickly thrust the boiling contents of his coffee mug into Scruffy's face. The thief howled in pain and tried to wipe the scalding coffee off his face with his left sleeve. Brad took advantage of the opening to the mid-section by kicking him hard in the stomach with a front snap kick, driving the ball of his foot deep into Scruffy's abdomen. Scruffy gasped for air like a fish lying on the bank of a river. Brad looked up at the big man who was rapidly advancing toward him. The big, red duffle bag was comically bouncing on his over-sized posterior every step of the way.

Thousands of hours of training in Hapkido had taught Brad that when he was in an altercation involving a gun, taking out the guy with the gun was priority number one. A gunshot wound could be mortal. The hot coffee and kick to the mid-section had given him a few seconds to reach in and grab Scruffy's right hand, the hand with the gun in it, with both his hands. Upon securing a tight grip, with lightning speed he stepped backward with his left leg and then twisted Scruffy's wrist backward and downward against the bone with all the might he could muster. The stepping was designed to throw his attacker off balance while he applied the wrist technique. Scruffy dropped his gun when his wrist broke, screaming even louder than before and directing a spicy assortment of vulgar Mexican profanities at Brad.

Brad followed that movement with a leg sweep to Scruffy's left leg, and Scruffy hit the ground with a thud. As Scruffy tried to raise his head, Brad brought a crushing stomp kick down on his head, banging Scruffy's head against the concrete stair floor. It was lights out for that *bandido*.

During this commotion, the big, burly fellow had managed to drop his bag and grab Brad by the throat, pushing him up against the wall and choking him. Brad was struggling to breathe. With only a few more seconds before he passed out, the Controller reached down with his right hand, grabbed the groin area of the giant attacker, and squeezed his attacker's family jewels with a vise grip. It was so painful that this gigantic fellow immediately released his grip on Brad's neck and began to lose consciousness.

As Brad held the groin grip and continued to squeeze, he pushed up and backward on the chin of his giant attacker with his left hand, driving the big guy's neck backward and downward. The giant Mexican fell backward and onto the stairs, like a huge oak tree being brought to the ground by a lumber jack. *Bonk! Bonk! Bonk!* He went sliding down the stairs banging his head on each concrete step all the way down to the bottom. He ended up sprawled out at the foot of the stairs, completely unconscious.

Another KO for Brad, and the day was still young. Brad's heart was pounding. He looked around with rage in his eyes. *Who's next? Who wants some?* Fortunately, there were no more bad guys coming down the stairs. The Controller took a few breaths to allow the rage inside to simmer down.

After taking a quick inventory of the situation, Brad determined that both men were out cold and would be so for a while. He ran downstairs, grabbed the Rossi revolver, and put it between his belt and the small of his back. Next, he quickly pulled the shoe strings from the shoes of the big, brawny Mexican fellow and tied his hands tightly behind his back. Once he had removed the huge belt from this downed giant, Brad tied his feet together. *Whoa, man, this is a big belt!* He remarked to himself as he looped it around the big Mexican's ankles several times. He removed the shoes from this mighty man and threw them down the hall as far as he could. Next, he did the same thing to Scruffy.

Brad then opened the huge, red duffle bag and saw that it contained about half of the payroll envelopes filled with cash. With two hands he proceeded with great effort to lug the big bag up the stairs. Once he had accomplished this feat, he opened the door into the second floor office and towed the bag down the hall to the payroll office. When he opened the door to the payroll office, he saw Consuelo and Severo in the corner on the floor. Their feet and hands were tied securely with duct tape, and duct tape was placed over their mouths as well to keep them quiet.

Brad looked at Consuelo. Eyes that were usually sparkling like glitter were now filled with tears and fright. Severo, a short man in his mid-30s, looked shaken up as well. Brad searched desperately for a pair of scissors. Finally, in the bottom drawer of Consuelo's desk, he found a pair and immediately proceeded to cut them loose. Once their hands were freed, each of them pulled off the tape that had kept them quiet during the heist.

"Oh, Bradley! They stole the payroll! They told us that they would kill us if we did not cooperate, and they had guns! One of them pointed a gun to my head!" She sobbed so uncontrollably that it affected her breathing.

Brad put his arms around her and calmed her. "It's OK, Consuelo. They are gone now. It's going to be OK. Did they hurt you?" Without looking up, Consuelo shook her head and continued crying. Brad turned to Severo. "Severo, what about you? Did they hurt you?"

"No, Brad. I am all right, *gracias a Dios*."

Brad grabbed the phone and called security. The phone rang and rang and rang, but no one answered. *Where could they be?* Brad did not want to create a panic, so he carefully weighed his next move. He needed to inform the right people about the robbery. *I wonder how many more there are.* He sat Consuelo down in her desk. She was starting to regain her composure slowly but steadily. "Consuelo, how many of them were there?"

"Four. There were four. Two men of average height, one big, tall man, and one *chaparrito*."

Brad realized that they must have split up. Two must have gone down the stairs on the right side, and the other two must have gone down the left side. He had the misfortune of running into the bigger pair. "Here is the bag that I pulled off the big man. I left both of them lying in the stairwell."

"What happened?" Severo asked with great curiosity. "Did you fight them?" Severo was wondering how Brad could have defeated the huge Mexican in hand-to-hand combat.

"Yes, but it was brief. Are you two well enough to stay here for now while I go get some help?"

"*Sí*, Bradley."

"*Claro que sí*," Severo assured Brad. "But tell me how you beat that *grandote*. He was a giant! Plus that other *muchacho*! How did you take them out?"

"I had a cup of *café* with one of them, and the other one is going to need some ice tonight," Brad said with a smile and a wink. He patted Severo on the back. "Let me go get some back-up. I shall return shortly. You two stay here and rest. Severo, please call the police and get them here *a la brevedad* so that we can file a report."

"*Sí señor*. I'll get right on it."

"Consuelo..."

"*Dígame usted.*"

"Please get this money back in the safe until we get things under control."

* * * * * * * * * * * *

Brad went down the other stairwell, but there was no sign of anyone. Just then, the administrative workers began to enter the office area. They were returning from the cafeteria where they had been eating breakfast. Most of them were going to get their toothbrushes and then go to the bathroom to brush their teeth.

Looking around downstairs, Brad saw nothing. Like a cheetah he jetted down the hall toward the middle stairwell to check on Scruffy and the tree trunk. He saw administrative workers pouring back into the office, but he did not hear any remarks about anybody being tied up on the floor. They all entered as if nothing had happened. He slowed down to a walk and then arrived back at the stairwell where he had fought the two *bandidos*.

"What?" Brad remarked to himself out loud. "They are gone!" Brad stood there for a minute, trying to figure out what could have happened in the interim since he had departed from the area where these two had been. He ran down the rest of the hall, passing through the HR, customs, and traffic areas. *No sign of anything out of the ordinary,* he thought. Everyone watched Brad with puzzled looks on their faces as he swiftly made his way through the halls.

Finally, Brad arrived at Victor's office. Lupita Anaya, Victor's assistant, saw the look of confusion on Brad's face. "Is everything all right, *Señor* Jenkins?"

"I don't know," replied Brad, still grappling with what could have possibly happened to the thieves. He was confounded. *Nobody seems to be aware of this but me! This is crazy!* The Controller took off down the hall again and headed outside toward the gate. Once he got there, he saw the security guard leader, Misael López, lying on the floor inside the guard shack. His hands were tied behind his back and his feet were bound with duct tape. Misael also had duct tape over his mouth. It looked really convincing.

Little did Brad know that Misael had done almost all the binding himself. One of the four thieves had merely completed the finishing touches on his way out. Brad pulled a box cutter out of the desk drawer in the guard shack and quickly cut Misael loose. "Are you OK, Misael? Has anyone gone through here within the last ten minutes?"

"*Sí, Señor* Jenkins. A man wearing a red bandana stuck a gun to my head and tied me up a few minutes ago. Right after that I saw him and three others run out of here and jump into a blue car parked across the street."

"Was one of them a real big guy, about this tall?" With his hands Brad indicated the dimensions of his giant Mexican attacker. Misael nodded to indicate his concurrence. The corrupt security guard could have won an Oscar for best supporting actor for his performance of a scared security guard.

"Misael, was that big *muchacho* walking?"

Misael again confirmed with a nod. Brad was perplexed as to how the two he had laid out could have recovered so quickly and escaped. Something was not right about this situation.

Just then, a Mexican police squad car pulled up, followed by another one. *They must be responding to the phone call Severo made,* Brad reasoned. Misael tried to hide his surprise at seeing the police show up so quickly after his fellow conspirators had left the premises. That was not supposed to have happened.

* * * * * * * * * * * *

The police made their inquiries of all those involved, documented the descriptions of the suspects and said that they would file a report and put out an APB on the blue car. However, they really did not have a lot of concrete information with which to work. Brad was still baffled by the situation.

The Controller could not understand what had happened to the two men he left sprawled on the floor. Even more curious, the blood he saw trickling from the heads of both Scruffy and the burly fellow had vanished. Someone had wiped down the area just like a CIA cleaner after a hit gone bad. No blood, no prints; nothing to go on except the descriptions of the four men and a small, blue car...and the gun he had removed from Scruffy! He turned that over to the police, hoping that his own fingerprints had not contaminated the *bandido*'s prints.

Victor had left the plant just after his meeting with Brad to attend a meeting with the owners of the construction company, GZZ-Mex *Constructores*. They were planning for the construction of a new building for AMA Monterrey. Lupita Anaya had given Victor's cellular phone number to Brad, and Brad gave Victor a call just after the police left. As Brad explained the situation to Victor, the stylish, bald *Director General* did not seem very worried.

"Brad, we are covered by insurance, so don't worry about it," Victor instructed nonchalantly. "Just file the proper paperwork and we will get our money back less a 10% deductible."

The fact that Victor would have such detailed knowledge of the insurance policy deductible related to payroll theft raised an eyebrow on Brad. That was something that fell within Brad's domain, not Victor's. *How would he know how much the deductible was? I don't even know what the deductible is for payroll robberies.*

When Brad mentioned that he had taken one of the assailant's guns, Victor suddenly became quite interested in the robbery. He wanted to know exactly how that had happened and hear Brad's description of the two men. The bald executive asked Brad if there were anything else Brad had removed from them.

"No, Victor, but if I had been thinking more clearly, I would have taken their driver's licenses. Then we would have nailed them for sure." Brad, frustrated and tired, rubbed his eyebrows as he fought to make sense of all this. "Victor, this incident highlights the need for switching to direct deposit. We need to make sure we don't have cash on the premises like this again." Victor agreed and asked Brad to follow up on it.

Having informed his boss of the incident, Brad walked upstairs to give the insurance agent a call. After he had handled the administration related to the robbery, he grabbed his suitcase and asked cost accountant Javier Peralta to drive him to the Monterrey airport for his trip back to El Paso. Brad planned on flying from Monterrey to Juárez and then taking a taxi across the bridge to El Paso.

During his waiting period to get onto the jet, he reflected upon the events of the day. *What a way to end my first week,* he grumbled. *Well, thank God that no one was hurt. This whole situation reeked of an inside job. I am going to keep my antenna up over the next few weeks.*

Chapter 6

Chinese at a Mexican Restaurant

April in El Paso was arguably the most delightful time of the year. Cool mornings gave way to pleasantly warm afternoons and evenings. Frequently during the day the coolness of a refreshing April breeze would gently and flirtatiously caress the faces of those whom it encountered, uplifting their spirits in a way that only Nature could. Desert flowers and the rest of El Paso's springtime gifts combined with the famous El Paso sunshine to create a unique beauty for the residents of this famous city of the Old West.

Brad awakened at sunrise the following morning, much earlier than any of the other members of the Jenkins family, and walked up to the North Hills Park to run for 30 minutes. As he completed lap after lap, the events of the payroll robbery which had occurred the day before played over and over in his mind. *That robbery went too smoothly. There had to be someone on the inside—maybe more than one person. The bandidos whom I laid out on the floor just vanished without a trace! No prints, no blood, nada! Who was the "cleaner?"*

Brad quickened his pace as the unanswered questions began to trouble him more. Sweat was pouring down his face. His breathing was steady but audible. He wiped his forehead with his right shirt sleeve as he pondered the situation further. *I don't understand Victor's reaction. He was too cool, too relaxed, as if this incident were no surprise to him. Something is amiss.*

The Controller returned home about 7:00 a.m. Looking at his house, one could learn a lot about Brad. His house was nestled in a nice, middle-class neighborhood of El Paso. Due to its elevated position, North Hills provided a cooler alternative to the lower valley regions of the "Sun City" during the blistering heat of the El Paso summers. Clean air, beautiful skies, and good neighbors characterized the North Hills living experience.

Brad's neighbors were friendly, hard-working people: firemen, teachers, middle managers, policemen, and military officers. They were the people that got the work done in life, and Brad felt comfortable living among them. His modest but attractive house was reflective of Brad's fundamental values. When it came to personal finances, Brad believed in living well below his means and saving the difference. Brad and Sofía were working toward eventual financial independence the long, hard, honest way.

For the Controller, material things were not the source of his happiness. His family, his good health, and his faith were what brought him joy in life.

* * * * * * * * * * * *

Brad put the coffee on to brew and then hopped into the shower. All the other Jenkinses were still asleep. After showering and dressing, Brad prepared a cup of delicious, hazelnut coffee for both Sofía and himself. He quietly entered his bedroom and put the steaming hot cup of coffee under Sofía's nose. The rich aroma gradually began to pull her out of her deep sleep. She kept her eyes closed a little while longer, savoring her last few minutes in bed.

"Mmmm...*¡qué rico!*," she remarked lazily, still unwilling to open her eyes and embrace the new day.

"*Su café, señora,*" Brad announced playfully, pretending to be her waiter.

Brad decided to let Sofía wallow in bed a tad longer while the wonderful scent of fresh coffee went to work on her sense of smell.

After enjoying a pleasant morning with his family, Brad looked up at the clock and saw that it was 2:30 p.m. "Oh, I have to go to my Hapkido class!" He quickly changed, jumped in his truck, and drove to his martial arts school.

Brad had been taking Hapkido for 11 years. On Saturdays the Controller had private classes. Brad was a Chodan, or first-degree, black belt and was currently training for his second-degree black belt. Liliana also studied Hapkido and was currently a red belt.

Hapkido was a Korean martial art designed for the streets, not for tournament fighting. It had lots of kicking, like Tae Kwon Do, another Korean martial art. However, Hapkido was known for its joint-locking and joint-breaking techniques as well as its circular movement. Depending on the perceived level of danger, the martial artist who had mastered the techniques of Hapkido could tailor his or her response to simply frustrate and stop the attacker or, in life-threatening situations, to permanently damage or even extinguish the life of the attacker. Many of the techniques were capable of inflicting debilitating structural damage on the joints of its victims. For those reasons, Hapkido was not a mainstream martial art in the sense that Tae Kwon Do, judo, and some of the other arts were.

Brad's Hapkido master was a kind and patient man, full of wisdom. Not all class time was devoted to physical techniques. He would take time to talk with his students and try to impart to them some of the things he had learned in his four decades as a martial artist. Two of the primary values he instilled in his students were a respect for others and reverence for life.

"It is to one's honor to avoid strife," he could be heard to say from time to time. "To the extent that it is possible, try to live in peace with others. If you must fight, use only that force which is necessary for the situation at hand. Remember, if you take a life, you can never give it back. Therefore, as a martial artist, you should strive to preserve life. Only in the most extreme and life-threatening situations, when there is no other alternative, should you take life. I prepare you each time you come into my school for the evil you will encounter in this world. You must use your knowledge and skills for the good of mankind, selflessly. Do not shirk your responsibilities as students of Hapkido, but do not abuse your abilities either." Brad held his Hapkido master in high esteem.

* * * * * * * * * * * *

After Brad returned from his Hapkido class, he showered and spent the rest of the afternoon playing hide-and-seek, wrestling and other games with his children as Sofía became engulfed in reading one of her favorite magazines. Sofía loved to read and was well-versed on many subjects. She particularly enjoyed books on health, religion and geography. Little Michael finally "ran out of gas" and fell asleep on the carpet in the middle of the den floor.

As evening fell, Liliana ran up to her Daddy and said, "Daddy, Daddy, may we have pizza tonight?"

"That sounds good. It is Saturday night, which means pizza night. Check with Mommy to make sure it's OK with her. Ask her if she would be kind enough to make us a salad, too."

Sofía agreed, so they ordered up the usual: one large pepperoni pizza and one large jalapeño and mushroom pizza from the Prima Donna Pizza Palace. While Liliana was watching TV, Brad tip-toed into the kitchen where Sofía was preparing a delicious salad.

"Why don't we go outside and watch the sunset?" Brad whispered with a sparkle in his eyes. Sofía nodded and followed him outside to the front entrance of their house. Brad stood behind his wife and wrapped his arms around her. She purred like a cat and snuggled in close to him.

Together, they looked up at the magical El Paso sunset. That evening Nature had painted a rainbow of colors across the heavens, stretching as far as the eye could see and leaving Brad and Sofía spellbound by its captivating aura. "El Paso is truly a city of unique beauty," Sofía said, lost in the romantic wonder of the moment.

Brad kissed Sofía softly on the side of her neck, giving her chill bumps. *"Ooohhh, me da cosquillas,"* she said in her flirtatious, teen-ager voice as she shrugged her shoulders and smiled. They were not sure how long they stood there, but it must have been at least thirty minutes, because that was the time it took for the pizza to arrive. When the Prima Donna Pizza Palace truck drove up, Brad and Sofía were still locked in their romantic trance.

The tall, lanky teen-ager hurriedly approached the front door. "Uh...excuse me. Did you guys order a pizza?" he said respectfully, realizing he was interrupting something special.

Sofía smiled and looked at the young man. "Yes, just a minute and I'll go get the money." She walked into the house with Brad and got her purse, and then walked back out to pay for the pizza.

As the pizza delivery boy hastily scurried back to his truck to go on to the next delivery, he slammed his car door, triggering Gino to start barking loudly, and causing little Michael to wake up crying. Once everything had calmed down, the Jenkinses stretched out in front of the television set to watch a movie and eat pizza.

* * * * * * * * * * * *

That night in a restaurant that definitely did not rate as one of Monterrey's swankiest, Victor and his usual crowd of *compadres* were living it up at a large table in the back. This particular restaurant, *La Joya Mexicana*, had the elements that brought Victor back time and time again: loud music, an abundance of alcohol, pretty young waitresses, and good Mexican food. Several of the AMA Monterrey plant managers along with Paco Delgado, Director of Purchasing, were present. Notably absent, as usual, was plant manager Jorge del Valle.

"I enjoy the distinction of being the *Don Juan de México*," Victor slurred, his words barely understandable due to his inebriated condition.

Pancho Zapata, who also found himself in a drunken stupor, managed to flimsily hold up his glass of Tequila and toast his long-time friend and boss. *"Brindo por el Don Juan de México. ¡Salud! ¡Salud!"* All the *compadres* seated around the table held their glasses up to toast in unison. *"¡Salud!"*

"*Oye*, Victor," Pancho asked, "why doesn't Jorge ever go out with us?"

"Jorge? Jorge who?" Victor replied with a groggy voice.

"Jorge del Valle. He is a plant manager, but he never likes to come celebrate with the *compadres.*"

Victor's face lost its look of drunkenness for a moment and turned sober. The other *compadres* heard Victor and Pancho's conversation and stopped speaking. "Jorge del Valle," Victor said with a scowl, "is not with us, because he is definitely *not* with us. He is not one of us. He is a treacherous, ambitious *traidor!*" Victor yelled as he hammered the table with his fist. The *compadres* became quiet.

Several others dining in the restaurant looked over at Victor. Victor turned to his onlookers and gave them a sour face. "What are all of you looking at?" he slurred. "Don't you know that it is impolite to stare? Go back to eating and to your boring dinner conversation!"

"*Cálmate, Victor. Tranquilito, tranquilito, mi carnal*," Pancho said soothingly as he patted his friend on the back and tried to calm him down.

"Victor," asked Walter Ruíz, a plant manager in his late 50s, "what did Jorge do to you? Why do you dislike him so?"

The other *compadres* elbowed Walter and kicked him under the table to get him to leave the subject be, but it was too late. Victor was already looking at Walter with anger in his eyes. "Just like the two-faced rat that he is, he smiles in my face when he sees me and then he stabs me in the back every chance he gets. That is why I 'dislike him so'," Victor said, mocking Walter.

Paco, ever the lively one of the group, quickly changed the subject. "*Compadres,* listen up. I'm not an accountant, but I now know that numbers can be dangerous. Let me tell you what happened to me last week-end that made me see the light about how dangerous numbers are." The pudgy purchasing director began with a smile on his face. "I am at the mall accompanying my wife Dulce while she does some shopping. I don't like to shop, as you all know, so I generally sit out on the bench while Dulce goes into a store to find whatever it is she is looking for. Anyway, while I'm standing outside one of the stores looking suave and debonair, as usual, I see this guy. I'll call him Scarecrow because he had a face so hideous it could frighten away birds. So, ole Scarecrow is walking through the mall, and clinging to his puny little arm is this beautiful girl. *La neta, compadres*, she was a *potranca*—absolutely gorgeous! Being the astute observer of human behavior that I am, I notice an imbalance in the nature of that relationship. So, I mosey over to give that beautiful girl a closer look at yours truly. Now, I know I'm no Hollywood movie star, but between me and Scarecrow, well, there was no contest."

Paco looked around the table to see the smiles of interest on the *compadres*. They were all ears, so he continued. "Well, as luck would have it, Scarecrow leaves this vision of beauty sitting on the bench right in front of me while he goes to get some ice cream. So, I say to myself, '*Paco, now's your chance, amigo. Make your move! Get her number!*' Of course, with my charm, I quickly strike up a conversation with her and learn that ole Scarecrow is just her boyfriend. She's still single! As we continue to chat I get her laughing and enjoying herself, and then at the perfect moment I tell her that she has the face of an angel and that she is the most beautiful woman I have ever seen."

"You are a smooth talker, Paco," Pancho Zapata cried out. "Yes, you are, you certainly are. You have a way with words."

"*Gracias, compadre.* When you got, you got it, and I got it," Paco acknowledged. "Anyway, back to the story, so right when I am about to get her number, I notice that she is looking up at someone to my left. I look up in the same direction, and lo and behold, guess who's standing there looking like Attila the Hun, or in this case, I should say Attila the Nun."

"Your wife!" they all shouted.

"That's right. There she is, in all her glory, looking down at me. If looks could kill, *compadres,* I would not be here with you gentlemen tonight. I don't know how much she has heard, but judging by the way she is looking at me, she has obviously heard way too much. To make matters worse, she has just bought one of those 44-ounce sodas filled to the rim with ice-cubes and cold soda. All right, so my wife gives me the mad-dog look, see, like this." Paco squinted his eyes and showed his teeth like an angry dog growling. "She walks over to me, pulls at the front of my pants and shorts, and dumps that soda and ice right in my drawers. Man, was that ice cold! She says, 'Maybe that will cool you off, hot stuff!' Then, she walks off madder than a hornet that has just been swatted at. So, I get up and start moving my legs up and down, shaking my derriere to the left and right, doing anything I can to get those ice cubes out of my shorts, but it was not working."

"Then, I notice that people in the mall had stopped and were staring at me. Some of them were thinking that I was hired to put on a dance show. Others were looking at me like I had been smoking dope or something. So, that's it for me. I take off running for the bathroom. As I am running, some of the ice cubes fall out of my drawers, slide down my leg, and get thrown in front of me. Before I can react, I step on a couple of ice cubes and start sliding across the mall floor. I keep sliding right into this big, 400-pound woman. The force of the impact knocks her right on top of me. Don't get me wrong, *compadres*. I like a big woman. There's nothing like a full-figured gal, but that was too much woman for me."

By now, Paco had the compadres in stitches. They were falling all over the table, dying with laughter, but still trying to hear the story.

"So there I am, *compadres,* lying on the mall floor with ice cubes in my underwear and this 400-pound woman is moving around on top of me, screaming as loud as she can and calling me a pervert and all other such names. Then, wouldn't you know it! Ole Scarecrow comes waltzing by me smiling and eating his cherry ice cream, and that gorgeous girl that was almost mine is hanging on to his arm. As she passes me, the beautiful girl turns back and gives me a sexy smile and blows me a kiss. She laughs as she walks away. I'm lying there watching her shake that booty all the way down the mall, and this hippopotamus is still on top of me crushing me to death. Finally, they get the hippo off of me and I am able to breathe air into my lungs. So, what did I learn from that day? I went through all that strife just to get a lousy telephone number. That's why I tell you, *compadres*, numbers are very dangerous!"

Paco's story had left everyone rolling with laughter.

"Paco, Paco," Victor said as he put his arm around his nephew, "I don't know what I would do without you, my long-winded *amigo*!"

* * * * * * * * * * * *

On Sunday evening Victor was seated in the green recliner in the back office of a warehouse in Monterrey. There before him on the floor were stacks and stacks of Mexican pesos—the equivalent of about $400,000 U.S. dollars. Victor had several of his personal crew, headed by his number one confidant *Chato*, on-site for security just in case.

Ri-i-i-i-ing! It was Victor's cell phone.

Victor looked at the caller ID, which showed that the call was coming from the U.S. Victor recognized the number. "Hello," he said nonchalantly.

"Was that your work?" asked a familiar voice in English.

"What are you talking about?" Victor replied innocently.

"The payroll robbery at the Monterrey plants—did you orchestrate that?"

"Why do you ask?" Victor responded, still playing the innocent one.

"Just answer the question!" said the voice authoritatively.

"So what if I did? We're covered by insurance except for 10%."

"Victor, we have bigger fish to fry," said the cool, calm voice. "The stock is now trading at $47. We need to stay focused on that stock price."

"I am focused on that!" Victor barked angrily.

"This incident drew unnecessary attention to you. It created noise that we don't need. Do I make myself clear?"

"Yes!" growled Victor. He did not like to be lectured. "I understand."

"Good. Then I will forget about this issue so we can re-focus on the big picture."

"Right. *Adiós.*"

Victor glanced over at Carmen Silva who was coiled on a red cushion on the floor busily dividing up the cash. For her efforts in coordinating the robbery with the outsourced *bandidos*, she would be rewarded with US $25,000 of the bounty and would continue to remain in the good graces of Victor Reyes, the Czar of AMA Monterrey. She looked up at Victor and produced her famous fake smile. Victor was not as happy, and his head was still reeling from last night's activities at *La Joya Mexicana* restaurant with the *compadres*.

"If it had not been for that boy scout Brad Jenkins, this would have been a cool $1 million dollars of which $850,000 would be sitting in my pocket after everyone's cut," he grumbled.

"Victor, darling, after everyone's cut you are still $350,000 dollars richer, so take heart," she said.

Victor thought about what she said, and he had to agree with her. "You know, you're right, Carmen," he said with a devilish smile. "I must admit that $350,000 dollars is not bad for a day's work. Not bad at all."

* * * * * * * * * * * *

On Tuesday Brad met Jorge del Valle for lunch at a local restaurant called *El Pueblito de Pablito* that specialized in *cabrito*, a dish made of charbroiled young goat meat for which Monterrey was famous. *El Pueblito de Pablito* had a charming architectural design that captured the essence of old Mexico. The inside of the restaurant looked like a small Mexican village back in the 1800s, with colorful buildings spanning the perimeter of the stucco walls inside the restaurant. The tables were strategically placed in the middle of the restaurant's interior, and the restaurant floor was covered in Saltillo tile to create the illusion that the customers were outside in a village square. The waitresses and waiters were dressed in attire reflective of the unique styles and vibrant colors of that colorful period in Mexican history.

Jorge was several years older than Brad and had a full head of black hair with streaks of grey, combed straight back and held there with styling gel. His hairline was about two inches above his eyebrows and ran straight across his forehead without a trace of recession anywhere, one of the lowest hairlines Brad had ever seen on a man that age. A full beard, kept neatly groomed and trimmed closely to the face, rounded out Jorge's facial appearance. Even though he was extremely intelligent, Jorge had a quiet, unassuming manner about him. His English was impeccable, noticeably better than Brad's Spanish. They generally ended up speaking in English, although Brad would always start out in Spanish out of respect for being in Mexico. The Controller felt that it was simply good manners to speak the language of the country in which he resided.

Both Brad and Jorge ordered *cabrito* and began chatting about their families and background. Jorge's wife Zayra was a successful doctor in Monterrey with a large practice in family medicine. Jorge's children were now fully grown, but in his office he still had pictures of them when they were little. The highly-regarded plant manager indicated to Brad how refreshing it was to finally have an American on the management team in Monterrey.

"Brad, I understand that you took your family and studied a few months in Beijing, China just before you came here. That is very interesting. What in the world motivated you to do that?"

"Well, I have always been fascinated by the Orient, Jorge, especially China. China is the oldest continuing civilization in the world and as such has a rich history. I had just completed a three-year contract in Juárez and decided that it was a good time to experience China."

"I see. So, how was China? Was it like what you expected?"

"In some aspects it was everything we expected, and in some ways it was very different. My wife is a great admirer of Chinese arts and crafts. She found a world of reasonably-priced treasures in small markets in the Chaoyang district of Beijing. We have some beautiful Chinese dolls and glass vases meticulously painted on the inside. Another aspect that really stood out about the Chinese is that they are very hard-working people. I respect their work ethic immensely. They work hard and are big savers."

"As a foreigner did you feel safe in Beijing?"

"Yes, we felt extremely safe. My hat is off to them in this area. My wife would go out by herself, and I did not worry about her. There was very little crime in Beijing. I wish Mexico City were half as safe."

"Mexico City—safe? That is wishful thinking," Jorge said with a sarcastic laugh. "They are now calling Mexico City '*la ciudad del miedo*' instead of '*la ciudad de México*.'"

Brad shook his head sadly as he reflected upon the crime in Mexico City. He was disheartened by the fact that such a magnificent city had such a horrendous problem.

"What about the construction and real estate development going on in China?" Jorge asked.

"Again, we spent all our time in Beijing, so I can only comment on the development going on there. I must say that the Chinese are really gearing up for the 2008 Olympics. They are investing huge amounts of capital in their infrastructure. It is amazing to see all the construction work going on in that city. I cannot wait to see the 2008 Olympic Games. Beijing will certainly showcase itself as a great world city."

"Yes, I am looking forward to that as well."

"We felt very fortunate to have had the opportunity to live among the Chinese and learn about their language and culture."

"Tell me, Brad, what do you think about Mexico's chances of competing with China for foreign direct investment? This issue is very much on the minds of Mexican business leaders. How can we compete against China's cheap wages?"

"Well, I don't think that Mexico can compete against China's low wages, Jorge. Mexico should not try to do so, either. China's wages are currently about 25% of Mexico's wages. Based on my first-hand observations when I was in China, there appears to be little upward pressure on wages for several years to come. From my viewpoint, it will take a lot more investment in manufacturing facilities to absorb all those unemployed workers that are in a transition phase as a result of China's structural reforms. Therefore, I don't see wages in China moving up very much for quite some time."

"Brad, then what are you saying? Do you think that China is going to take all the foreign investment away from Mexico?"

"No, I'm not saying that at all, Jorge. I do feel strongly that Mexico can compete, just the way individual companies compete against other companies in the free market. They carve out a niche, they focus on their strengths or they develop new strengths, and they attack their competition where there are opportunities."

"What do you suggest?" Jorge inquired with interest. This was a subject about which he had thought a great deal.

"Well, Jorge, first of all, I think that Mexico should continue investing in its people, especially in the fields of mathematics and natural sciences."

"I agree wholeheartedly with you, Bradley," said Jorge with a nod. "Investing in people is critical for *any* country. I hope that *mi querido México* makes this a passionate national priority."

"So do I, Jorge. It is in the interests not only of the great Republic of Mexico, but also of every nation in our hemisphere. America struggles with the same problems, as we have seen our manufacturing jobs move from the U.S. to Mexico, to Central and South America, as well as to Asia. Dealing with that is a huge problem for us, one that I do not think that we have addressed properly."

Jorge squeezed the lemon strip into his iced tea and took a big sip. "Speaking of this hemisphere," Jorge said, "Mexico already has a great advantage that China will never have. Mexico and the U.S. not only share the same hemisphere, which in itself is important, but they are next-door neighbors."

At that moment the delicious *cabrito, arroz* and *guacamole* arrived. Steam was coming off the succulent meat. The two men paused to taste the food. It was absolutely delicious.

Jorge wiped his mouth and elaborated on his comment. "Close proximity to the largest market in the world is a decided advantage logistically for Mexico. For U.S. multinationals, the whole supply chain is more easily managed in Mexico rather than China. Would you not agree?"

Brad nodded as he polished off the last of his Diet Coke. He asked the waiter for another diet soda: "*Joven, ¿me trae otra Coca Light, por favor?*"

"*Sí señor, enseguida se la traigo.*"

"There is another element to what you just mentioned about both countries being in the same hemisphere that goes beyond the realm of business," Brad added. "It touches on national security." Jorge perked up and edged closer to the table to hear what Brad was about to say.

Brad continued: "I think that Mexico is strategically very important to the U.S. for bolstering security in the Western Hemisphere. As China emerges as an economic powerhouse, she will also channel a lot of money into her military. That's already happening as we speak, and it is making China's democratic neighbors nervous. That military build-up will be much more profound as we move forward in time."

"Do you foresee China developing into a military power similar to Russia?"

"I think China's military strength will surpass that of Russia in time. I venture to say that Washington is probably quite concerned about China's increasing military might. We can see that in Washington's cautious overtures as China emerges as the great superpower she will become in this century. For example, America has maintained an embargo on arms exports to China since the 1989 Tian'anmen Square incident."

"Wait a minute, Bradley," Jorge said with a perplexed expression. "Are you saying that while American companies continue to invest billions and billions of dollars in China every year, thereby strengthening its economy, at the same time America fears China militarily and has an arms embargo against China?"

"Yes," Brad acknowledged.

"Pardon my criticism of your country, but that seems illogical. On one hand, the U.S. is trying to contain China militarily, right? You are attempting to prevent the transfer of military technologies to China due to both national security interests and to the U.S. commitment to its hegemonic role of ensuring peace and security in the Pacific region. On the other hand, your country is giving China the economic means to do exactly that which it is trying to prevent."

"You have a valid point, Jorge," Brad admitted, "and that is an issue with which I am sure my government is grappling. The Chinese are increasing their contacts between the Chinese military and the militaries of Latin American countries each year. I think that is one of the reasons why America spends more than $100 million dollars each year in the Western Hemisphere region on foreign military financing."

"How do you know all this, Bradley?"

"Let's just say that I stay well informed."

"I should say so," Jorge added, surprised at Brad's intimate knowledge of such facts.

"We Americans believe that democracy and free markets promote peace, stability and economic prosperity," Brad said with conviction. "Washington has its eye squarely on Beijing's actions here in the Western Hemisphere. America's aim is to continue to encourage democracy, free markets, and economic integration in the Western Hemisphere with free trade accords."

"Yes, like NAFTA and CAFTA," Jorge added.

"That's right. However, having said that, I think that it is important to point out that America welcomes China into the international community as a strong, *peaceful* nation that can use her abundant resources to help with her new international responsibilities. America wants China as an ally to help in making this world which we share a better planet."

"Hmmmm…." Jorge mumbled skeptically. "It appears that your country has its work cut out for it," he said with a cautious smile.

"Perhaps you are right, but I have confidence in our Secretary of State. She is a gifted diplomat and will be a guiding force in helping China and the U.S. develop a relationship that focuses on both our mutual interests."

Jorge smiled. "Brad, perhaps you missed your calling."

"What do you mean, Jorge?" Brad asked curiously.

"You should have been a diplomat, not a businessman. The U.S. Department of State needs more people working abroad with your mentality. You have a good head on your shoulders, you have a firm grasp of global business, and, perhaps most importantly, you understand what it takes to get along in this world with other cultures. That is what America needs more of if it is to continue to be a super power and maintain good relations with other nations."

"Thank you, Jorge," Brad said modestly. "I appreciate those kind words, but I am just an accountant."

Jorge continued: "You are more than that, *amigo mío.*" Both men finished what was left on their plates. "I have a lot of confidence that we will continue to see true progress in Mexico," Jorge added. "Our progress thus far in the fight against corruption and the effort to promote transparency is encouraging. Granted, we are a long way from where we need to be, a long way. However, in the last 10 years or so I have seen accelerated progress in this area, and that is important for strengthening the belief of Mexicans in our democratic government. It shows them that we are moving more to a democracy that truly allows the power to be vested in the Mexican people, and not in the rich elite of Mexico. Mexicans want a government that is not only elected democratically but that governs democratically."

Brad smiled, "I agree with you, Jorge. There is still work to be done in the governmental and legal institutions so that the opportunities offered by democracy and free markets are enjoyed by all Mexicans, but I believe Mexico is on the right path and I applaud her progress. Without a doubt, the *maquiladora* industry has been fundamental in promoting the growth of a middle class in Mexico. I believe that we will see in Mexico, as we have seen in America, that the emergence of the middle class will help provide equality of opportunity in the Mexican economy, which has been dominated by economic elites and powerful families for so many decades. I share your conviction that Mexico has a bright future ahead of her and will continue to lead Latin America as a model for democracy and free markets. I might add that, as an American, I am proud to have Mexico as my next-door neighbor in this hemisphere."

Jorge smiled and patted Brad on the back. "And I am proud to have America as my neighbor."

The friendship between these two businessmen from different countries and different cultures was beginning to blossom. This luncheon had been instrumental in strengthening the trust in their relationship by showing how closely aligned their philosophies were. Jorge wiped his mouth with the blue cloth napkin. "This is very interesting, Brad. I invited you to this restaurant *muy mexicano* for a traditional Mexican lunch. However, based on our conversation, the lunch appears to have been more Chinese than Mexican," Jorge said with a chuckle.

Jorge turned to the waiter: "*Joven, la cuenta, por favor.*"

Chapter 7

Business Could Not Be Better

As the weeks turned into months, the star of CEO Rick Less shone brighter and brighter in the electrical products industry. He often appeared on TV business shows and was treated with the adulation of a Hollywood celebrity. His picture had appeared on the cover of many of the major business magazines, and he was frequently quoted in the business press. The 48-year-old executive was now among the superstar CEOs whose charisma and presence, coupled with outstanding corporate performance, projected them to stardom within the world of the business elite.

Since Rick Less had taken over as CEO of AMA a little less than three years ago, the stock had jumped from $22 per share to $55, very close to the magic number of $60 per share which Rick felt was the proper value for AMA. He used the power of that increase in stock price as a valuable currency to purchase more and more companies in his growth-by-acquisition strategy. AMA had issued 60 million shares at $30 two years ago and 50 million shares at $50 recently, raising a total of $4.3 billion to further fortify AMA's war chest and fund acquisitions.

With this huge amount of capital, AMA continued to make acquisitions at a blistering pace. The latest acquisitions were made of relatively large, privately-owned businesses which were marginally profitable.

During the time in which Rick had been at the helm of AMA Electric International, the acquisitions had boosted revenue from $4 billion per year to current revenues of $8 billion per year. It had taken AMA Electric International 75 years to grow to $4 billion in sales. Then along came Rick Less, who doubled the size of AMA in less than three years, an incredible feat by any standard. Operating profits increased in line with revenues, from $340 million to $700 million.

AMA's ability to issue stock was fundamental to its ability to purchase companies and continue driving up revenues, profits and, accordingly, the all-important stock price. The increasing stock price allowed AMA to purchase private, low-priced stocks cheaper and cheaper as the AMA stock price spiraled upward. In addition, the weak electrical products market this year had hit the smaller players in the industry hard. Rick moved in for the kill and gobbled up these struggling companies at bargain prices in a series of rapid acquisitions.

Success in AMA's acquisitions had a snowball effect. The additional sales of the acquired companies increased AMA's overall sales and earnings. This increase in earnings, in turn, increased AMA's stock price. Sales of AMA stock at higher stock prices provided more capital to acquire more companies. The newly acquired companies then added more sales and earnings, driving the stock price even higher. The sequence of events continued snowballing AMA into a bigger and bigger company. The financial press hailed Rick Less as a brilliant business strategist.

Through synergies in terms of a reduction of duplicate headcount, shared sales force resources, and good manufacturing execution, AMA was able to make these acquired businesses even more profitable. At the operational level, COO Harry Allen drove the "lean manufacturing" effort at the manufacturing facilities which provided productivity gains across all of AMA's global operations. CFO Bryan Taylor was expanding the lean manufacturing effort internally in the administrative area as well as with suppliers and customers.

"Business could not be better at AMA Electric International," the illustrious Rick Less was often heard to say when speaking to the financial press. "The economic downturn which has recently begun to affect our industry should not adversely impact AMA," he assured. "On the contrary, our growth-by-acquisition strategy was designed so that we should prosper because of any weakness in the market. The weak will die, and the strong will grow stronger."

* * * * * * * * *

One Friday evening Brad was sitting at the dinner table as the Jenkins family ate supper together. Since they had been in Monterrey, they had developed the custom every Friday night of ordering tacos that were delivered to their house. These were not just ordinary tacos. They were sirloin beef tacos cooked on an open grill that were so succulent and tender that Brad's mouth watered each Friday night when Sofía called to place their order. They came with fresh, homemade, corn *tortillas*; a spicy, guacamole sauce; and *pico de gallo*. Sofía usually requested two orders of *quesadillas* which were made with flour *tortillas*. *¡Qué rico!* It was Mexican food at its best.

As they sat at the table enjoying their meal, Sofía mentioned to Brad that she had seen several advertisements in the local newspaper for different job openings at AMA Monterrey. "I saw an advertisement for a receptionist position which specified that the candidates must be females between 18 and 25 years old, and it even required that they be nice looking or '*de buena presentación.*' Doesn't Mexico have laws that prevent discrimination based on sex and age?"

Brad had taken a big bite out of his *quesadilla.* He pulled the *quesadilla* away from his mouth, but streams of hot, delicious Swiss cheese were still running from his mouth down to his *quesadilla.*

"Look at Daddy's mouth!" said Liliana teasingly.

Brad smiled and wiped his mouth with his napkin. "*Perdón*," he said while he cleared his throat. "I believe that you're right, *mi vida.*"

"I thought so," Sofía said confidently. "In addition to the receptionist position, I also saw an announcement for machine operators in AMA Monterrey's die cast plant. There the ad specified that the candidates must be males between 20 and 35. I can't believe that your company would just violate the labor law so blatantly. What they are doing is illegal, and it is not right, either. Women, men, and senior citizens should not be discriminated against."

Brad nodded his head as he polished off his *quesadilla.* "I agree wholeheartedly with you, *mi vida.* I saw this practice in Juárez as well. Unfortunately, it is very common in Mexico. In fact, I have some friends in Mexico City that are in their forties and fifties, and they are terrified of losing their jobs for fear of not being able to obtain another job. They have commented to me that the market treats them as if they were over the hill, when in fact they are at their peak in terms of maturity, stability, and knowledge. It is a crying shame."

"It appears to me to be a violation of Mexico's labor laws and of these people's human rights to seek dignified work. For goodness' sakes, Mexico is a modern-day democracy with free markets. Democracy requires that there be equal opportunity for all to compete in the job market and improve their socio-economic standing in life. The fact that this kind of discrimination still exists is absurd. You should say something to the Director of Human Resources on Monday. Even if other companies in Mexico do not respect the law, your company should. Change begins with one person. AMA should set the example for other Mexican businesses."

Brad nodded his head in agreement with his wife. "You are absolutely right, Sofía. What we and other companies are doing is immoral. It's not fair; and it is against Mexican law. On Monday I shall discuss this with Carmen Silva, although she does not strike me as a very ethical person."

"Why do you say that? You have never mentioned her to me before."

"She just rubs me the wrong way. There is something about her that is sinister. Nevertheless, you have made an important point, and I shall follow up on it." Brad looked over at Liliana and little Michael who were very quiet, which was an unusual situation. Brad knew that they really liked the scrumptious beef tacos. "Don't talk so much," he said playfully and winked at them. Their faces shone with contentment. They did not say a word, but instead just looked up and smiled at their daddy and kept on eating.

Brad mentioned to Sofía how well the finance members were progressing with their English. Through funds available in the finance department budget, Brad was sponsoring on-site English instruction for his staff every morning at 7:00 a.m. This had been a big hit at AMA Monterrey because it provided a practical way for his staff to enhance their English-speaking skills. He looked at his wife and, smiling, asked her if she remembered how vigorously she had worked at her English when they were newlyweds.

"You mean Mommy did not speak English when you got married?" asked Liliana in disbelief.

"No, Sweetie. Mommy was just 18 years old when we got married and had spent her entire life in Monterrey. I was working for another company in Atlanta at the time, so she moved from Monterrey to Atlanta and began studying English."

"What school did she go to?"

"We did not have enough money for her to go to school back in those days, Love. In fact, we did not even have any furniture at all. We slept on a lumpy old mattress your granddaddy gave us. One week-end back in 1991 we drove to my old university in Athens, Georgia, and purchased some English books at the university bookstore. Then, I started teaching Mommy English on the week-ends. During the week…"

"'Mommy English?'" Liliana said with a puzzled look on her face. "What is 'Mommy English?'"

"No, Sweetie, let me re-phrase that. I started teaching English to Mommy."

"Oh, OK," Liliana said as she laughed. "Now I understand."

Brad chuckled. "I shall try to be more precise with my diction," he said apologetically. "As I was saying, during the week, Mommy studied English grammar very hard and spoke in English with everyone whom she encountered. Nobody on my side of the family spoke any Spanish except Nana, so Mommy had ample opportunity to practice her English. Then one day, at a bookstore in Atlanta, we found another book for people who wanted to learn English. This particular book had tiny cards with words that you use around the house, like 'table,' 'bed' and 'glass.' Mommy cut out all the cards and taped them all over the house. I remember that I would shave in the morning and look into the mirror and the word 'mirror' would be taped to it. I would walk into the kitchen and see 'oven' taped to the oven. I would reach over to turn on the lamp, and guess what I would see taped to the lamp?"

"Lamp!" said Liliana with a big, proud smile.

"Yeah, wamp!" chimed in little Michael.

"I knew that Mommy was doing her best to learn English as quickly as she could, so I tried to be patient and understanding. As the days went on, though, your mother got a little carried away with this idea of taping those little words to everything. Everywhere I turned there was a little card with a word. Finally, I got so tired of seeing cards everywhere that I did something to show Mommy how far she had taken this idea of hers. Mommy walked into the bedroom late one evening and saw me lying in the bed with a card taped to my forehead which said, 'Tired husband.'"

Sofía and Liliana burst into laughter.

"Daddy, did that really happen?" asked Liliana.

"Yes, it did." Brad looked across the table at Sofía. "Do you remember that, Baby?"

"*Sí, mi amor.* That seems like so long ago."

"Now Mommy speaks English very well, doesn't she Daddy?"

"Yes, she does. Your mother is so smart that now she speaks English as well as some native-born Americans."

"Mommy is smart *and* pretty, isn't she Daddy?"

Brad looked at his daughter and reached over to stroke her long, brown hair. "That she is," he said with that calm, reassuring voice that always made everything seem right.

* * * * * * * * *

The wife of Victor Reyes, Montserrat Amparán de Reyes, was a grand woman. She was intelligent, compassionate, and quite attractive for a woman in her fifties. In her family, marriage was for life—period. Members of the Amparán family did not enter marriage "to see if it worked out." Marriage was "for better or worse, for richer or poorer, until death do you part."

The Amparáns did not have money, as did some of the other fine old families in Monterrey, but they had a nobility that money does not buy. Their nobility was bred into each Amparán by parents who were kind, virtuous, and hard-working. The Amparán name had never been marred by graft nor greed. It was a good name, and the Amparáns were people of honor.

Unfortunately, while still in college Montserrat had fallen victim to the charm and charisma of one of the masters of deception, Victor Reyes. For over 30 years she had been married to this disgraceful scoundrel whose whole world revolved around one thing: pleasing himself. Montserrat always wanted to believe in her husband in spite of signs that he may be out on the prowl. Victor was so clever in his dirty dealings that even for an objective soul it would have been hard to discover his true nature.

Therefore, that Friday when Victor had told Montserrat that he had to go out of town on business for the week-end, she believed him. According to Victor, there was going to be a supplier's convention in Cuernavaca. He needed to evaluate some new suppliers for AMA Monterrey and would be back on Sunday evening.

Cuernavaca was a quaint, charming city about an hour's drive south of Mexico City on Highway 95. It was known as "The City of Eternal Spring" because it had moderate temperatures year-round and was always spring-time green. As far as the eye could see, one could encounter flowers and beautiful greenery. Cuernavaca was a romantic place. It was a city for those who wanted to celebrate the grandeur of being in love.

Victor had reserved a room in one of Cuernavaca's most charming hotels. This hotel consisted of cottages spread all over a large tract of land that, in essence, was a big, beautiful garden. The area was overflowing with flowers, trees, and rich vegetation. It was a paradise of nature.

On Saturday morning, Victor and the lovely Lolita Loya arose together, showered, and ventured over to the hotel restaurant where a delicious breakfast was being served in the main patio.

"Oh, Victor, this place is so beautiful," Lolita said as her eyes took in the abundant natural beauty of her surroundings. "I have never seen a place as marvelous as this. Thank you for bringing me here!"

"*De nada, preciosa*," Victor said as he gazed into Lolita's eyes. "Cuernavaca is indeed a natural paradise. I wanted us to see it together." He slid his hand across the table and placed it on hers.

Lolita leaned over and kissed Victor on the lips. "*Te amo tanto, mi amor.*"

Victor hired a driver to show them the sights of Cuernavaca. Everywhere they went, they encountered the same natural beauty. Lolita marveled at the colonial-style European architecture of the mansions located throughout the city. Many of the wealthy families in Mexico City had second houses in Cuernavaca to which they escaped on the week-ends and on holidays.

That evening Victor and Lolita were sitting outside their cottage in a wooden swing, rocking back and forth. Both of them sat there quietly, looking up at the stars.

Lolita, who was resting her head on Victor's left shoulder, had a pleasant smile on her face which Victor noticed.

"What are you thinking about, *preciosa?*" Victor asked as he looked down at Lolita.

"I was just thinking, Victor, about how wonderful it would be if I were married to you. Nothing in the world would make me happier than to be your wife. We could have children and we could raise them together, and we would not have to hide our love from anyone."

Victor kissed Lolita gently on the cheek. "We have talked about this before, Lolita. You know that I want you to be my wife, but right now that is not possible. We will get married one day, though."

Lolita picked her head up and turned around to look directly into Victor's eyes. That was the first time Victor had ever said that they would eventually get married. "Promise me, Victor," she said. Her eyes were full of joy. "Promise me that we will get married one day!"

Without blinking an eye, Victor smiled and said, "I promise."

"Oh, *mi amor,* that makes me so happy!" Lolita screamed with emotion and gave Victor a big, loving hug.

Victor sat there, basking in the adoration of Lolita, his most prized possession. She was truly a beauty. However, there wasn't a kernel of truth in his promise to Lolita. No matter how beautiful she was, he would never even entertain the thought of breaking up his marriage with Montserrat.

Victor was a complicated man, and it was difficult at times to understand him. There was one commitment, however, that burned in his soul; a commitment that not even the lovely Lolita Loya could ever influence. That was a promise that a seven-year-old boy made to himself over 45 years ago. Amidst tears and heart-wrenching pain, a distraught little boy vowed that he would never abandon his family. Never.

And what of this promise to Lolita? It was just a tool, a mechanism of convenience, like so many others he possessed, that he used to get his way whenever he needed it. For the moment, it served its purpose by reassuring Lolita and by making her happy so that she, in turn, would give him what he desired that week-end: the heated passion of the voluptuous and sensual Lolita Loya.

* * * * * * * * *

That following Monday work began once again at 7:30 a.m. for Brad. Upon arriving he began to answer e-mails from corporate headquarters. Atlanta was on EST, which was one hour ahead of Monterrey. After about twenty minutes, he recalled his conversation last Friday evening at the dinner table with Sofía about the manner in which AMA Monterrey was discriminating against workers based on their age and sex. He grabbed his copy of the Mexican Federal Labor Law, the *Ley Federal de Trabajo*. He turned to Article 3 and confirmed that indeed no Mexican company could discriminate against an applicant "based on race, sex, age, religion, political doctrine or social condition."

With his copy of the law in his hand, he walked down to the first floor to visit the pit viper Carmen Silva. When he respectfully entered her office, she was coiled at her desk drinking a cup of coffee. She looked up at Brad with her famous fake smile. Brad began to explain his views on the discrimination issue to Carmen, showing her the AMA Monterrey advertisements for open positions that Sofía had cut out of the paper.

Just as a snake's first line of defense against predators was to stay motionless, Carmen's trademark smile faded and was replaced by stillness. When Brad was finished, her snake eyes were glowing. She was furious and ready to strike. "How dare you march in here and preach to me about how to do my job, Bradley! Do you think that I did not already know everything you have just told me?"

Brad remained calm and gave thought to his words before he spoke. "Carmen, if you are conscious of the fact that we are guilty of sex and age discrimination in our hiring procedures, then my question to you would be the following: why are we doing it?"

"Why don't you ask that question to all the other companies in Mexico? Every company does this, Brad! You worked in Juárez for years, so you should know that. We are no different. Nobody cares about this issue! Have you ever heard of a discrimination case being brought against a Mexican company?"

Throughout Carmen's verbal assault, Brad had maintained his composure just like the gentleman he was. He respectfully waited for her to finish her ranting, and then he rebutted. "We live in a rules-based society, Carmen. If the Mexican labor law says that we cannot make a distinction based on age or sex, then we should not do so. It is as simple as that. Adherence to the rule of law is a fundamental component of democracy. I know that other Mexican companies engage in the same practice, but that does not necessitate that we do the same. We should set the example."

"Bradley," Carmen said with irritation quite notable in her voice, "you are making a big to-do about nothing. Let me repeat myself: nobody cares about this issue."

As Brad had learned from his first conversation about the company car, Carmen did not like to lose arguments. He saw that he was not getting anywhere with her. "Your position is unfortunate, Carmen…"

"Oh, please, Bradley," she said sarcastically.

Brad stood there for a minute, staring into her hypnotic, dark, snake eyes. The pit viper was beginning to cross the line with him. "Carmen, I do not appreciate your tone of voice. It is unprofessional. I came to talk to you about this to protect the company on this issue and help us to do what is right. Perhaps Mexico has not yet come to terms with this incongruence between her labor law and her labor practices. Nevertheless, that does not change the fact that what we are doing is wrong, both legally and morally. Every qualified applicant deserves a chance to compete for a position in our company. That is the law in the U.S., and we obey it. It is also the law here in Mexico. I had hoped that my bringing this to your attention would result in AMA Monterrey being a leader in Mexico in terms of compliance in this area. I was wrong. I will re-visit this issue later with the proper company officials in Atlanta."

That comment caused Carmen to do a complete about face. "Bradley," she said with her superficial sweetness, "I am not saying that we will *never* address this. There is no need to bring Atlanta into this. All I am saying is that we have other, more pressing issues right now, like staffing up for the new production lines to be transferred. We will get to this eventually, I assure you. *No te preocupes.*"

Brad was shocked by how easily she could switch from cold to warm. It was a scary sight. Obviously, he did not take her comments at face value. "I hope so, Carmen," Brad said diplomatically but firmly, "for the good of AMA Monterrey, and for the good of workers all over the great Republic of Mexico. *Con permiso.*"

After Brad had left her office, an evil smile surfaced on Carmen's face. *You are such a boy scout, Bradley Jenkins,* she thought. *I'll tell you one thing, you self-*

righteous gringo. If you think you are going to tell me what to do, you are mistaken.

* * * * * * * * * *

Bryan Taylor was the CFO of AMA Electric International. Rick Less hired this 44-year-old financial executive almost three years ago when Rick took over the leadership of the company. The former CFO for AMA, Herbert Schwartz, 59, was still a few years away from retirement age when Rick came aboard. However, Rick was adamant about having his own hand-picked team to be able to take AMA to the next level. A key player on his team would be the CFO. So, he made Schwartz a sweet offer in the form of an early retirement package, and the conservative CFO took it and bowed out gracefully. The change in CFOs appeared to be a very normal, natural succession and raised no eyebrows on Wall Street.

The relatively young, new CFO Bryan Taylor had begun his career as an auditor with Dodds Drucker Matthews, or DDM, the same firm that served as AMA's outside auditors. He spent twelve years at DDM, rising to Senior Manager in the audit department. On one heart-wrenching day, the managing partner for DDM walked into Bryan's office and advised him that he would never make partner in the firm. According to the managing partner, Bryan just did not have what it took to bring in new business and help the audit firm grow. Bryan was devastated.

Tired of the long, grueling hours and frustrated by his inability to make partner, Bryan left DDM and went to work as Corporate Controller for one of DDM's clients, Weatherproof Action America Corp., a $500 million manufacturer of weatherproof products. He spent eight laborious years at Weatherproof but was never tapped for the coveted CFO role, even though that position had been available two times.

After the second time the CFO position had been filled, Bryan was told by the CEO of Weatherproof that he was never going to get the nod as CFO. Although he was a fine accountant, he just did not have the background in operations that was needed to be an effective CFO. After all, the CEO had told him, Weatherproof was a manufacturing company, not a service company. The top finance person had to have a manufacturing mentality. Bryan was furious, but he had no choice but to accept the CEO's decision or leave. That same day on which he had been given the bad news by the CEO of Weatherproof, he updated his résumé and sent it out to several headhunters. Then one day, out of the blue, he was approached by Rick Less for the CFO position at AMA Electric International.

Bryan, who had been earning $275,000 in salary and bonus at the time he interviewed with AMA, was elated at the opportunity to move up to a CFO role. When Rick offered him a commanding $500,000 base salary plus a potential bonus of 100% of his base, Bryan almost fell out of his chair. The bonus, emphasized Rick, was tied directly to the stock performance of AMA Electric International. If the market price of the stock increased by at least 25% year-over-year, Bryan would receive a $500,000 bonus. If not, he received nothing. Bryan was floored by the offer. He finally was going to be a CFO, and he could potentially earn $1 million that year! It was the opportunity of a lifetime for him. He quickly accepted the offer and said "*hasta la vista*" to Weatherproof Action America Corp.

The superstar CEO felt that Bryan would be the team player he needed in the CFO role. Buzz Blakely, Rick's head of security and long-time confidant, had done considerable research on Bryan. Buzz's research determined unequivocally that Bryan fit the profile that Rick was looking for in his new CFO.

Rick and his right-hand man COO Harry Allen went to great lengths to ensure that the bonuses of not only the new CFO but of all the corporate officers were directly tied to the performance of AMA's stock. That would guarantee that everybody's attention was focused on that all-important stock price. Rick wanted to make sure that his team of "A players" was happy....and loyal. When it came to hitting the corporate earnings goals, Rick's standing orders were to "do whatever it takes." The cunning CEO had assembled his executive team and structured their compensation package to motivate them to do just that.

Chapter 8

The Man with the Golden Glow

In the months that he had been there, Brad Jenkins had made many improvements to the administration and to the operations of AMA Monterrey. He had already made a name for himself within the AMA organization as a very competent financial executive. However, he was still struggling with a major issue at the Monterrey facilities: the unreliability of the inventory figures in the MRP inventory system. The more Brad worked with the inventory, the more he realized that the inaccuracies were pervasive. The bills of materials (BOMs), routers, and standard costs contained countless errors. Many had not been updated for the production lines that were transferred down to Monterrey before he had arrived.

His seasoned experience made the Controller aware that this was a serious problem that had to be remedied immediately. However, in order to correct the problem over an aggressive time frame and make sure that the improvements were sustainable, Brad felt he needed to put together a cross-functional team of experts with hands-on experience. He needed an immediate and sustainable solution which could only be achieved by functional experts within AMA.

After talking with the plant managers, manufacturing engineers, planners, and cost accountants, Brad approached Victor Reyes and Victor's boss, COO Harry Allen, with a plan to enhance the integrity of the inventory database in a timely manner that would, indeed, make the improvements sustainable. The plan involved recruiting a functional expert from the U.S. plants in the following areas: manufacturing engineering, materials planning, cost accounting, and logistics.

Brad referred to the U.S. and Mexican personnel assigned to this project as the "Inventory S.W.A.T. team," and he made sure that his outstanding cost accountant, Javier Peralta, was assigned to the team. The Controller went to work on the project. Over the 12-week period, the inventory S.W.A.T. team executed very well to the project timetable. This bi-national team accomplished the objectives of cleaning up the inventory, BOM, router, and standard cost databases. They also transferred that knowledge to the Monterrey team and put processes and procedures in place to ensure that the integrity of the data would be maintained. Javier Peralta was a key player in the project. As a result of his efforts, Brad rewarded him with a promotion to Cost Accounting Manager.

Atlanta was thrilled with Brad's continuing contribution to the success of the Monterrey operations. The corporate officers were well aware by now that Brad was the man who made things happen south of the border. Whatever problem he encountered, he resolved. The Monterrey personnel said that Brad had a definite aura of success about him. They playfully called him "the man with the golden glow."

* * * * * * * * *

The day after the inventory S.W.A.T. team concluded its successful project, Paco Delgado, Director of

Purchasing, came bursting into Brad's office unannounced. "*Oye*, Brad, *¡qué onda!* What are you working on? You look so serious behind that desk."

"Excuse me, Paco, but don't you ever knock?" Brad inquired after Paco's startling entrance.

"Why? What are you going to say if I knock?"

"I would probably say 'come in.'"

"Of course you would, Bradley. You know you would, and I know you would, so why go through that? It's a waste of time."

"No, Paco, it is good manners."

"Manners, bananers, Bradley. Look, you know how the CFO Bryan Taylor is trying to take waste out of the administrative processes? Well, that's what I did a long time ago. I just applied Japanese thinking to the process of walking into someone's office and took out the waste, or *muda*, of knocking."

"On the contrary, Paco, when it comes to manners, the Japanese are extremely respectful."

"Bradley, please! Let's don't argue! You make me feel like I am at home with my *vieja*. Lighten up, *compadre*. Look, what I came in here to say was that you knocked a home run by cleaning up the inventory database. Everybody is happy now that they can trust what is in the system. So, take it easy for a while! You gringos work too much. You need to learn how to enjoy life more, *amigo mío*. You just need to spend more time with me and the *compadres*!" shouted Paco with his usual intensity. "*¡Caray!* How old are you?"

"I am 42 years old."

"Well, you need to loosen up a little bit. Don't worry. I'll help you in that department. I will introduce you to some lovely *señoritas* who will make you feel 20 years younger!"

"Thanks, Paco, but I love my wife and I...."

"I love my wife, too," interrupted Paco with a smile, "but that does not mean that I can't have a little fun on the side, eh? Look at me," Paco said as he patted his large, round, bulging belly. "I am too much man for just one woman. Hah! Hah! Hah! *La neta*, Brad, I could introduce you to some *mamacitas*....*ay-ay-ay*...I know these twins named Angelina and Josefina. They would make you realize that being 42 is twice as good as being 21!"

Brad smiled. "I am very happy with my own *señorita* with whom I have lived for 14 wonderful years, Paco. Thanks anyway."

"*Híjole*, Brad. You are such a boy scout! But that's OK...I like you! Well, I gotta go. I have people to see, things to do, and people to do things to!"

* * * * * * * * *

The next morning Brad was sitting at his desk working when his phone rang.

"*Buenos días, Señor Jenkins. Habla Lupita, la asistente del Ingeniero Reyes*," said a kind voice.

"*Buenos días*, Lupita."

"*El Ingeniero Reyes* wants to speak with you as soon as possible. Could you come down to his office at your earliest convenience?"

"Certainly, Lupita, I'll head down to his office right away."

Brad grabbed his pen and pad and made his way downstairs to Victor's office. When he arrived, he was met by Lupita. She always perked up when the Controller came around.

"Thank you for coming, *Señor* Jenkins," Lupita said with uplifted spirits. "*El Ingeniero Reyes* is on the telephone. I will let him know that you are here."

"*Gracias, Lupita.*"

Brad sat down on the couch outside of Victor's office while Victor finished his phone call. Brad could not help but overhear the conversation.

"The construction on the new plant has been delayed a couple of weeks.........I know we have already bought the cement.....*ni modo*, we will just have to wait. Just don't buy any other materials yet, and put the *muchachos* on something else. I'll talk to you this week-end. *Adiós.*"

Brad thought to himself: *That's strange. Why would Victor be involved with purchasing materials for the construction of the new plant? The builder should handle that...*

"Brad, *¡buenos días!*" Victor said with a hearty voice as he greeted Brad with a pat on the back. "*Pásale.*" The two went into Victor's office and sat down at his table. "*¿Quieres un café?*"

Just as he said that, Lupita walked in with a cup of hot, black coffee, exactly as Brad liked it. "*Aquí tiene, Señor Jenkins.*"

"*Muchas gracias, Lupita.*" Brad took a sip of the delicious mocha coffee.

Victor began chatting about the key performance indicators for the month to see if there were any way to improve the current month's forecast. Atlanta had announced that they needed to improve the actual performance for the quarter by eliminating a projected shortfall in profitability.

Victor and Brad hammered away at the expense items for about two hours, making periodic phone calls to various plant managers during the meeting. They were able to carve out a total savings for the rest of the month of about $300,000 for all five plants by whittling down planned MRO purchases, travel, and premium freight.

As Victor was escorting Brad to the door, Brad stopped and turned to him. "By the way, Victor, I wanted to make a suggestion that I think would help us in our production line transfers."

"What's that?"

"I know a really good project engineer who has strong experience handling projects involving transfers of production. His name is Ted Alston. He is a little older than I am with good credentials, including an MBA from one of the best universities in Texas."

"That is interesting that you say that, because the project manager we had, Jack Dawson, has left the company."

"Yeah, I heard about him. That was unfortunate."

"He was not a team player, Bradley. We need to find a replacement for him so that we can coordinate the transfer of all the production lines we have scheduled. So far, Atlanta has not come up with anyone who can serve as the intermediary between the transferring plants and Monterrey. How well do you know this guy, *¿cómo se llama?*"

"Ted."

"*Sí*, Ted. How well do you know him?"

"I know him very well. Ted is very personable, mild-mannered, and he gets along well with people. He also speaks pretty good Spanish. I am sure that he would fit in well here. He lives in El Paso, and the great thing is that he is available right now."

Victor looked directly at Brad. With a very serious tone, he asked: "Is Ted a team player, Bradley? You know how important that is to me."

"He is definitely a team player, Victor," Brad said with confidence. "I can vouch for that. I have seen him in action. He understands the importance of working as a team and does not get caught up in petty office politics."

"¡*Qué bien!* Tell him to send a résumé to Harry Allen and me *a la brevedad*. If you say he is good, then he must be. I trust your judgment."

As Brad made his way back to his office on the second floor, he was happy about the prospect of working with Ted Alston, a good friend and a very talented project engineer. Brad was also glad to see that he and Victor were working so well together. Victor listened to what he said and valued his input. In spite of all that, he still had this uncomfortable feeling about the emphasis Victor put on being a team player.

* * * * * * * * *

The stockholders of AMA Electric International were elated. With the rise of the AMA stock price during Rick Less' tenure, the net worth of the stockholders had skyrocketed. These investors thought very highly of AMA's top executive and, naturally, they wanted to ensure that Rick stayed at the helm of the company. None of the CEOs in the competitor companies were able to come close to creating the value that superstar Rick Less had created for AMA's shareholders. Rick was the very best, the crème de la crème. He could do no wrong in the eyes of the stockholders.

These investors had channeled their money into the company for one reason: to make more money. They really did not care if AMA made electrical products, feminine products, yo-yos or peanut butter. They invested in AMA to increase their wealth, and Rick Less was making them lots of money very quickly. Rick's meteoric rise to power was amazing. The CEO was playing to the greed and lust for money of the shareholders, and they gave him extraordinary leeway to manage the company as he saw fit. Nobody dared challenge him.

The Board of Directors of AMA Electric International had made several large grants of stock to Rick and other top AMA executives in the form of bonuses which vested immediately. The better the company did financially, the more stock they received in their executive compensation plans. It was easy for Rick to convince the Board to award him stock because of his outstanding track record with the company and his super hero status with the stockholders.

* * * * * * * * *

Zulema Palma was another one of Victor's ladies on the side. However, there was an abysmal difference between Zulema Palma and Lolita Loya, almost as marked as the difference between Victor Reyes and Brad Jenkins.

To look at Zulema, one could quickly surmise that she was of European ancestry. She had long, blonde hair and milky-white skin. Her green eyes, high cheek bones, and dainty, pointed nose gave her the look of a super model.

Zulema's grandparents had immigrated to Mexico from Spain in the1950s and started a successful chain of *panaderías*, or bakeries. Once the bakeries had taken off, her grandfather channeled the cash that they generated into several restaurants and some apartment buildings. Within time the businesses grew to provide a strong cash flow which afforded a luxurious lifestyle for Zulema's father, Ricardo, as he was growing up.

Unfortunately, the pampered lifestyle made Ricardo weak of character. He was a lazy young man who chased after pleasure and gave no thought to tomorrow. During his twenties he developed a bad drinking problem that became so notorious that everyone in the family knew he was a terrible lush.

Zulema was six at the time of her grandfather's death. At the age of sixty-four he died of a heart attack while sitting in the back of one of his restaurants going over the accounting books. Without a word, he just keeled over on the table. That marked the beginning of the end for Zulema's father Ricardo.

Ricardo inherited the bakeries and the apartment buildings. Zulema's aunt inherited the restaurants. During the early years of her life Zulema enjoyed all the luxuries that money could buy. She became accustomed to the good life as a young girl and relished it. Her father was a terrible example for her, and her mother was not much different from him. Thus, while there were plenty of material comforts and luxuries in her house, there were none of the things that make a house a home.

As time passed, Ricardo's drinking and womanizing left little time to nourish the family bakery business. One by one, the bakeries began shutting down due to poor management. Within time Ricardo had to sell both apartment buildings. Finally, by the time Zulema was twelve, her father declared bankruptcy. She had gone from an upper class lifestyle to rock bottom over the course of six years.

Terrible financial hardship ensued and dominated Zulema's life throughout her teens. She grew angry and embittered. *Why has life done this to me?* she often asked herself. *It's not fair! I should be rich! I deserve to be rich!* Zulema cried herself to sleep many nights, cursing her misfortune.

Because of the difficult financial situation, Zulema had dropped out of high school to work as a waitress. She worked at several restaurants over the years and hated every minute of it. *This is beneath me*, she complained to herself a thousand times. Then she met Victor.

One Saturday night Victor was living it up with his *compadres*, and Zulema greeted him and his party as they entered the restaurant. From the moment Victor's eyes fell upon her, he knew he had to have her. He assigned Chato, his number one man *de confianza*, to learn everything he could about this sultry blonde bombshell. Taking advantage of that information and Zulema's feelings of the unjust manner in which life had treated her, Victor was able to quickly win her over. As time progressed the voluptuous blonde became the object of his desire.

Zulema loved living life to the fullest, pampered by what money could buy. Victor showered her with beautiful clothes, a luxury car, expensive jewelry, and eventually a luxury apartment. The blonde vixen had exacted her revenge on the cruel world which had shamed her and her family. She was back on top again, this time living it up even more extravagantly than ever before.

At the time Victor met Zulema, he was in his mid-forties. Being a master at judging others, he knew that Zulema was not in love with him, but he could have cared less. He was well aware of the fact that she was with him only for the lifestyle which he provided for her. By the same token, Zulema was supremely aware that Victor only wanted to be with her for one thing, something which she provided amply and richly on demand. In many ways, she was much like him. The two used each other for what each wanted. It was a sad case of two individuals with a deep sense of inner poverty that was camouflaged to others by the luxurious lifestyles which they lived.

* * * * * * * * *

Victor Reyes always carried two cellular phones which reflected the two sides of his life. One was the public side he wanted everyone to see: the successful executive and family man. His wife, children, and AMA employees called him on that phone. The other was the dark side where his greed ran rampant and his lusts knew no bound. His *muchachas* on the side, Chato, and others in his secret world called him on that phone.

Zulema was bored that Friday and had been pestering Victor all day long on his private cellular phone. Given that she did not work or study, Zulema had lots of free time. Victor paid all her bills as well, just as he did for all his girlfriends. In fact, Zulema was by far his most expensive habit.

The 28-year-old blonde with the fabulous figure had not seen Victor in almost two weeks. She knew that it was not wise to let Victor stay away from her too long. Victor needed to be reminded of the reason she was such a treasure. Zulema also wanted to use her charms to convince Victor to upgrade her European sports car to the latest model. She had laid her trap and was attempting to lure Victor to her lair. As usual, all it took was a few sensual words over the phone to evoke the needed response and send Victor running at light speed.

As Victor made his way out the door of his office that busy Friday afternoon, he informed his assistant Lupita Anaya that he was "going to visit a vendor to resolve some issues." Lupita, who had worked for Victor for several years and had studied his conduct during that time, suspected that Victor was off on another one of his escapades. She was well paid, though, and so she kept quiet. Lupita simply concentrated on doing her job to the best of her ability. Victor suspected that she was on to him, and so he rewarded her silence and discretion with good bonuses and raises each year. She stayed out of his way and let him live his lifestyle of the rich and shameless.

Lupita was a single mother and lived with her two parents who were retired. As a result, she had others to think about which caused her to be more practical as opposed to the idealistic Controller Brad Jenkins. Nevertheless, she had the utmost admiration for Brad and secretly hoped that one day she would meet a man who possessed his diplomacy, honor, and virtue. In her mind, Brad was the perfect man.

As Victor was driving to Zulema's house in his luxury sedan, his *muchacha* hotline rang again. He glanced at the caller ID and realized that it was his newest girlfriend Jackie Villalobos. Jackie worked in the administrative office of the small, struggling Monterrey law firm of Guerrero and Pompa. The 18-year-old had been with Victor for just a few weeks.

"*¡Hola, Victor!* Where are you?" she said with an innocent voice full of the joy of youth.

"*Hola, mi amor.* I am on my way to meet a supplier," Victor prevaricated so easily.

"Victor, I want to see you. Can we have dinner tonight?"

Victor smiled devilishly. He was going to be with Zulema this evening, so he could not be with Jackie. He reveled in his promiscuous lifestyle. *I am the Don Juan de México*, he mused. *So many women, so-o-o-o little time.*

He had told his wife Montserrat that he had a business dinner, so he could use the same excuse with Jackie. "*Mira, mi amor*, tonight I have a business dinner. What about Saturday night?"

"Oh-h-h, all right. I guess I will have to wait even if it kills me. What do you want to do on Saturday?"

"We can grill steaks and, well, I think you get the idea," Victor said with a naughty laugh.

"You are such a bad boy, Victor! OK, I'll get the steaks. You bring the sizzle."

Victor liked the sound of that. *"Muy bien, mi amor. I'll see you around 6:30 p.m. tomorrow."*

Finally, Victor arrived at Zulema's apartment complex. When she opened the door, he was reminded why he paid so much for her expenses. What a sight to behold she was. The sultry blonde was wearing a gold-colored, silk nightgown, diamond earrings, and gold sandals. The inviting smell of her exotic perfume rolled off her body, seducing Victor and drawing him inside her apartment.

That entire evening had been planned to suit her purpose: an evening of passion followed by the sales pitch for her new sports car. The night went just as she had planned. She played Victor like a fine-tuned guitar. Blinded by his lust, he consented to the new car and even gave her more than her normal spending cash for the month.

Sadly, Zulema was becoming more like Victor with each passing year. She was learning to master the art of deception and manipulation. At the rate at which she was progressing, soon the student would become the master. Zulema needed to keep her guard up, however, because Victor's time was being increasingly invested in the arms of the lovely Lolita Loya.

Chapter 9

Be a Team Player

On the following Monday champagne was flowing in the luxurious Atlanta office of superstar CEO Rick Less. "We have hit the mark!" Rick exclaimed with pride to the group of AMA Electric International executives gathered in celebration of the momentous event. "With great passion we have doggedly executed what many called a pretentious plan to drive our stock from $22 per share three years ago to our goal of $60 today. Congratulations to everyone!"

"Cheers!" said Harry Allen as he raised his glass to toast the phenomenal accomplishment of AMA.

"Cheers!" the others joined in merrily.

Alice Starnes, Rick's executive assistant, rolled in a large vanilla cake shaped in the form of "60". "The first piece goes to our visionary leader, Rick Less," she said slicing a very large piece and placing it on a saucer.

"Whoa, Alice," Rick said teasingly, "you just added another hour to my jogging time tomorrow morning!" The others laughed heartily. The joy and deep sense of accomplishment had everyone in a jolly mood, and with good reason. The executives in that office had much to celebrate. Each one of them had become filthy rich because of the stellar performance of the AMA stock.

The richest of all, however, were the *compadres*: Rick Less, Harry Allen, Bryan Taylor, and Victor Reyes. With 1,670,000 shares of AMA common stock, Rick was now the "$100 million dollar man." Harry owned

1,100,000 shares worth a cool $66 million, and Bryan followed with $31 million. Victor Reyes did well in his own right. His stock was now worth $28 million.

However, all this wealth was paper wealth. In order to convert it to cash, they had to start selling their stock. That was exactly what the executives had in mind, keeping within the constraints of insider-trading laws. Slowly but surely, they would begin to turn paper profits into cash in the bank.

* * * * * * * * *

The instant that Brad walked into his office, the phone rang. Brad looked down at his watch, which showed that it was only 7:30 a.m. *Wow, it certainly is early for a phone call.* He picked up the phone.

"Brad Jenkins," Brad answered in typical fashion.

"Brad, good morning this is Harry Allen," said the polished Chief Operating Officer.

Immediately upon hearing Harry's voice, Brad pictured Harry in his mind. He was a tall, distinguished-looking man. His robust physical appearance was a deep contrast to his calm, collected nature. The successful executive had a full head of thick, silver hair, always held in place by gel and neatly parted to the side. Harry's even temperament under pressure was legendary at AMA. In fact, for an April fool's joke last year Rick Less had instructed Harry's executive assistant to replace his business cards that read "Harry Allen, COO" with "Harry Allen, COOL" because of his uncanny ability to maintain his composure. At the Atlanta corporate office, Harry was known as the King of Cool.

"Good morning, Harry. By the way, congratulations to all the folks on hitting the $60 mark for the stock."

"Yes, that was a great achievement. Now, we need to make sure we hold it there," he said as he thought about the $66 million he was going to make as he systematically sold off his stock. "Brad, I received your email on this project engineer, Ted Alston. His background looks good, and Victor tells me that you speak highly of him."

"That's right, Harry. Ted has solid project management experience, and he works very well with people. I have known him for ten years."

"How good is his Spanish? I have received résumés from people before that could not speak a lick of Spanish but claimed to be bilingual."

"Ted's Spanish is pretty good, Harry. I would say he is somewhere between functional and fluent."

"Well, good, let's get him here to Atlanta. Tomorrow he can interview with some of the divisional VPs of operations that will be moving production lines to Monterrey in the coming months. If they feel comfortable with him, and if Victor gives us a thumbs up, we'll bring him on board quickly."

"Sounds good, Harry."

"Well, you are doing a great job for us down there, Brad. If you say someone is good, that carries a lot of weight with me. You are a straight-shooter, and everybody knows that. In fact, everybody I talk to thinks very highly of you. You have proven yourself to be a key to the execution of our operating strategy in Mexico. I wanted you to know that I am counting on you for the future of the Monterrey organization. That's why I have authorized a pay increase for you. Your new base salary is $160,000 a year."

Brad was shocked. "Harry, thank you. I really appreciate this."

"No need to thank me, Brad. You have earned it. Keep up the good work, and don't forget what we talked about today. One more thing: keep in mind what Victor Reyes has told you about being a team player. That is critical to your continued success with this company."

"I understand, Harry," said Brad with a smile. "Take care." Brad hung up the phone, feeling as if electricity were running through his body. *Wait until I tell Sofía. She will be so happy. $160,000 a year!*

At the same time that he was reveling in his pay raise, he could not help but think about those daunting words that rolled off Harry's lips at the end of the conversation. *"Keep in mind what Victor Reyes has told you about being a team player." Be a team player—there it is again. I have never been in a company that focused so much on that phrase. What exactly does Harry mean by being a team player?*

* * * * * * * * *

The next day Ted Alston interviewed at AMA Electric International headquarters in Atlanta. Everything went exceedingly well. Ted then flew to Monterrey to interview with Victor. After a probing interview, Victor gave the go-ahead to hire Ted. By the end of the following week, Ted was in Monterrey working on the next line transfer, which was going to be huge. Atlanta was closing an entire die casting plant in Memphis and sending it to Monterrey.

Victor was happy to finally have that project engineer position filled with a *gringo* whom he felt he could trust. Brad had earned Victor's respect. A recommendation from Brad was a good indicator that Ted would fit right in with the team of *compadres*.

Brad's excellent work over the last few quarters had made Victor look very good in the eyes of everyone. In particular, Victor was elated with the success of the S.W.A.T. team inventory project. He felt that now was the time to bring Brad in a little closer to the inner circle of his *compadres*. He stopped by Brad's office to invite him and Sofía to dinner that Friday evening at his ranch located just outside of Monterrey. Brad thanked Victor for his help with the salary increase and graciously accepted his invitation to the dinner.

* * * * * * * * *

Victor's ranch was about 30 minutes outside of the Monterrey city limits. The ranch was fondly named "*La Pachanga*," or "The Rowdy Party," by Victor due to the numerous big bashes, wild fiestas, and other social events held there over the years. When Brad and Sofía arrived at *La Pachanga* that evening, Victor and his wife Montserrat gave them a tour of the place.

After their tour, Brad and Victor grilled steaks and hamburgers while Sofía got to know Victor's wife. Montserrat was a proper and soft-spoken woman, very much the opposite of her outspoken husband, who was quite the extrovert. She, like her husband, was also in her early fifties. Her lovely skin showed that the years had been kind to her. Montserrat had maintained her youthful figure through a vigorous exercise regime.

At the grill, Brad sipped a diet soda while Victor drank tequila.

"Brad, you did such a great job getting our inventory records straightened out and re-establishing integrity in the materials database."

"*Gracias*, Victor, but I was just orchestrating the efforts of some very talented people. They are the ones that deserve the credit, not I," Brad said humbly.

"You are right, they do deserve a lot of credit, but it was you who put this together and drove the project every week, making sure all the resources were focused on their tasks," Victor said with a smile. By then he had drunk more than his share of tequila.

"You also helped me fix the problem with the forecasting accuracy so that we could move ahead with the Memphis project. Every thing I have asked you to do, you have done well. All the plant managers are singing your praises. They call you 'the man with the golden glow.' Hah! Hah! Hah! I think that's kind of catchy. *De veras*, Bradley, you have become a valuable member of my team."

"*Gracias,* Victor."

"'The man with the golden glow'," Victor repeated to himself. "*¡Me gusta!*"

"I'm just an accountant, Victor," Brad said in his usual modest manner.

"Bradley, when you first told me that you had studied some of your Spanish in Mexico City, I thought to myself: *Oh, no, this guy is a chilango-light. I don't trust those chilangos.*" Suddenly, Victor paused and looked inquisitively at Brad: "Do you know what a *chilango* is, Brad?"

"Yes, that is what some people from northern Mexico call people who live in Mexico City, usually used disparagingly," Brad replied, offended by Victor's comments about the residents of Mexico City. Two of Brad's good friends and his father-in-law were from that great city.

With his travels, Brad had learned that there were good and bad people everywhere. He believed that people were defined by their actions and words, not by where they lived, what color their skin was, how much money they had, or what language they spoke. He had met people all over the world who were kind, honest, hard-working—people with good values who tried to live honorable lives. Thus, to categorically state that all people from a certain area, such as Mexico City, or China, were good or bad, was to make a gross misrepresentation about the human race. Given Victor's drunkenness, however, Brad opted to divert the conversation to more pleasant topics.

Victor chuckled. "You know, Bradley, I think that Paco Delgado is right about you. He says that you talk like people used to talk in those black-and-white movies a long time ago. You are always so formal and so proper. Nowadays, I just don't hear many people talking like that. I wish they did, though. My wife is like you in that respect. The fact that she was so well-spoken was one of the things that attracted me to her. Oh, yeah…another thing: you never curse, either. Why is that?"

"I just think that a man should control himself, even when provoked," Brad replied.

Victor was surprised by Brad's economy with words. He had expected a much lengthier explanation.

Brad just smiled and took another sip of his soda. "You have a really nice place here, Victor. I am sure that you have had many good times at *La Pachanga*."

Victor put his left arm around Brad and pointed with his right hand which held his bottle of tequila. "You see all this, Bradley? Every peso I used to buy this place came from hard work. I never told you how difficult it was for my family. *Mi papá*, that sorry old *desgraciado*, left us when I was just six years old. Can you believe that?" Victor asked, slurring his words a bit. "He walked out on his wife and children!"

Brad wanted to ask why, but he felt it more prudent to keep quiet.

Victor elaborated. "He ran off with some *muchacha* half his age, and he left *mi madre, que descanse en paz,* alone with five children. My oldest brother was nine at the time. He became my new father. He quit school and started working at whatever he could, and he brought his money home to *mamá*. I will never forget that day. That is why I will never leave Montserrat. *¡Nunca!* I will never break up our family, even though my children are grown. Soon I will have grandchildren. *La familia,* Bradley, *es lo más importante en la vida.*"

"I am sorry to hear that you had such a difficult childhood, Victor. It appears that you overcame your initial obstacles, though. Look at you now."

"That's right, Bradley. That day when my father walked out on us changed me forever. I vowed that I would make it, and I have. I started working when I was eight, and I have never stopped. I put myself through college. Incidentally, that is where I met my wife."

"She seems to be quite a lady, Victor. Congratulations, you are a lucky man," Brad said with the sincerity that only an honest man can exude.

"She is, Bradley, she is," Victor said with emotion, slurring his words drunkenly. "When she met me, I had nothing but *ganas*. I had no money, no car, no house, but I had *ganas* to improve my lot in life. Montserrat is the one who inspired me to start my own company when I was working for one of the metal foundries. I was in my early thirties. So, I started a company that made metal for air conditioners. After a while, I parlayed that into other businesses, taking some gringos as partners. Maybe I will tell you about that one day. Then, I started the first manufacturing plant of what is now AMA Monterrey. It took me ten years to grow it to the five facilities we currently have. Now, over two years, Atlanta wants to double it! That is why your role here is so important, Bradley. I am so proud of the job you have done," Victor said, swaying a little as he spoke. "Did I tell you that already? I'm not sure if I did or not. This tequila is beginning to affect me," he said laughingly, knowing full well that he was quite inebriated.

Soon the meat was ready. Brad helped Victor walk over to the picnic table and sat him down. Then, he brought the meat over. As the two couples feasted on the delicious meal before them, Victor did not say much. He was groggily swaying back and forth over his plate and struggling with cutting his steak. Montserrat mercifully reached over and cut it for him.

During their time together at *La Pachanga*, Brad could see how much Victor's wife actually loved her husband. Montserrat appeared to be a lady with a lot of class. She was polite, well-mannered, and quite articulate. At times, she changed to English and spoke with great facility with Brad in his native tongue. Regardless of which language she spoke, her conversation centered around two things: her husband and her family. Not once during the conversation did she mention any of the material things that Victor's wealth had afforded her.

As the evening came to a close, Brad and Sofía thanked Victor and Montserrat for their hospitality. Brad helped Victor up to his house and into his bedroom, and then he and Sofía drove back to Monterrey. During their return trip, they talked about how much they had enjoyed that evening with Victor and Montserrat Reyes. They arrived at their house at around 11:00 p.m. Sofía's mother had been taking care of their two children. "The children have been asleep for about an hour," she whispered to Sofía as they entered the house. Since it was so late, Sofía's mother stayed the night at their house.

Without Brad's realizing it, that evening had been a major step forward for him in Victor's eyes. Brad was now more that just a team player. Now, the Controller was practically one of the *compadres*.

* * * * * * * * *

Brad spent the rest of the week-end with his family. On Saturday morning the Jenkinses went to the grocery store and bought rice, *frijoles*, *tortillas*, cookies, milk and other food items for their monthly visit to the *San Cristóbal* Orphanage. During Brad's first week in Monterrey, *El Cuerpazo* gym owner Rogelio had told Brad about the orphanage, which was located close to the gym.

Rogelio knew of the difficult plight of the orphanage. The donations were oftentimes not sufficient to fund the expenses and provide a dignified lifestyle for the children. That very week Brad had begun his monthly visit to bring food to the children there. On the first Saturday of each month he had continued faithfully supporting the *San Cristóbal* Orphanage.

Unknown to Brad was the fact that Lolita Loya's mother lived right across the street from the orphanage. In fact, *Señora* Aurora Loya was good friends with *Hermana* Lucila, the kind, elderly woman who managed the orphanage. Oftentimes *Señora* Loya volunteered to help out at the orphanage. She knew that Brad Jenkins came by periodically to donate food, but she had never bumped into him. She hoped that one day she would run in to him on his visits.

Once the Jenkinses arrived that Saturday morning, they were greeted by *Hermana* Lucila. "*Buenos días,*" she said with a warm smile.

"*Buenos días, Hermana* Lucila," said Sofía. "We have some more food for the children."

"Ah, *¡qué bueno!* Please, come in."

Each member of the Jenkins family carried in packages of food including little Michael, who carried in a bag of corn *tortillas.* Once inside they chatted briefly with *Hermana* Lucila and then graciously said their good-byes.

"*Que Dios los bendiga,*" *Hermana* Lucila told them as they walked out.

The Jenkinses climbed into the mini-van, and Brad started up the engine.

"Mommy," said a sweet voice in the back. "Why do we give food to those children every month?" Liliana asked.

"Well, Sweetie, we do so because your father and I believe that we should always try to help the poor."

"But why?"

"Because if it were not for the grace of God, you would be one of those children in there who has lost her parents and does not have much food to eat. Remember, love is unselfish and it means that you think about others. Some people, such as these children, really have a tough life. That's why we should do what we can to help those in need."

"OK. Mommy. I understand now."

"Then you have learned one of life's most important lessons, *hija,*" said Sofía with her beautiful smile.

* * * * * * * * *

Those legs. Those long, luscious legs of the lovely Lolita Loya. Victor Reyes could not get his mind off them.

As Brad reviewed the key performance indicators during his presentation in Victor's weekly staff meeting that following Monday, Victor was engulfed in a fantasy about his number one *muchacha*. Finally, he could stand it no longer. His wanton desire for Lolita dominated his every thought. Forget about business. He had to see her!

Victor interrupted Brad in the middle of his presentation. "OK, Bradley, that should do it for today. I have to get out of here and run see the construction company GZZ-Mex about the details of the new plant. I told them I would be there before 4:00 p.m., and it is already 3:30. *Muchas gracias a todos. Nos vemos el próximo lunes a las 3:00 de la tarde.*"

With that, Victor stood up, grabbed his notepad, and rushed out of the conference room. He scurried down to his office and darted into his private bathroom. In a very hurried manner, the *Don Juan de México* closed the door, brushed his teeth, and gargled with mouthwash. "Ah-h-h-h!" he said approvingly as he smelled his fresh breath. Then for the final touch, he slapped some expensive cologne on his cheeks, neck, and bald head.

Now he was ready for Lolita. He grabbed his keys and dashed out the door. "I am going to meet with GZZ-Mex," he hastily told Lupita Anaya on his way by her desk. A few seconds after he had whisked by her, she could smell the heavy scent of cologne still lingering in the air. Victor could not fool her. She knew exactly where he was headed.

Back in the conference room, Brad was pulling together his papers and shutting off the overhead projector, or *cañón*, which he used in conjunction with his laptop computer to show his key performance indicator files on the screen. When he had finished, he looked up and saw that everyone had returned to their respective offices to continue with the day's work. All, that is, with the exception of one person: the ever-comical and irreverent Director of Purchasing Paco Delgado who was seated all the way at the end of the 30-foot conference table.

Paco picked up his coffee cup and walked over to Brad. "Bradley," he said with a serious look on his face, "we need to talk."

"*Claro, Paco,* what do you wish to discuss?" Brad inquired politely.

"We need to talk about transparency."

"Transparency?" Brad repeated with a puzzled look.

"*Sí, compadre,* transparency," Paco affirmed. "You always say how important it is to be transparent in everything. No offense, Bradley, but I say that too much transparency is not a good thing."

Brad zipped up his computer carrying case and cast a leery eye at the five-foot four-inch Paco. Brad knew him well enough by now to know that the fun-loving *chaparrito* was up to something.

"I am not quite sure I follow you, Paco. May I ask you to elaborate?"

"Oooh, yes, you may," said Paco, poking fun at Brad's eloquent diction. "In your country, you simply have too much transparency. For example, my wife Dulce and I have cable TV, and we were watching one of the American channels the other night. During one of the commercial breaks, a drug company showed a commercial which at first was very nice. There was this family laughing and having fun in the outdoors, surrounded by flowers and trees. It was great. Then, at the end, they start in like a machine-gun rattling off all the side effects that their product could cause. They begin with the little side-effects that really don't scare you much. Then, when you have tuned them out, they slip in the bad ones. That night they started by saying that their pill could cause headaches and nausea. No big deal. Shoot, my wife gives me those symptoms at least once a week. Then they move into the personal stuff like problems urinating, viral infections, seizures, nose bleeds, constipation, diarrhea…By the way, how in the world can you have constipation and diarrhea at the same time?"

"That is beyond my understanding, Paco," Brad said in jest.

"That's what I'm talking about. So, now this drug company, or *pharmaceutical* company as you would say with your big words, hits you with the really bad potential side effects like kidney trouble, cirrhosis of the liver, sexual inadequacy, and possible death. Death! Can you believe that? Who is going to buy a drug like that if they tell you it may kill you? Maybe that might turn on the psychos of the world, but not a normal person. Are you with me?"

Brad nodded his head.

"The worst thing is that of all the things they say on that commercial, the one thing my wife hears is 'sexual inadequacy.' So she looks at me and says, '*Oye, Paco*, that drug causes sexual inadequacy.' Then she gets real serious, and she gets right in my face, looks me in the eye, and she asks me, 'Are you on that drug?' *¡Híjole!* That comment was hitting below the belt…literally. But anyway, that's just too much transparency."

Brad laughed heartily.

"So, for the sake of people like me, take it easy with that transparency stuff. Too much transparency is not good for you."

* * * * * * * * *

Over the next three weeks Brad worked with his good friend Ted Alston on the project to move the Memphis die casting plant to Monterrey. Ted and Brad actually wrote a production line transfer procedure for AMA which they presented to Victor Reyes and the Monterrey plant managers in the weekly staff meeting.

"That is an excellent procedure, Ted," Victor commented after Ted had finished with his presentation. He looked around at the other plant managers in the room. "I especially want to emphasize the last part—making the transfer invisible to the customer. We have to maintain on-time deliveries and quality throughout the process. The customer should never know that the line has been transferred from the U.S. to Mexico. That is how good we must be. Above all, I want each of you to give Ted all of your support. We must make production line transfers a core competency of AMA Monterrey so that we can continue to grow the Monterrey operations."

With Victor's support, Ted and Brad put the plan into action as they oversaw the transfer of the production lines and 500 jobs from Memphis to Monterrey. The lines were transferred smoothly while Victor maintained on-time delivery levels to existing customers at 99%. This was a huge improvement over past production line transfers at AMA, whether it had been within the U.S. or abroad. Victor was now beginning to look very good in Atlanta's eyes. Atlanta executives could rely on the fact that if they transferred a plant to Monterrey, the transfer would occur without a hitch, and that production and service would be as good as or better than in the U.S. Victor highly valued Brad's work and was impressed with Ted's performance. The future looked very bright.

After the success of the Memphis line transfer, Harry Allen called Brad again. "Victor tells me that the Monterrey folks call you 'the man with the golden glow,'" Harry said playfully.

"I have heard that on occasion," Brad said modestly.

"Well, are you 'the man with the golden glow'?" Harry said, still needling Brad.

"If you choose to regard me as such," Brad said modestly.

"Well, I do. It is a fitting tribute to you, Brad. How long have you been with AMA now?"

"My start date was in April of last year, so it has been a year and four months."

"Well, in that short period of time your contributions to Monterrey have exceeded all of our expectations for you. Just keep on doing what you are doing. Our ability to transfer the new plants we pick up in the U.S. to Monterrey is a critical part of our low-cost operating strategy, and Monterrey has done that exceptionally well—better than Hungary and better than China."

"We have a great team down here, Harry."

"Yes, you do," Harry admitted, "but I'll tell you straight out, Brad. Before you came aboard, Monterrey was not able to execute to plan like it is doing now. Atlanta is singing your praises. I think that you even have the corporate officers convinced that you are 'the man with the golden glow.' Now, let's get to the bottom line. I have authorized Atlanta payroll to bump your salary up again, this time from a $160,000 base to $175,000. I am also awarding you a $50,000 incentive bonus for the outstanding contribution you have made to the success of the AMA strategy execution. The other top executives and I want to ensure that your pay is commensurate with the value that you bring to the organization."

"Harry, I really appreciate this."

"It is just good business sense. We want to keep you happy so that you can continue with your fine financial leadership in Monterrey."

Brad was tremendously elated, not only by the raise and bonus but also by the fact that his efforts had been recognized. When he called Sofía and told her the good news, she screamed with joy. "I'm going to go to the mall this afternoon and buy some new clothes to celebrate!" Sofía said ecstatically.

"OK," Brad said calmly, "but let's try to keep a level head about this. I know I am making a lot of money, but I do not want that to change us. It's all right to get a few things, but the rest of it we should invest. Remember: wisdom dictates that we live well below our means and save the difference. We need to continue doing that, so let's not get overzealous because of this raise. Right now they are showering me with money, lots of money, but…"

"That's right. *¡Es mucho dinero,* Bradley!" Sofía said enthusiastically. "Just think about it. Fifteen years ago we were sleeping on an old lumpy mattress with no furniture in a cramped, one bedroom apartment; just a clock radio and a phone. Now, look at us!"

"…but," Brad reiterated, grounding her enthusiasm, "you never know what the future has in store."

"OK, Mr. Controller," she said teasingly.

"And by the way," Brad added. "I was just as happy fifteen years ago with just that old lumpy mattress and no furniture as I am now. We were rich back then, as we are now, in what makes life worth the living: love and good health. Everything else is just gravy."

"*Sí, mi amor. Tienes razón,*" Sofía agreed. She adored her husband.

* * * * * * * * *

This year was developing into a tough year for AMA Electric International. The dreaded economic illness of weak demand had afflicted the entire electrical products market. For some companies, the disease had proven fatal.

America's ongoing war against terrorism had caused ballooning U.S. deficits. For a while, the government had been able to finance the deficits by drawing down on its international reserves and selling U.S. bonds. Unfortunately, the large budget deficits had continued, pressuring the central bank to monetize the deficit by expanding the money supply excessively, and the inevitable result was inflation.

This inflation, in turn, caused uncertainty about real interest rates, resulting in a risk premium that sent interest rates up higher. However, as any American home owner knows, high interest rates are the death knell for buying and selling houses, whether they be new housing starts or sales of existing homes. The higher the interest rates went, the more the demand for housing fell. The weak demand for housing had a direct impact on the electrical products used in building houses and office buildings.

For AMA the weak demand was both a blessing and a curse. At first this softness in demand for electrical products had worked in AMA's favor. The industry-wide downturn had squeezed the margins of AMA's competitors. It had put some of the smaller players out of business and left others weak and fighting to survive.

Rick was an astute business strategist. He knew that cash was the lifeblood of a business. If a company ran out of cash and had no access to borrowings, the game was over. Armed with a war chest of cash from two major stock issuances at a time when other companies desperately needed to get their hands on cash, Rick had become the predator. He picked up many of the struggling industry players at rock-bottom prices. However, the weak demand had finally begun to take its toll on mighty AMA in all segments of its business.

Further complicating AMA's plight was the difficulty it was now beginning to have in assimilating the dozens of small companies that it had acquired. This indeed was a troubling dilemma, because the fast and effective integration of new businesses was a well-publicized core competency of AMA. Try as it may, AMA personnel at the plant and corporate level simply could not keep up with the torrid pace of acquisitions that the executive officers were driving. Sales orders during the first quarter, or Q1, of the current year had been less than expected. Q2 was even worse. Now AMA was looking at a substantial decrease in sales during Q3. This would be a disaster! A decrease in AMA's sales would shock Wall Street analysts, who were looking for continued growth and profitability.

The biggest acquisition to date for AMA was Mertrico Electrical Manufacturing and Supply. Surprisingly, six months after being acquired the Mertrico fittings business was still in the red. Mertrico simply had not provided the boost to earnings which were projected by the acquisition team. When the latest earnings were reported for the Mertrico division, Rick Less was furious. He immediately called a special meeting with his *compadres*, COO Harry Allen and CFO Bryan Taylor.

"I cannot believe this, Bryan!" Rick barked at the CFO. "We spent a year studying Mertrico and convinced ourselves that it would help drive up our profits. Then we spend $500 million to buy it, and it continues to lose money for six straight months! What is the matter with Mertrico? We are already into the third quarter, Bryan. Why can't this business turn a profit?"

"Rick," Bryan said feebly, "sales prices have dropped so low that they won't cover the fixed costs. The whole electrical fittings industry is in the tank due to excess supply in the market. There simply is too much industry capacity. Until demand picks up for Mertrico's products, I am afraid it will continue to perform poorly."

Rick looked at Harry. "Harry, for crying out loud, do something about this! Cut overhead until demand returns. Get rid of some of those people who are making us lose money!"

"OK," Harry said calmly. He was seated across the desk from Rick with his arms folded, unshaken by Rick's raving. "I'll start reviewing salaried headcount figures, perqs, travel expenses, and other areas where we can make some quick improvement in that business."

"Good, put a travel freeze in place and start getting rid of people," Rick said firmly. "On second thought, let me help you with your headcount reduction efforts. Get the Mertrico president and sales VP in my office this week. I am going to give them their walking papers. They're history!"

Harry nodded his head in silence. Bryan looked at Rick, but the CFO did not say a word. He was noticeably uneasy.

Rick beat him to the punch. "Bryan, I want to see those NS-60 sales go up in Mertrico," Rick said solemnly, trying to keep his wrath at bay.

"By how much?" Bryan asked reluctantly.

"We need to get those sales up at least enough to generate a profit, Bryan." Rick, who had been sitting behind his desk with his legs crossed, stood up and walked over to the other side of his desk where Harry and Bryan were sitting. "Gentlemen, we cannot afford to let this acquisition lose money. It is our biggest and most visible purchase to date. Wall Street's eyes are following us very closely on this one. Remember: we have gained a reputation as being experts at growing profits through acquisitions, at being able to assimilate and manage those acquired assets better than the competition. That is how we got the stock to $60 per share. We picked this company up at a bargain price because it was not making money. The Street expects us to be able to turn it into a money maker. We have the talent on board to do it, so let's get to it. I have a $100 million pay-out riding on keeping the stock at $60."

Chapter 10

In Pursuit of Profit

The announcement of the closure of the Arkansas plant was made that day by executive management in Atlanta. The AMA Electric International press release indicated that it was "part of an on-going effort to rationalize production facilities acquired as a result of AMA's growth-by-acquisition strategy."

However, Brad knew the real reason: cheap labor. The cost for direct labor in Monterrey was the equivalent of U.S. $1.25 per hour straight time vs. $12.50 per hour in Arkansas for the same job. Even if you added benefits, the cost of the Mexican labor fully loaded was only $2.80 per hour.

The Arkansas plant closure was part of COO Harry Allen's overall "LCR" strategy. In performing the due diligence in its acquisitions, Harry's team looked at companies with many manufacturing plants in industrialized nations such as the U.S., Canada, Germany, and the United Kingdom. A preponderance of plants located in those high-wage nations made a potential acquisition all the more appetizing.

After the purchase was completed, Harry's team of project managers would go to work shutting down plants in the high-cost regions and moving them to low cost regions, or LCRs. There were three current LCRs to which production was being transferred. Plants located in North America were closed and sent to Monterrey,

Mexico. Plants located in Europe were transferred to Hungary, and plants in Asia were shut down and sent to China.

As he ate the crisp, tasty *flautas* covered in *salsa roja* that Sofía had made for lunch, Jorge del Valle poked his head into Brad's doorway and knocked. "Oh, I see you are eating, Bradley," he said with his normal diplomacy. "Forgive the intrusion. I'll come back later."

"No, it's quite all right, Jorge," Brad replied as he crunched a *flauta*. "Please come in."

"Thank you, Bradley," Jorge said, noticing the disheartened look on Brad's normally cheerful face. "I just wanted to pop by and say hello. Did you see the announcement about the Arkansas plant?"

"Yes, as a matter of fact I did. I was just reflecting upon that," Brad commented rather somberly. "Even though I have been in this business of working abroad for U.S. companies for 10 years, I always feel sympathetic for the Americans who lose their jobs in these types of plant closures. I know exactly how it feels for a family to lose their source of income due to competition from low-wages. I have been on both sides of this coin."

Brad's thoughts drifted back in time. He recalled how difficult it was for his family as he was growing up in the 1960s and 1970s. "My father worked in the textile industry in the Southeast, and more than once a plant in which he was working was closed and moved to a Southeast Asian country." Brad shook his head as those unwelcome feelings returned. "One of my most vivid memories as a youngster was the anger I felt at a Georgia textile mill that had taken my dad's job away. With one simple decision by management acting on the insatiable desire for profit maximization by any means, our economic stability was shattered."

Jorge respectfully remained quiet and nodded his head. He could tell that Brad wanted to talk, so he took a seat in front of the Controller's desk, crossed his legs, and prepared himself to listen actively.

"Things were different back then, however," Brad continued, almost as if he were talking to himself. "Due to the fact that most of the fighting in World War II had taken place in Europe and Asia, the infrastructure and economies of those two regions were devastated after the war. As a result, those countries had needed years of reconstruction to rebuild their economies. With a few exceptions, that left global competition basically unchecked for U.S. manufacturers in the late 1940s, 1950s, and 1960s. Business was good in America, and families prospered over that period. That was the labor environment in which my dad had worked during the first part of his career."

Jorge rested his chin on his left hand and gave Brad his undivided attention.

"Workers back then did not see this global threat coming, Jorge, especially because it began so quietly and subtly. As the European and Asian economies recovered and their manufacturing capacities improved, the U.S. began to feel the heat of competition. America responded to the competition by pursuing low wages for labor-intensive jobs in developing countries. Manufacturing facilities began to close in the U.S. and migrate to low-wage countries."

Jorge nodded in agreement. "That trend has accelerated over time and has continued right up to the present day. In fact, I see no end in sight for the perpetual pursuit of cheap labor, all in the name of profit maximization by any means necessary."

"Yes, 'the primacy of shareholder interests,' as they like to call it," Brad said sneeringly as he polished off his last flauta.

"Like it or not, Bradley, job losses are the reality of free markets. Either we can recognize what is happening in the global economy and deal with it pro-actively by re-positioning ourselves and our own skillsets, just as you have done, or we risk falling victim to these structural changes of the free market. That is the cold, hard reality of capitalism and global competition."

Brad looked sincerely into Jorge's eyes. "But is it morally right?" Brad asked his friend. "Those workers in Arkansas who are losing their jobs are the very ones who actually have done the work over the last 23 years at that plant that created the value and made it what it is today, yet they had little or no voice in the decision to close the plant. It was not their fault that AMA came knocking at their president's door seven months ago."

"I understand your point. It is very sad," Jorge lamented. "Turk Haziz, the VP of operations over my division, told me that the strategic planning group in Atlanta did their homework and knew that the company desperately needed an infusion of cash. It was no surprise when the president indicated he would consider selling his two-plant company at a bargain price. He was tired of the long hours and ready to cash out and retire to the Florida Keys."

"After the acquisition was a 'done deal,' the Arkansas plant was marked for death," Brad said grimly.

"That's right," Jorge agreed. "It was just a matter of time before the Arkansas plant would be shut down and all the production lines transferred here to Monterrey."

Brad looked Jorge directly in the eyes. "Make no mistake about it," he said in earnest. "I believe strongly in capitalism and the benefits it brings to society. I am a staunch supporter of free markets and economic integration in the global community. Free trade not only expands economies and reduces poverty, but it also mitigates corruption and strengthens democracy."

"Assuming, that is, that a country has a well-defined legal system that protects personal property," Jorge added. "Without a strong adherence to the rule of law, you will have problems similar to what is happening in China with respect to violation of intellectual property rights."

"Good point, Jorge. With a strong legal system, free markets and competition generally bring out the best efforts in people and in companies."

"Nevertheless, Bradley, as much as you and I believe in free markets, I believe we are both painfully aware that they are not without their shortcomings."

"Like the situation in Arkansas," Brad pointed out.

"Exactly."

"That is my point precisely," Brad emphasized. "Should corporations not also exist to serve society while at the same time providing that necessary profit to its shareholders? Do corporations not have a responsibility to the American public beyond maximizing profits by any means as espoused in the primacy of shareholder interests? Should the maxim of placing shareholder interests above all other interests not be balanced with the role of the corporation in society?"

"Those are very good questions, Bradley. Certainly, the object of a business is to make a profit. That is a worthy goal and the only way that a business can continue as an ongoing entity without governmental intervention. However, the means by which a company makes that profit should be examined by society. The management of a corporation should be held accountable for its actions, morally as well as financially."

"That's right!" Brad said with conviction. "It is morally right and proper for a company to make higher profits when it creates something new and helpful to society, such as a cure for a disease or some useful device. That company should be rewarded for its courage to take a risk and invest its hard-earned money in something that has the potential to benefit mankind. That is the beauty and greatness of capitalism! It challenges and liberates people, regardless of their backgrounds, to bring to market things that enhance the quality of life, and it rewards them financially for that effort!" Brad said passionately.

"However," Jorge interjected, "I think you are struggling with the issue of whether it is right for a company to continue to reap high profits by taking advantage of the workers who have helped build the company into a successful enterprise, similar to what AMA is doing. Am I right?"

"Yes, you are," Brad confirmed. "How can AMA ever expect its employees to give 100% to the company when, with the decision of a few profit-maximizing executives at the top, hundreds of jobs of loyal American workers are eliminated and those families' livelihoods disappear overnight, only to send those same jobs to Mexico, China, or Hungary where the work can be done cheaper? Where is the justice in that?"

"It is a tough pill to swallow," Jorge acknowledged.

"I believe adamantly that in America there is an unhealthy focus on short-term earnings by CEOs. This is a dangerous problem that needs to be addressed urgently. Prudent management dictates that corporations make decisions that are focused over a longer horizon than just next quarter's earnings." Brad breathed deeply and then exhaled in frustration. "I simply cannot comprehend why this destructive focus on short-term earnings is not a high-priority item on the national business agenda. Businesses leaders, government oversight bodies, and accounting organizations should be passionately hammering away at this problem, making it visible and finding solutions. But they are not!"

"Not like they should, Bradley. Of that there is no doubt. Good management requires taking into account the interests of *everyone* involved in generating a profit, not just the absentee owners who buy and sell AMA stock or the corporate executives in Atlanta who are going to get huge bonuses for short-term profit improvement."

"Jorge, wouldn't you agree that people and relationships are what create value in a company?"

Jorge nodded his head. "Indeed I do."

"Therefore, just as an individual's quest for accumulating wealth must be tempered by honorable conduct, so should a corporation's quest for profit maximization," Brad stated unequivocally. "Greed, whether it resides in a person or in a company, has a way of warping viewpoints and justifying actions that otherwise are harmful to mankind."

"The best capitalists know how to balance the rights, rewards and weaknesses that are inherent in free markets with their own responsibilities to society," Jorge said. "They understand the bigger picture of what life is really about and realize that this balance is necessary if capitalism is indeed to enhance the well-being of a town, a state, a nation and a planet."

"That is the essence of leadership," Brad concluded.

"Unfortunately, Bradley, from my perspective there does not seem to be much concern among AMA executives about its employees. To Atlanta, AMA employees are just numbers in a headcount figure. They are simply costs that can be reduced, not the assets that have created the value at AMA."

Brad sighed sadly. "Unfortunately, I do not have the answers to this dilemma. Certainly, Jorge, as we have discussed in the past, investment in education is a key component of the solution. Mechanisms also need to be put in place to deal with the brutalities of free markets. I only pray that the men and women who are leaders of businesses, the captains of industry, are asking themselves these same questions and looking for real solutions."

Brad recalled that universal truth in life: you reap what you sow. "You know, Jorge, I believe that if you live an honorable life and treat people the way you want to be treated, then things will generally go well for you. However, if you use others for your own selfish aims and then cast them aside heartlessly, it will eventually be your downfall. This is just as true for businesses as it is for people. Although the workers in Arkansas will never know it, my heart goes out to all of them who received the news today that they are losing their jobs in the relentless pursuit of profit by AMA Electric International."

* * * * * * * * *

That night Brad arrived home and was greeted at the door enthusiastically by the other three Jenkinses. He kissed his wife and picked up his children, one in each arm. Still holding his children in his arms, Brad walked into the kitchen, accompanied by Sofía. He eased down in one of the chairs and placed his briefcase on the floor. Sofía brought him a glass of fresh-squeezed lemonade and they chatted about her day while Liliana and little Michael climbed all over their tired father.

Feeling rejuvenated after his refreshing beverage and relaxing conversation with Sofía, Brad changed into a tank-top shirt and shorts and walked into the backyard to practice his Hapkido kicks and katas. Liliana joined him. She had begun practicing Hapkido when she was only four years old, and now she was a red belt. Her natural flexibility had been enhanced by years of diligent stretching.

As Brad paused to stretch in a Chinese split, the sweat pouring off his face, he watched Liliana go through her katas. She was poetry in motion. Her kicks were fast, sharp, and powerful for her little frame. Her movements reflected the flowing, circular movements which were a fundamental part of Hapkido. She flowed through the katas like water running over rocks in a stream. At times her movements were slow and gentle, and at times quick and intense. Brad took comfort in the fact that by the time Liliana became a grown woman, she would be able to handle herself in just about any altercation she might encounter.

When they had finished practicing Hapkido, Brad lifted weights. Tonight he was focusing on his shoulders and trapezius, or traps as he called them. Within forty-five minutes he had completed his routine. Liliana ran up to her father quickly. "Daddy, would you play on the trampoline with us?"

Even though Brad was fatigued, he gladly accepted her daughter's invitation. "Sure, Sweetie. I'll race you to the trampoline!"

Once they had climbed onto the trampoline, they all held hands and began jumping up and down as they moved in unison to the right. Liliana and her brother were shouting and laughing merrily. As Brad picked up the pace, Liliana began to protest. "Daddy, not so fast!

Not so fast!" she screamed as she laughed, enjoying the challenge of trying to keep up with her father.

Soon they were jumping out of synch, and they all fell one-by-one to the trampoline mat. They continued to play this game until they could jump no more. They lay on the trampoline utterly exhausted, breathing heavily from all the jumping. Shortly, their breathing returned to normal, and a silence fell upon them. They all looked up at the beautiful, clear, moonlit sky.

"Daddy, why did God make the stars?" Liliana asked with that wonderful curiosity that children have.

"I'm not sure, Love, but I know there must be a reason."

"You don't know? I thought you knew everything!"

Brad chuckled. "No, Sweetie. There is a lot that I do not know. However, I do believe that God is the Creator of everything, and He had a master plan in that creation. When I look at the stars, I realize how great He is to have created the heavens."

"Yeah, it's beautiful. Oh, look Daddy! There is a shooting star or a comet or something! Look!" She pointed up toward the sky.

Brad looked up and saw the bright light shooting across the heavens. "Wow, that is beautiful."

"Where? Where?" asked little Michael anxiously. "I wah see the shoe star!"

Liliana giggled. "Shooting star," she said, still laughing, "not shoe star."

Michael snuggled up next to his father in the middle of the trampoline. Brad put his arm around his son and kissed him on his forehead.

"Hey, what about me?" said Liliana, playfully jealous as she curled up next to her father on the other side.

Lying there under the stars, Brad's thoughts drifted back in time to the night on which Liliana was born. He recalled how overwhelmed with emotion he was when the nurse handed him his newborn daughter. All he could do was smile and look down at the tiny, precious bundle of life in his arms. With little Michael, the experience of creating life was equally as powerful. As his children grew, the journey of life began to make more sense to Brad. He grew to understand more fully the unselfishness, patience, and forgiveness implicit in loving another person.

Liliana looked over at her father. With a look of surprise she asked her father, "Are you crying, Daddy? Why do you have tears in your eyes?"

Brad rolled his head over to the right to look at his daughter. "Moments like tonight are the only ones that really matter, Sweetie: the special moments that are sprinkled throughout your lifetime that make life worth living."

Liliana cuddled closer to her father and closed her eyes.

Soon, all three had fallen asleep on the trampoline. Their dog Gino was lying on the ground next to the trampoline, faithfully guarding them. There they slept peacefully underneath the beautiful heavens.

Around 10:00 p.m. Sofía came walking out into the backyard, wrapped in her nightgown. *"Mi amor,* wake up! It is 10 o'clock. You need to take a shower and go to bed. Help me get the children inside."

Brad quietly got up, still groggy from being rousted out of a deep sleep. He yawned and stretched, which helped to wake him up. Then, he carried Liliana inside while his wife carried little Michael. He took a quick, hot shower, brushed and flossed his teeth, and collapsed into his bed. Sofía reached over and kissed her husband gently on the lips, pulled the covers over him, and turned out the bedroom lamp.

Chapter 11

Whatever it Takes

By early the next week all the Monterrey personnel assigned to the Arkansas project had arrived at the AMA plant in Arkansas to begin executing the production transfer plan. Brad received a call on Wednesday afternoon from one of the project engineers and Brad's trusted Cost Accounting Manager, Javier Peralta. The two were having a rough time.

"*Caballeros,* how is the prep work going?" Brad inquired optimistically, trying to dispel the gloom in their voices.

"Not very good, Brad. The people here are not cooperating with us," Javier replied gloomily.

"I am sorry to hear that, gentleman," Brad said. "In what way are they not cooperating?"

"Well, they still have not given us access to their system so that we can begin working on our audit of the bills of materials, routers, and standard costs. Their engineers never have time to meet with us, either. *Son bien gachos con nosotros.* We have been keeping our cool, but our patience is wearing thin."

"OK. First of all, I will talk with their plant manager, Bill Sawyer, and make sure that we get the support there that we need. Bill is a good guy, and I'm sure that he will help us to get his people to cooperate."

"Secondly, let's step back from the canvas of this situation for a minute and try to look at this situation through the eyes of the Arkansas employees. For just a couple of minutes, I would like to ask you gentlemen to think about how those people in Arkansas feel. Put yourselves in their shoes. Let's suppose that Atlanta announced last Friday that they were shutting down Monterrey and sending all the production to China. How would you feel?"

"Very depressed," Javier said. "I'm sure I would feel like the company didn't care about me."

"Now add to that the possibility that you had worked for 10 or 15 or maybe even 25 years at the company and had no prospects of finding a job anywhere near that pay level in the future. Then, an engineer and an accountant from the new Chinese plant come to visit the Monterrey operations to review your systems before they transfer everything to China. How would you feel about the situation then?"

"I know that I would be very angry at the company," said the project manager.

"In your heart, would you want to help the Chinese employees?"

"No, I would not."

"OK. Now that we have been able to see things through the eyes of the Arkansas employees, we can understand why they are not finding time to meet with you and why they are not cooperating in other areas. They feel hurt, maybe even betrayed by their own company. It is nothing personal against you. It is just the reality of the global market place in action, and sometimes that reality is tough to deal with if you come out on the losing side. With respect to your relationships with these fellow workers, just treat them the way that you would want to be treated if you were in their places. I will do my job and get on the phone with the plant manager as soon as we hang up. If there is not a marked improvement in the level of cooperation by tomorrow morning, please call me back."

"OK, Brad. *Oye, muchas gracias.*" The two looked at each other when the phone call was over, smiled and nodded at each other. Without a word being spoken, they communicated to each other that they were working for someone truly unique in the ferocious warfare of global business.

Immediately upon hanging up with his Monterrey team, Brad telephoned the Arkansas plant manager, Bill Sawyer, whom he knew fairly well. He very diplomatically explained the situation and solicited the plant manager's support, which he received. The next morning Bill Sawyer called Brad back to advise him that everything was back on track. He thanked Brad for working through him rather than going to his superiors in Atlanta on this issue.

"No problem, Bill. I just did what I would have wanted you to do if I had been in your shoes. You have been dealt a tough hand, and I feel for you and your people. Thank you for your support in making this project a success."

* * * * * * * * *

During the last week of September, the end of the third quarter, the number-crunching Wall Street analysts appeared on all the business news channels to make their earnings projections for the final quarter and the year for the best known companies as well as the companies to watch. Among those companies to watch was AMA Electrical International. The consensus was that AMA would make $190 million in operating profit before taxes in the last quarter, or Q4, and $700 million for the year on sales of $8 billion.

The numbers were staggering. Rick Less and Harry Allen continued to feel pressure to report quarterly earnings in their financial statements that were on target with Wall Street analysts' predictions. It was as if Wall Street were determining the company's earnings goals and then management was reacting to achieve those targets.

During the weekly profit status meeting that Friday with Rick Less, Harry Allen, and Bryan Taylor, Rick led off as usual. "The consensus on The Street is that AMA will earn $700 million this year. Harry, get the word out to your operating VPs that we need $190 million in operating profit this quarter. Assign them their relative portion. Base the distribution on Q3 OP."

Bryan interjected. "Our preliminary forecast submitted this week projected about $100 million in OP, and that's our best case scenario. We are off by about $90 million, Rick—almost half the profit that The Street expects."

"Does that $100 million profit include NS-60 sales?" Rick asked.

"Yes, it does," Bryan replied with gloom in his voice.

"Well, we need to come up with the shortfall. Harry, get with JT Terrence and get more aggressive with the VISTA system billing. Look at current operational costs and see if there are any grey areas where we can capitalize them. Cut expenses—you know the drill. Bryan, take a look at the restructuring reserve. Do whatever it takes to hit that number. All three of us in here have too much riding on this not to hit that number."

Harry folded his arms across his chest, looked down at his feet and nodded stoically. "We'll take care of it," said the silver-haired executive reassuringly.

Bryan spoke up, nervously. "Rick, our cash flow position is deteriorating rapidly."

Rick looked at Bryan with intense eyes. "Bryan, I thought you were working on that $500 million line of credit with the group of bankers you took down to Monterrey a few months ago."

"I am. Fortunately, I think we will be able to get the loan—unsecured. Also, I suggest that we pay Series C and D preferred stock dividends in common stock rather than cash. That will save cash and help take advantage of the high price of the common stock."

"Very good, Bryan, I knew I could count on you. Let's look at a new stock issue while the price is at $60. With the proceeds from the stock issue, we can pay down the line of credit."

"Joe McGhee in Treasury is working on that with the investment banking firm of Stanley Wharton Rutz."

"Good. OK, gentleman, let's get to work."

* * * * * * * * *

The following Monday, Harry met with his seven operating vice-presidents and advised them of their new operating profit targets. Also in attendance was John "JT" Terrence, VP of Distribution and a long-time friend of Harry's. Prior to the meeting, Harry had met with Bryan Taylor to do just as Rick had requested. He allocated the profit targets out to the divisions based on their respective profit in the third quarter. Thus, the best performers had even more pressure heaped on them.

"This is what Wall Street expects, this is what Rick expects, so this is what we have to do," Harry stated firmly. "You are the best managers in the business. I know we can find a way to execute better and hit this. It's $90 million more in total profit for the quarter. I know that's a lot, so do whatever it takes. That comes straight from Rick."

There were groans and some mumbling as the figures were read, because the new targets were much greater than the optimistic forecast they had submitted the prior week. However, all of them knew that if they could not hit those targets, then Harry would find someone who could. Earlier that year the VP of Operations over the plastics division failed for two consecutive quarters to make his numbers. He was out the door the same day that the second quarter ended. It was an unwritten rule at AMA: either you hit your numbers or you were off the team.

Even though they thoroughly disliked being put under the gun by their Chief Operating Officer, the operating VPs knew that they would be hard pressed to find a compensation package which equaled what AMA offered. AMA paid top dollar for the best and showered them with stock options and stock grants. The VPs were getting richer as each month passed. They were not about to let anything happen which would cause them to lose their well-paying jobs. Life was too good.

Since Rick and Harry had come aboard, the operating VPs had become adept at learning how to manage their numbers to ensure that they met the expectations of "The Street." Brad had seen and challenged how the operating VPs used the "cookie jar" approach to temporarily park good accounting results until they needed them. These unethical managers had learned other techniques as well. Those techniques were, in reality, highly questionable accounting practices which deviated from the conservatism that should abound in good financial reporting.

The operational VPs were always able to justify to themselves "fudging the numbers." Somehow, they were able to rationalize their questionable accounting practices within their analytical, results-oriented minds. The divisional controllers who worked for the operating VPs were put under the same intense pressure to cooperate, to be "team players," and to find ways to help their respective divisions make the number that Wall Street was expecting. The controllers were also rewarded handsomely for doing so. Sometimes it was a huge bonus of cash, but more often than not it was a bonus of AMA stock. Even the 401(k) match was given in company stock. Rick Less went to great lengths to ensure that compensation packages, performance goals, and executive attitudes gravitated around the value of AMA stock.

* * * * * * * * *

The sultry blonde Zulema Palma was feeling nervous and depressed. She had not heard from Victor in several days, which did not bode well for her relationship with her financial backer. Reliable sources had informed her that Victor had been with Lolita Loya twice this week, yet he had not even given Zulema one lousy phone call. Things seemed to continue spiraling downward for her and her *amante*.

Walking over to the mirror, she looked at her beautiful, wavy, blonde hair and perfect complexion. Not only was she genetically blessed with young-looking skin, but ever since she was a small girl she had gone out of her way to protect her skin from the ravages of the sun. The result was creamy-white skin that was so beautiful that she was the envy of girls ten years younger.

What is it that Victor does not see in me? Am I not beautiful and sexy? Do I not shower him with affection when he is with me?

Just as long as she was his number one and he kept the cash flowing into her bank account, Zulema could accept the fact that Victor would never be satisfied with one woman. What terrorized the blonde vixen was being cut off by Victor and having to return to her life of poverty. She had anxiety attacks when those horrifying thoughts crept into her mind. That fear fueled her hatred for Lolita.

Picking up her phone, she called Victor on his private cellular phone. *"Hola, Victor. ¿Cómo estás chiquitito?"*

"Uh, I am in a meeting right now, *mi amor*," Victor replied as if he were talking to his wife Montserrat. Zulema recognized that tone and realized that Victor must be with one of the people in his "other world" that never crossed over into her world with him. "I'll call you back in a little while."

Victor hung up the phone, and then turned his attention back to the two gentlemen seated at his table. They were conducting the weekly status meeting on the Arkansas plant production transfer. "Bradley, the Arkansas project is moving forward ahead of schedule. GZZ-Mex has exceeded my expectations again by finishing the construction of plant number seven already, so I would like for us to begin moving production lines to Monterrey next week. That is a week ahead of what we have here in the project management template." Victor turned his head to Ted Alston. "Ted, do you feel comfortable with that?"

Ted took a deep breath, then smiled and nodded his head. "I think we could accommodate that with a little OT this week-end," the friendly Texan said.

"¡Muy bien! Then let's do it! Ted, you call Bill Sawyer in Arkansas and I'll let Harry Allen know that we're ready to begin moving the lines." Victor stood up, indicating that the meeting was adjourned. *"Muchas gracias, caballeros."*

After Ted and Brad had walked out of Victor's office, he closed the door and called Zulema back. She picked up the phone in her luxury apartment and checked the caller ID. It was Victor!

"*Chiquitito, ¿qué onda?*"

"How are you this fine morning, *mi reina*?"

Good, thought Zulema. *He's in a pleasant mood.* "I have missed you the last few days, *mi amor*. Let's do something!"

"Now?" asked Victor, a little surprised. "I am in the middle of work."

"But you are the boss, *el gran jefe*. You can do whatever you want, *chiquitito*. Come see me. I'll make it worth your while," Zulema tempted Victor with her inviting voice.

The mere sound of her words made Victor's mouth water. He looked down at his watch. It was almost noon. *Well, I need to take a lunch break anyway,* he decided. "*De acuerdo, mi reina.* Why don't you order some food and I'll be there in about thirty minutes."

"Wonderful!" Zulema exclaimed happily. "I'll be waiting for you. I hope you slept well last night!"

"Heh-heh-heh," Victor laughed devilishly. "I'm on my way!" Victor closed his cellular phone and headed out the door. He looked over at Lupita and declared flippantly, "I'm going out for a snack. I will return in a couple of hours."

"*Sí, Ingeniero,*" replied Lupita respectfully. Whenever her boss darted out the door with that much enthusiasm, she knew that there was only one thing he had on his mind.

Victor was already out of the entire building before Ted and Brad had made it back to Brad's office. While they were walking up the stairs, Ted remarked sarcastically, "Victor and I have very divergent points of view on GZZ-Mex. Those bums exceed my expectations when they show up for work."

"What happened this time, Ted?" Brad inquired with concern.

"Those GZZ-Mex jerks didn't show up for work two times this week, Brad," he griped. "Can you believe it? I simply don't understand it. We have constant problems, poor quality and horrible service, and yet Victor always defends them. What's more, Victor uses GZZ-Mex on everything from re-painting old walls to building our new manufacturing facilities," he grumbled.

Ted was right. Without fail Victor used the same local construction company, called GZZ-Mex *Constructores*, on all the work for AMA Monterrey. This irritated Brad because GZZ-Mex seemed like a poorly-run construction outfit. Ted was not the only critic of GZZ-Mex. The AMA Monterrey engineers and others who worked with GZZ-Mex frequently complained of their unreliability and the poor quality of their work. Sometimes they complained to Victor, and he, very reassuringly, told them not to worry. GZZ-Mex would "make it right."

Another aspect about GZZ-Mex made Brad even more skeptical. Victor Reyes always insisted upon managing the construction of the new plant sites himself. He was adamant about it and would not allow Ted, Brad, or anyone else to be involved.

It all reeked of something that Brad had seen in *maquiladora* companies in Juárez. *No, not that! Not here! My life is going so well,* he thought. His deep, gnawing concern about GZZ-Mex was beginning to eat away at the pit of his stomach.

After a brief silence, Brad spoke. "Ted, although GZZ-Mex's poor performance is a constant source of agitation for us, your very capable project management skills always compensate for the inadequacies of GZZ-Mex. I think that is the main reason Victor likes you so much. He knows that come Monday morning, Monterrey will be ready for the first lines of production of cellular phone connectors from Arkansas."

"Brad, I appreciate the vote of confidence," Ted said in his Texan drawl. "I guess I should not complain so much. Victor has given me a great opportunity down here."

"That's the spirit!" Brad said, patting Ted on the back as they walked into his office.

Brad and Ted worked through the week-end to get all the details finalized for the transfer of the Arkansas plant production to Monterrey's plant number seven. The following week the Arkansas production lines began to move to Monterrey. Again, the project execution was outstanding. By the end of the month, the entire plant had been transferred flawlessly, and it was "invisible to customers," just as Victor had instructed. AMA Monterrey had proven once again that it was a magnificent production site and could handle all the investment that Atlanta could send it.

* * * * * * * * *

That month the Controller also pushed ahead on the rigorous compliance work related to the Sarbanes-Oxley Act, nicknamed "SOX" by many accountants. SOX was legislation passed in 2002 in response to the large accounting frauds that had occurred in recent years. Its purpose was to raise the responsibility of the people involved in the financial reporting process of publicly-traded companies.

Atlanta had named Brad as the leader of the SOX Section 404 compliance work for Monterrey. That part of Sarbanes-Oxley dealt with management's assessment of internal controls and required that public companies provide evidence that controls in their business existed and were effective. Brad set up a meeting with Victor Reyes, the plant managers, and functional directors in Monterrey to explain the importance of the project and solicit their support for the people that would be involved in the internal control documentation.

"You have all heard me talk about internal controls a lot," Brad said to the group. "Internal controls are processes which give us reasonable assurance that we are safeguarding our assets and effectively mitigating the risk that our financial reporting will contain material misstatements…"

"Speak Spanish, or English…just don't speak that accounting mumbo-jumbo," said the irrepressible Paco Delgado from the back of the room. He loved to needle Brad, especially in front of others.

Brad paused for a minute to re-group his thoughts. "Perhaps I have tailored this presentation to a group of accountants rather than a cross-functional group. Forgive me," Brad said humbly, and then he continued. "Really, this is something that companies should have been doing all along—focusing on good, basic internal controls in all our processes. SOX now makes it the law that AMA management must document these controls, review the documentation, and then test the controls to ensure that they are functioning as documented. Then, our outside auditors, Dodds Drucker Matthews, will come in and perform their own testing of the internal control structure."

"We have to write down all of our controls in everything we do? That sounds like a lot of work for nothing, Brad," Victor said cynically. He caught Brad completely off guard with his comment, but he did not stop there. "In the end, all that work will not change a thing. It won't change whether someone will try to commit a fraud. It may make it more challenging, but smart people will *always* find a way to beat the system. No amount of documentation or testing will change that fact, especially if collusion is involved," he said almost triumphantly.

Brad looked at Victor and paused for a moment before continuing. He carefully weighed his words. Victor's comments certainly were not appropriate for the *Director General* of AMA Monterrey, and they were undermining his attempt to promote the importance of complying fully with the spirit and the letter of the SOX law. However, he knew that Victor had a valid point. With the advances in technology that had taken place in the last twenty years, currently it was difficult to detect frauds caused by the really clever crooks.

Brad regained his composure and continued. "The most important point that I can make to all of you today about internal controls is that they are not just the responsibility of the finance department. Internal controls are the responsibility of everyone. That includes all of you. Each manager here is responsible for ensuring that internal controls in his or her area exist, are documented and are complied with everyday. Now, with Section 404 of the Sarbanes-Oxley Act, you are going to have to prove it." Brad continued to discuss the work to be done over the next few months.

The managers, a little bewildered, looked around at each other. Finally, Pancho Zapata, the ever-nervous plant manager of plant number one, spoke up. "*Oye,* Brad. What does Sarbanes-Oxley have to do with...uhhh... manufacturing in Mexico? That law is for the United States...for the United States. Why do we have to worry about it? We are in Mexico."

"Good question, Pancho. SOX is indeed a U.S. law, but it has a direct impact on the Monterrey operations, on what we are doing, because the financial results of everything we do here in Monterrey are consolidated and reported through AMA Electric International in the United States. AMA is a public company and sells its stock to millions of investors through one of the stock exchanges in the U.S. It is registered with the Securities and Exchange Commission, or SEC. Therefore, all of its world-wide operations are subject to this law. Does that answer your question?"

"*Sí. Sí-sí-sí. Gracias, Bradley,*" Pancho replied in his typical nervous fashion.

Victor once again ruffled Brad's composure. "Well, if it is the law, then I guess we have to comply. However, I do not want us losing focus of what puts food on the table: manufacturing electrical products. We do not earn one peso for documenting internal controls. Bradley, do what you have to do to comply, but remember that I need you to be focused on the profitability of these operations."

Brad nodded his head, acknowledging Victor's instructions. The disappointment on his face was obvious. Ever the gentlemen, he gave Victor his due respect as the top executive in Monterrey. Regardless of Victor's opinion, however, Brad intended to push ahead fervently with SOX Section 404 compliance. Even if documenting controls did not pay one peso, not documenting these controls and falling out of compliance with Sarbanes-Oxley could have catastrophic repercussions.

* * * * * * * * *

Over the next few weeks Brad spearheaded the Sarbanes-Oxley, or SOX, Section 404 internal control documentation and testing. The Controller selected team members from various areas in the company, not just finance, who understood financial and operational controls well. These core team members were the leaders who facilitated the process within each functional area by helping lead the documentation of the controls of each transaction cycle.

What Brad learned, however, was that many people were spending a tremendous amount of time documenting hundreds of procedures and processes instead of performing their normal jobs. The SOX Section 404 work was terribly burdensome for his own staff, and the fall-out was the same in purchasing, materials planning, customs, HR, and every other area. Poor Brad was the brunt of attack for the entire Monterrey organization. He accepted that criticism, however, since he was the leader of the project.

Finally, the SOX work became so overwhelming that Paco Delgado erupted in anger. He marched upstairs to Brad's office.

"SOX sucks!" Paco screamed as he waltzed into Brad's office.

"Don't you knock?" Brad said on that occasion, as he did on every occasion that the short, pudgy Director of Purchasing burst rudely into his office.

"Knocking is *muda*, Brad. We already talked about that. Look, my people are working 12-14 hours a day, but they're not working on purchasing our much-needed materials for these operations. Do you know what they're working on, Bradley? Can you guess?"

Brad looked at Paco's face which was red as a beet. "I would venture to say that they are probably documenting and testing controls for Sarbanes-Oxley."

"That's right, they're working on SARBANES-OXLEY, or SOX as you accounting nerds like to say. Sarbanes-Oxley! Sarbanes-Oxley! Sarbanes-Oxley! That's all I hear!" Paco was screaming at the top of his lungs. "My people have important work to do, Bradley. They don't have time to sit around documenting things that are second nature to them. It's a waste of time!"

"Paco, I understand your anger, but please calm down before you give yourself a heart attack," implored Brad.

"Heart attack? Oh, don't worry about that, Bradley. I have a pill for that," Paco said as he held up a yellow pill. "*Sí señor*, I have been watching those American channels on cable TV every night, remember? Well, those drug companies are changing my life! Yeah! When I am stressed-out, I take this yellow pill, but when I am depressed, I take a white pill. I take a pill when I can't get to sleep, and then if I can't wake up in the morning, I take another pill. I'm taking this purple pill to lose weight, see?" Paco showed him the small pill. "And, I'm taking this pill to stop smoking. Here, look at it. When Spring comes, I won't worry about my allergies, because I have a pill for that. Look at me! I'm worse than you gringos."

"Whoa, Paco, you need to calm down," Brad said as he stood up, walked over to the Purchasing Director, and gently sat him down. "Paco, I am concerned about you. Are you really taking all that medication?"

"Sure I am. What about you? Don't you take medication?"

"No, Paco, I don't. I focus on the preventative side such as eating properly and exercise."

"Oh, that's right. I forgot that I was talking to Mr. Perfect. Don't tell me—you're high on life, right?"

Brad chuckled. "Yes, I guess I am. Seriously, Paco, you seem to be really stressed out. Talk to your doctor about the combination of all the medication you are currently ingesting…"

"*Taking*, Bradley, *taking*! Most people *take* medicine. You're the only one I know that *ingests* medicine," said the wise-cracking Paco. "You and your fancy words, Bradley, you're killing me with them."

"Indubitably," Brad said just to spite him.

"See! That's what I'm talking about! Oh, the inhumanity of it all! Listen to you! What was that word? In-du-bi---what? What kind of a word is that? Look, I'm making a new company policy. From now on AMA Monterrey personnel cannot use a word with more than four syllables. OK? That's the limit. If you use words with more than four syllables, you will be fined…$100 pesos. I'll get Victor to send a memo out on it tomorrow."

Paco's craziness had Brad laughing again. "Paco, *amigo mío*, you really have a gift," Brad said as he pat his fellow director on the back. "Now, getting back to Sarbanes-Oxley…"

"Wait," Paco interrupted, "let me get my yellow hypertension pill if we are going to talk about Sarbanes-Oxley. OK."

Brad continued, "I understand the misery that this work is causing everyone, Paco, because I more than anyone else am living it. I have to personally review each control objective and assessment that is written— for all the functional areas. Then, I have to ensure that they are tested by someone in my group."

"Wow, I did not realize that. That *is* a lot of work. Here—let me give you one of these grey pills so that you don't fall asleep."

"You are very kind, but no, thanks, Paco," Brad said graciously. "SOX is the law, Paco, and so we must comply. Sarbanes-Oxley has a noble intent, which is to strengthen investor confidence in the financial statements of public companies. Over the last few years we have lost that confidence."

"I understand that, Bradley," Paco said in a serious tone. "However, I have to ask you straight out. Do you actually think that all this work will make a difference? I mean, look at us. For the last few weeks we have not been doing our jobs. We have been working for the U.S. government as professional control documenters."

Brad nodded his head. He could empathize perfectly with Paco.

"Do you think complying with Sarbanes-Oxley will stop accounting frauds?" Paco asked.

Brad took a deep breath and then responded. "No, Paco, I don't. However noble its intent, it will not prevent accounting frauds."

"Well, then, you're the 'man with the golden glow.' You have all the answers, so what's the answer to this dilemma, golden boy?"

"Paco, I certainly don't have all the answers, but I will voice my opinion on what I *do* think will make a difference."

"Great, tell me. I'm all ears! Well, actually I'm all stomach," Paco said looking down at his big belly and patting it, "but I'm listening."

"I do not believe that America, or any country for that matter, can change morality through legislation," Brad said. "In my humble opinion, the only effective way to deal with the root cause of accounting frauds rests in the strength of the family structure. Parents should raise children with good values such as honesty and a concern for the public good. That must be instilled in children at an early age and nurtured throughout their formative years. Then, when the children become adults, they will have the wisdom to know right from wrong and the discipline to do what they know is right. However, I feel that passing a law such as Sarbanes-Oxley will do little to change the behavior of would-be adult criminals."

"I agree with you totally. So what do we do given that scenario? Do you, as the project champion, still expect us to kill ourselves trying to do our jobs and document and test all these controls?"

"For the time being, Paco, we must," Brad said somberly. "However, I know that many financial professionals in the U.S. are expressing the same frustrations that we feel, that SOX Section 404 is too burdensome. I would expect that in the future there will be some modifications to this law to bring the perceived benefits more in line with the costs in terms of everyone's time."

"In other words, I need to take another one of these green pills and get back to my computer," Paco said as he stood up and patted his robust belly.

"Take it easy on those pills, Paco," Brad admonished. "Hey, why don't you start a good work-out program? I can help get you started."

"I have, Bradley. I have been doing a lot of running," Paco said proudly.

"That's great, Paco. I am impressed. The more time you dedicate to exercise…"

"Yeah, boy," Paco interrupted. "I run after women of ill repute, chase after hotties, and, when I catch them, well, since you are such a boy scout I'll just leave it at that."

Brad shook his head in disapproval. "Paco, you are a handful."

"Just a handful? More than that, Bradley, my boy," Paco said in his typical pert manner as he walked out the door.

Chapter 12

Revelations Made over Burgers and Fries

That particular Tuesday was a pleasant day in October. Summer was gracefully bowing out, and autumn was timidly beginning to show her presence. The forecasted high for the day in the industrial powerhouse of Monterrey, México, was a moderate 70 degrees Fahrenheit.

Brad had chosen plant number two, the electronic products plant, for his morning plant walkthrough. Javier Peralta, his trusted Cost Accounting Manager, was accompanying him on the tour. He made his way slowly through the rows of work tables in which workers, mainly teen-age girls and young women, were busy assembling plastic components and wires into plastic connectors. With a friendly smile and a *"buenos días"* he greeted the people who were creating value for the stockholders of AMA Electric International that day. The production workers generally smiled back at him and greeted him cordially. By now, most of the workers knew that he was the Controller.

Over the months, the workers had come to know this likeable American who was easily approachable. Brad stopped several times on his tour to read the production boards, which showed the daily production goal and the actual production for each production line. "Today is another good day in the electronic connector plant," he commented to Javier.

He sporadically chatted with the workers, especially those who approached him to make a comment about a particular problem or bring him up-to-date on certain issues that he was working on at the time. His work on the S.W.A.T. inventory team project had brought him into close contact with a variety of production workers and material handlers, and he knew many of them by name.

As Brad was finishing up his tour, his good friend and plant manager Jorge del Valle walked up to him. "To whom am I indebted for the honor of this visit?" Jorge greeted Brad in his usual elegant diction.

"Good morning, *señor*. How are you?" Brad replied with a friendly smile.

"I am getting hungrier by the minute," Jorge said with a bright smile. "Would you care to join me for lunch?"

"I would be delighted to, Jorge. Are you free at noon?"

"Oh, noon," Jorge said as he scratched his beard. "I forgot that your stomach is still on American lunch time," he chuckled. "My stomach is on Mexican lunch time, which is around 1:30 or 2:00 in the afternoon. However, considering my appetite today, I can make an exception."

"Good. I shall see you at noon, then," Brad confirmed. He and Javier returned to their desks and continued with the day's work. The Controller looked forward to lunch with his colleague *Ingeniero* Jorge del Valle. Each time they met, they talked of family and engaged in interesting dialogue on business and world events. By now the two good friends had come to realize that they were very much alike and shared many mutual interests. Over time a level of trust had been built between the two men that would prove to be pivotal in the history of AMA Electric International.

* * * * * * * * *

Prompt as always, Jorge stuck his head in Brad's office at 12:00 sharp. "Are you hungry?" he inquired.

"Yes, I am. Where would you like to go?"

"How about Heriberto's Hamburgers? I know how much you Americans like those charbroiled burgers," Jorge said with a smile.

"Sounds great! Let's rock-and-roll."

There was a nice, two-story Heriberto's Hamburgers restaurant just about a mile down the road. They walked in the restaurant, and Brad ordered the *paquete número tres*: a charbroiled half-pound burger with cheese and jalapeño peppers, fries and a diet soda. Jorge ordered the same but without cheese, and they walked upstairs to a booth in the corner of the restaurant on the second floor. They tried to sit as far away as possible from the children who were playing happily in the two-story, indoor playground.

"Production looks good today in your plant," Brad said as he removed his hamburger from its foil wrapping.

"Yes, Bradley, we are having a very good month. The new maintenance engineer we hired has put together a preventative maintenance program that has improved our uptime by 7%."

"Wow! That is great. Give that man a raise!"

"Indeed. What is it that you say in America? 'An ounce of prevention is worth a pound of cure'?"

"That's right, Jorge," Brad replied, pleasantly surprised to learn that Jorge was familiar with that American expression. "You know, that holds true in many areas of life: health, finances, and security."

"I agree. There is a lot of wisdom in that simple phrase," Jorge said as Brad went to work on his burger. "Bradley, ever since our first conversation at *El Pueblito* restaurant, I have watched you and observed you in many different situations. Through our conversations, I have come to know you fairly well." Jorge grabbed two French fries. "*¡Qué rico!*" he exclaimed as he dipped each one of his salted fries in ketchup and slowly chewed it, savoring the flavor. "I love the French fries at Heriberto's. They are absolutely delicious!"

Jorge grabbed three more and devoured them. "Bradley," he said as he wiped his mouth with a napkin, "the reason I am telling you these things is because I would like to share something with you that, unfortunately, is not as palatable as these French fries. It deals with AMA Monterrey. I wanted to disclose this to you a long time ago at *El Pueblito,* but I realized that such a disclosure would have been premature at the time. Now, I think the time is right. However, I will need your assurance that everything I tell you will be kept in the strictest confidence—just between you and me, OK?"

"Certainly, Jorge. Rest assured that whatever you tell me here will stay between you and me...and the French fries," Brad said trying to make light of a situation that was beginning to make him uneasy. He was dreading whatever it was that Jorge was about to say.

Jorge smiled and took a deep breath as he looked down at his soda. After a moment of silence, he looked back at Bradley, but his expression had turned from his usual cheerfully optimistic look to a very serious and grim appearance. "Victor Reyes is the most corrupt person I have ever known. The darkness of his depravity knows no bounds."

Brad, who was holding his hamburger with two hands, immediately lost his appetite and placed his burger on the table. He felt his stomach begin to tighten and his heartbeat increase. Jorge continued. "I have been working here for several years, and I have seen things that have made me so angry that I once even called Harry Allen, Victor's boss, to report it. *That*," Jorge emphasized, "was a huge mistake."

"Why do you say that, Jorge?" Brad asked as he tried to appear calm.

"Because all Harry did was to pacify me and tell me to stay focused on the bigger picture. He said that I should expect corruption in Mexico and that I should try to get along with Victor, to be part of the team. In my judgment that was not a proper response for our Chief Operating Officer. What Harry said angered me, as well. Not everyone in Mexico is like Victor. You, of all people, know that."

"Yes, I do know that, Jorge."

"Anyway, I wanted to tell you what I have seen, with the hope that you will look into it. I report up through Victor and to Harry, but you report up through finance. That gives you an advantage. If you need to get internal audit involved in this, they cannot block you from doing so. Another advantage you have is that you see all of the financial details in the accounting records, and you are exposed to other administrative issues that I don't see. Thus, you may be able to do some digging and report something with more corroborating evidence than I did."

Brad sat at the table with a sullen look on his face. Although he appeared calm, inside him there was a whirlwind of emotion reacting to what he was hearing. The most condemning part of the situation was that he really was not surprised to hear this. In the back of his mind, he had seen things which led him to believe that problems of corruption might be quite prevalent at AMA

Monterrey. However, his workload had not given him much time to think about that possibility.

"The only reason I wasn't fired when I reported those conflicts of interest about Victor," continued Jorge, "was because Turk Haziz, the VP of operations over my division, defended me. Fortunately, Turk has a lot of clout in the organization, so Harry backed off. However, since then I have been on Victor's personal 'black list,' and he has been looking for an opportunity to get rid of me."

"Jorge, you are very good, perhaps the most talented person here in the Monterrey operations," Brad said trying to console his friend. "It would be a huge loss for you to leave the company. In fact, I see you as Victor's successor one day."

"*Que tu voz sea de profeta*, Bradley. I appreciate the vote of confidence."

"Getting to the specifics, what are some of the corrupt things that you have seen going on here?" Brad felt that gnawing feeling in his stomach beginning to grow as he prepared for Jorge's revelations.

"Well, they are conflicts of interest and fraud involving Victor. I only reported two issues to Harry: the pallet company and the cafeteria. That was about a year ago. I am sure that Victor owns both of those companies, but I cannot prove it. Also, since then I have seen other things that cause me to think that he owns other companies with which AMA Monterrey does business."

The Controller still had not divulged his own deep-rooted suspicions about Victor to Jorge. He continued to probe. "Jorge, what makes you think that Victor owns the pallet company?"

"Simple. They have terrible quality, high prices and lousy service. We complain to Victor about them all the time, yet he never makes a change in the company. In fact, he even defends them vigorously."

Brad's heart sunk even lower. That sounded exactly like GZZ-Mex *Constructores*, the construction company.

Jorge continued to articulate the web of corruption involving the infamous Victor Reyes. "As far as the pallet company is concerned, one of my material handlers, Nacho González, has told me that his cousin works for the TCR pallet company. TCR stands for *Tarimas y Cajas Regiomontana,* or Pallets and Boxes *Regiomontana.* According to Nacho, his cousin sees Victor at the TCR office all the time. He says everybody knows that Victor is the owner, and his son-in-law Fernando Grajeda is the manager."

"I have had experience investigating conflicts of interest like this before," Brad revealed. "I can have someone go to the Monterrey office of the Public Registry of Property and Businesses and request a copy of the *acta constitutiva,* or corporate charter, and other corporate records, which are public record. Then we can see who the stockholders of record are. If Victor is involved in these companies, maybe he was careless enough to have his name listed as a stockholder."

"Maybe," said Jorge doubtfully, "but he is so shrewd and crafty that I doubt he would be that sloppy. He probably uses *prestanombres*, or fronts, which serve as intermediaries. Legally, this intermediary owns the stock, but in reality someone else controls the company, like Victor in this case. Victor controls the awarding of business to the company, so he controls the company. Nevertheless, you are right. All that information is available to the public. I don't know why I didn't think of that before. You are very clever, Bradley."

"Not so clever, Jorge, just experienced. Now, what do you know about the cafeteria company?"

"Wait a minute. I haven't told you the really shocking thing."

"What's that?"

"Well, after my conversation with Harry got me nothing but heartache, I began a little investigation of my own."

"What do you mean 'heartache', Jorge?"

"Ever since I reported those conflicts of interest, Victor's attitude toward me has been very combative. He has done his almighty best to be my nemesis. I am sure that Harry told him that I had reported those potential conflicts of interest."

Brad sat there, listening intently to every word that rolled off Jorge's lips.

"As the months went by I began talking more with Nacho, my material handler, about the pallet company. The quality of those pallets was terrible, I mean really bad. Nacho had conversations with his cousin who works at TCR, and then reported back to me in confidence that TCR was actually coming in at night, picking up the pallets that AMA received, and taking them to the TCR warehouse. Also, my shipping supplies expenses continued to increase much higher than my shipments. They were way out of proportion. So I suspect that they were taking the same pallets that they had already sold to us."

"How do you know that they were doing that?" Brad asked, trying to remain objective.

"We have proof because we marked the pallets with special, unique codes in red ink in the corners. We kept, and still keep, a log of all the pallets that we receive from them and from other vendors. In some cases, they have sold us the same pallet more than 10 times."

Brad laughed out of disbelief. "You have got to be kidding me!"

"I wish I were, Bradley. Perhaps now you can understand my indignation toward Victor," said the well-seasoned plant manager. "They did not stop there, however. In response to our complaints about the poor quality of their pallets, TCR began stealing our good pallets that came from shipments of raw materials and then selling us those as well. The audacity of it enrages me."

"Sounds like TCR's cost of goods sold is close to zero," Brad remarked facetiously.

"Exactly, their raw materials cost them absolutely nothing, because they steal them. It is a very corrupt but profitable little racket. My plant alone spends about $20,000 per month on pallets from TCR. If the same thing is happening at other plants, then we are looking at around $140,000 per month with the two new plants."

Brad made a quick calculation in his head. "That's about $1.7 million dollars per year in sales with very little cost."

"Now you are beginning to understand why I said that Victor is the most corrupt person I know. We're just getting started, though. There's more."

"OK, you have me worried now."

"The cafeteria company," explained Jorge, "serves the worst food I have ever tasted in a maquiladora plant. As you know, maquila plants usually do not have good food anyway because management limits the amount they are willing to spend, so the cafeteria company cannot buy the choicest ingredients with which to prepare the food. However, here the food is absolutely horrendous. The hygiene is poor, the cuts of meat, the vegetables; everything about it is ridiculously cheap. The people complain to Carmen Silva, the Director of HR, and yet she does nothing. By the way, I don't trust that snake."

"Yeah, I know what you mean," Brad confessed. "I do not have a very high opinion of Snake Eyes, either. What makes you think that Victor owns the cafeteria company? It could be somebody like Carmen getting kickbacks under the table from the cafeteria vendor."

"I don't think so, Bradley, and here is why. The cafeteria manager is the father of one of Victor's girlfriends…."

"Oh, no!" said Brad, laughing out of frustration.

"It just so happens that this particular girlfriend, Lolita Loya, is Victor's favorite. Someone pointed her out to me once when she walked into the cafeteria, and she really turned heads as she made her entrance. She is about 20 or 21 years old. I have seen Victor bringing her father and brothers to work early some mornings in his car. My sister-in-law's family lives in the same apartment building as Lolita. My niece sees Victor sneak in and out of there all the time. It is a nice apartment building. I am sure that it far exceeds Lolita's economic means, so Victor is most likely paying for it."

"So you think that Lolita or her parents are the *prestanombres* for the cafeteria service, and that the true owner is Victor?"

"Either that or Victor owns it outright."

"Did you tell Harry the part about the girlfriends?"

"Yes."

"What did he say?"

"He said that it had nothing to do with work."

"Well, again, I don't agree with Harry. If a man is not faithful to his wife, a person to whom he has made a promise before God to be faithful, how can we expect him to be faithful to the company? You cannot. Being faithful to your spouse is not only an act of love, it is an act of honor. It is living up to a promise. So is being a good steward of company assets."

"That's the way you and I think, Bradley. However, Victor is one of those *macho* Mexicans who thinks that it makes him a man to be with lots of women. There are a lot of those types in Mexico."

"How many girlfriends did you say that Victor has?"

"That I personally know of? Two, but I am sure that there are more. The other one is several years older than Lolita. Her name is Zulema Palma. I don't know much about her, except that she is a beautiful blonde. My people tell me she looks like a super model."

"Well, this is absolutely terrible," Brad said somberly. "If your observations are correct, then I am extremely disappointed in Victor. More than that, however, I feel terrible for Montserrat, Victor's wife. Sofía and I had dinner with Montserrat a few months ago, and she seemed like a grand lady. Hearing this is disheartening."

Jorge finished the last of his French fries. "I know Montserrat, too, and I agree with you. She is a good woman. Victor does not deserve her."

"What I cannot understand," admitted Brad still looking distraught over the news of Victor's actions, "is why someone with as much money as Victor would engage in these types of business deals when he is already rich. What is the motive? AMA paid him $28 million dollars when they purchased these operations three years ago, which, by the way, I think was really on the high side."

Jorge looked directly at Brad. "Victor Reyes does these things for the same reason that he runs around on Montserrat. That *desgraciado* has an unbridled lust for money and women that will never be quenched."

Brad looked down at the table and shook his head. "Selfish greed," he said softly, as if he were speaking to himself. This conversation had pulled the rug out from under his dreams for a smooth tour of duty in Monterrey.

Everything had been going so well. His family was happy, he was happy, and he was doing outstanding work for his company, making $175,000 per year. He had established himself as the man with the golden glow who could handle any problem that arose in the Monterrey operations. Now, all of that was about to change.

Chapter 13

Accounting Hocus Pocus

When Brad returned to the office, he walked in, sat down and began running his fingers through his brown, graying hair. He wanted to grab the phone and talk to Sofía. No matter what the problem was, he always felt better after he talked to her. She had a gentle way of putting his problems in perspective and making them seem so distant. The Controller sat there for several minutes staring at the wall as he began to reflect upon what Jorge del Valle had just revealed. As much as he did not want to, he believed Jorge.

The rest of the day Brad did something he had never done before at work: he watched the clock. It felt as if time were moving in slow motion. Brad checked his emails: 15 new messages and 112 opened messages. He quickly went through the important messages, answered them, and deleted the rest. After what seemed like an eternity, the clock mercifully struck 5:30 p.m. Brad grabbed his briefcase and headed for the door. A drive in rush-hour traffic that normally should have taken 45-50 minutes was completed in only 35 minutes. When Brad met Sofía at the door and saw her face, the worry began to dissipate. She had that kind of medicinal, calming effect on him.

"Dad-dy! Dad-dy! Daddy's here, little Michael!" Liliana called joyfully as she came running up to meet her father. She still had her school uniform on, consisting of a white cotton blouse and a navy skirt with long, tan socks.

"Hey, Dad-dy!" little Michael said as he came running up wearing only a smile and holding his diaper in his hand.

"*Lo siento, señor,*" said a middle-aged Mexican woman apologetically as she ran behind the toddler. Margarita had recently begun working for the Jenkins family in a role that was a combination of maid and nanny.

Brad looked at his son, trying to hold back a smile. "Son, mind your manners, young man. You know that you are not supposed to run around the house naked. Now, put your diaper on and get dressed."

"Yes sir."

"But first, give me a BIG hug." Brad held his hands out as little Michael ran and jumped into his father's outstretched arms.

"Doubles!" Liliana shouted as she looked up at her father, now holding little Michael.

Brad shifted Michael to his left arm and crouched back down to pick up Liliana in his right arm. He stood upright once again and walked into the kitchen, setting them both down in the kitchen chairs. It was good to be home.

* * * * * * * * *

Margarita was an inspirational woman who was especially good with the Jenkins children. Her own children were grown and already on their own. The friendly but strong-willed woman had weathered a heart-breaking tribulation years ago when her husband left her while she was still in her early 20s with three young children. Through sheer tenacity and the supernatural power of a mother's love, she had miraculously managed to raise them by herself while working long hours at meager wages. In Brad's eyes, that was quite an accomplishment. He admired Margarita's invincible spirit.

Brad paid Margarita about 50% more than the going wage for her work; in addition, he gave her medical insurance, an employment benefit rather uncommon for domestic help in Mexico. He also provided a nice room for her and even paid for her cable TV. Margarita knew that the Jenkinses treated her very well because they were good people. Through her hard work and loving service, she expressed her gratitude.

"May we go outside and play, Daddy? Please, pretty please?" implored Liliana.

Little Michael seconded the motion. "Yeah, I wah oway!"

Brad wanted to play with them as well, but he felt compelled to talk with Sofía about the day's events and the things Jorge del Valle had told him. Margarita volunteered to take them outside to play on the trampoline.

Brad closed the sliding door, poured himself a glass of water, loosened his tie, and sat down at the kitchen table. Then he began to describe to Sofía the conversation with Jorge. As Brad went through the details, Sofía experienced the same reactions as Brad had earlier that day. Finally, when Brad had finished, Sofía asked the logical question: "What are you going to do?"

"My gut tells me that Jorge is right on target. As the Controller, I feel that I have to act on this information. However, experience has taught me well…."

"Bradley, you are not in internal audit," Sofía remarked firmly. "Why do you want to get in the middle of this? You will only end up causing a war between you and Victor."

"Look, Sofía, I simply cannot ignore this as if I were never made aware of potential conflicts of interest violation of fiduciary duty, and fraud. If this is in fact happening, I cannot allow it to continue…not on my watch."

Sofía simply shook her head and stared down at the floor.

"Besides," the Controller said with a stone-cold look, "there may be bigger problems."

"What do you mean, *mi amor*?"

Brad closed his eyes and rubbed his eyebrows firmly, and then he sighed heavily. "I'm not sure yet."

"*Mi vida*, I just don't want you to get involved in this," Sofía said tenderly. "Victor really likes you, and AMA is paying you a lot of money—$175,000 a year plus a $50,000 bonus. That's $225,000 a year that you may just throw away if you engage Victor on this. Besides, we are happy here, *mi amor*, and my parents are delighted that we are in Monterrey with them. I just don't want you to go out of your way to bring an end to this."

Brad was irritated by Sofía's lack of support, but he understood her completely. She had a valid point. Half of him agreed with her, but the other half just could not let it go.

Sofía knew her husband, and she realized that her pleas were futile. Brad lived his life honorably and expected others to do the same. Corruption of any form angered him. As surely as night followed day, she knew that her husband would not allow that kind of unethical behavior to occur under his administration.

After a short pause, Brad continued, now more calmly than before. "Tonight I'm going to give José Luis

Serrano a call. He is the partner for the local accounting firm Dodds Drucker Matthews here in Monterrey that handles our audit. He also does fraud investigations. I am going to ask him to check a few things out for me related to these alleged conflicts of interest and the scam Victor is running with the pallets. Apart from what Jorge told me this afternoon, there are some other things I myself have seen that don't look right, either. I will have José Luis take a look at those issues as well."

"OK, *mi amor*, but this makes me so sad. Everything has been going so well, and now it looks like things could get ugly, especially if you confirm your suspicions."

Suddenly, the sliding door to the backyard opened up and little Michael came running in, followed by Gino. Michael, who had taken off his shirt, ran and jumped in Brad's lap. Gino came walking up to the table. His keen canine olfactory sense enabled him to smell the goodies that had been on the table a couple of hours ago, with only crumbs remaining.

"Gino! *¡Fuera! ¡Salte de aquí!* Get out of here!" Sofía yelled angrily at the poor dog as he scurried to get out.

"Hey! Take it easy with my dog, Sofía! He is not doing anything wrong," Brad scolded.

"Yes, he is! He is stinking up the place! *¡Fuera perro apestoso!*" she shouted as Gino lowered his ears and head and then scooted outside. She closed the door firmly.

Margarita, seeing that Michael was safe with his father, quickly returned outside to sit by the trampoline with Liliana as the eight-year-old continued to jump.

Little Michael sat up straight in his father's lap. Brad whispered in his ear just loudly enough for Sofía to hear, "Hey, son, would you take a good gander at that pretty lady sitting across the table! She's the best-looking thing I have seen all day!" Little Michael just grinned from ear to ear.

Sofía's eyes brightened and she flashed that million-dollar smile of hers. Brad gazed into her deep, brown eyes. Their earlier disagreement had faded away.

* * * * * * * * *

Around mid-afternoon of the following day Brad decided to talk with Paco Delgado about the metals surcharges that were becoming more of an issue on a global basis. Due to the unprecedented demand for steel, aluminum, and other metals world-wide, the manufacturers of these metals had increased prices dramatically. Much of the demand in metal markets was being driven by the ever-increasing construction occurring in China.

In Beijing they were getting the city ready for the 2008 Olympic Games, which Beijing would proudly be hosting. The Beijing government wanted the capital city to shine so that it could take its rightful place as one of the prominent cities on the global map.

In Shanghai, Shenzhen, Guangzhou, and other industrial parts of China, American and other foreign companies were constantly building manufacturing facilities to capitalize on the abundant cheap labor. Brad called these factories the "Chinese *maquiladoras*" because the production of this sector basically was exported out of China back to Europe and the U.S. similar to the Mexican *maquiladora* program. It was amazing to see so much pent-up demand for construction unleash itself on one country. The giant had awakened.

Unfortunately for China and the rest of the world, this excess demand had resulted in much higher costs for metals. That had a direct impact on the manufacturing costs of AMA Electric International Corporation. In response to this unwelcome situation, corporate accounting and purchasing in Atlanta were working with AMA's manufacturing facilities globally to set up procedures to record in the accounting records the amount of this additional cost, called a metal surcharge. The intent was to pass this metal surcharge directly on to AMA's customers. Like many other companies around the globe, AMA was not prepared to absorb this additional cost for metal.

Brad called Paco to make sure he was in his office and could receive him before he walked down to his office. "Sure, come on down, Brad. I always have time for you, my gringo friend!" Paco said in his typical lively fashion. "Oh, and don't worry about knocking, either. Just come on in when you get here. I don't get offended so easily like somebody in this organization, although I won't mention the name of this American," Paco said playfully.

Brad quickly made his way down the stairs, through the HR and traffic areas and then to purchasing. When Brad walked into Paco's office, the chubby *chaparrito* was working away at his computer.

"Don't you knock?" Paco inquired.

Brad stopped in his tracks and folded his arms across his chest in a non-verbal protest. "Paco, you told me not to knock on the phone," Brad clarified.

"Of course I don't want you to knock on the phone. I want you to knock on the door, Bradley," the quick-witted Paco replied. "But I am a forgiving person, so I won't hold it against you. So, why don't you sit down and take a load off those big, smelly feet of yours."

Bradley smiled, shook his head, and took a seat. "You are one of kind, Paco…thank goodness."

"Hey, I resent that, Bradley!" Paco said with playful indignation. "Now, I'm going to get real gringo on you and go straight to the point." Paco advised Brad that he had already received guidance from corporate purchasing on his role and responsibility in helping to isolate and capture this metals surcharge expense. He would have to ensure that all the purchase orders were broken out between the normal cost of the metal and the additional surcharge due to excess demand. Brad highlighted the importance of getting this done ASAP.

Given the seven manufacturing plants now operating in Monterrey, the amount of expense to be captured and passed on to customers would be substantial and could save AMA Monterrey hundreds of thousands of dollars over the year, based on Brad's preliminary figures. Brad would have his accounts payable staff trained to assist in the collection of these amounts.

"*Mira,* Brad, I guarantee you that all the manufacturing companies in Monterrey will be doing the same thing," predicted Paco. "Monterrey is famous for keeping expenses down. Some people call it being cheap, or as we say in Spanish, *codo*." Paco pointed to his elbow, which also meant *codo* in Spanish. "Have you seen the mountain range *Cerro de la Silla* here in Monterrey?"

"Of course," Brad replied. "That is a very well-known landmark in Monterrey. It looks like a horse saddle."

"*Correcto*, my pale-faced amigo," Paco teased. "Well, we *regiomontanos* say that the *Cerro de la Silla*, or horse saddle, was formed because the first person to settle in Monterrey lost a peso coin in the mountains and started digging for it. The fellow could not find it, so he continued to dig and dig for that measly peso. He dug so much that, after a few months, he looked around and realized he had dug out part of the mountain so that it now looked like a horse saddle." Paco burst out laughing, pounding on his big belly as if he were playing the drums. He was quite a character. "We know how to pinch our pennies, or in this case our *centavos*."

Brad laughed. Even though the joke was not that funny to Brad, he could not help but laugh because of the contagious manner in which Paco was laughing.

Paco managed to regain his composure, bringing his roaring laughter down to a contained chuckle. "Mexicans, especially the *chilangos* in Mexico City, say that we *regiomontanos* in Monterrey are so cheap that when we want to get drunk, instead of spending money on beer and liquor, we grab hold of a light post and spin ourselves around and around until we feel like we are drunk. That way we can get drunk for free!"

Brad's chuckle turned into a hearty laugh.

"*Regiomontanos* know how to save money, Brad. That's why I know that everyone in this city will be passing this additional metals cost on to their customers. No company here will eat this charge. And you say that all of this extra cost is due to those *chinos cochinos*, those dirty Chinese?"

Paco's disparaging remarks about the Chinese offended Brad. "Paco, why do seek to vilify the hard-working Chinese people? They are simply trying to advance economically, just as we Americans are…just as you Mexicans are. I admire their spirit, and I think it is not becoming of you to criticize them for wanting to improve their lot in life. I have a lot of good friends that live in Beijing, and I do not appreciate your derogatory comments about the Chinese."

"Well, excuse me, Mr. United Nations," the pudgy Paco said defensively.

"Paco, all I am saying is that we all must live together on this planet, and that means we need to be respectful of others and treat them in a dignified manner, just as we expect others to treat us with the same decency."

"OK, Bradley, I'll stop noodling you...I mean needling you about the Chinese," the irreverent Paco said with that cocky smile of his.

"Getting back to the purpose of this meeting," Brad said trying to take control of the direction of the conversation, "the increase in cost of the metals is due principally to excess demand being experienced in China. There is ...."

Paco interrupted Brad. "Bradley, Bradley, Bradley. Why is it that every time I talk with you, I feel like I am watching one of those old, black-and-white movies from the 1930s? You never use foul language, you are always so polite that it makes me gag, and you use these fancy words. *¡Caray!* I feel like I have just had a vocabulary lesson every time I speak with you. When you leave I have to jot down all these new words to learn before I see you again."

Always a good sport, Brad just sat there and chuckled. He knew that Paco loved to tease him.

"OK, *compadre*," Paco said, "let's get this metals surcharge accounting set up quickly. *¡Híjole!* Those *chinos cochinos*— first they steal jobs from us Mexicans. Then, they make us pay higher prices for metals because they are building more factories for more of the production that they are going to take from Mexico. The next thing you know, they will be making *tortillas* in China and selling them to us here in Mexico!"

* * * * * * * * *

That afternoon *Señora* Aurora Loya was visiting her daughter in the luxury apartment funded by Victor Reyes. Her mother was making the lovely Lolita Loya a dress as they chatted and drank coffee.

"*Mamá,* you don't have to worry about making me dresses," Lolita said lovingly to her mother. "Victor buys me all the clothes I need."

"I know, *hija,* but I still like to make you dresses. I have always made you at least two dresses a year, and I do not intend to stop now," said the attractive *señora.* Then she stopped sewing and looked up at her daughter. "Lolita, *hija,* are you happy with Victor?"

"*Sí, Mamá.* I am very happy with him. Why do you ask?"

"I don't know, *hija.* It's just that, well, Victor is married, and you are so young and beautiful. What plans does he have for you? I mean, do you intend to live like this forever?"

"*Claro que no, Mamá,*" Lolita said with conviction. "Victor is the most wonderful man I have ever met. Have you forgotten about what he did for this family when we were down and out?"

"Of course not, *hija,* it is only that…"

"Remember, *Mamá,* nobody wanted to help us back then, not even our relatives."

"They did not have the means to help us, Lolita," her mother pointed out, but that was only an excuse. The fact was that none of the Loyas' relatives stepped up to help out as they should have.

"We were in terrible shape," continued Lolita. "Somebody could have done something, but they did not care. Then, like an answer to a prayer, Victor came into my life, into our lives, and he gave us money so that we could eat and lead a dignified life. Victor paid for the medical treatment for Teresa so that she could get her diabetes under control. He put Pablo through that detoxification center to get him off drugs, and he paid for the back operations for *Papá*, and then he gave them all well-paying, decent jobs. Nobody else helped us except for Victor. He is a good man, *Mamá*, and he treats me like a queen. I love him, and I know he loves me."

Señora Loya nodded her head in agreement. "I remember all of Victor's kindness, Lolita, and I am very grateful to him for his benevolence. I just am worried about you, *hija*."

"Me?" Lolita said with a surprised tone in her voice. "I am perfectly fine, *Mamá*. You mustn't worry about me."

Señora Loya tried to be careful not to alarm Lolita, so she thought about how she might express her concern more tangibly. "Lolita, you and Victor have been together now for more than two years, and yet he is still married to his wife of thirty-some odd years. Don't you think that if he really loved you that much he would do the honorable thing and end his marriage with his wife so that you two could have a legitimate relationship? My fear is that Victor may never marry you, and…well…you deserve to be married and have a family of your own, Lolita."

All of a sudden the Latin beauty's face lit up like a bright light. "*Mamá*, I have not told you yet, but I have good news!"

"What is it, *hija*?"

"When we were in Cuernavaca, Victor told me that he *would* marry me! He promised me that he would!"

"*Qué bien, hija*," her mother responded, trying hard not to let her skepticism drown out Lolita's joy. However, her mother had lived almost 60 years, and she knew how men like Victor operated. "When is he planning on leaving his wife?"

"I don't know, *Mamá*," Lolita replied, annoyed by her mother's question. "He did not say. All I know is that I believe him, just like I believed him when he told me he was going to help us and he did. Victor always does what he says he is going to do. He will marry me, *Mamá*. I know that he will!"

Señora Loya put her sewing down and hugged her daughter. "I hope so, *hija. Ojalá que sí.*"

* * * * * * * * *

As that final quarter progressed and AMA Electric International approached its December year-end, there was not much improvement in profitability. Wall Street had predicted that AMA would have an operating profit of $190 million for the quarter and $700 million for the year. Internal estimates indicated that AMA was still off from analysts' estimates by about $45 million for the quarter, even after Harry Allen put the pressure on the operations VPs and their divisional controllers to come up with numbers that would hit Wall Street's forecast for AMA. In spite of a depressed electrical products market, Rick Less and Harry Allen were determined to meet the Street's earnings expectations. Atlanta abounded with creative accounting ideas.

When Rick first took over as CEO almost three years ago, he had immediately made changes to two accounting reserves: the reserve for bad debts and the creation of a restructuring reserve. By doing so, AMA took a "big bath" and charged the expense of the reserve to Rick's first year, which he could easily blame on his predecessor. During that first year as CEO, he instructed CFO Bryan Taylor to increase the reserve for bad debts by an additional $100 million to serve as a cushion for the future. Bryan made sure that his worksheets provided ample evidentiary support for the increase, although in reality it was not justified at the time. Rick simply wanted the charge to hit expense that first year as insurance. That way he would not have any additional charges to the reserve as his sales increased, and he could write off uncollectible sales to that reserve in the future without an impact to a future year's profit.

Also, during his first year Rick charged an expense of $75 million to earnings of that year for future expenses that were related to the restructuring of the company. To the financial press he called this a "restructuring reserve." Those expenses stemmed from future plant closings in the U.S. and Europe and the relocation of those production lines to low cost regions in Mexico, China, and Hungary. These future expenses would consist of severance pay, stay-for-pay agreements, travel expenses, and other related expenses.

In reality, the reserve far exceeded the actual costs anticipated. That difference was to serve as another cushion that could be used to make up for future shortfalls in income when actual profitability lagged behind what Wall Street analysts were expecting. However, to cover himself with the external auditors, Rick directed Bryan Taylor's finance group to come up with defendable, but grossly exaggerated, worksheets which supported the $75 million reserve charge. Bryan and Corporate Controller Steve Adams were able to convince the auditors at DDM that the accounting treatment was correct, partly because of the atmosphere of trust that existed between the accounting firm and AMA. Since both Bryan and Steve used to work for DDM, it was "all in the family." They trusted each other more than they should have. The concept of professional skepticism that a good auditor should always cling to was somehow shoved to one corner.

After these two accounting entries had been made, Rick had created for himself $175 million in excess reserves that he could use in the future to "manage the earnings" of AMA, to manipulate the profitability and align it with Wall Street's expectations. All the expense for this $175 million cushion had hit the first year, and of course Rick was more than happy to pin the blame on the outgoing CEO. Rick secretly called these questionable accounting practices AMA's "Wall Street insurance policy."

That was three years ago. Now, Rick was going to have to use that Wall Street insurance policy. Rick had set up AMA's normal conference call with Wall Street analysts to give an outlook for the fourth quarter. During that conference call, Rick announced that AMA Electric International and the outside auditors had "scrubbed" the accounting books looking for possible write-downs from asset impairments and other accounting issues before they closed the books for the year.

What they found was that the restructuring reserve, instead of being too low, was actually now overstated. Under Harry Allen's leadership in operations, AMA's outstanding execution of their strategic plan had given better-than-expected results for the transfers and plant consolidations. Accordingly, Rick revealed with great pride that AMA was reversing $45 million of that $75 million reserve for restructuring, which meant that it would increase operating profit by $45 million. What he did not reveal, however, was that he had finally closed the gap on the $45 million difference between AMA's forecast and Wall Street's forecast for AMA earnings, all in an effort to keep the stock price at $60 per share.

During the follow-up question and answer session, a skeptical Wall Street analyst from a large investment firm asked the CEO if the decision to reverse the $45 million in the restructuring reserve had anything to do with less-than-expected results for the final quarter.

"Nonsense!" replied Rick Less adamantly. "The fourth quarter is looking great. As a result of our outstanding manufacturing execution, we will hit our numbers again. The strong, continued growth in all our business segments will result in record profits. AMA is the best operating company in the electrical products industry when it comes to manufacturing execution and plant consolidations. That is exactly why we were able to decrease the reserve we initially set up several years ago for these same plant consolidations."

The same analyst that asked that pointed question noticed that Bryan Taylor was suspiciously quiet during the conference call. Rick and Harry did all the talking as they carried the Wall Street analysts down a fairy path into the never-never land of accounting hocus-pocus.

At the end of the conference call, after they had put on the "Rick and Harry Show" for the analysts, the three executives walked back to Rick's office with a feeling of accomplishment. Rick turned to Harry and Bryan and said with a cynical smile, "If the company can't make money, we'll make it for them!"

Rick and Harry laughed out loud, but it was not a laugh of joy. It was a dark, sinister laugh, the kind of laugh that was heard frequently behind the closed doors of the CEO's suite at AMA Electric International.

* * * * * * * * *

When Brad read the e-mail from corporate about reversing $45 million in expense from the restructuring reserve, he was angry. By now he had seen enough of the company's accounting practices to know that this was more of AMA's accounting hocus-pocus. *Corporate appears to be smoothing earnings again! I am convinced that they reversed this reserve to cover part of the shortfall in profit this period.* However, knowing it was one thing and being able to prove it was another. It was reasonable to assume that Atlanta had covered itself with lots of spreadsheets justifying the decrease in the restructuring reserve. In the end, it was an accounting estimate, although it was a big estimate.

As time passed, Brad was becoming more and more dismayed with the questionable accounting practices of AMA's executive management. These types of practices convinced him that, if the allegations of Victor Reyes' conflicts of interest turned out to be true, it would be useless to go to corporate with that information. For the moment, he would wait to see what the investigation revealed. Tomorrow morning he would meet with José Luis Serrano, the expert in fraud auditing. Rick Less, Harry Allen, and Victor Reyes would soon learn, much to their chagrin, that they had grossly underestimated the resolve of the Controller.

Chapter 14

The Discovery of an Empire

Three days had passed since Brad had spoken with José Luis Serrano about the potential conflicts of interest that Jorge del Valle had reported. José Luis was the partner for the Monterrey office of the accounting firm Dodds Drucker Matthews. Brad had called José Luis during the evening due to the confidential nature of the issue. The Controller did not want to risk having someone overhear his conversation. Brad and José Luis had agreed to meet and review a plan of action to investigate several companies which Brad feared may be owned or controlled by Victor Reyes.

They met at 7:30 in the morning at the DDM office in an upscale section of Monterrey known as Del Valle. Although Monterrey had a desert-like climate, Del Valle was always green in more ways than one. Del Valle boasted an abundance of vegetation and an abundance of money. José Luis closed the door to his office so that the two financial executives could begin.

"José Luis, I cannot overemphasize the need for absolute confidentiality on this issue. Please do not allow anyone, not even the other partners or your secretary, to be privy to this investigation. I do not know where this may lead, and I have seen signs that tell me that there may be much bigger problems within AMA than just conflicts of interest in Monterrey. I am hoping that my instincts are wrong," Brad said with a note of dejection, "but they usually are right on the money."

"Certainly, Brad, absolutely no one else will know about this investigation. I shall go about my business with the utmost secrecy. You have my word."

"Thank you, José Luis. A good friend of mine, Miguel Dávalos, who is also an audit partner in the Juárez office of DDM, told me that I could trust you implicitly with this assignment. Miguel said that you have strong experience with fraud investigations."

"Ah, yes," José Luis said with a smile as he recalled his long-time friend and colleague Miguel. "That is correct, Brad. I am a certified fraud auditor here in Mexico. I have done some fraud investigations, or what we call forensic accounting, for some of the largest companies in Mexico. With this assignment I have an advantage, since I am also the audit partner in charge of AMA Monterrey. I know the company quite well."

José Luis paused to take a sip of coffee. The veteran auditor looked about ten years older than Brad. He had a kind face, but it was a tired, deeply lined face and showed the effects of 30 years of grueling 16-hour days in the rigorous public accounting profession. The lack of sleep, the thousands of cups of coffee, and the constant stress to meet deadlines had taken their toll. José Luis was not very tall, measuring no more than five feet six inches in height. He was wearing his shiny, black, wing-tipped dress shoes, a trademark of accountants. José Luis jokingly told Brad that his body reflected the Mexican economy back in early 1995 when the peso plummeted: his hairline suffered from a deep recession and his waistline from uncontrolled inflation.

However, according to Brad's trusted friend Miguel Dávalos, José Luis' looks and his mild-mannered persona were deceiving. He was an expert in forensic accounting, one of the best fraud auditors in all of Mexico who could give anyone in the U.S. a run for their money as well. José Luis had an easy, down-to-earth manner about him that Brad warmed up to quickly.

José Luis felt that this was an opportune moment to talk in general about frauds and why they occurred. He explained that there had to be some sort of pressure to commit a fraud coupled with the opportunity. "The first element is some sort of pressure which, in my experience, has generally been financial pressure. For example, living beyond your means is the biggest cause for financial pressure that I have seen. You rack up high credit card debt and bank loans, and then all of a sudden you realize that you have dug yourself into a deep hole. You get desperate. Your creditors are harassing you for payments. They call you at home and make your life miserable. That can drive you to steal from your company if you are of weak character.

"Also, a complicated medical illness can create substantial financial pressure. If, God forbid, cancer struck someone, and the family did not have insurance or the insurance did not come close to covering the actual bills, then that person might be motivated to commit a fraud. Or, it could be just plain greed. Some people are so selfish that the desire to have more and more is cause enough for them to commit a fraud. Those are the ones that I especially enjoy catching.

"There are other types of pressure, such as when someone is in an adulterous relationship and has to support more than one family. Those situations require a lot of cash. That is, unfortunately, a common problem here in Mexico. Wealthy, successful men are tempted by the beauty and charm of a young, beautiful girl, and the cash drawer opens."

Brad's eyes opened widely as his mind raced back in time to the conversation with Jorge del Valle in which he asked Jorge why Victor, being so rich, would take advantage of the company through conflicts of interest and fraud. Jorge's words echoed in Brad's mind:

"Victor Reyes does these things for the same reason that he runs around on Montserrat. That desgraciado has an unbridled lust for money and women that will never be quenched."

José Luis unknowingly interrupted Brad's thoughts. "Does Victor gamble or use drugs?"

"Not that I know of, José Luis. However, according to Jorge del Valle, Victor does have at least two girlfriends."

"Two girlfriends? And a wife?" asked the veteran fraud auditor in disbelief.

"At least two, probably more."

"Where does he get the energy?"

"Or the money. Except, in Victor's case, he is rich already."

"Who knows, Brad. He may have burned through all his cash because of his lifestyle, or he may have businesses on the side that are in financial trouble. I have seen cases in which apparently rich and successful people were on the brink of bankruptcy because of the poor performance of their side businesses."

"Well, Victor spends an enormous amount of money on clothes, houses, cars…."

"….and apparently women," José Luis interjected jokingly. "That's what I am telling you, Brad. People who live this jet-set lifestyle sometimes are in such deep financial trouble that they live every day wondering where they will get the additional cash to support their expensive habits."

There was a short pause as José Luis took some notes. "*Bien*, Brad. We have discussed the pressures that can contribute to a fraud, and it appears as if some of them do apply to Victor Reyes—the extra-marital relationships and the expensive lifestyle. Also, he may have some businesses that need an injection of cash."

"Or perhaps it is simply due to the fact that he is greedy," Brad added.

"Perhaps so. Now I want to look at whether or not you feel he has the opportunity or the ability to perpetrate a fraud at AMA Monterrey."

"All right," Brad said as he pulled his arms up and back in a long stretch.

José Luis explained that due to the fact that Victor, who was currently serving as General Director, had owned the Monterrey business for 10 years prior to its being acquired by AMA, there were certain potential risks. For example, if Victor still exercised a considerable degree of influence over the operations, then he could easily circumvent internal controls and defraud the company. Brad agreed that managing a privately-held company was much different than managing a publicly-held corporation subject to SEC regulations.

"Brad, how much influence does Victor have over the AMA Monterrey operations?"

"One of the first things I noticed was that Victor commands a tremendous amount of power and influence over those operations, more than his position as General Director warrants. In fact, he rules the operations with an iron fist, somewhat like the power a fascist dictator would wield. All of the managers at the plant, except for Jorge del Valle, live under the frightening shadow of Victor's wrath. Jorge calls Victor the 'Czar of AMA Monterrey.'"

"Not good," José Luis said solemnly as he shook his head and continued taking notes. "Not good at all."

Brad continued. "Another thing that probably contributes to his power is the fact that all of the current functional directors and plant managers also worked for Victor when he owned the company. Atlanta corporate headquarters did not make any changes after they acquired the Monterrey operations."

"Atlanta did not send anybody from corporate to work in the Monterrey operations? That is very unusual with an operation of this size," commented the veteran accountant as he continued to capture notes on his little pad. José Luis tensed his black, bushy eyebrows again and frowned. "Brad, just from this overview of the facts, I am already concerned. You have motive and you have ability. If he can rationalize this in his mind, then we have a dangerous situation."

Brad agreed. He spent the next hour with José Luis going over his notes from the conversation with Jorge del Valle three days ago at Heriberto's Hamburgers. He also discussed his own concerns of other potential corruption. In addition to the concerns over the TCR pallet company and the cafeteria company that Jorge had mentioned, Brad had independently identified several more companies that he suspected. The first included the bus company that took the workers to and from the manufacturing plants. These expenses were paid for by the company, and the rates were high. They had used the same bus company for many years and had never once bid the service out for quotes to see if the bus rates were competitive.

José Luis took another sip of his coffee. *Yuk,* he thought as he moved the coffee cup away from his mouth quickly. It had been more than an hour since he had poured that cup of coffee. His facial expression vividly showed his displeasure. He made a quiet, growling sound to complain to himself that the cold substance in his mouth, which bore only a faint resemblance to the once rich cup of hot coffee, was now quite foul-tasting. Almost painfully he swallowed the coffee. "This conversation has outlasted the coffee," he expressed with a scowl, trying to make light of his unpleasant experience as he moved his tongue around the inside of his mouth to rid himself of the taste which was still lingering. He cleared his throat and forced a smile.

The second company that Brad had been eyeing skeptically was the Mexican freight company, VR Fletes. VR Fletes brought the raw materials from Laredo, Texas, to Monterrey and then shipped the processed finished goods back to Laredo. Brad revealed to José Luis two things which drew his attention to this freight company. First of all, the initials were the same as those of Victor Reyes. Could it be that Victor has the brass to use his own trucking company that bore his initials? Secondly, the fact that the Manager of Traffic and Customs was Victor's niece was not good.

"Ooh!" exclaimed José Luis melodramatically. "The plot thickens."

Brad smiled and continued. "By the way, the Director of Purchasing, Paco Delgado, is Victor's nephew."

"Does the corporate office know about these family relationships?" José Luis asked in astonishment.

"I don't know."

"Brad, if this were a Mexican privately-held company, which it once was, that might be acceptable. However, this is a subsidiary of a publicly-held American company, and such relationships are bad corporate governance."

"I agree totally, José Luis. I have not made an issue of the family relationships thus far, though."

A third company Brad was concerned about was the security company. This company provided the security guards for AMA Monterrey and installed and monitored the security surveillance system.

"Why do you suspect them, Bradley? Do their prices seem out of line with the market?"

"No, their prices are a little high, but they are competitive. However, they never change the guards assigned to AMA. At most security companies, the security guards of these outside security firms are rotated every month or two to another client to mitigate the risk of the guards developing any relationships with workers that could lead to collusion and theft. Ever since I have been here, the same guards have been assigned to the same shifts at the same plants. I am not even sure this security guard company has any other customers. It is something that has always bothered me. Another thing that has stayed on my mind since the first week I started working here was that these guards were totally ineffective in stopping the payroll robbery that occurred on Friday of my first week. They were all interviewed by local police and by the insurance claims investigator. They saw nothing, at least, they said they saw nothing. That just does not make sense to me. Somebody had to have seen something. Somehow the payroll bandits knew where the closed-circuit TV monitors were and managed to spray paint them just before the robbery, yet none of the guards noticed anything."

"The robbery situation does sound suspicious. The fact that Victor has never changed the guards is unusual and poor policy, Brad. Why haven't you complained?"

"Because I have had bigger fish to fry—namely restoring order to the inventory, facilitating the transfer of production lines from the U.S. to Mexico, reconciling the intercompany accounts, enhancing the forecasting accuracy, and other major problems that had plagued the AMA Monterrey administration for quite some time. I just have not taken the time to look into this. Let me add something else I don't like about the security company. Having his own little security firm to monitor the closed circuit TV and other security issues would put Victor in the perfect position to ensure that he did not get caught as well as to conduct other surveillance. Victor appears to be a very controlling individual. Having the ability to see all over the Monterrey manufacturing campus seems to me like something that Victor would want. Putting all this into perspective, I now even suspect the security guards and Victor in the payroll robbery we had when I first started at the company."

"I see where you are going," said José Luis. He caught on fast. "His security people would see and control all the movements of the facilities. They would have eyes and ears everywhere. That would also allow him to do some of the things like what Jorge del Valle reported with the pallets—stealing them at night and reselling them the next day."

"Victor has total control over these facilities to do as he pleases and get rich off his little companies with no one to stop him. However, in the interest of justice I will not jump to conclusions. I'll let you do your investigation, and then I'll draw my conclusions when we have all the facts—*todos los pelos de la burra en la mano*."

"That's right. We need to remain objective. Now, are there any other companies that you suspect, Brad?"

"Yes, there is one final company that concerns me, José Luis, and this may be the biggest one of all. It is a construction company called GZZ-Mex *Constructores*. This company is absolutely horrible in terms of service. Yet Victor defends their shoddy work and lousy service vehemently. This company does all the work for the AMA Monterrey buildings. They build all the new buildings, perform any improvements to existing buildings, and they do anything slightly related to construction. We are talking big bucks, too—millions of dollars over the last two years. To top it off, just like with the other companies, there are never any competitive bids for us to know if we are getting a decent price on the work. Victor does not allow anyone to become involved with the construction work negotiations. He handles it all."

"Well, that certainly does sound suspicious. At the very least it is a bad business practice," José Luis said as he finished his notes.

"I don't know if this is related, José Luis, but I would like to put it on the table anyway," Brad commented with a note of concern. "If you will recall, at the beginning of our conversation this morning I said that I was not sure how high up this may go. Well, Victor Reyes has strong connections with the top two officers in the company, Rick Less, the CEO, and Harry Allen, the COO. From what I have been able to gather, Rick, Harry, and Victor have worked together in various ventures over the years. Victor has always handled the Mexican side, and Rick and Harry have always handled the U.S. side."

"Hmmm…..that is very interesting. It sounds like Victor is their Mexican connection," observed José Luis, slowly raising his eyebrows, then lowering them, as he moved his right forefinger over his lips and then began tapping his lips like a drummer. The drumming stopped abruptly. "That gives them a very nice mechanism to do a lot of things, theoretically speaking."

José Luis took a few more notes. He was like a veteran homicide detective finishing up a visit at the crime scene, a detective who had seen it all. However, the homicides that he had seen were those in which greed and deceit killed companies, not people. In his world, the world of fraud, the criminals used journal entries and computers rather than knives and guns.

As Brad said good-bye, José Luis shook his hand and smiled. He had a good feeling about Brad. *This American seems like a good, honest man*, José Luis thought as Brad left his office. *You could see it in his eyes. He is also a courageous fellow.* A look of concern gradually overtook the smile on the face of José Luis as he realized the gravity of the situation. If what the veteran forensic accountant suspected were true, his client was indeed in the middle of a dangerous web of deception designed to make Victor Reyes an even richer man and would put this American Controller in harm's way.

* * * * * * * * *

Brad had made such an impression on José Luis Serrano that the veteran auditor decided to clear his schedule for the next two weeks and devote himself to work exclusively on the AMA Monterrey investigation. José Luis and Brad had given the investigation a secret code name, *"El Pelón,"* or "Baldy," named especially after the principal of the investigation: *Señor* Victor Reyes. No one except for the Controller knew that José Luis was working on this investigation.

In his usual low-profile style, José Luis went about looking into each company that Brad mentioned. With the RFC number, the equivalent of the federal taxpayer ID number in the U.S., José Luis was able to acquire a generous amount of information on the companies in question. Through third party interviewers, he discreetly verified Jorge del Valle's allegations. He visited the

Monterrey office of the Mexican Public Registry of Property and Businesses to request a copy of the corporate charter and other corporate records to identify the stockholders of all the companies under investigation. He spoke "off the record" with some of his long-time acquaintances in *Hacienda's* SAT office, the Mexican equivalent of the IRS in the U.S., to further his understanding of the companies.

The more the expert auditor dug, the more interested he became in the investigation. His focus and urgency to complete the forensic accounting work within two weeks had been justified. *When I meet with Brad, I will have some interesting news to report,* he thought.

Finally, after two arduous weeks of forensic accounting, the veteran fraud auditor was ready to meet with Brad. It was a rainy Saturday evening, and Brad was eating dinner at home with his family when the phone rang.

"*Bueno*," answered Brad in a chipper voice.

"Bradley, this is José Luis Serrano."

"*Hola, José Luis. ¿Cómo estás?*"

"*Bien, Bradley. ¿Y tú, qué tal?*"

"I am enjoying this rainy Saturday with my family. We have spent all afternoon watching movies. How is '*El Pelón*' coming along?"

"That is precisely why I wanted to call you today. I know that tomorrow is Sunday, but would you have a couple of hours for me to come by your house?"

"You mean you have finished?"

"Yes, I have."

"*De acuerdo.* Why don't you drop by around 3 p.m. tomorrow? I will ask Sofía to prepare one of her famous pecan pies for us to nibble on as we chat."

"*Muy bien*, Bradley," José Luis replied. Brad could tell by the upbeat sound of his voice that the veteran fraud auditor had a big grin on his face. "I'll see you tomorrow at 3 p.m. at your house."

* * * * * * * * * *

The next day José Luis arrived right on time. He and Bradley sat at the dining room table while Sofía brought some coffee and pecan pie. The aroma of the pie was mouth-watering. *"Ah, Sofía, muchas gracias,"* José Luis said as he put a big bite of pecan pie into his mouth. *"¡Qué rico!* Bradley, after this investigation we are going to have to have our regular audit meetings here so that I can continue to enjoy your wife's culinary talents!"

"My wife does indeed make a scrumptious pecan pie," Brad concurred.

Just then, José Luis felt something wet on the back of his neck and shoulders. Brad looked behind this chair and saw little Michael dressed in his training pants, cowboy boots, and black Stetson cowboy hat. The energetic toddler was squirting the 53-year-old audit partner with a lime-green squirt gun.

"Pow! Pow! Pow!" he said with a tough little bad guy voice. Brad chastised his son for the action. "Son! Do not shoot your squirt gun at *Señor Serrano.* You are getting him wet. Holster that weapon, cowboy!"

"OK Daddy," the little cowboy said as he blew at the tip of the barrel and put his gun back in his play holster. José Luis just chuckled and pulled out a white handkerchief to dry the back of his neck. Then he folded the handkerchief and put it neatly back in his pocket, drank another sip of the delicious coffee, and looked over at Brad. "Not to worry, Brad," he said in his typical good-natured manner. "I have four children and nine grandchildren. This is not my first gunfight, nor will it be my last."

Brad smiled in relief.

"Now," said José Luis with a more serious tone of voice, "I have some very interesting news to report. It appears that you have stumbled onto something really big." There was a dramatic pause. José Luis took another bite of the rich, delicious pecan pie, washed it down with a sip of coffee, and returned his attention to Brad. "Brad, you have discovered an empire. Victor Reyes has either a direct or an indirect interest in every one of the companies you mentioned."

"I knew it!" Brad said emphatically. He did not know whether he should be happy about confirming that his suspicions were accurate or sad about what this finding implied concerning his future with AMA. He sat there in his chair for a few seconds, trying to come to terms with what José Luis had just confirmed. Then, he looked at José Luis and said very calmly, "The dream is over, and the nightmare is about to begin."

While he was taking another sip of coffee, the veteran fraud auditor looked up from under his black, bushy eyebrows and saw the disappointment in Brad's eyes. In a gentlemanly gesture to recognize the difficult road ahead for Brad, he quietly set the coffee cup down on the table and slowly nodded. There was a respectful moment of silence.

José Luis then continued to discuss his findings. "I brought a rough draft of the full report, but let me just give you the highlights. Let's start with the pallet company—*Tarimas y Cajas Regiomontanas*, or TCR. Victor owns this outright. Next, the cafeteria company. Victor's girlfriend, Lolita Loya, serves as the front, or *prestanombre*, that owns that company, but Victor obviously controls it through the awarding of business. Now, the bus company: Victor is the sole stockholder."

José Luis paused and took another bite of his pecan pie. "This is goo-oo-ood pie, Bradley. Now," he continued, "the Mexican freight company VR Fletes: Victor's daughter is the stockholder of record, but obviously that is just another front. The other company we researched, the security company, is owned by another one of Victor's daughters. All of these companies have two elements in common: they were all formed right around the time that Victor started the manufacturing plants, which are now AMA Monterrey, and they all have only one customer. That customer is…"

"AMA Monterrey," interjected Brad.

"*Correcto*," said José Luis. "Victor has his own little gold mine going on here, and AMA Monterrey is footing the bill."

"Conflicts of interest," Brad said sadly, "are one of the most common breaches of fiduciary duty in the Mexican *maquiladora* industry. This one takes the cake, though, but it all makes sense. Victor had the power and influence to control the awarding of business to whomever he desired while he was the owner of the manufacturing plants, and he never relinquished that influence when he sold the company to AMA. Also, by not changing any of the management when AMA bought these operations, he has been able to maintain his iron-fisted grip over the operations."

"Wait, that's not all. I have saved the best for last," José Luis said in a tone which resembled a TV announcer trying to mass market the latest and greatest kitchen gadget for $9.99. "Do you remember your concerns about GZZ-Mex *Constructores*, the construction company which everyone complains about?"

"Yes, what is the story with those sorry bums?"

"Your instincts were correct, Bradley. Victor Reyes is a stockholder of GZZ-Mex, along with a U.S. company called R & H Holding Corporation. Victor owns 49% and R & H owns 51%, a controlling interest."

"That makes sense to me," Brad exclaimed nodding his head in confirmation. "There were too many red flags about that company for Victor not to have an interest in it. What about R & H Holding Corporation? Who is behind that company?"

"We could not tell from the records available here in Mexico. Nevertheless, just think about it, Bradley: R & H. Doesn't that ring a bell?"

"R & H, R & H…hmmm…" Just then Brad's face changed from a puzzled look to a look of enlightenment. "R & H: Rick & Harry—Rick Less and Harry Allen!"

"*Así es*. My own thoughts were along similar lines. However, now this is getting into the interior of the US, which is out of my practice area. You will need to get someone else to trace that one down."

"I know just the guy," Brad said, thinking of his old high school friend Chuck Simpson who was now a private investigator in Brad's home town of Columbus, Georgia. "I'll get him working on this tomorrow. If Rick and Harry are involved in this company, then that would add a whole new element of danger to this situation."

Brad sat back in his chair and looked off at some distant spot on the wall. "You know, Victor has been friends with Rick Less and Harry Allen for about 20 years. If Rick and Harry are the controlling owners of GZZ-Mex through this front called R & H Holding Corporation, then Victor could be just a puppet. This web of corruption could go straight to the top of AMA management. If that is the case, who knows what depravity is occurring at the corporate level on a global basis." Brad looked back at José Luis, who cocked his head to the left, raised the tired eyebrows of his time-worn face, and nodded slowly indicating that he concurred wholeheartedly.

"Well," said the veteran auditor, "it would not surprise me. GZZ-Mex was formed just over two years ago, about nine months after AMA Electric International bought these Monterrey operations."

"That's right, and it coincides exactly with the time that AMA announced its strategic plan to relocate U.S. manufacturing operations to low cost regions, particularly to Monterrey," Brad added. "This all makes perfect sense, now. Rick, Harry, and Victor knew that they were about to embark on a plan which would entail the building of several new buildings and the renovation of the existing five buildings, so they set up this little company exclusively for that purpose."

"Brad," José Luis added, "we reviewed over $12 million in GZZ-Mex invoices in only 18 months! That's a nice chunk of change, even for a millionaire."

"...and no other bids have ever been solicited from any other construction company for any of the work performed," Brad added.

"My off-the-record conversation with my contacts in *Hacienda* confirmed that, like the other companies, GZZ-Mex has no other customers except for AMA Monterrey."

"It fits the model."

"I did some rough calculations, Bradley, and I estimated that Victor is pulling in about $10 million per year in business with all these companies, including his portion of GZZ-Mex. He has his own empire of conflicts of interest. Brad, I strongly suggest that you be very careful with your next step. If you caused Victor to lose $10 million a year, well, let's just say that you would be in a dangerous position down here in Mexico. You represent a huge threat to him."

Brad leaned back, picked up his coffee cup, and moved the cup in a circular motion, stirring the little bit of coffee still remaining at the bottom the cup. "That's right, but I have the advantage," Brad said with a sparkle in his eyes.

"What's that?"

"Victor is not on to me yet. He does not realize that I know all this. Therefore, I have the element of surprise on my side." Brad smiled and winked at José Luis.

"Indeed you do, Bradley," José Luis affirmed, smiling, as he winked back. "Indeed you do."

Chapter 15

The Past is Ever Present

The next day Brad decided to bring Jorge del Valle up-to-date on everything he had discovered. After all, it was Jorge who had first brought this to Brad's attention. Given the heavy demands of work that day, they decided to get a quick bite at their favorite burger place: Heriberto's Hamburgers.

With a grumbling stomach, Brad ordered his usual, *paquete número tres*, and Jorge ordered the same without cheese. The two good friends walked upstairs to their usual spot and began devouring those delicious char-broiled burgers. Brad quickly walked Jorge through all the conflicts of interest that had been proven during the investigation.

"Believe it or not, Brad, none of this surprises me," the well-spoken engineer said. "If you recall, I told you that Victor Reyes was the most corrupt person I knew. His selfishness is like a teen-ager's stomach."

Brad looked at Jorge with confusion written all over his face. "I am afraid that I do not quite follow you, Jorge."

"Wait until your kids are teen-agers, and then you will understand. They will eat so much that you will think that their stomachs are bottomless pits," he said smiling.

"Oh, OK," Brad chuckled. "I'm with you now. Yeah, that sounds like a fair comparison, because Victor is looting this company. Once I finish investigating the

R & H Holding Corporation, I will have to decide how to move forward with the information I have."

"I suggest that you go straight to Eric Johnson in Internal Audit," Jorge advised. "He seems like a stand-up guy."

"I agree with you, Jorge. Eric will not let this get covered up, that's for sure. He has been down this road before in another company, and he denounced the corruption vehemently there. He will not back off from anybody at AMA."

Brad reached down and grabbed a couple of French fries, dipped them in ketchup, and drew them close to his mouth.

"BRADLEY!" shouted an irreverent voice right behind Brad, startling the Controller and causing him to accidentally flick one of his fries to the right. It was the saucy Paco Delgado.

"Did I scare you, Bradley my boy?" he said as he sat down at their booth, delighting in the full knowledge that he most definitely had spooked his favorite American.

Brad gave Paco a stern look, and then graciously said, "Won't you join us?"

"Bradley, I think you need to visit the optometrist, my gringo friend. I already *have* joined you," said the crass *chaparrito*.

Jorge cleared his throat as a gesture of his disapproval of Paco's lack of tact.

"What's the matter, Jorge, do you have a French fry stuck in your throat?" Paco said playfully. Jorge just shook his head and took another bite of his hamburger. Jorge did not have much tolerance for Paco's immaturity.

Brad and Jorge watched as Paco unwrapped the foil on his two, massive "Double Heriberto" hamburgers. He took the top buns off of each one. Then, he grabbed the two patties from one hamburger and put them on his other hamburger. Now, he had one hamburger with four beef patties. Paco noticed that his two colleagues were fixated on his creation. "Oh, this is part of my new high protein diet. Check it out: One hamburger with four beef patties. I'm trying to bulk up," he explained.

"Paco, are you serious?" Brad asked innocently.

"Of course I am! It pains me to say it, Bradley, but you are starting to rub off on me. I actually joined a gym over the week-end. So that I can whip myself into top form, I put myself on this high protein diet. The question is: can the world stand it if I get any sexier?" Paco said with a smile.

As Brad was about to recommend some healthy diet tips, he heard a disgruntled female voice to his right.

"Oh, no! Ketchup stains," said the attractive young lady as she pulled the French fry off her blouse.

All three looked over at her. Brad realized that the young lady's troubles were his doing.

"I'm terribly sorry, miss. I'm afraid that I accidentally threw...I mean, well...I was startled and..."

"I know," said the pretty young lady, laughing. "I saw what happened. It was funny to see you jump like that. You ought to get those French fries registered as a lethal weapon. Look, you got me right over the heart." She showed her onlookers the ketchup stain on her blouse, and her healthy contours nearly caused Paco's eyes to pop out.

"That's terrible," Paco said apologetically. "Please overlook my clumsy American friend's inadequacies, *señorita*. He is sort of spastic."

Brad just shook his head with a dry smile.

Paco looked back at the attractive brunette. "May I offer you my personal cleaning services?" he said beaming with a piquant expression.

"Paco! Don't embarrass yourself," Brad scolded. "You are in the presence of a lady." Brad reached into his wallet and pulled out a 100 peso bill. "Please allow me to pay for the dry cleaning charges on your blouse, miss. It's the least I can do after such a clumsy mishap."

"Don't worry about it, *señor*. I think it will come out in the wash."

"Please, miss, I insist," Brad said as he gently placed the red $100 bill on the table.

"You're an American, aren't you?" said the pretty lady.

"Yes, I am."

"My name is Raquel," she said with a flirtatious smile.

"*Mucho gusto*, Raquel. My name is Brad Jenkins, and these two gentlemen are Jorge del Valle and Paco Delgado. We work together at AMA Monterrey."

"*Mucho gusto*," Raquel replied, still smiling. All her attention was focused on Brad, something which did not sit well with Paco. "I work down the street at the library."

"Ah, so she has looks *and* brains," said Paco in an attempt to step back into the limelight of the conversation.

Raquel rolled her eyes at him as if to shoo him away. Then she turned back to Brad. "Do you eat here often, *Señor* Jenkins?"

"Yes, as a matter of fact I do. I get these hankerings for a hamburger, and it brings me here."

"Well, I just may start eating here more often," Raquel said.

Pudgy Paco, undaunted by his failed attempts to win over the attractive brunette, was not about to give up so easily. He walked over and sat down in Raquel's booth directly across from her.

With that act, Paco had violated her space. Wanting nothing to do with him, she looked at him and said, "Well, you certainly are …"

"Irresistible?" Paco interrupted with a suave and debonair smirk on his face.

"No!" Raquel replied with a scowl, repulsed by the less-than-handsome Paco.

"Irreplaceable?"

"Definitely not!"

Paco looked over at Brad. "Hey, Bradley, why don't you toss me a couple of your fancy words that begin with 'irr.' I'm all tapped out."

"Let me help you," said Raquel firmly. "You are irreverent, irresponsible, irrational, and, judging from your diet," she said as she glanced over at his hamburger with four patties, "probably irregular."

Jorge and Brad tried to contain their laughter. "Paco," Brad said, "you look irritated."

"Yes, Paco, and I believe that your differences with this young lady are irreconcilable," Jorge added. Both he and Brad were cracking up.

The defeated Paco rolled his eyes to the left and then the right, not moving his head, trying to think of what to do. "*Con permiso*," he said respectfully as he stood up from the table, "I'm going to the bathroom…to irrigate." He walked to the back and entered the bathroom.

"You'll have to excuse our colleague, Miss Raquel," said Brad. "Sometimes he gets a little overzealous around pretty young women. *Con permiso*." With that, Jorge and Brad went downstairs and headed out to the parking lot, as Raquel's eyes followed Brad all the way to his car.

"Paco is hopeless," Jorge said playfully as they got into the car and drove off.

* * * * * * * * *

As Brad and Jorge were walking into the AMA Monterrey building, Victor Reyes was walking out. "*Buenas tardes, caballeros*," he said in his best business voice. He was not pleased to see his arch-enemy Jorge fraternizing with his Controller.

"*Buenas tardes*," they replied, somewhat uncomfortable that they had bumped into the villain himself just after having discussed his corporate crimes at lunch.

Victor had told his assistant Lupita Anaya that he was going to attend "a business luncheon" that would take all afternoon. Of course, Lupita suspected that Victor was off on another of his escapades, and she was right. Victor spent all that afternoon at the apartment of his *amante* Zulema Palma. The tempting blonde vixen was making sure that she got plenty of time with her sugar daddy so that she could strengthen her loose grip over him.

Around 2:30 p.m. Victor's private cellular phone rang. He reached over to answer it. It was Lalo, one of his *compadres* who worked at the Monterrey office of the Mexican Public Registry of Property and Businesses.

"*Oye, Victor, te están investigando hasta los chones aquí*. This one guy has been in here asking for the corporate charters on all your companies. Why are they investigating you?"

A look of shock came over Victor's face. He moved the phone to his other hand and sat up in the bed. "What is the name of this *pelado*?"

"He signed in under the name of José Luis Serrano. I have a copy of his voter registration credential if you want me to check him out."

"Yeah, put Chato on it. I want a full report on this *cuate* within 48 hours."

"You got it, Victor."

"*Oye, Lalo, muchas gracias.*"

"*Para servirte, Victor.*"

Victor hung up the phone and lay back down in the bed. Zulema, noting the worried look on Victor's face, rubbed her fingers gently over his chest and inquired: "*¿Qué te pasa, chiquitito?*"

"*Nada, mi reina.* Just something I need to look into." He smiled at his voluptuous blonde bomb shell, she smiled back at him, and they went back to what they were doing before the phone call had so rudely interrupted them.

* * * * * * * * *

That evening Brad decided to give his long-time friend Chuck Simpson, PI, a call to follow up on R & H Holding Corporation, the 51% owner of GZZ-Mex. Brad wanted to know if the company was legitimate or, as he suspected, a front. He also wanted to know if by chance Rick Less was the "R" and Harry Allen was the "H" of R & H Holding.

Chuck was a private investigator and an old friend of Brad's from high school. After Chuck's parents had died tragically in a plane wreck while coming back from a vacation in Hawaii, Chuck moved in with Brad's family and spent the rest of his senior year with them. The accident had devastated Chuck, but Brad had been there to help him through that rough period. Consequently, Chuck had a fierce loyalty to Brad. They were like close brothers.

After high school, Chuck joined the army and did his basic training at Fort Benning, Georgia. He trained at the famed United States Army Infantry School, the greatest infantry center in the world, where he developed into an outstanding combat infantryman. Later in his military career he trained in advanced tactics and skills warfare at Benning's Ranger School. He had proven his military prowess in the first Gulf War as well as in certain covert operations to which the American public was not privy.

After 15 years of dedicated service to his country, Chuck returned to Columbus, Georgia, and opened his own private investigation service. Over a period of several years he had built a strong client base and a lucrative practice. Chuck was very quick to tell others that his success was directly attributable to the leadership, discipline and sense of honor that he had developed in the military. The excellent contacts that he developed during his military career were also a decided advantage in getting information in his career as a PI.

Chuck was happy to hear from Brad. The workload of both had caused them to lose contact with each other over the last few months, something uncharacteristic of their relationship. They generally were in communication via e-mail or telephone at least once a month.

"Brad, my boy, you are getting too busy down there in Taco Land," Chuck chided Brad. "How are Sofía and the kids?"

"They're fine, Chuck, thanks. How are you and Mary doing?"

"Oh, Mary's doing fine. She finally opened that flower shop a couple of months ago."

"Good for her! I know she must be on cloud nine. That is something she has wanted to do for so long."

"Yep, she saved and saved to get enough start-up capital. You know how she hates to be in debt. Now she has her own website and everything. I'm happy to say that her business is doing pretty well."

"That's great, Chuck. Please tell Mary how happy we are for her."

Brad and Chuck continued to chat for a few minutes. After catching up on events, Brad explained the R & H Holding situation in detail to Chuck.

"How did you get yourself into this mess, boy? I thought an accountant's life was supposed to be boring."

"Well, you know me, Chuck. There's never a dull moment."

"That's for sure, Brad, my boy," Chuck said, as images of Brad's past quickly went through his mind. "OK. I think I've got the gist of what you need. I'll get right on it."

* * * * * * * * *

While Chuck Simpson, PI, was investigating R & H Holding Corporation, Victor Reyes had his own team of PIs investigating José Luis Serrano, the veteran forensic auditor from the Monterrey office of Dodds Drucker Matthews. Over a 48-hour period that had begun on Sunday, Victor's PIs conducted a quick but thorough investigation of *Señor* Serrano. They were fervently trying to understand why he was investigating Victor.

What Victor learned was that indeed José Luis was a specialist in the fraud audit department of DDM. José Luis was well-respected both within DDM as well as in the audit community at large. However, try as they may, Victor's PIs could get no details as to why this veteran fraud auditor was investigating the bald, egotistical *Director General* of AMA Monterrey. Victor had contacts high within the ranks of DDM, but no one there had a clue as to what was happening.

That made Victor even more nervous. Over the years, this unscrupulous businessman had made many enemies within the Republic of Mexico, both in his professional and in his personal life. He pondered whether someone from one of his past business deals had hired José Luis to try and get some dirt on him to blackmail him. Then again, perhaps it was one of the dozens of women whom he had romanced on the side and then discarded when he grew tired of them. There were many people with a motive to do damage to his reputation.

However, never in a million years would Victor have suspected that José Luis was working for his own Controller, Mr. Brad Jenkins. That would have been inconceivable. Brad was Victor's right hand man and was personally responsible for much of Victor's success professionally over the last 18 months. For the moment, Brad was safe.

* * * * * * * * *

Chuck Simpson, PI, worked intensely on the investigation of R & H Holding Corporation. After about a week, he called Brad at his house.

"What do you have for me, Chuck?" Brad inquired with much anticipation.

"Jackpot, my boy! It's just like you thought: R & H Holding Corporation is owned by Rick Less and Harry Allen. Lucky for me I live close to AMA's corporate office. I visited the address you gave me that was listed on the registration at the Mexican Public Registry of Property and Businesses. Check it out: the address is a metal foundry business located south of Atlanta in Peachtree City."

"Yes, it has been a long time, but I remember Peachtree City. It's just a few exits south of Atlanta off of I-85."

"That's right. Anyway, R & H Holding also owns a large security alarm company which provides service to the greater Atlanta area, including service to AMA Electric International headquarters in Atlanta. R & H also owns the 1,000,000 square foot distribution center just north of Atlanta in Lawrenceville, Georgia. Guess who the current tenant is?"

"AMA Electric International."

"You got it. That's not all. R & H also owns a travel company located in downtown Atlanta. Take a guess who their number one client is."

"Don't tell me: AMA."

"Right again. These jerks are milking your company for everything they can get out of it. They have perfected the art of creating conflicts of interest."

Brad took a deep breath and then exhaled slowly. "Now the muck is beginning to appear all over the place, which paints a dangerous picture for me and my family. I am going to have to think about what to do."

"Muck? Did you say muck?"

"Yes. Muck: slimy dirt or manure. What is the matter with 'muck'?"

Chuck began laughing. "Bradley, my boy, you are one of a kind. You and I have been friends for over 25 years, and yet I have never once heard you use profanity, not one little curse word. You are squeaky clean."

"Look, Chuck, did you take pictures and get all this information documented?"

"Affirmative."

"Way to go, Chuckie. I appreciate it. Please send me the information via express mail to my house here in Monterrey."

"Just remember that when you get my bill, buddy!" Chuck said with a laugh.

"OK, Chuck. Send me the bill, but in a different envelope. I will wire you the money. And Chuck…"

"Yeah, Bradley?"

"Keep a low profile on this one. It could get dangerous."

"Roger that. You watch your six, Bradley. I don't want you to get iced over this. You've gotten yourself into a real pickle. If you need me, you know how to reach me."

* * * * * * * * *

It was business as usual the next morning at AMA Monterrey. Brad was reviewing the monthly cash forecast when he heard a soft knock at his door. He looked up and saw Enrique Navarro, the IT Manager who was a member of Brad's staff. Enrique was a tall, mild-mannered gentleman in his early 30s. He and Brad got along well because they were so alike in many ways.

Brad saw a lot of himself in Enrique. Enrique was a family man with a wife and a four-year-old girl to whom he was supremely devoted. Enrique was an athlete as well. He rose each morning at 4:30 to go to a gym close to his house and lift weights. After his weight training, he did 30 minutes of cardio-vascular work, took a shower, drank a glass of fruit juice, and then drove straight to the office. Every day Enrique carried out this same routine, regardless of what time he had gone to bed the night before. People at the company really liked Enrique. He had the rare gift of being great with people and great with information systems.

That morning, however, Enrique did not have his normal chipper look on his face. He stood in the doorway smiling, but the smile was unable to hide the signs of worry that wore heavily on his face.

Brad opened up the dialogue. *"Buenos días, Enrique. Pásale.* What is going on in the computer world this morning?"

Enrique smiled again. "I have something to discuss, Brad, but it is rather confidential. May I close the door?"

"Certainly. *Con toda confianza,"* Brad said reassuringly. Enrique closed the door and walked in. "Now, what's on your mind?" Brad inquired.

Enrique sat down, put his elbows on his knees and held his hands together. Leaning forward he rested his chin on his hands, looking at Brad with a nervous smile. Finally, he spoke. "There is something unusual that I have noticed in the VISTA sales system. Since the beginning of the year, I started seeing a notation appear in a field that we have never used before in the sales invoice screen. The field is so inconsequential that only a computer tech guy like me would ever notice it. It popped out one day on a daily exception report that VISTA generates."

"What was the notation?" Brad asked curiously.

"In a field in the lower right-hand side of the invoice screen was the code 'NS-60.' I thought it was a mistake, so I called the Lawrenceville, Georgia, distribution center to ask what it meant. I spoke with one of the warehouse workers who is a friend of mine. We had worked together on a couple of projects involving the Monterrey operations and the Lawrenceville DC. Anyway, I wanted to make sure that the data entry clerks had not made a mistake by keying data into this previously unused and blocked field on the invoice computer screen. At the time, my friend told me that it was a new designation to indicate some special type of sales…"

"What kind of special sales?" Brad interrupted.

"I'm not sure, Brad, but my friend at the Lawrenceville DC mentioned that JT Terrence, the VP of Logistics, had told him that all invoices coded as 'NS-60' were to be segregated and shipped to a special warehouse. It seemed strange to me, so I wrote a query to start tracking this each month just out of curiosity. As I said earlier, we had never used this data field before, and I had never received any notice from the corporate systems department that we were going to activate this new field."

"That's odd," Brad interjected, "because corporate policy requires you to be notified by e-mail if they are going to modify a screen in the VISTA system."

"Exactly, Brad. Everyone knows that policy, which is why I became keenly interested in this situation. I believe that somebody overrode corporate policy to make this change. That is really what whetted my appetite, because I wanted to catch them. So, each month I have been running this query. The sales amounts coded to 'NS-60' have grown dramatically since January. Back in January the NS-60 sales were $2 million."

"Wait, is that $2 million for just Monterrey or for the entire company?" Brad inquired.

"It's for the entire company, but that was just the tip of the iceberg."

"Wonderful," Brad said with sarcasm. "Please continue while I look for my aspirin for the headache I am about to get."

Enrique chuckled. "Call Paco Delgado. I'm sure he has the right pill for you," he said, poking fun at the chubby *chaparrito*. Then he continued with his revelation. "In February these weird NS-60 sales jumped to $4 million, then $6.5 million in March. In April there was more than $10 million coded as NS-60. These types of sales have continued to increase each month. Here is a print-out of these sales by month since January."

Enrique handed Brad a VISTA system print-out. His eyes got big when he saw October's NS-60 sales amount of $100 million followed by $125 million in November. "Wow!" Brad exclaimed. He sat back in his chair and studied the progression from $2.4 to $125 million once again. Then, he looked up at Enrique. "Enrique, you old blood hound! I think you have really stumbled onto something here."

Enrique smiled modestly with pride.

"What do you think theses sales are?" Brad inquired.

"Well, last week I called my friend again at the Lawrenceville DC. Brad, I don't want to give his name because I promised him I would not disclose his name if this ever came up."

Brad smiled and nodded his head. "I understand, Enrique."

"Funny thing, though: another warehouse worker that answered the phone told me that my friend was not working there anymore. So, I called his home number, and he told me that he had been let go because business was slowing down. That didn't make sense, though, because sales are at record highs. My friend wasn't too upset, however, because the company gave him three months' pay as severance. It was like a long, paid vacation for him. After we got caught up on things, as an aside I asked him about those NS-60 sales. According to my friend, during the first part of the year Atlanta had contracted several new warehouses to store the NS-60 shipments. In the second quarter, the warehouse workers stopped shipping any inventory marked NS-60. He indicated that the Lawrenceville DC had filled up the new warehouses."

"What?" asked Brad with a surprised voice. "I did not know that we had these warehouses full of inventory, and I receive a weekly e-mail of all Monterrey finished goods inventory by warehouse. Another thing that seems odd: it doesn't make sense that we would build up inventory so much. Harry Allen, the COO, has been diligently working on making the supply chain as lean as possible. Why would he have the AMA plants overproducing and building to stock, thereby increasing our finished goods inventory, when he is trying to match production to sales demand to decrease working capital tied up in inventory? That just doesn't add up."

Enrique continued, "My friend told me that they continued to key in hundreds and hundreds of small and medium-dollar invoices into the VISTA system during each month, but they never shipped anything. Nobody really understood what was going on. My friend became curious and started asking questions, and the next thing he knew he was laid off. To this date, the Lawrenceville DC is continuing this practice. As you know, Bradley, the VISTA sales system feeds directly…"

"…into the general ledger, which in turn reports sales for the period in AMA's financial statements issued to the American public," Brad interrupted matter-of-factly. "That means that if those sales are not real, then AMA is committing an accounting fraud of enormous proportions!"

"*Así es*," Enrique affirmed.

"Enrique, you have done this company a great service by bringing this forward. Don't worry, I will take it from here. You are out of this."

"Why, Brad? I want to help."

"You already have helped more than you realize, Enrique." Brad gave Enrique a big brotherly smile and said, "Look, Enrique, this could get dangerous, very dangerous. If what I suspect is true, this is a serious issue that could result in some powerful people going to jail. I don't want you involved in that. You just go home tonight and give your wife and little girl a kiss. You have done your job. Now, let me do mine."

Enrique looked somewhat perplexed, but he trusted Brad. "OK, Brad. If you need any more information, just let me know."

"Now that you mention it, Enrique, you can help. As soon as you can, please write a query to produce a report that will show me the monthly sales by customer for these NS-60 sales. I need to see this information by customer so that I can find out if these customers exist."

"*De acuerdo*, Brad. I'll do it before I leave," said the young IT manager.

"*Muchas gracias, Enrique, y gracias por la confianza.*"

"*De nada*, Brad. I will e-mail you an electronic version of the file."

"No, Enrique, please—no e-mails. I don't want an electronic trail of what we are doing. For the time being, let's keep a lid on this. Right now we have the element of surprise, and I want to keep it that way. Just print me out three copies: two for me and one for you. Take your copy to your house tonight and put it in a safe place."

"OK. Let me get to work on it." Enrique jumped up and headed out the door to his office to start writing the query.

Brad leaned back in his chair again and looked off into the distance. *Can this be real? I don't want to jump to conclusions, so first I need to confirm my suspicions. I must talk with Beth Wright in the credit department at Atlanta corporate HQ. She is the only one there whom I can trust on this issue.*

* * * * * * * * *

Early the next morning Brad called his long-time friend Beth Wright, the Corporate Credit Manager in Atlanta. Just to be on the safe side, he made the call from a public telephone using a pre-paid card. Atlanta was one hour ahead of Monterrey, so Brad calculated that Beth should just be sitting down at her desk with her first cup of coffee. Beth and Brad had attended graduate school together and had worked for the same accounting professor as grad assistants. They had continued to maintain close contact over the years.

"Hello, this is Beth Wright," she answered in her typical upbeat, professional style.

"Hey, Beth."

"Bradley? Is that you?"

"Yes. How are things going?"

"Fine, Bradley. How are Sofía and the kids? It has been a while since we have talked."

"They are fine, thanks. How are Tom and your two aquatic daughters?"

"They're all doing well; very busy, of course, but doing well. Theresa and Sue are still swimming competitively. Theresa placed first this past week-end in the Georgia state swim meet."

"Wow, that's great. She takes after her mother, the prettiest blonde-haired fish I know."

"Bradley," Beth said somewhat bashfully. "It has been many years since I swam competitively. Nowadays I am lucky if I make it to Panama City Beach once a year."

"Well, that does not sound like the swim team star I used to know," Brad said teasingly. "I recall many a time that you said 'I'll be swimming an hour a day even when I am a blue-haired old lady.'"

Beth smiled as she reflected on those good times. "Well, with this demanding job and being a wife and mother, somehow those laps in the pool have become a distant memory. I just don't spend much time in the water anymore."

"But you are still bathing everyday, aren't you?" Brad joked.

"Of course I am, silly," she said laughing at Brad's wit. "Oh, Bradley, I really miss those college days. Oh well, what's going on today south of the border?"

"Well, Beth," Bradley said changing to a more serious tone, "I am quite concerned about some things I have been seeing in the VISTA sales system. I don't want to get you involved any more than you need to be, but you are the only one I can trust on this issue."

"Sure, Bradley, how can I help?"

"I am trying to understand the nature of some unique sales transactions that I have seen recorded in the VISTA sales system this year. There are a large number of transactions that are tagged NS-60 in a field of the sales screen. This field appears to be relatively new. It was just activated this year. What do you know about this?"

"Wow, Bradley, you are as sharp as ever. You are the first person to ever ask about those NS-60 sales. Not even the internal auditors have ever questioned them." Beth turned to the wall and lowered her voice. "I have had my concerns about these sales transactions as well."

"Oh, really?" Brad replied, intrigued.

"Yes. As you know, I have been working in the credit department ever since I got out of grad school, so I have a good historical perspective of what goes on here. Well, when Rick Less took over as CEO of AMA Electrical International, one of the first things he instructed Bryan Taylor to do was to increase the reserve for bad debts from 1.5% to 4% based on some analysis which I never participated in and which I still have not seen. That's 4% on the $4 billion in sales that year."

"Yes, I am aware of that questionable decision. Talk about taking a 'big bath.' Rick Less created an additional $100 million fund which he could manipulate if he wanted. Do you think that the amount was warranted?"

"Not at all, at least it was not warranted back then. Reserving bad debts at 1.5% of yearly sales, which was about $60 million, was perfectly sufficient at the time. Before Rick Less joined us, the quality of our sales was much better. We generally collected 98% or 99% of what we sold. Of course, AMA was a much more conservative company back then. There was no reason to increase the bad debts reserve when Rick started. However, Bryan Taylor was able to convince the internal and external auditors that we were being conservative and that we did not want to overstate the net value of our receivables, so they were happy with the reserve as stated."

"OK, I am with you so far."

"Now for the part that really makes me uncomfortable. JT Terrence, VP of Logistics, meets with me every month to review the bad debt reserve and talk about our problems in collections. Each month I discuss the NS-60 sales to customers which have been past due for greater than 180 days, but he never lets me write them off. Oddly enough, with the year-end accounting close right around the corner, he and Bryan Taylor told me last week to write off about $100 million against that reserve we created when Rick Less took over three years ago."

"I get it. We write off the fictitious sales against the reserve, and there is no impact to profits because we took the hit to expense three years ago when Rick Less set up the reserve. That year was a bad year for the company, but it looks like Rick wanted to set up this reserve for future write-offs that really did not exist at the time."

"Brad, why do you think the NS-60 sales are fictitious?"

"I have my reasons, Beth, but the less you know about this, the safer it will be for you."

"Oh, Bradley, you are starting to scare me. Is everything OK?"

"Beth, look, I'm not sure what I am stepping into here, so it is best that I keep you out of it as much as I can. I have a list of the NS-60 customers by month, but I do not recognize a lot of the customers. What can you tell me about them?"

"Well, most of the NS-60 sales are to new customers with whom we have never done business before. There are a lot of them, probably somewhere between two and three thousand customers. However, we have about 27,000 customers. Ever since Rick Less took over as CEO, AMA has been constantly acquiring new companies. With those companies come new sales accounts. Also, the sales guys are always bringing in new business. Maybe that's why the auditors have never noticed this situation."

"Of course," Brad concluded, almost as if he were talking to himself. "It blends in perfectly with the acquisitions. It is actually quite clever." There was another short pause as Brad thought about how to proceed. "Beth, I need you to do me a favor."

"Sure, Bradley," Beth said, her voice now reflecting her concern. "What do you need?"

"Please send me all the information you have on the top 25 customers by sales dollars that fall into this NS-60 category. I need the company name, address, telephone number, contact, anything you have on them. Print that out and send it via overnight mail to my home address in Monterrey. You still have that address, don't you?"

"Did you get your Christmas card last year?"

Brad smiled. "Yes, the one with Frosty the Snowman break dancing. I'll never forget that one."

Beth laughed heartily. "Wasn't that cute? I just loved it! This year I'll send you something more serious, like Santa bungee jumping off the Golden Gate Bridge." Beth and Brad both burst out laughing.

Once the laughter subsided, Brad returned to his point. "Beth, please send the information to that same address, and let no one know what you have done."

Chapter 16

This is Your Wake-up Call

The next Saturday morning Brad was in his home office working on trying to put all the pieces of the puzzle together. At 10:30 a.m. the doorbell rang. Brad went downstairs and, as he expected, it was the delivery person from the express mail service. He signed for the package, which was from Beth Wright. Subsequently, Brad hurried upstairs, unwrapping the package as he climbed the stairs.

Once he was in his office, he began to pore over the list of the top 25 customers in the NS-60 sales category. Most of the addresses were in Georgia, Alabama, South Carolina, and Florida, with a couple located in Phoenix, Arizona. None of the names or addresses of the companies on the list rang a bell with Brad. He picked up the telephone and dialed a 706 area code.

"This is Chuck," said the voice on the other end with a heavy southern accent.

"Chuckie, this is Brad."

"Brad, you ole son of a gun. What's up?"

"Well, since it is a week-end, I'll get right to the point. I have another assignment for you."

"Hang on. I was just fixin' to clean my .45. Let me get to my office so I can take some notes. How have things been going with your *compadre* Victor Reyes?"

"Well, he's still living the lifestyles of the rich and shameless, but that's not what this call is about. This goes higher up in the organization."

"Did you ever report that information on the conflicts of interest to internal audit?"

"Not yet. I really do not know whom I can trust right now. Until I do, I am not going to report anything to anybody. I am trying to put together the pieces of a bigger puzzle, and I am getting closer by the minute. Now, I need your expertise again."

"OK, buddy—shoot."

"Well, I have a list of 25 companies that I would like for you to check out. I'll give them to you in a minute over the phone. I don't want this going over the Internet."

"Good thinking, Brad. The Internet is too easily compromised."

"I have a strong suspicion that these companies may not exist. They could be fronts or they could simply be non-existent, ghost companies used to fraudulently inflate the sales and profit of AMA. I don't want to get into the details, but I just wanted to give you a heads up that they probably are ghost companies. I need proof, so I would like for you to check them out for me and get me some documentation to prove my hunch."

"No problem, Brad, my boy. Why don't you give me the names, addresses and all that info?"

Brad proceeded to dictate the list of companies to Chuck, being careful to ensure that Chuck wrote down all the information correctly. When they had finished, Brad thanked Chuck and asked him to get back to him with something definitive as soon as possible. Time was of the essence.

* * * * * * * * *

The same week-end that Brad Jenkins was putting the pieces together of the suspicious NS-60 sales, Victor Reyes' wife Montserrat was visiting her sister in San Antonio, Texas. That provided Victor with the perfect opportunity to spend some time on the prowl.

There was no one with whom Victor would rather be than the lovely Lolita Loya. He had called her the past Wednesday afternoon and told her that he would be taking her to dinner at a small restaurant just outside of Monterrey called *La Sabrosa*. The specialty of *La Sabrosa* was delicious, grilled *fajitas,* one of Lolita's favorite dishes.

Victor picked the Latin beauty up at her apartment on Saturday evening after he left one of his secret businesses, the TCR Pallet Company. Lolita looked ravishing in her tight, red dress with matching red sandals. Then again, Lolita did not need much to glow. Nature had done the rest.

The *Don Juan de México* escorted his most prized possession to his car, and they drove for about 45 minutes until they came to *La Sabrosa* restaurant located on the outskirts of the industrial metropolis of Monterrey, Nuevo León. That night there was a *mariachi* band playing at *La Sabrosa*. As was his custom, Victor motioned them over to this table, slipped the young musicians 200 pesos, and asked them to play "*Morenita Mía*" in honor of the voluptuous *morena* seated across the table from him. While the *mariachis* played, Victor gently took Lolita's hand and held it throughout the song. She could not take her eyes off of Victor. She was deeply in love with him.

Ri-i-i-i-i-ing! The romantic moment was interrupted by a phone call on Victor's *muchacha* hotline, the phone that handled communications from the dark side of his life. He looked down at the caller ID and saw that it was Zulema. "I'll be right back, *preciosa*," Victor said apologetically to Lolita. He stood up and headed away from the *mariachis* toward the men's bathroom and answered the phone angrily. "*Bueno*," he barked, knowing very well who it was.

"*Hola, chiquitito*," said a sultry voice on the other end. "*¿Qué haces?*" She knew that Victor was out with Lolita—again.

"I told you that I was going to be entertaining a vendor tonight, Zulema. Why have you called me?"

"I just miss you, that's all. Please don't be mad, Victor." Zulema was a little worried that she might have crossed the line. The blonde vixen needed to backpedal and let him get back to his tomcat ways. "I'll call you tomorrow, *¿sí?*"

"All right!" Victor snapped back at her. He despised the fact that Zulema always called him—day and night. He was beginning to tire of her possessive nature. *Maybe she should not be in my stable anymore*, he mused. He turned off the *muchacha* hotline so that he would not be interrupted anymore that night, especially not in the presence of Lolita, his finest filly. He quickly returned to his table so that Lolita would not be suspicious.

"Is everything OK, *mi amor*?" she inquired innocently.

Victor smiled and placed his hand gently over hers. "*Sí, preciosa*. It was just a problem at one of the plants. Nothing to be alarmed about," he said in a shameless prevarication.

The entire evening proved to be a wonderfully romantic experience for Lolita. Victor just sat there in utter awe of her beauty. The very virile Victor could not stop thinking of what was to come once they returned to

Lolita's apartment, which they finally did around 11 p.m. The lights went out in Lolita's apartment as soon as they got there and did not come back on until the next day.

* * * * * * * * *

Over the next two weeks Brad took Chuck Simpson's advice and kept a low profile, although not a day went by without his thinking about the NS-60 sales. Finally, Chuck called Brad one Thursday evening around 8:30 p.m. Brad was out in the back yard practicing his Hapkido weapons katas. He was on his fifth kata, double nunchakas and staff, when Sofía stuck her head out of the sliding glass door and said, "*Mi amor, te habla por teléfono Chuck.*" Brad stopped immediately and made his way into the house, wiping the sweat off his face with the inside of his right elbow.

"Hello, Chuck?"

"Bradley, my boy. How's life in Taco Land?"

"Fine, Chuck. Hey, what did you find out about those 25 companies?"

"Shoot, son, what's the deal? Not even a 'how's it been, Chuck' or 'how's the wife, Chuck?' You just get straight down to business."

"Please forgive me, Chuck. I am just a little anxious to hear about those companies. How have you been?"

"Cut the chit-chat, boy! I've got something important to tell you!" Chuck said teasingly as he reversed his position, trying to vex Brad. "Well, I have to hand it to you. You nailed this one. Every single one of these companies is a ghost company. None of them exist! Not one of them."

"Are you sure, Chuck? Did you get corroborating evidence?"

"Of course I'm sure! I looked at public records, made tons of phone calls, and tried to visit every one of those cotton-pickin' companies. None of them exist. Your CEO is running a big scam. But I have to hand it to that buccaneer. He is a slick one."

"What do you mean?"

"Well, I had some people send letters to four of those 25 companies trying to apply for a job under an assumed name, and they all got answers back. So, somehow those guys have all the mail re-routed to a central location so that any mail could be answered."

"Yes, that makes perfect sense," Brad surmised. "If the external auditors ever wanted to confirm an accounts receivable balance with one of the companies, they would be sure to get a response from whoever is handling the mail for all of the fictitious companies."

"Yeah, that's right. How much has allegedly been sold to these companies this year?"

"Conservatively, I calculate cumulative sales to these NS-60 companies to be around $400 million for the year. Of course…"

"Pack your bags, boy!" Chuck interrupted. "You had better get your family out of there now! I mean roll out of there tonight like a hurricane! If those sorry dogs in Atlanta who are behind this find out that you are on to them, they will take you out. Especially if you are the only one who knows about this. They won't even think about it. Are you sure the auditors are not on to them?"

"I don't think so, Chuck. They have created a paper trail of documents that looks so legitimate that it is very unlikely that someone could ever hope to put the pieces together. By the way, I fell on to this piece by luck. My IT manager did a little investigation on his own and put me on this trail. Otherwise, I am unsure whether it ever would have been detected."

"Well, give that man a cee-gar. He deserves it. Just make sure he doesn't get whacked for this. If I were you, Bradley, I would call in the Feds on this one now. You have enough evidence to get the FBI or the SEC to open an investigation, don't you?"

"Yes, I think I do. I still wish I had some proof as to who is calling the shots on this, but I am confident that Rick Less is the mastermind behind it all. Harry Allen, I am sure, is heavily involved as well. Those two are pretty much inseparable."

"Just get out of there and get your family to a safe place, somewhere where they can't track you until you can get this information into the hands of the Feds," Chuck reiterated with notable concern in his voice. "Even after that, it is going to be dangerous for you, Sofía, and the kids. If they prosecute these crooks, you will be the key witness. Your testimony could ruin some powerful people. Have you thought this thing through, Bradley?"

"Well, not completely. I have been so focused on trying to unravel this puzzle that I haven't thought much about what would happen after I obtained proof. I just know that it will not be safe for us until we get these crooks."

"I understand, buddy. You got yourself in another pickle, but this one is a red-hot pickle. Just keep it together. I'll help you anyway I can. You know that you can count on me."

"Thanks, Chuckie," Brad said weakly. His stomach was beginning to feel queasy. "I'll get back to you soon."

"Watch your six, Bradley. Do you hear me?"

"Roger that, Chuck."

Brad hung up the phone and sat there in the kitchen thinking about the situation in which he now found himself. He had discovered that AMA management had grossly overstated sales and profits, to the tune of at least $400 million dollars. The amount was a material misstatement that would definitely affect the decisions of investors if they knew about it. Worse than that, it was a lie to the American people.

American citizens—grandparents, young couples, hard-working Americans—were putting their trust into what AMA management was saying. They were making important decisions with their life-time savings. That was money that was supposed to take care of them in their retirement years so that they could live a dignified life. Most importantly, they were relying on the accounting information that AMA published to help them to decide what to do with their savings. Brad knew that he had to do something to prevent this fraud from continuing and resulting in the bankruptcy of AMA. He had to determine what to do with this information. Should he go to corporate internal audit or straight to the FBI?

* * * * * * * * *

Before he left for work the next morning, Brad called José Luis Serrano, the veteran fraud auditor. The Controller asked José Luis to meet him at *La Chulada* restaurant for lunch, but he did not explain why. In his usual punctual manner, José Luis showed up right at 1:00 p.m. Brad went straight to the point of the meeting. He brought José Luis up to speed on his research, describing all the ways in which AMA was manipulating its financial statements—the change in accounting policies, the reversal of the $45 million expense in the restructuring reserve. Then he dropped the bomb on the fraud auditor about the $400 million in fictitious sales manufactured through a maze of paperwork and deceit.

José Luis was floored. The investigations he had conducted a couple of months ago had shown him how corrupt Victor was. This news, however, was above and beyond anything he imagined that AMA was capable of doing. The scope of the abuse had expanded from a greedy General Director in Mexico to a world-wide fraud of massive proportion. Brad also disclosed the fact that Rick Less and Harry Allen were indeed the owners of R& H Holding.

If the news on the accounting fraud were made public, the AMA stock could suffer a sales frenzy that would send it into a fatal downward spin. The result could leave millions of investors holding a stock trading for a fraction of its current $60 sales price. However, if this accounting fraud were not stopped, it would probably bankrupt the company, leaving AMA stockholders and employees in a much worse position.

"How could this be happening, Brad? Our Atlanta office has been on this audit for years."

Brad explained that the fraudulent sales were very cleverly buried in a maze of voluminous transactions, collusion, and false documentation. Those calling the shots had left no audit trail in writing. They were using mid-level managers and lower level employees to do their dirty work in excruciating detail, with all the supporting documentation to legitimize every aspect of the fraud.

Many of those employees involved did not understand the gravity of what they were doing because they could not see the big picture. They did not know the magnitude of the deception. The secrecy of the inner circle of executives involved in the fraud was bound by greed in the form of huge salaries and lots of stock grants and stock options that were tied to the stock price. Rick Less had everyone singing harmoniously to the same tune, a melody called "Whatever it Takes to Please Wall Street."

José Luis sat there in the restaurant booth looking down at his coffee and stirring it slowly. *"Ah, caray.* This paints a very bad picture, Bradley. I would be remiss if I did not warn you of the grave danger in which you now find yourself. You must protect your family at all costs. If these unscrupulous people find out that you have this incriminating information in your possession..." José Luis's facial expression conveyed his fear of what might happen to Brad. There was no need for him to finish his sentence. Brad knew well what the consequences would be.

José Luis and Brad were so engulfed in their conversation that they did not pay any attention to the tall, husky man seated directly across the restaurant from them. Although he was not within listening distance, he watched intensely as the two accountants discussed the shameless acts being committed by AMA Electric International to defraud the American public.

After they had finished their lunch, Brad and José Luis agreed to stay in close contact and said their good-byes. As soon as they walked out the door, the mysterious, husky man stood up and dropped a crispy green 200 Mexican peso bill on the table to the right of his half-eaten plate of *guisado.* He then exited the restaurant quickly. The bright Monterrey sun struck his eyes painfully. The stranger squinted and put his hand up to block the sun as his body reacted with a loud, violent sneeze. "Ah-h-h-h-choo!" He wiped his nose with his handkerchief and continued walking through the restaurant parking lot at a hurried pace. His eyes were locked on to José Luis just like a jet fighter pilot locks on to his aerial target.

José Luis walked briskly over to his modest, late model sedan and drove slowly out of the parking lot. The stranger pulled out right behind him in a heavy-duty pick-up truck with a big, silver cattle guard in front. The stranger's phone rang, and he struggled to reach down and grab it. The call was an unwanted distraction. Finally, he managed to pull the phone out of the carrying case clipped onto his belt buckle. *"Bueno,"* he grumbled into the slim, silver cellular phone.

"Salazar, ¿qué onda? Do you have him in sight?"

"Sí, Chato. Andamos en la Avenida Insurgentes. I'm right on his tail."

"Bien, Sal. Take care of this problem discreetly."

"Sí, jefe. No se preocupe. No le voy a fallar."

* * * * * * * * *

That evening Brad was lifting weights with Sofía in the garage while Little Michael and Liliana were in the back yard playing on the trampoline under the watchful eye of Margarita. Brad and Sofía were listening to a local Monterrey news channel on television as they worked through their weight-lifting routine at a quick pace. An anchorman was rattling off the day's events in a pleasant, flowing Spanish. Brad was assisting Sofía from behind as she did leg squats with a 45-pound barbell and a 25-pound plate on each side of the barbell.

The words of the Mexican anchorman caught their attention:

"In local news, a Monterrey businessman was involved in a tragic automobile accident today. José Luis Serrano, a partner with the local office of the international accounting firm of Dodds Drucker

Matthews, died this afternoon when the car he was driving at high speed ran head-on into a cement post. Señor Serrano suffered a severe concussion and internal bleeding and was rushed to La Virgen de Guadalupe Hospital where he was pronounced dead on arrival. Funeral arrangements have not yet been announced by the family..."

"Oh no!" Sofía said sadly, her face vividly expressing the horror of the news. "Poor José Luis. I can't believe this!" She buried her face in her hands and wept. Dumbfounded by the news, Brad's face turned to stone. His heart began to race and his breathing became heavy and audible. He gritted his teeth, flared his nostrils, and shook his head in disbelief. Sofía looked up at her husband. "*¿Qué te pasa, mi vida?*" she whispered.

Brad did not answer immediately, because he was still thinking about his conversation earlier in the day with his now deceased friend.

"*¿Mi amor, estás bien?*" Sofía asked, her voice reflecting her concern.

Finally, Brad spoke, but all the while he looked at the cement wall in the garage. "I had lunch with José Luis today at *La Chulada* restaurant. This accident must have happened right after our lunch as José Luis was returning to his office, but…"

"But what, *mi amor?*"

"It just does not make any sense. José Luis was a notoriously slow and careful driver. I have never seen anyone so devoted to driving safely. Everywhere he went, he drove like an 80-year-old man going through a school zone. On one occasion he commented to me that he had not been cited for a traffic violation for over 25 years. He was proud of that. Yet, the news just reported that he was traveling at a high rate of speed. Why would a man who habitually drove as carefully as José Luis ever drive at a high rate of speed and crash into a cement post? Something is not right."

"Maybe someone was chasing him," Sofía remarked.

Brad thought for a moment. Sofía's comment would logically explain what happened. "You may be right," Brad said as he slowly nodded his head, "and I think that I know who may be behind this."

"Who?"

"Victor."

"Victor? Victor Reyes? *Mi amor*, from all that you have told me Victor sounds like a really despicable man, but a murderer? Do you actually think he is capable of having someone killed?"

"At this point, I do not know what to think about Victor. He is incredibly selfish and greedy, that much I do know. However, if indeed José Luis's death was not accidental, then who would have the most to gain if José Luis were out of the picture?"

"Probably Victor, but you are assuming that he knew that José Luis was investigating him. Do you think he knew?"

"I did not think Victor had a clue about the investigation before, because he has not changed at all in his behavior toward me. With this, however, I am beginning to change my mind. Come to think of it, Victor probably has contacts all over Monterrey. Perhaps someone tipped him off about the investigation."

A look of fear appeared on Sofía's beautiful, *morena* face. "Bradley, *mi amor*, I'm scared! If Victor knew that José Luis was investigating him, then he probably has asked the question of who hired José Luis. He may be on to you, Bradley. If he had José Luis killed, we could all be in great danger right now!" Sofía rested her head on Brad's shoulder, slipped her hands around her husband's arm, and squeezed tightly.

Brad gently caressed his wife's long, curly hair. "Baby, let's not jump to conclusions. A man like Victor must have lots of enemies, from his business dealings as well as his running around with other women. There is a good chance that, if Victor knows about the investigation, he thinks one of his enemies hired José Luis to dig up some dirt on him. At this point I do not think he suspects me. I am certain of one thing, though. No one else knew that it was I who hired him."

"What about when he was paid? Could that have given any clues to Victor?" Sofía asked.

"No. The invoice for his services appeared just like all the other invoices we get for DDM's audit services, so there was nothing out of the ordinary when he was paid. José Luis Serrano was a man of honor and, accordingly, I am supremely confident that he would have never betrayed my trust."

The Controller wanted to believe that he and his family were safe. Nevertheless, prudence dictated that he not discard the remote possibility that Victor knew that Brad was the one behind the investigation. For a while he sat there quietly with Sofía on the weight bench.

The pressure was beginning to mount for Brad. He had been holding on quite well up to this point, dealing quietly with this heavy burden of the investigation. However, the death of his friend, the veteran auditor José Luis Serrano, was a foreboding of stormy weather ahead. *This is your wake-up call,* Brad thought to himself. *You could be next.* The clock was ticking. Now more than ever he knew that he needed to take action *pronto*.

Chapter 17

A Tale of Three Saturdays

The following weekend superstar CEO Rick Less invited Bryan Taylor to his home to grill some steaks. Rick and Bryan sometimes played golf on the week-ends, but there would be no golf this week-end. This was a special occasion.

Looking at his house, one could learn a lot about Rick. His home was located in the beautiful Atlanta suburb of Buckhead. Some of Atlanta's wealthiest residents lived in this prestigious area. Rick's neighbors were successful doctors, lawyers, corporate executives and business owners. Some had lived in Buckhead for more than a generation. They were hard-working people who had done very well economically in life, and their properties reflected their financial achievements. Rick felt comfortable living among them.

Rick lived in a magnificent 5,000-square-foot home situated on a half-acre of land. The exterior of this two-story home was colonial red brick. The front and back yards were immaculately landscaped by a private gardener who came by twice a week. There was an array of flowers lining the flower bed which ran along the front of the house. The front door opened to a grand entrance with a spiral staircase that led up to the living quarters upstairs. The house contained hardwood floors throughout, large bay windows, and spacious rooms. From the granite-covered countertops in the kitchen to the gold-covered spigots in the bathroom, Rick's house abounded in elegance and exquisite taste.

His gorgeous home was reflective of Rick's fundamental values. The CEO believed in living well and enjoying life to the fullest. Success was measured in dollars. One had to balance finesse and diplomacy with brutal aggression and a killer instinct if he or she expected to win at the game of life, and Rick considered himself a master at the game.

By the time Bryan had arrived, Rick had already thrown the steaks on the grill. Rick's wife Ruth greeted Bryan at the door with a kiss on the cheek. She was dressed in her golf attire. "Bryan! How are you, dear? Do come in, please. Rick is in the back grilling."

Ruth Less was anything but what her name implied. A charming Southern Belle who had lived in Atlanta all of her life, she was a respected dentist, as were her father and her father's father. This was the second marriage for both her and Rick

"Thanks, Ruth. I'll just walk on back there if you don't mind."

"Make yourself at home, Bryan. May I offer you somethin' to drink?"

"Yes, I'll take a gin and tonic, Ruth. Thank you."

Bryan was a little nervous. He hardly ever visited Rick's home, and he wondered what had prompted the invitation. The CFO made his way out to the grill area in the back yard with his drink in hand. Ruth grabbed her golf clubs, put them in the back of her Mercedes-Benz, and drove to the country club to try and get in nine rounds before darkness fell.

Rick was working away on the steaks. He was dressed in navy-blue Bermuda shorts and a red, designer short-sleeved shirt. The smoke and the mouth-watering aroma of the steaks sizzling on the grill overwhelmed Bryan as he walked over to Rick.

"Bryan, I'm glad you could make it," Rick said casually.

"I saw Ruth on her way out to shoot the back nine at the club," Bryan commented, notably tense. "It's a shame we are not out there today."

"That is why I love Atlanta. Here we are in December, and it is 70 degrees outside. Isn't it great?"

"Yes, I really enjoy the weather here. It won't be long before the cold weather hits us, though."

"Winter always comes every year, Bryan, but the key is to be in the position where you can best weather it," Rick said with a smile. That provided a perfect lead-in to Rick's purpose for having Bryan come by his house. "Bryan, I wanted to chat with you about something that I need your help on to make it a success."

A look of surprise came over Bryan's already nervous face. "Oh, really? What do you have on your mind, Rick?"

"Well, I have been noticing that you have not been yourself lately."

His boss's comment made him feel uncomfortable. "What do you mean, Rick?"

"It is just that recently you have seemed distant, preoccupied, even a little nervous. Is everything all right?"

"Sure, Rick, everything's fine. Maybe I have been just a little worried about work. All these accounting practices we are engaging in to hit Wall Street's numbers are stressing me out a little, that's all."

Rick smiled as he looked down at the steaks and flipped them over. Flames leaped up and tried to nip him on his nose. "Whoa!" he said playfully as he quickly whipped his head back to avoid the flames. Then he tossed a little water on the source of the flames, and the problem was remedied.

Bryan elaborated in a soft, respectful tone. "Ever since the industry went into a recession, it seems like we have gone overboard trying to compensate for our lack of profitable growth. When it started I thought that it was just going to be for a couple of months, until industry demand picked up and we were able to better assimilate some of our recent acquisitions. I mean, the economic slump had been going on for a while when it finally started to affect our profitability, so I thought the market would soon be turning the tide."

"We all thought that, Bryan."

"Now, well, I am unsure as to how this will end up, Rick. This has been going on for quite some time now. When I think about what occurred at some of the high-profile companies where the executives got caught in accounting scandals, well, I just get...yeah...nervous. To be frank, I am concerned that we may get caught, too. What do you plan on doing if our true profitability does not pick back up soon?"

Rick smiled and looked away from the grill directly at Bryan. He knew that Bryan was having second thoughts, and that was exactly why he had invited him to his house. "I plan on getting rich, Bryan, very rich," the charismatic CEO replied flippantly with an arrogant smile. "You'll be rich, too, my friend. Stop worrying. This recession has lasted a little longer than I originally envisioned, but it just requires that we be a bit more creative and a little more careful. We stay the course, and we get rich."

Bryan looked off in the distance, beyond Rick's backyard, to a quiet stream about 100 yards away. "I hope you are right, Rick."

"Of course I'm right," Rick said confidently. "Bryan, you know better than anyone that we have hidden those false sales so well that it would take thousands of audit hours to crack this case. As far as the reversals on the reserves, well, the outside auditors have already signed off on it. It took a little salesmanship, but you were able to convince them of our position. We have done such a good job hiding all this that it is highly unlikely that even the best auditors will discover our accounting creativity. The odds are better that you will win the lottery than that we will get caught in these accounting practices."

"Fraud, Rick. It is accounting fraud." Bryan looked down at the ground, his spirits still low. He kicked a small acorn a few yards across the grass. "The fictitious sales *are* buried in a maze of small transactions," he admitted, trying to convince himself that he believed that they could pull it off. "We have well-constructed documentation supporting all of it. It is actually quite easy to hide these types of transactions, especially the way AMA has been doing it: a series of thousands of modest sales transactions throughout the year mixed in with the other hundreds of thousands of transactions. The way we have orchestrated this is actually quite clever," the CFO said, smiling with pride and feeling a little better about the problem.

"That's right, Bryan. You have done a marvelous job with this curve ball that the economy threw at us, and I won't forget it. We just need to stay on top of this until the demand comes back."

Bryan nodded his head in agreement. "If you add up all the false entries, they represent hundreds of millions of dollars in extra sales over a year's time. Not even our hotshot VP of internal audit, Eric Johnson, has a clue about this, and he made partner at his audit firm in eight years. Hah!" he said proudly. Because Bryan had never been given the coveted position of partner, he had always been rather jealous of Eric.

"Exactly!" Rick said reassuringly as he patted Bryan on the back. He put his arm around his CFO's shoulder and looked him in the eyes. "Bryan, on paper you are now a wealthy man because you are a team player. Our collective economic futures all depend on holding the stock at $60. We can have confidence in the fact that it will function just as we have planned as long as the circle of trust between you, Harry, and me is solid and unshakable. If that circle of trust is broken, then we all fail."

Bryan nodded and took a deep, relaxing breath.

"Remember, Bryan, this is a temporary problem. I said that a year ago, and I still believe it. We are engaging in these accounting practices, or accounting frauds as you so aptly phrase it, on a temporary basis, just until we can weather the storm of this weak demand in the industry. You have been working long enough to know that demand in almost any industry always comes back, especially in the electrical products industry. When it does, our sales will pick up and our true profit margins will improve."

"Right," said Bryan affirmatively. "Over time our actual sales should increase so that AMA systematically reduces the fictitious sales. Within a couple of years, all the fictitious sales will have been replaced by real sales. The problem will no longer exist, and no one will be the wiser. I know that will probably happen, Rick. It's just that I am a little nervous, that's all."

"It's OK to be nervous, Bryan, as long as you keep your wits about you," Rick said emphatically. "This weak market *will* eventually pick back up, and our true sales will pick up. That is inevitable. As that happens, we back off the fictitious sales little by little as real sales replace them, and our problem goes away. To Wall Street it will look as if we have leveled off in our sales growth. The stock price may not stay at the high it is now. I will probably lose my status as the hottest CEO in the industry, but who cares? By then I will have sold all my stock. I will be a rich man with $100 million dollars in the bank. You will be rich as well! That's what the name of the game is in capitalism: getting rich."

Rick held up his drink and toasted with Bryan: "To getting rich!"

Bryan forced a smile. "To getting rich," he echoed.

Rick continued hammering away at Bryan's doubts. "Bryan, nobody is going to find out about what we are doing. There's no way that they can. Nobody ever catches the smart ones; not the auditors, not even the SEC."

Ever the master at reading people, Rick knew that he had not yet closed the sale. The well-seasoned orator continued calmly and confidently. "Let's say, Bryan, just for argument's sake that they do stumble upon our little plan. It will never happen, I assure you. However, to completely alleviate your fears, let's go down that hypothetical road. Even if the Feds were to detect the fraudulent reporting, we would not be convicted. There is no written evidence linking you, me, or Harry to the fraud. It has all been done by verbal instruction to mid-level managers. If we stuck together, maintaining the circle of trust, and no one divulged anything to the Feds, they could never prevail in their case. That's why it is so critical for you to stay strong with me on this."

"Why do you say that the Feds could never prevail, Rick?" Bryan asked.

"Legally, Bryan, the question the Feds would be faced with is this: If the financial statements are fraudulent, who is responsible for it? How are the prosecutors going to prove that you or I or anybody else knew what was going on? Remember, the prosecutors must have enough evidence to prove *beyond a reasonable doubt*, Bryan, *beyond a reasonable doubt*, that we knew about the fraudulent transactions and that we conspired to carry it out. The Feds simply will not be able to do it. They would have to prove what is in our heads, which they cannot do. There would be no publicly-available evidence that we knew of or directed fraudulent activity at AMA. It has all been verbal—nothing in writing and nothing recorded. No e-mails, no voicemails, nothing, Bryan—except Sarah."

Bryan smiled. "Oh yeah—Sarah. Don't worry about her. If anyone ever even got close to discovering us, Sarah would disappear. I know she represents a slight risk, but without her I cannot keep up with what is real and what is not."

"I understand. She is a vital part of this. Anyway, getting back to what I was saying: without corroboration, whatever the Feds had would be purely circumstantial and would not result in evidentiary support for a conviction. I have done my homework on this, Bryan, with one of the best lawyers in the business, a gal that specializes in SEC issues. She assures me that an insider in AMA would have to testify against us, and the Feds would need written evidence in the company's files. One witness will not suffice; the Feds would need a paper trail as well. But there is no paper trail, Bryan. So relax."

"Rick, what do you think about the increased responsibility under Sarbanes-Oxley? Now with the CEO and CFO certifications that you and I have to sign and with the Section 404 assertions on management controls, I have lost more than one night's sleep wondering what our responsibility for AMA's accounting practices is under SOX. It's a different ballgame now."

"CEO certifications?" Rick scoffed. "Bryan, please! It is ridiculous to think that a CEO can guarantee the accuracy of the financial statements. That would take thousands of hours of my time each year. I am a CEO. I am not an accountant anymore. My job is to strategically guide this company, not to tick and tie the accounting figures. Does Congress want me in the trenches doing accounting work or 25,000 feet above strategically directing the company? Those politicians that passed Sarbanes-Oxley just wanted to generate some good public relations for themselves so that they could get re-elected. They wanted to show their voters that they were making an effort to take care of the problem with the accounting scandals. Accounting frauds are not new. Ever since business has existed there have been accounting scandals. This CEO certification has no teeth. It is not realistic to expect that CEOs can guarantee the financials."

"I suppose you are right, Rick. Even if they did catch us, which they won't, they could never convict us."

"Now you are beginning to see the light, Bryan, so stop worrying. Everything is going to be fine."

Bryan sat there pondering the warped but cunning genius of Rick's plan. He knew that transactions well hidden would be difficult to audit, especially if buried in a voluminous structure such as AMA's maze of hundreds of thousands, maybe millions, of transactions. The financial executive also knew that the SEC regulated over 6,000 public companies and reviewed only 15% or 20% of the filings in a given year. As he thought about it, he had to admit to himself that Rick's plan seemed infallible.

That Saturday was a dark day for the accounting profession, a profession devoted to faithfully serving the public through its unwavering commitment to facilitating the orderly functioning of commerce through integrity in the financial reporting process. Bryan Taylor was an accountant who had risen to the highest level in his profession. He was Chief Financial Officer of a multi-billion dollar company. However, he had allowed his fear and desire for personal gain to accommodate Rick Less' wicked web of deception.

In the defining moment of his career, the veteran accountant did not have the courage to do what was right and denounce the fraud, the lies, and the deception. Instead, he fostered it. The American public was depending on accountants like him to watch out for the public interest, to protect them from evil, self-serving scoundrels like Rick Less. Bryan Taylor proved that day that he was a selfish coward unworthy to practice the noble profession of accounting.

* * * * * * * * *

That same Saturday afternoon, Brad was focused on his family as usual. The day before, Sofía had gone to the grocery store to purchase food for their monthly visit to the *San Cristóbal* Orphanage. As usual, the Jenkins family arrived early that morning to deliver the food.

Hermana Lucila knew them well by now, and greeted them with a hug. She was very grateful for their faithful financial support of the orphanage.

"*Buenos días*, *Hermana* Lucila," Liliana said as they entered the orphanage. "Today we brought lots of potatoes, bananas, *tortillas*, chicken and….oh, yeah, lots of cheese! We even brought some milk this time. May I put it in the refrigerator?"

"*Claro que sí, hija. Pásale*," said the kind old woman.

As was the custom, each one of the Jenkinses carried in packages of food. By now little Michael was three-years old and was getting bigger every day. He always tried to impress his father by carrying the heaviest food item. This time it was the milk. "Yook, Daddy. Yook at me," he said as he struggled to carry both milk jugs into the orphanage building.

"That's great, son!" Brad said. "You are getting so strong, Big Guy!"

"Yeah," little Michael replied proudly.

"*Hermana* Lucila, I have a special treat for you today," Liliana said mysteriously. She went out to the minivan and then returned holding a chocolate cake. The Jenkinses shouted out: "*¡Feliz cumpleaños!*"

Hermana Lucila was surprised and deeply moved by their thoughtfulness. "*Muchas gracias*," she said with a big grin. "How did you know that my birthday was today?"

Brad smiled warmly and gave her a mischievous look. "Oh, a little bird whispered it in my ear," he said playfully. "Guess who prepared that cake?"

"I don't know. It looks so delicious."

"I did!" Liliana shouted. "It is only my third cake!"

"That is wonderful, Liliana. I feel honored."

Liliana beamed with pride as she cut a piece and handed it to *Hermana* Lucila.

"Mmmmm…*¡delicioso!*" said the kind woman who had devoted her life selflessly to the children of the orphanage.

The Jenkins family continued chatting a few more minutes with her and then bade her farewell so that she could get on with her work. Just when they were about to walk out the door, *Señora* Aurora Loya walked in the door. She recognized Brad immediately.

"*Hola, Señor* Jenkins. Do you remember me?"

Brad looked at her and knew that she looked familiar, but he just could not quite place her. She was remarkably attractive for an older woman. Then, it hit him. She was the lady he had rescued his first week in town.

"Yes, I remember you. It has been a while, has it not?"

"*Sí, Señor* Jenkins. Almost two years ago, because my grandchild will be two in April, and he was born the night you rescued me from those hoodlums."

Sofía was looking on with interest. Brad introduced the two and *Señora* Loya explained how Brad had defended her that fateful night from the *bandidos* who sought to rob her. "You are very lucky to have such a good man for a husband," she said to Sofía as she patted the Controller on his arm.

"I know," Sofía acknowledged, looking up at Bradley and smiling. "My husband is a wonderful man."

Shortly thereafter, they said their good-byes. "*Que Dios los bendiga,*" *Hermana* Lucila told them as they walked out.

The Jenkins family passed a stunning young lady walking into the orphanage on their way out to the car. After they had climbed into the mini-van, Sofía turned to Brad and said, "*Mi amor*, why didn't you tell me about helping that woman?"

"I just didn't want you to worry," Brad said as he kissed her hand.

"Daddy, did you really beat up some bad guys that were trying to rob that lady?" inquired Liliana.

"I just did what I would expect anyone else to do in the same situation, Sweetie."

"Wow, that's cool! I would love to kick the bad guys in the face one day," Liliana exclaimed as she moved her leg in a make-believe side kick.

"Let's hope you never have to, Love. However, we cannot rely on hope alone. That's why you train in Hapkido—to be prepared for that moment should it ever arise."

Inside the *San Cristóbal* Orphanage, the girl of extraordinary beauty who passed the Jenkins family walked into the building and kissed her mother on the cheek. "*Hola, Mamá*," she said.

"*Hola, hija*," said her mother.

"Who was that *norteamericano* who was in here?"

"Oh, that was *Señor* Jenkins, the *norteamericano* that defended me from those *malvados* that attacked me a while back. Don't you remember when that happened?"

Lolita nodded her head.

"*El Señor* Jenkins and his family come in to the orphanage once each month to bring food for the children. I wish there were more people like him. This orphanage needs all the financial support it can get."

The Latin beauty paused for a minute to reflect upon the American whom she had heard so much about but had never seen until that morning. "*Mamá, el Señor* Jenkins is a good man, isn't he?"

"*Sí, hija*, he is a very good man."

* * * * * * * * *

On that same Saturday the mood at Zulema Palma's luxury apartment was not as cheerful as it was at the Jenkins home. Zulema lounged around her apartment all afternoon staring at those horrible photos. They had confirmed her greatest fear: history was repeating itself.

Victor had not called her for two weeks…again. This time she did not call him either, just to see if he would notice. He did not. In spite of Zulema's relentless advances in recent months and her earnest attempts to re-kindle the fire that she once shared with Victor, the *Don Juan de México* was spending more and more of his time with her arch enemy Lolita Loya. The writing was on the wall. Zulema, who was at one time Victor's number one girl, was being pushed aside by the breath-taking, voluptuous Lolita. The materialistic blonde vixen, who was now about to turn twenty-nine years old, had seen this coming. Slowly but surely, it was happening. She was convinced of it, because she had done the same thing to Victor's number one *muchacha* who had preceded her—Esmeralda Olivas. Victor never spoke of Esmeralda anymore.

As his women aged and he tired of them, Victor cast them aside like an empty soft drink bottle and cut them off financially. None of them dared think of exacting vengeance on Victor by telling his wife Montserrat. They would have to face Chato, Victor's confidant who enforced certain conduct in the dark side of Victor's life. Chato had a reputation for being merciless and cruel to the enemies of his *patrón* Victor Reyes.

Two weeks ago Zulema had paid her trusted private investigator to follow Victor and get an update of where her financial backer was spending his time. That afternoon her PI had delivered dozens of photos to her showing Victor and Lolita together at different places. She looked at the photos and fear gripped her. She began mumbling colorful expletives under her breath. As much as she hated to admit it, Lolita was incredibly photogenic. Zulema hated Lolita's beauty. She fixated on the look of joy which appeared on Victor's face as he gazed at Lolita in each one of those photos. *I remember when I was the only one who could make him smile like that*, she recalled.

Now, Zulema faced a formidable threat to her plush lifestyle. If Victor lost interest in her as he had done with Esmeralda, there would be no more cash, no more designer clothes, no more sports cars, no luxury apartment, or any of the excesses to which she had become accustomed over the last seven years. That simply could not happen. She deserved to be rich! It was her destiny.

In a maniacal fit of rage, the beautiful bombshell threw the photos across the room, and they spread out all over the place, covering Zulema's den floor with Lolita's radiant face. Lolita was everywhere. Then, Zulema jumped off her couch and, with a crazed look in her eyes, began ripping up all the photos and screaming. "*Nunca! I will never let that estúpida ruin this for me,*" she vowed. Cursing Lolita, she proclaimed her bitter hatred for the Latin beauty: "*¡Maldita Lolita! ¡Te odio! ¡Te odio!*"

The angry fire of jealousy and hatred that was consuming Zulema filled the room with its destructive presence. She carried on with her violent, emotional tantrum for quite some time, screaming and crying and ripping up the photos like a mad woman. After a while, the fury within her subsided, and she sat lifelessly in the middle of the floor.

There she sat for hours staring at the wall and thinking. Her beautiful face was void of emotion, as if she were in a mystical trance. *I must come up with a way to get Lolita Loya out of the picture so that I may regain my rightful position with Victor*, she thought. Eventually, an evil, depraved smile formed slowly on her face. She nodded her head and vowed stoically to herself, "When I finish with her, *la maldita Lolita estará solita.*"

Chapter 18

Man of Honor

Brad spent most of the following Monday trying to make sense of everything that had happened and trying to determine what he was going to do. The information he was sitting on was highly explosive. Apart from handling routine functions such as approving check requests and reviewing accounting reports, he just sat in his office and thought through all the sordid details of Victor Reyes' lifestyle, the mammoth accounting fraud he had uncovered, and José Luis Serrano's untimely death.

Poor José Luis, Brad thought. *His children and grandchildren looked devastated at the funeral. They all think that his death was an accident. I don't think that it was.*

Most of all, however, he thought about his family. Although he felt that they were safe for the moment, he was now beginning to fear for their safety. His family was everything to him. If something were to happen to them...

"BRADLEY!" cried out Paco Delgado as he waltzed in to Brad's office unannounced without even as much as a knock at the door. Brad jumped in his seat, startled by the unexpected and scandalous intrusion, and spilled his Diet Coke on his face and shirt. Paco realized he had spooked Brad once again. He loved it. "Sorry, *compadre*, I didn't mean to scare you!" he said with a laugh that betrayed his superficial intent to show empathy.

"Don't you knock?" Brad said as he always did with Paco's insensitive interruptions, more irritated by Paco's lack of protocol today than usual.

"Ooooh, touchy today aren't we? What's the matter, Bradley, did you lose some money in the stock market? Maybe you are a little constipated because you didn't eat your bran muffin this morning at breakfast?" He laughed again, but he saw that his jokes were not cheering Brad up. Then, he realized he had caused Brad to spill his soft drink all over him. The short, pudgy Paco walked around to the other side of Brad's desk, grabbed his own tie, and began to dry the soda on Brad's face.

Brad pushed away. "Paco, what are you doing?" he asked distrustfully.

"Bradley, don't get excited. I don't have the hots for you or anything like that!" Paco declared, laughing heartily. "I am just cleaning you with one of my disposable ties."

"Disposable ties? What on earth is that?"

"Take a look at this thing, Brad," Paco said as he held out his tie, now soiled by soft drink stains. "Look at this: a purple tie with pink polka dots! What kind of tie is this? This is for clowns!"

"Well, then, why do you wear it?" Brad asked with a perplexed look on his face.

"Because my wife bought it for me! She loves purple and pink. She's crazy about those colors, and so she buys me these funky ties that look like they came from a pimp store on Broadway."

"If you don't like the ties, then you should just be honest with her. Tell her that you don't like them, and then don't put them on."

"Oh, no! Don't start with that transparency stuff again. I told you a while back to take it easy with that transparency stuff, Bradley. Too much transparency is not good for you, remember?"

Brad reflected back on that conversation. "Oh, yes, I remember."

"Unlike some other people in this room, pretty boy, I don't look like a movie star, so I have to work a little harder to keep my lady happy. I have tried to 'just be honest with her,' but then she wouldn't speak to me. Not only would she not speak to me, but she wouldn't do the 'cha-cha-cha' with me for a month! I am *not* talking about trotting across the dance floor either, if you know what I mean."

Brad laughed. "Yes, I understand."

"So, forget about the honesty and transparency stuff. When you live in the world of Paco Delgado, you have to make these ties disposable. I just make sure that I spill something on them, or I 'accidentally on purpose' lose them, or sometimes I just burn a cigarette hole in them. That buys me about a month of time before my wife goes out and buys me another one of these disgraceful pieces of cloth. I tell you, Bradley my boy, the things I do to keep my wife happy."

Paco was relieved to see that he had brought a smile to Brad's face.

"Let's see, now, why did I come in here to see you? It certainly wasn't to clean your face with my tie, although I thank you very kindly for allowing me to use my disposable tie to do so. Oh, yeah, I have an idea for a project to generate about $50,000 a year in favorable PPV by changing the vendor for plastic pellets we are using for the tie wraps in the plastic plant. I wanted to seek your enlightenment on the issue. Hey, how do you like that big word: 'enlightenment?' See, first the exercise program and now the fancy words. You're really starting to rub off on me, my gringo friend."

"Well, is that good or bad?"

"The jury is still out on that, Bradley. You are a really square guy, but then again, you are an accountant. You accountants are supposed to be nerds. I tell you one thing, though. If those fancy words can help improve things for me at home, then maybe I won't have to wear too many more of these disposable ties!"

* * * * * * * * *

Around three o'clock in the afternoon the doorbell rang at the luxury apartment of the lovely Lolita Loya. When she opened up the door, there was a huge arrangement of red roses and baby's breath for her. She thanked the delivery person and brought the flowers inside.

She flashed that dynamite smile of hers and remarked to herself how beautiful the flowers were: "*¡Qué bonitas flores!*" She opened the card, which was obviously written by the person at the floral shop. It read: "Hoping that you will accompany me tonight on an unforgettably romantic evening at the *Hacienda del Norte* Hotel at 8:00 p.m. room 410. *Te amo…*Victor."

Oh, Victor, you are so romantic, she thought. *Of course I'll be there!*

* * * * * * * * *

That night, after a hard work-out and a delicious dinner with his family, Brad sat down with Sofía on the couch in the TV room. She was watching her favorite *novela*, or Spanish soap opera. Liliana liked this one very much as well. They both sat glued to the TV as the events unfolded.

When there was a commercial break in the *novela*, Brad looked at Sofía. "Hey, Baby, could we talk in private for a few minutes?"

"*Sí, mi amor*," she said as she reached for the remote control and handed it to Liliana. "Is everything OK?"

"I don't want to alarm you, but I wanted to talk with you about what is going on at work. I have been thinking about the fraudulent financial reporting that I have uncovered. It looks like this goes all the way to the top. It does not stop at Victor Reyes."

"You mean Rick Less and Harry Allen are crooked, too?"

"No doubt about it. I already had found out that Rick and Harry have several large conflicts of interest both here in Monterrey and in the U.S. They are using a holding company called R & H Holding to do business with AMA on many levels, and they have never disclosed any of their related party-transactions."

"Oh, my," Sofía remarked with concern.

"The more I dig, the more corruption I uncover. I am convinced that the pressure to falsify sales has been coming straight from those two so that the stock price would continue to go up. Each of them owns more than a million shares of AMA stock that they were granted by the board of directors for allegedly turning the company into the top performer in the industry. Over the last few months they have begun to systematically sell their shares of stock. They are doing it very discreetly. They sell 15,000 shares one month, 10,000 shares the next month and so on. They are doing some serious profit taking, because the value of these shares is at an all-time high: $60. It was at $22 per share when Rick Less started, so he is raking in big profits on these stock sales.

I estimate that he has already realized $38 million in profits from the sales of his AMA stock."

"What do you mean about the accounting fraud?" Sofía inquired. "What else have you discovered besides the conflicts of interest?"

Brad had been waiting for the right moment to break the news to her, and now seemed like that moment. He told her about the $400 million in fictitious sales and the other accounting hocus-pocus going on at the corporate level.

"Unless something miraculous happens, these guys are going to bankrupt the company, and then employees will have no pension for retirement and AMA stockholders will be holding worthless stock. The reason that our stock has had such a stellar performance this year, in the midst of an industry recession, has been because of this dastardly fraud and accounting hocus-pocus that corporate has been getting away with for quite a while. None of the other companies in our industry are making money. The demand has weakened sales to such a degree that sales are down and profit margins are weak in all segments of the industry."

"You say that Rick and Harry have all those shares of stock, but they are selling just small amounts. Why don't they just sell it all at once?"

"These guys are very clever, Sofía. They know that the SEC tracks insider trading. If the SEC sees some major movements by corporate officers with their own stock, they may launch an investigation, and that is the last thing Rick and Harry want." Brad put his hand on Sofía's shoulder and rubbed it gently.

"So then what? What will you do?" she asked, her beautiful, brown eyes unable to hide her growing anxiety.

"Well, I am going to report this to internal audit tomorrow. The VP of internal audit, Eric Johnson, seems like an honest man. I have not mentioned any of this to him…yet. When I was attending the last AMA controllers' conference in Atlanta, Eric and I had a cup of coffee at a nearby coffee shop. He described to me how he had left a well-paying job at his prior company. Eric said that he had detected some significant irregularities in the financial statements of the company and reported it to the board of directors, but nothing was ever done about it. So he walked."

"He did not have a job after that?"

"No, he didn't. He was unemployed for a while, and then he was hired by AMA as the VP of Internal Audit."

"Why don't you just quit? We have plenty of savings, *mi amor,* most of it in liquid assets. We could live for years comfortably, which we won't have to do. You are a very talented financial executive. I know you will get another job, this time with a good company. There are good companies out there. You know that better than I."

"I probably will quit, *mi vida*, but I have to report what I know to internal audit, and then they will have to report it to the board of directors. It will most likely be my final act as the Controller of AMA Monterrey."

"Is it safe? Won't Rick and Harry try to stop you from reporting this?"

"Once I report the fraudulent financial reporting to Eric and give him the documentation, he will go to the SEC or the FBI if he does not get support from the Board of Directors. However, there will be no future for me at this company as long as Rick and Harry are here."

"This is very serious, Brad."

"I know it is, *mi vida*," said Brad calmly. "That is why I want you and the children to fly to Austin to lay low with your sister Isabel for a few days. It is probably best that you leave the country tomorrow. Nobody will expect it."

"Aren't you coming, *mi amor?*"

"Not right now. I don't know what is going to happen. I may resign or they may fire me. At any rate, I do not want my family to be a target. When José Luis died, it was a wake-up call for me. I am sure that Victor had something to do with it. He, Rick, and Harry know how much I love my family, and you and the children are the only vulnerable place for them to attack. So, once these *desgraciados* realize that I have this incriminating evidence in my possession, they may try to scare you guys…or worse, to keep me from testifying."

Finally, the gravity of the danger was clear to Sofía. "No, no, Bradley. Please, don't do this," she pleaded. Her big, beautiful eyes filled with tears. "It's not worth it! Forget about this corrupt company! Just quit!" She placed her hands on Brad's chest and looked up at him, trying to force a smile in spite of her tears. "Why don't we go to Cancún for a winter vacation, just the four of us? We can spend two or three weeks there just having fun at the beach. The children would love it, and you could put an end to this once and for all."

Brad took a deep breath and looked lovingly into his wife's eyes. "A lot of good, honest people work at AMA. Honor dictates that I fulfill my obligations as Controller. This philosophy of indifference that currently abounds within the ranks of accounting is exactly what has caused the finance people to stand by while this fraud has mushroomed into the mammoth deception that it has become. You know me well enough to realize that it is not within me just to stand by and let this happen. Perish the thought!"

Sofía began sobbing uncontrollably as she shook her head. "No, Bradley! Just walk away, *por favor. Te lo suplico.* Something terrible could happen to you, just like with José Luis Serrano."

"Sofía, please, Baby, calm down and hear me out on this." It taxed Brad considerably to see her anguish. "If I don't get these guys behind bars, we will never be safe. Over the last few days I have been thinking a lot about this situation, trying to keep a clear head so that I could make the wisest decision for our family. I have concluded that as long as these crooks know that I can put them behind bars, we will always be at risk. I have to end this."

There was a long silence between the two as Brad caressed Sofía's back. He looked back down at Sofía as she raised her head to meet his eyes. Wiping the tears from her eyes with both his hands, he smiled tenderly and kissed her lips, tasting her tears. "I tell you what you ought to do," he said with a smile. "Go get yourself a sexy new bikini and buy lots of suntan lotion, because we *will* take that vacation in Cancún soon. When this is over we will be playing in the sun and drinking tropical fruit juices as we look out over the beautiful, blue Carribean Sea."

Sofía nodded her head slowly as if to tell him that she was scared but that she would support him, whatever he decided to do. That was one of the things she loved so much about her husband: Brad Jenkins was a man of honor. Amidst the darkness of human depravity, Brad was indeed the man with the golden glow.

* * * * * * * * *

At 8:00 p.m. that evening the voluptuous Lolita Loya arrived at the *Hacienda del Norte* Hotel. There had been instructions given to the front desk to have a key waiting for her. Lolita looked ravishing. Instead of the skin-tight, sexy outfits that she normally wore, tonight she had on a long, light blue evening gown that was a birthday gift from Victor. She was also wearing a pearl necklace and pearl earrings.

The hotel desk clerk lavishly expressed his admiration for Lolita's beauty: *"Qué bella se ve, señorita. Esta noche brilla usted más que la luna."*

"Muchas gracias," said the Latin beauty, smiling and anxious to rendezvous with Victor for what promised to be a sensationally romantic evening.

She took the elevator to the fourth floor, and then walked to suite 410. That particular hotel room was the romantic "Honeymoon Suite." Slipping the electronic key into the door lock, Lolita quietly opened the door and walked in, hoping to surprise Victor and shower him with her sweet kisses. Once she was inside, she tiptoed through the living room area to the bedroom, which was closed. She reached for the knob, but hesitated before she opened it. Voices inside the bedroom startled her. *Oh, no, I hope that I do not have the wrong room!* Then she recognized one of the voices. It was Victor's. She also heard a woman's voice in there. Her heart began to race and her stomach tightened.

Almost as if she were paralyzed from the shock, she remained frozen in her tracks at the door. The sensual moans and groans coming from the bedroom coupled with amorous comments by Victor left no doubt about what was occurring behind those closed doors. Finally, she could bear it no longer and opened the bedroom door without making a sound. There, before her very eyes, the man whom she had loved with every ounce of her heart and soul was in bed with another woman. Her whole world crumbled before her.

"Victor, how could you do this to me?" she said, as she began to sob uncontrollably.

Victor stopped his nocturnal activity and lifted his head up. "Lolita!" He jumped out of bed and put a towel around him. "Lolita, *preciosa*, let's talk about this, please!"

Lolita looked Victor straight in the eye. With tears of painful indignation streaming down her *morena* cheeks, she said very softly: "You never really loved me, did you?"

Victor put his arms around the Latin beauty. "Lolita, I love you, only you. Zulema means nothing to me!"

"Victor!" exclaimed Zulema, trying to pretend to be crushed by Victor's words. "You have been the love of my life for seven years. How can you say that you don't love me, *chiquitito*? Who is this *India María?*"

"Shut up, Zulema," Victor barked. "You just keep out of this!"

Lolita headed for the door, still weeping painfully. The Latin beauty was distraught with grief.

"Lolita, please don't go, *preciosa*. We need to talk. I can explain this. It is not what it appears to be!"

Lolita stopped suddenly and turned around. Trying to regain her composure, she wiped the tears from her eyes and cleared her throat. "What? What could you possibly say to explain this, Victor?" she said angrily. "You were with another woman right before my eyes! I can never believe anything you tell me again…"

"No, *preciosa*, please listen to me. You are the only woman for me. I love you…"

"Liar! If you had really loved me, this never would have happened. I know, because I really love you, and I could never even think of being with another man."

Zulema had gotten out of bed and put on her bathrobe. Events were unfolding exactly as she had hoped. She was ecstatic, but she had to hide her delight. The sultry blonde vixen quietly walked up to Lolita and, putting her face inches from Lolita's, asserted her claim on her man. "*I* am Victor's woman. Who are you?" Then she turned to Victor, "Who is this *María*, Victor, your maid?"

Lolita did not take kindly to the insults of someone she did not know, especially this lewd woman who was with her beloved Victor. "Listen to me, you tramp…"

"How dare you!" shouted Zulema as she grabbed Lolita by the arms and started to grapple with her. Lolita defended herself well by grabbing Zulema's hair and jerking her head violently to the left and right like a puppet.

Victor stepped in and broke up the scuffle. "Zulema! I told you to stay out of this! Go into the bathroom! Now!" Zulema, whose beautiful blonde hair now resembled a ball of fur, knew that she should back off for the time being. The damage she wanted to cause had been handsomely done, and she did not want to botch things at this point. She walked off quietly, but used sign language to express herself once more to Lolita.

Lolita turned around and started for the door again. Victor grabbed her arm and pleaded for her to stay. "*Preciosa, por favor, no te vayas.* Please don't go! *Te amo.*"

"Let go of me, *descarado!*" the broken-hearted Lolita cried as she jerked her arm from Victor's grasp. In between her sobs, she laughed out of desperation. "You know, you really had me fooled, Victor. I truly believed that you were different from any other man. I thought you were a good, kind, benevolent man who cared about others. But now I see you for what you are: a sanctimonious old hypocrite." With that condemning judgment, Lolita turned and marched out the door.

Victor stood there, numbed by what had just occurred. How did Lolita happen upon him and Zulema? For more than two years he had taken meticulous care to ensure that Lolita would never cross paths with him when he was with one of his other women. How was this possible?

Then, as if a light had been turned on, he realized that there could be only one logical explanation: Zulema! That scheming, manipulating she-devil! She had to be the one responsible for this. He turned around and ran toward the bathroom.

Inside the bathroom, Zulema was still doing her best to convince Victor that she was devastated by what had just occurred, but it was a futile attempt. Victor grabbed her, yanked her out of the bathroom, and threw her to the floor. "Ouch," she said rubbing her right elbow and shoulder, "Victor, you hurt me."

"It was you, wasn't it? You were the cause of this, you insidious, jealous tramp! I should have gotten rid of you long ago!"

Zulema got back up on her feet and turned on the drama. "That is not true, Victor. I love you with all my heart," she vehemently declared. *"Te amo, Victor, te amo."*

"Quit groveling! You don't love me! You love my money. I know, because you and I are the same. I'm no genius, but I can read people, and I know when someone is trying to con me. The only thing you ever wanted from me was my money, you manipulative witch! At least be straight with me for just this once."

"Victor, that is not true. I don't care about your money! All I want to do is to be with you, *mi amor.* Please don't say those things." She put her arms around Victor and kissed him on the lips. "Stay with me tonight, *chiquitito,*" she begged with her smooth, sultry voice as she caressed him enticingly.

Victor looked at Zulema with fury in his eyes and then pushed her away with great force. Zulema fell to the floor and remained there, crying tears that now had become real. The acting was over.

The *Don Juan de México* dressed as fast as he could and ran out the door in search of Lolita. He had to find her and make things right.

Chapter 19

Timely Communication

The next morning Sofía went to a public phone, just as Brad had instructed, and made two phone calls. First, she called her parents who were visiting her sister Janet in Greenville, South Carolina. Sofía's mother Clara answered the phone. She described to her mother in general terms what had happened.

Her mother was shocked and fearful for her daughter's safety, but her fears were allayed when Sofía explained that they would be leaving Monterrey to seek refuge with her oldest sister Isabel in Austin. She told her parents that it was imperative that they stay in Greenville until things were safer for them to return to their home in Monterrey. Much to her relief, they sensibly agreed to do so.

Next, Sofía called Isabel in Austin, Texas. Isabel said that she would be waiting for Sofía and the children at the airport in Austin when they arrived. Isabel and Sofía were not just sisters; they were the very of best friends and stayed in close contact even though they lived hundreds of miles apart. Brad knew that Isabel would be very supportive of Sofía over the next few days.

At lunch time Brad left the office. Instead of going to get something to eat at a nearby restaurant, he went home for lunch and then secretly took his family to the airport. Sofía, who was a dual citizen, used her Mexican passport to purchase the tickets. She would not use her U.S.

passport until she arrived in the U.S. Since Mexicans use their mother's maiden name as part of their legal name, this would make it more difficult for anyone to trace the purchase of the tickets.

Once Brad had seen Sofía and the children safely aboard their plane for Austin, he went out to a public phone and called Eric Johnson, the VP of Internal Audit. He used Sofía's prepaid calling card. He did not want to leave an audit trail of whom he was calling on his company cellular phone.

"This is Eric," said a friendly, professional voice.

"Eric, good morning, this is Brad Jenkins. I'm sorry to trouble you, but I wanted to talk with you about something very important."

"Sure, Brad, how can I help you?"

Brad then began explaining the wicked web of deceit that the accounting *bandidos* had woven within AMA Electric International. He described to Eric in detail the technical support for his findings. It took him about 20 minutes to cover the issue thoroughly. When he finished, there was a long pause on the other end of the line.

Finally, Eric spoke. "Whoo-eee!" He was obviously knocked off his feet by the news. "You know, Brad, if the FBI knew about this, they would have a jet in the air bound for Atlanta tomorrow."

"Well, I think that they need to find out about it, Eric, but I just wanted to go through the proper channels. That's why I thought the best thing to do was to start with you. I went back and forth on this. I was not sure whether I should go to you first or go straight to the Feds."

"You did the right thing. I appreciate your giving me a chance to do my job. I have to admit, Brad, I am impressed! How did you figure all this out and still get your regular work done?"

Brad thought for a minute, and then answered the question. "Signs of it were just staring me in the face everywhere I turned. Twenty years of accounting experience develops seasoned judgment. I'm sure you know what I am talking about, Eric.

"Oh, yes," affirmed Eric. "Some people might call it a sixth sense. If something does not appear right, you sense it."

"You just have to look beyond the numbers," Brad added.

"Well," said Eric, "you have just re-arranged the rest of my week. I am going to get on a plane tonight and fly down to Monterrey to look at your documentation. Brad, I believe you on this. You have a lot of credibility within the company. For you to come forward with this information, well, let's just say that it will not hold you in good stead with Rick and Harry if they are in on it. I need to step in and do my job now. I'll see you first thing tomorrow morning, but I recommend that we meet at your house rather than in your office. I'll stay at the Regal Hotel tonight."

"Very good, Eric. I'll pick you up at the Regal around 8:00 a.m. tomorrow."

* * * * * * * * *

That evening Buzz Blakely, the head of security for AMA Electric International, was relaxing in his recliner and watching television. His wife of 45 years, a third grade teacher at a nearby elementary school who was nearing retirement, sat at their kitchen table grading papers. It was another quiet, peaceful evening at the Blakely residence.

Buzz first began working for Rick Less about ten years ago when Rick was a divisional vice-president at his prior company. Back in those days, Buzz was struggling to obtain gainful employment. At the time he was fifty-five years old and unemployed, but he did have good experience with the National Security Agency. Unfortunately, after his thirty years at the NSA, he had drifted from one job to another, never really landing anything worthwhile. It was difficult for a 55-year-old unemployed man to get a good job in the security field. Then he met Rick.

Rick liked to control people. To the unscrupulous CEO, it was all part of the game at which he was a master. For him to be able to control people, he needed something compromising on them, such as an affair, illegal drug use, or any number of vices that a person can fall into in today's world. Buzz Blakely was the man who got him that information. Whether it was photos of indiscretions, taped conversations of corruption, or bank records of misappropriation of funds, Buzz could get the information. Over the years Buzz had proven to be fiercely loyal to Rick and had gained his trust. Rick paid Buzz exceedingly well for his diligent work and loyalty, to the tune of $350,000 a year.

At 9:30 p.m. Buzz's cellular phone rang. "Who could it be at this hour?" his wife asked as she grabbed the next student's exam and started grading it.

Buzz did not reply to her but instead answered the phone. "Buzz Blakely."

"Mr. Blakely, this is Mark Watson," said Buzz's young assistant.

"Yes, Mark, how are you?"

"I am fine, sir. Please forgive the late call, but I have some big news to tell you, Mr. Blakely."

"Yes, I gather as much. What have you to report?"

"Well, just now I was doing my daily review of Eric Johnson's phone conversations, and I heard something that sounds like big trouble. He was talking with Brad Jenkins, that Controller down in Mexico. I have the tape with me. Should I bring it over to your house, Mr. Blakely?"

"Do you think that the issue is that urgent?"

"Yes, sir, I do. I really do."

"OK, Mark. I'll be waiting for you."

* * * * * * * * *

Brad arrived at the Regal Hotel at 8:00 a.m. on Wednesday, just as he had agreed. Eric Johnson was waiting for him in the lobby. The distinguished-looking, middle-aged, African-American executive was dressed in a blue pin-striped suit, a white button-down shirt, and black wing-tipped shoes—the accountant's uniform. The corporate vice-president was tall and had a slim, athletic build, similar to Brad's, and his suit was tailored with an athletic cut. His gold-colored, wire-rimmed glasses fit him to a "T". He was immaculately clean-cut—the consummate professional.

"Brad!" he said as he walked toward the Controller waving his hand.

Brad hustled over to Eric. "Hey, Eric, thanks for flying down," Brad said in a grateful tone of voice as he shook the corporate officer's hand. "Shall we go?"

Eric smiled. "Yes, I am anxious to look at what you have."

The two accountants arrived at Brad's house around 8:45 a.m. As they walked in, Brad's maid Margarita greeted him and his guest and brought them a cup of coffee. "*Muchas gracias, Margarita*," Brad said with a smile.

"Where is your wife?" Eric asked, surprised not to see Sofía.

"She and the kids flew back to the States yesterday just to be on the safe side."

"Man, you *are* concerned about this, aren't you?"

Brad nodded slowly. The solemn look on his face clearly communicated to Eric the gravity of the situation.

"Well, let's get to work," Eric said as he turned on his laptop computer. The career auditor spent all morning reviewing Brad's work papers, memos to file, and other corroborating evidence. He engaged in detailed dialogue with Brad. He was surprised to see the convincing information on the R & H Holding company implicating Rick Less and Harry Allen in several undisclosed conflicts of interest. Of most interest to him, however, was the information on the mechanisms AMA had used to generate the $400 million in fictitious sales.

"Good night, Brad. I think you are right about these NS-60 sales. This is unbelievably good audit work. How many years were you an auditor?"

"Just two, but I have kept an auditor's sense of skepticism throughout my career, and it has served me well. Nothing that I ever dreamed of, however, could have approached the sophisticated corruption I uncovered at AMA Electric International."

* * * * * * * * *

Victor Reyes was visibly shaken by what had happened last night at the *Hacienda del Norte* Hotel, but his anguish was nothing compared to the awful throes of betrayal from which Lolita Loya was suffering. She was utterly devastated.

In the midst of her pain she kept asking herself how someone could commit such a treacherous act against love. For Lolita, love was that uplifting, celestial state of the heart which gave meaning to life and served as a guiding light. Love was the most beautiful thing that existed.

Her love for Victor had been true, faithful, and unselfish. Yet he had not valued the purity of that love. What was worse, he had scorned her love by giving himself to whoever that vulgar, blonde-haired woman was. *Who knows how many times they had been together before last night*, she wondered. Now, there was nothing to do but pick up the pieces and start over again. However, the Latin beauty was certain of one thing at that moment: she had to get away from the long arm and watchful eye of Victor Reyes. She had to leave Monterrey.

Wednesday morning the voluptuous *morena* returned to her luxury apartment to gather her things. As soon as she arrived, the apartment manager did as instructed and immediately phoned Victor on his private cellular phone, the one which received all the calls from the dark side of his life. Victor ran out of his office like an Olympic sprinter without even bothering to give Lupita the usual line that he was going to see a supplier, or to talk with GZZ-Mex *Constructores*, or any one of a dozen cockamamie excuses he had used over the last few years as he set out on his romantic interludes.

By the time that Victor arrived, Lolita had packed her possessions. She left all the dresses, shoes, jewelry, and other gifts that Victor had given her over the last two years in their respective places. She wanted no tangible memory of the mirage of benevolence and affection of that traitor to love. Dignity dictated that she leave them.

Victor ran up to Lolita's door and opened it with his key. "Lolita, *preciosa*, please, let's talk." He saw that she had already packed. "Please don't do this, *preciosa*. Don't leave me."

Lolita continued about her business silently. She had shed so many tears since last night that her soul felt empty and void of any human emotion. There were no more tears to cry. Then, at the worst moment, Victor's cellular phone rang. He muffled a few expletives and looked at the caller ID. It was Harry Allen. He had to take this call.

He pulled himself together and walked into the guest bedroom. "Yes, Harry, what's...what's going on?"

Harry noticed immediately the uncharacteristic weakness in Victor's voice. "Are you all right, Victor?"

"Yes, yes, Harry. What can I do for you?"

"Victor, I have Buzz Blakely sitting here with me, so I am going to put you on the speaker phone. Talk loudly so that we can both hear you over the speaker." Harry pushed the "speaker" button on his phone. "OK Victor, can you hear us?"

"Yes, I hear you fine," Victor confirmed in a strong voice.

"Well, Buzz has an interesting tape that I have just heard. It is a phone conversation yesterday between Brad Jenkins and Eric Johnson, the Vice President of Internal Audit. In that conversation, Brad revealed to Eric a lot of sensitive information about our plan."

"You mean...the NS-60 sales?" Victor inquired, now fully focused on the phone call.

"Yes," said Harry with disgust, "that, the conflicts of interest, and more. Brad knows...well...pretty much everything, and he claims to have documentation of it all."

There was a silence over the line. *This is the last thing I need right now*, Victor thought in anger.

"Victor?" Harry cried out.

"Yes, Harry, I'm here. Look, are you sure about this? Brad Jenkins has been my right arm down here for almost two years. He is a huge asset to these operations."

Buzz Blakely interceded. "We have strong reason to believe that Mr. Jenkins has everything he claims to have, Mr. Reyes. From our intelligence gathering, we know that Mr. Jenkins is not a man given to exaggeration. He is a straight shooter."

"I know that Brad Jenkins is a straight shooter!" Victor barked.

Hearing Brad's name caught Lolita's attention. She made her way closer to the door to hear the conversation.

"Be that as it may, Victor, we need you to step in and resolve this situation."

"Don't you want me to talk with Brad first?" Victor inquired, still shocked by the news.

"There is no use in it now, Victor. He has already gone straight to the one person whom we do not have on our team—Eric Johnson. In fact, Eric flew down to Monterrey last night to meet with Brad. Also, it was Brad that hired that fraud auditor down there to investigate you."

"What? It was Brad? I don't believe that!"

"Yes, unfortunately it's true. It's all on this tape, Victor. Look, I can send Buzz down there this afternoon if you need him."

Victor was more vexed now than ever. It was difficult for him to believe that Brad had gone behind his back and delved into his dark side. The corrupt Victor had always thought of Brad as a team player. "No, that won't be necessary, Harry. I have more contacts here than the CIA, DEA and FBI put together. I'll handle it. I have to say, though, that I am very disappointed to hear this."

"I know you are, Victor, and so was I when I heard the tape. I hate to think of those operations without

Brad's driving force. But it has gone way beyond that now. Let me make myself perfectly clear, Victor, just so there is no doubt about our predicament," Harry said with the same cool with which he handled every emergency. "If Brad has the information that he claims to have, and if he gets it into the hands of the U.S. authorities, then not only will we lose out on a fortune, but we will be indicted and could face jail time. Is that clear enough?"

"Crystal clear, Harry," Victor said with dejection. "Don't worry. I already know how I am going to handle this."

"Very good, Victor. Keep me posted."

"Adiós."

Now Victor had to shift back to the other crisis at hand—the lost love of Lolita Loya. Not knowing that Lolita was just outside his door, Victor turned his head to the den and yelled out, "Lolita, *lo siento*. I have one quick phone call to make and then I'll be with you, *preciosa*." Victor dialed one of his *compadres* who was a sergeant at one of the Monterrey police stations.

Lolita leaned over to the doorway as close as possible without being seen so that she could hear Victor. At this point, she no longer trusted the deceptive man in the next room, and she did not like the tone of voice that he used when he spoke disparagingly of Brad. The Latin beauty knew that *Señor* Jenkins was a good man, and now she appreciated that fact even more. Her eyes widened and her lower jaw dropped as she heard the details of Victor's plot.

When Victor had finished his phone call, he walked back into the main room. The bald 54-year-old looked around, but there was no sign of the voluptuous *morena*. Her suitcases were gone and so was she. He had seen the lovely Lolita Loya for last time.

* * * * * * * * *

Around noon Eric Johnson turned to Brad and said, "We have more than enough right now to open up an investigation. The normal procedure would be to hire an outside law firm, one that specializes in SEC issues, to come in and run the investigation. I know a good firm in Washington. However, given the fact that it looks like this goes all the way to the top, I am unsure whether that would be prudent. If Rick Less, Harry Allen and Bryan Taylor are involved, as it appears that they are, they would just hire one of their buddy law firms, pay them off, and cover the whole thing up."

"That's exactly what would happen," agreed Brad. "Those scoundrels are so clever that I doubt that there is anything in writing to link them to these irregularities; at least I have not been able find anything. Once news of this is revealed, Rick will probably instruct his accomplices to destroy as much evidence as they can."

"Well, that could get them up to 20 years in prison under Section 1102 of the Sarbanes-Oxley Act, so they had better be careful. The bar has been raised since SOX was passed, and the penalties and criminal liabilities have gone up accordingly."

Ri-i-i-ing. Both Brad and Eric looked at their cellular phones. "It is mine," Brad clarified. "*Bueno*," he answered in a Spanish that was beginning to sound native.

"*Señor* Jenkins?" answered a soft, lovely voice on the other end.

"*Sí*, this is Brad Jenkins."

"This is Lolita Loya. We have not met, but I know a lot about you. You are the man that saved my mother in front of *El Cuerpazo* gymnasium. Three hoods attacked her and tried to steal her purse. Do you remember?"

"Yes, Lolita, I do remember that. In fact, I saw her again recently."

"*Sí, Señor Jenkins*. Thank you for helping her."

"It was my duty to help her, Lolita."

"I also know that you help feed the children at *San Cristóbal* Orphanage. *Señor* Jenkins, I know that you are a good man. That's why I had to call you." There was a silence over the phone. Lolita was having difficulty continuing.

"Lolita, are you all right?" Brad asked, concerned about what was happening.

Lolita wiped her nose with a paper tissue. "Not really, but that is another story that I will not trouble you about. The important thing is for me to tell you what I overheard this morning." Lolita continued, now in better control of herself. "Victor Reyes and I had been in a romantic relationship for over two years. I thought that he loved me…" Lolita almost lost it again, but she quickly regained her composure.

"I am still here, Lolita," Brad said compassionately. "Are you sure that you are OK?"

"Yes, thank you, *Señor* Jenkins. *Lo siento*. I will try to be brief. This morning I overheard Victor talking to someone on his private cellular phone. Victor said that he was going to send over several policemen to take you to jail. Then, once you were in the jail, someone on the inside was going to kill you and your *compañero*, *Señor* Eric. I cannot remember his last name."

Brad felt like he had been kicked by a Missouri mule. *Kill me? Kill Eric?* "Lolita, are you sure about this? Perhaps you misunderstood."

"No, I am positive. Victor fears you, *Señor* Jenkins. His boss, *Señor* Allen, fears you, too. Victor knows that you have some information which could hurt him and his boss. He plans on killing you both and then making it look like a prison fight. You have to leave now! *Por favor, Señor* Jenkins, *váyase ya.* You are a man of honor, and I do not want anything to happen to you. Your family needs you."

Brad sat there quietly as his mind raced through what Lolita said, what he needed to do, and how quickly he could get out of there. "Lolita, thank you very much for warning me about this. I will not forget your kindness. I can sense that Victor has hurt you very badly, and I am sorry for that. Victor has hurt a lot of people."

"I know," the Latin beauty replied with profound sadness. "Victor is not the man I thought he was. He is a bad person."

"He is indeed," Brad said, and then shifted gears. "Look, Lolita, I know it is hard for you to see this now, but time will heal what is hurting you at this moment. Please do not allow a worthless scoundrel like Victor to keep you down. You have your whole life ahead of you. You need to push on and make a contribution to society."

"*Gracias, Señ*or Jenkins, *y Que Dios lo bendiga.*"

"*Igualmente, Lolita.*"

Brad closed his cellular phone and put it on the table. He was silent as he digested what Lolita had so nobly had the courage to tell him.

"Lolita Loya?" said Eric, intrigued by the phone call. "What was that all about?"

Knock! Knock! Knock! The sound of heavy knuckles striking the wooden door startled both Brad and Eric. Brad's heart began to pound.

"*Yo contesto, Margarita,*" Brad instructed as he headed for the door.

He looked out the window and saw two police vehicles. His heart went into overdrive and adrenalin rushed through his veins as he thought about what Lolita had said those officers were coming to do.

"Eric, it is the Monterrey police. Lolita Loya called me to warn us that there is going to be serious trouble. There is a plot to kill us. Please, grab all the documentation on the table and put it in your audit bag." He turned to Margarita and asked her to clear the area and return to her room.

"*Sí, señor Brad*," she said, her voice trembling with fear.

There was another knock at the door. "*Policía. ¡Abra la puerta!*"

Chapter 20

Hap-what?

The police continued to bang violently on the door. One of them threatened to knock the door down. "*¡Abra la puerta o la vamos a tumbar!*" Outside the house, Brad's black Holland shepherd Gino was barking ferociously at the cops.

Brad opened the door, very carefully positioning himself sideways to make it hard for them to grab him. He quickly surveyed the scene. There were three policemen at the door. Two policemen had medium builds and appeared to be in their late 20s. The third was a mean-looking, stocky, dark-skinned *moreno* of indigenous descent who appeared to be in his mid-40s. He was the one who had been yelling at the door and appeared to be in charge. They were all armed with .38 caliber pistols, but their guns were holstered. There was one more officer still sitting in the second patrol car.

"*Buenas tardes señores,*" Brad said very calmly and respectfully, struggling to keep his nervousness at bay.

"*¿Es usted el Señor Brad Jenkins?*"

"Yes, I am Brad Jenkins. How may I help you?"

"You are under arrest!"

"Arrest?" cried Brad in disbelief. "What is the charge, officer?" Brad looked back at Eric, who had managed to put all the work papers in his audit bag. Poor Eric looked terrified.

"I asked what the charge was, officer," Brad stated firmly. "You barge into my house with no search warrant, and then tell me I am under arrest but will not tell me why."

"*¡Usted cállese!*" screamed the officer rudely for Brad to shut up as the officer began to take the handcuffs out. The other two officers started moving around Brad, hoping to form a circle around him. Brad slowly and tactically moved to the left, to prevent them from surrounding him. Gino was jumping at the sliding glass door in the kitchen, barking like a mad dog at the policemen and scratching the glass.

"Don't move, *gringo*! *¡No te muevas!*" shouted the stocky policeman in charge. He grabbed Brad's right hand with his left hand and moved his other hand over to put handcuffs on Brad's wrist. With the speed of lightning honed by years of Hapkido training, Brad instantly grabbed the officer's left hand with his own right hand while stepping forward with his left foot under the officer's shoulder. He raised and twisted the officer's left hand inward toward his chest. He now had a very effective shoulder lock on the officer, who could not move without risking a shoulder dislocation. It was a severely painful shoulder lock.

Brad kept a vise-like grip on the lock. The stocky policeman felt the pain from the shoulder lock running like electricity through his entire arm. He was totally immobile and did not know what to make of this technique, which he had not seen before. His face reflected his fear that, at any moment, Brad could move and dislocate his shoulder. While maintaining the shoulder lock on the cop in charge, Brad surveyed the situation. The Controller saw that he would have to debilitate these crooked cops if he were going to get away unharmed. Thoughts of his phone conversation with Lolita Loya echoed in Brad's mind:

"Victor said that he was going to send over some police to take you to jail. Then, once you were in the jail, someone on the inside was going to kill you and your compañero, Señor Eric."

The Controller looked back at Eric. "Let my dog inside! He is in the backyard. Open the sliding door in the kitchen!" Eric hurried into the kitchen and opened the sliding glass door. The beautiful, black Holland shepherd bolted into the house.

Maintaining his vise-like shoulder lock on the stocky officer, Brad did the same spin again stepping to the rear 180 degrees, turning, and again stepping forward another 180 degrees, all at the speed of light. Brad moved much too fast to allow the officer to even think about a counter move. The first spin had locked the shoulder joint, but this second spin broke the officer's wrist, then his elbow, and finally pulled the officer's shoulder out of its socket. The once macho officer fell to the floor, screaming in agonizing pain. Brad had rendered the leader helpless; now on to the rest.

The other two officers had never seen a move like that before, either, and were temporarily stunned. The one to the left suddenly advanced toward Brad, raising his black night stick to strike Brad in the head. Brad swiftly kicked him hard in the ribs with a stepping side kick. Eric, who was frozen in fear all the way across the grand entrance room, could hear the officer's ribs crack as Brad drove his foot into the officer's side with unforgiving fury.

The second cop fell to the floor, pain emanating from his ribs each time his rib cage expanded to allow oxygen to enter his lungs. Gino pounced on the fallen cop and sunk his teeth into the cop's right arm, just as he had been trained to do in El Paso during his protection training. Gino had a deep bite on the officer and held it. The officer dared not move for fear of Gino's jaws applying more pressure, which would sever his arm from the rest of his body. He was effectively neutralized.

Brad looked at the third cop, who had recovered from his initial shock and was going for his gun. His trembling hands were complicating what should have been an easy movement. Before the third cop could pull the gun out of his holster, Brad stepped in and kicked him in the groin with a front snap kick. "Ohhh!" he cried out painfully as he bent over. Without hesitation, Brad took advantage of the cop's bent over position by thrusting his right knee with tremendous force into his nose while he anchored the cop's head from behind with his hands interlaced. He pulled down on the cop's head at the same time he drove his knee upward and into his face. The cop's nose and other facial bones shattered into pieces like a ceramic coffee mug smashing onto a concrete floor. The officer, overwhelmed by the pain, fell to the ground and passed out on the floor.

Quickly, Brad surveyed the rest of the room. His heart was racing, yet he remained calm and focused. He realized that he had not yet disarmed any of the officers, so he was still vulnerable to a gun attack. With the coolness and focus of a Special Forces commando, Brad took advantage of the fact that the third cop had passed out and quickly removed his pistol from its holster. Then, he pointed the revolver at the second officer still lying on the floor. Gino still was holding a strong bite on his arm, so Brad turned his attention to the stocky cop whose shoulder had been dislocated.

"*¡No se mueva!*" Brad warned as he approached the stocky cop, still on the floor wallowing in agony and cursing Brad under his breath. "Get on your back. *¡Rápido!*" Brad screamed.

"*Sí, señor.*" The stocky cop pleaded pitifully for his life. "*¡Por favor, no me mate! ¡No me mate!*" Brad cuffed him while the cop screamed even more from the movement of his dislocated shoulder and broken elbow and wrist. Brad removed the weapon from the cop's holster as well the back-up pistol strapped to his ankle, and slid them both over to Eric, who retrieved them nervously. He then grabbed the man's wallet and removed the driver's license, throwing the wallet back on the robust belly of the stocky cop. Brad knew that the officer would never have full use of his arm again. There would always be a nagging pain to remind the dirty cop of this fateful day when he severely underestimated the Controller.

Brad approached the other two officers, removed their weapons, and took their driver's licenses. The lessons learned from the payroll robbery had served Brad well today. This time, he knew who the bad guys were because he had their licenses, and he planned on using that information to his advantage.

Kicking the remaining weapons across the floor to Eric, he asked him to hold on to them. Suddenly, Eric yelled out, "Brad, look out! Here comes another one!" Eric raised his arms as if he were under arrest. He was scared to death and did not know what to do.

Brad commanded Gino to "sit and stay" behind the door. He ducked out of sight as Eric stood there motionless with his arms raised. The fourth cop, who was waiting in the squad car for what should have been an easy arrest, became suspicious when his partners did not come out. The cop entered the house slowly and cautiously, with his gun drawn and pointed, ready to fire. Suddenly, Brad came out from behind the dining room wall and kicked the fourth cop in the stomach with a swift and powerful round-house kick. The kick knocked the wind out of the cop's lungs, and he bent half-way over. Seizing the opportunity, Brad grabbed the pistol with both hands and swiftly twisted his attacker's shooting arm to the right and under Brad's left armpit. He extended his attacker's elbow until he locked it out under his armpit. The pistol was aimed safely away from everyone.

Just then, Gino launched at the fourth cop and bit him squarely in the posterior. The fourth cop screamed in pain and fired his weapon several times. The shots landed safely away from the others into Brad's living room wall.

"¡Ay Dios mío!" screamed Margarita so loudly from her room far in the corner of the house that Brad could hear her. She had lain down on the floor and placed her hands over her ears when the gunfire started. Margarita was petrified, la pobrecita.

Brad held the officer's elbow in a locked position under his armpit and maintained a tight grip with both hands on the cop's gun. Suddenly, with great speed he pulled up on the cop's shooting arm, pulling against the elbow joint with a quick and forceful action. The elbow, which was locked, made a popping noise as it snapped backward like a branch being broken. The officer screamed again with intense pain.

Brad slammed his left elbow into the cop's face, sending teeth flying all over his entrance hall. Gino still had a wad of the fourth cop's posterior in his mouth and was not about to let it go until Brad gave him the command to release his bite.

Then, Brad swept his left leg up under the cop's right leg, just along the calf muscle, and sent the officer to the ground. Unaccustomed to falling to the ground, the cop failed to break his fall properly, and his head hit on the marble floor of the entrance hall, rendering him unconscious. Brad disarmed the cop and kicked the gun over to Eric, who was standing still with his lower jaw hanging down, amazed at what was happening before him. *How did Brad learn to fight like that?* He could not believe what he was seeing.

Brad quickly handcuffed the fourth cop and removed the back-up weapon strapped to his ankle. He also took the driver's license. Eric collected all the weapons in a pile in Brad's kitchen. Then Brad walked over and grabbed the stocky police officer, still lying handcuffed on his back. He pulled the driver's licenses out of his pocket and spread them in his hands like a deck of cards until he found the stocky cop's license. "Tell me, Gabriel Torres of 351 Coronado Drive. Who sent you?"

"*No sé, señor,*" he replied meekly.

Brad twisted the elbow that had already been broken. "Ah-hhhhh!" the officer shrieked in agony. "*¡Ya no! ¡No más, por favor!*" he pleaded.

"Do you remember now?" Brad inquired firmly but calmly.

"*Sí, sí, ya me acuerdo,*" said the stocky cop, now bawling like a baby. "*Fue el Señor Victor Reyes. ¡Sí! Fue Victor Reyes.*"

"What were you going to do to us after you arrested us?"

"Take you to the jail and let the inmates beat you up real bad. That's all I know, *señor.*"

Brad paused for a few seconds to catch his breath and looked over at Eric, who was still quite shaken by the incident. He looked back at the men lying on his floor, moaning in agony. "You are all a bunch of corrupt cops! You are a disgrace to the honorable profession of law enforcement!" Brad said with an angry voice, still trying to catch his breath from the fighting. He spoke slowly and looked them right in the eye, pointing to them one by one. "I am going to keep all of your drivers' licenses, so I know who you are and where you live. Don't forget that! However, I'll make a deal with you. If I never see you again, I'll forget this ever happened. But, if I *ever* have any trouble out of any of you again, I am coming after all of you one by one with my own little army. *¿De acuerdo?*" The two cops who were still conscious nodded reluctantly, whimpering from the excruciating pain of their injuries.

Brad and Eric dragged them out to Brad's storage shed in the back. It was a short but painful commute for the four police officers. The other two who had passed out were beginning to regain consciousness. After they were all seated inside the shed, Brad looked at them and said with a stern tone of voice, "I will send some people to let you out in a couple of hours so that you can go to the hospital to have those injuries treated medically."

Pausing and looking at each one of them in the eyes one-by-one, Brad pulled out the driver's licenses from his pocket and showed them to the crooked cops again. "Remember, I know who you are and where you live. Don't make me come after you!" Then, he locked them inside the shed. The misery of the pain pulsating from their broken bones and dislocated joints caused them to moan and curse profusely.

Margarita came running out in a panic. *"Señor Brad, ¿qué sucedió? ¿Está usted bien, señor?"*

"I am fine, Margarita. What about you?"

*"Qué horror. Pues...este...*I think that I am all right,*"* she said feebly.

"Margarita, these were some bad cops that wanted to harm Eric and me. Don't worry; they will be taken care of shortly." Brad handed her a wad of red, 100 peso bills. "*Mire*, Margarita, here is several months' salary. I want you to take a vacation. I have your cellular telephone number and will call you in a few days. For right now, please get your things and return to your house. Do not come back to this house until I tell you it is OK, *por favor*."

"*Está bien, Señor Brad.* What about your dog?"

"Oh, that's right! Gino! Would you mind looking after him for a few days, until I can figure out what is going on around here?"

"*Sí*, of course, *Señor* Brad." Margarita called a taxi and then went into the back to get her things. Gino would be in good hands with her.

Eric sat there in a chair overcome with astonishment. "Man, I can't believe what I just saw. What was that shoulder-dislocating, arm-breaking freaky stuff you did to those dirty cops?"

"Hapkido," Brad said as he quickly grabbed some of his own things.

"Hap-what?"

"Hapkido. It is a Korean martial art."

"Well, Bradley, you really did some serious damage to those Mexican cops." Then, he began to laugh. "I don't think that they will ever forget you!"

"Eric, I do not like to fight. People get hurt whenever there is a fight." Brad turned around and looked Eric straight in the eye. "However, if I have to fight, I fight to win."

"You can say that again!" Eric said as he laughed heartily. "Remind me never to get on your bad side, Brad."

Brad continued to gather his things. "Eric, please get your things and let's get out of here. There may be more of these *desgraciados* on their way. Oh, don't forget those audit work papers. Somebody was probably going to come in to search my house while we were in jail getting our lights knocked out."

* * * * * * * * *

Eric grabbed his valuables and the audit bag quickly and threw them into the back seat of Brad's company car. Then they both took off.

"Where are we going?"

"We are getting back to the U.S. as soon as possible. Look, those cops were dirty, and they were going to throw us into prison. That would have been the end of us."

"Why do you say that?"

"Lolita Loya, Victor Reyes' girlfriend, or I guess I should say, ex-girlfriend, tipped me off. Some of Victor's goons would have taken care of us in jail."

"She told you that on the phone call you received just before the police arrived?"

"That's right."

"Did you say that Victor Reyes was behind this? Are you serious?"

"Yes. Lolita said that she had overheard Victor talking on the phone this morning."

Eric looked across at Brad as the Controller was driving. "They have laws down here just as we do in the U.S., don't they?"

"Yes, they do, but I know enough about Mexican prisons to know that two Americans like us would be grade A American beef in the joint. We would not have made it out of that jail alive. Some of Victor's guys on the inside would have stabbed us or beaten us to death the first night, before we could have arranged bail. If he really is intent on taking us out of the picture, then while we are still out on the street, he could have us whacked at a traffic light for $100 dollars or even less. You don't understand how easy it is to get killed here when you mess with the wrong people. Most of the time they never find the killers."

"That is because the cops don't want to find them, right?"

"That's right. Many times the killers are cops themselves. You have to be careful, because it is difficult to know who is honest and who is dirty." Brad turned off the boulevard and began to make his way into the downtown area.

Eric glanced over at Brad with a puzzled look on his face. "Brad, if that is the case, how has an honest Controller like you managed to stay alive so many years down here?" said Eric laughing.

"Because I mind my business, I watch my back, and I have allies that watch out for me."

"Well, I have to say one thing. You really handled yourself well back there. Whoa! I am still freaked out by it. I want to learn some of that Hap, what do you call it?"

"Hapkido."

"Yeah, Hapkido. I want to study that." Eric turned toward Brad again and, with a very serious tone of voice, asked, "Let me ask you something, Brad. How does a middle-aged, workaholic Controller find time to study the martial arts?"

"If it is important enough, you will find time to do it," Brad replied.

Finally, Eric put the question to him: "Do you work for the CIA?"

"The CIA?"

"Yes, the CIA. The Company. The Agency. Are you one of those farm boys from Langley, Virginia, with a license to kill that is using this job as a cover?"

Brad chuckled. "Eric, I am just an accountant."

Eric looked back at Brad with a skeptical look on his face. "You're just an accountant, huh?"

Brad smiled and grabbed his cellular phone. He called his trusted friend and Cost Accounting Manager, Javier Peralta, on his cell phone.

"Javier, look, I don't have much time to talk right now. I am in a tough situation and I need to get out of Mexico right away. I was just attacked by a bunch of crooked cops at my house. They wanted to arrest me and take me to jail. I have good reason to believe that Victor Reyes wants me dead."

"*¿Qué? ¿En serio, Brad?*"

"*Sí.* I am dead serious, no pun intended."

"*¡Híjole!* Are you OK?"

"Yes, thank you. Those dirty cops, however, did not fare so well. I left all four of those *desgraciados* handcuffed and locked in the shed behind my house. Do you recall the building to which I am referring?"

"Yeah. Did you take out all four cops by yourself?"

"Well, I had a little help from Gino, my puppy dog," Brad said smiling and looking at Eric.

"Bradley, I don't understand. Why does Victor Reyes want you dead? That's crazy. You are his right-hand man."

"I'm sorry, Javier, but I don't have time to get into that right now. Just be forewarned that Victor is a dangerous man. Stay away from him."

"*Sí, entiendo,* Bradley. By the way, are those cops OK? Are any of them dead or anything?"

"No, they're not dead, but they have had better days. They will need to get to a hospital soon. Look, I hate to trouble you, but I need a favor."

"Sure. What can I do?"

"Is your brother still a cop?"

"Yes. He is a lieutenant now," Javier said proudly.

"Good. Would you please go with him to my house and remove those scumbags from my shed? The key is under the mat out back. Your brother will probably need to take several officers with him. The guns of those crooked cops are all inside my house. The front door is locked, but I left the key under the ceramic pot to the right."

"No problem, Brad. I'll get on it now."

Brad smiled. "I owe you one, *amigo*."

* * * * * * * * *

Behind closed doors at his office at AMA Monterrey, Victor Reyes was talking on the phone with the police sergeant who had sent the four crooked cops to Brad's house. "What do you mean they never came back?" Victor barked while throwing papers off his desk furiously. "Are you telling me that four armed cops cannot handle two gringo accountants? Those guys are accountants, *contadores*, nerds! They spend their time making journal entries and playing with their computers! They were unarmed, too, and you had four cops strapped with service revolvers! How could your men be so incompetent?"

"*No sé,* Victor. I don't know what happened," said the Sergeant on the other end of the phone, trembling with fear. "The two *norteamericanos* just disappeared."

At that moment Victor recalled an incident in which Lolita Loya told him about how Brad had thwarted an attack by three assailants trying to mug her mother. He had completely forgotten about that situation. Maybe Brad really was a good fighter...or maybe these cops were complete nincompoops. "Did you go to the gringo's house to look for your men?"

"*Sí, señor*. But they were not there. Nobody was home."

"*Mira, compadre*, I paid you $20,000 US dollars to handle this for me, not to sit around all day polishing the seat of your pants, so go handle it!"

"*Sí, señor*. I will personally see to it. *No se preocupe*."

"You had better see to it!" Victor said as he slammed the phone down in anger.

* * * * * * * * *

After Victor had calmed down, he called COO Harry Allen back in Atlanta on his private cellular phone. "Harry, the plan failed. I don't know what happened, but it looks like Brad Jenkins and Eric Johnson got away."

"What? You are kidding me, aren't you?"

"No. I know it's hard to believe. Those incompetent cops botched the job."

"Victor, Brad knows way too much! With the information he has in his possession, our whole plan may go down the drain. I am not about to let that happen."

"Cut the drama, Harry. It's not like you are the only one with millions to lose," Victor barked back angrily.

"Look, Victor, let's put the petty wrangling to one side. We have been through a lot together over the last twenty years, but we have always managed to come out on top. We can handle this problem as well. It's simple: just make sure that those two accountants don't get across the border. You take care of things south of the Rio Grande…."

"*Río Bravo*, not Rio Grande!"

"Whatever!" shouted Harry. He took a moment to regain his composure, and then he continued. "You just make sure Brad Jenkins and Eric Johnson don't cross that border. Just in case they do, I'll have Buzz Blakely, my head of security, and his crew staked-out at border crossings and at the airports on this side of the border. You know better than I that it will be a whole lot easier to take care of this on your side of the border."

"OK, Harry."

"Good. Well, let's get on it."

"*Adiós.*"

Chapter 21

There's a Bounty on Your Booty

Brad looked over at Eric as he drove his company sedan through the streets of Monterrey. "Victor will probably be expecting us to take this car on the *autopista*, the toll highway, to the U.S.-Mexican border. That would be a big mistake, because they know this car. The plates are registered in the company's name, so I am sure that Victor will alert all the dirty cops and state troopers between here and the border. We can't take a plane, either; it's too risky. They can trace our departure and arrival electronically. We need to ditch this car, take a taxi to the bus station, and catch a bus to Laredo. From there, it should be safe for you to take a plane out of Laredo to be with your family. I may take a bus. At this point I am not sure how I am going to travel."

"That sounds good to me, Brad," the VP of Internal Audit said. "I trust your judgment; you know Mexico much better than I do. Do you think that Rick Less and Harry Allen had something to do with that situation with the cops at your house, or was it just Victor?"

"Eric, I am sure that Rick and Harry are orchestrating this whole thing. When I first found out about Victor's little empire—the conflicts of interest and that sort of thing—I thought I had solved the problem. However, now I realize that Victor is just a puppet. The real crooks are calling the shots from Atlanta, Georgia."

Eric nodded his head in agreement. "I see what you mean. This is a scary situation, Brad. We need to be very careful."

"Somehow they know we are on to them, Eric, and they are not going to take any chances. Think about it! We are down here in Mexico. Anything could happen to some foreigners in another country, and it is easy to cover it up down here if you have enough money. If they want to get us out of the picture, they will want to do it before we get back to the U.S. It would be a lot harder for them to cover their tracks in the U.S., but even that could be done if the price is right. Right now I am just worried about staying alive and making sure my family is safe. We need to get this information to the SEC and the FBI as soon as possible and then drop out of sight and let them do their job. We can talk about it on the trip to Laredo."

Brad needed to find an inconspicuous place to park his company sedan. He was about three minutes away from the downtown hotels. He could park the car in the underground parking lot of one of the large hotels and nobody would be the wiser. It would be easy to grab a cab from there as well.

Within minutes the Controller found a suitable hotel and was immediately greeted by a friendly valet driver. After indicating that he preferred to park his car himself, Brad drove below and found a very secluded area in the far northeast corner of the bottom floor. *Perfect!* The two accountants grabbed their valuables, abandoned the car, and quickly made their way back to the surface street. From there they summoned a taxi.

The taxi brought them to the Monterrey central bus station in a little more than twenty minutes. Fortunately, it was a weekday, so volume was not as heavy as on the week-ends when hundreds of Mexican families left the prosperous, industrialized city and ventured out to spend time with loved ones in surrounding pueblos.

"Victor would never expect us to take a bus," Brad sad confidently. "I'm sure he is anticipating that we will travel by plane or by car."

"Yes, you even surprised me on this call, Bradley, but I trust your judgment."

Eric was following Brad's lead. The corporate officer was now outside the English-speaking circles of five-star hotels, swank restaurants and first-class airline travel. He was now with *la raza*, the hard-working majority in Mexico that would probably never know the luxurious lifestyle of Mexico's rich. These were the salt of the earth, the backbone of the great Republic of Mexico, the ones who got the work done so that their country could keep on functioning. In spite of the hardships and obstacles they encountered in their everyday lives, they never lost that invincible passion for life so characteristic of the Mexican people.

There was a bus leaving for Nuevo Laredo in two hours, but there was another one leaving for Reynosa in 30 minutes. Brad turned to Eric and said quickly, "Change of plans. Let's take the bus to Reynosa. My wife has family there, and there is a bus leaving in thirty minutes bound for Reynosa. We can get something to eat there and lie low until nighttime. Then, we can take a taxi across the bridge into McAllen, Texas, and then fly out of Harlingen. How does that sound?"

"Yeah, that's fine. I'll follow your lead." Eric leaned over and rested his elbows on his knees. His head was hung low.

Brad could see that the situation was beginning to wear on Eric. He was probably in worse shape than Brad because he neither spoke the language nor knew the country. Brad patted him on the back. "Don't worry, Eric. We are going to get back to our families safely. One day we will be reminiscing about this adventure over charcoaled hamburgers with our families, laughing about it. You know, I may even write a book about it," he said with a wink and a smile.

* * * * * * * * *

Shortly thereafter they were on the road to Reynosa. The bus was very comfortable. The seats were large and roomy with plenty of leg space, much better than the economy seats on planes to which he was accustomed. Brad and Eric took a seat at the back of the bus where no one was sitting. After a while a young, friendly *señorita* began making her way down the aisle, serving the passengers coffee and cookies. The refreshments hit the spot. Both accountants were hungry, tired, and needed a jolt of caffeine.

The bus headed northeastward toward Reynosa, and Brad began to speak in a hushed tone to Eric about their strategy. "As soon as we are in McAllen, I need to call an FBI buddy of mine. I knew him when he was a cop in Atlanta. He is a good friend and has excellent connections within the Justice Department and with the SEC." Brad noticed that Eric's spirits had not improved much since the bus station. "How are you holding up, Eric?"

Eric sighed heavily and rolled his head toward Brad. "I'm OK, I guess," he said with a grim smile. He had not said much for a while now. "Hey, how is it that you know so many federal agents? Are you sure you are not some sort of a secret agent?" he said half-seriously.

Brad smiled but did not respond to the question. "I also need to call my wife and make sure that my family is OK," Brad said. "Atlanta does not know where my family is, thank goodness, but within time they could figure it out. I think they are fine for now. You ought to get in touch with your wife soon, but don't tell her where you are. They may be a target as well."

"It just dawned on me, Brad, that you may be right. I had not thought about that. I need to tell her to get the children to a safe place."

"How many kids do you have, Eric?"

Eric smiled as his thoughts went out to them. "Three. I have two girls and a boy. They are all teen-agers now."

"Wow, three teen-agers," Brad said, teasing his friend and fellow accountant. "You are a braver man than I thought."

"They are all great kids. Sharon and I are very fortunate. They have all turned out so well."

"Yes, you are, my friend, and soon you will be with them again."

Eric sat there for a couple of minutes as myriads of thoughts ran through his head. "Brad, you don't think they have a tap on my home line, do you?"

"Eric, at this point I am not sure, but I am not willing to take any chances. Somehow they found out you were coming down here. They probably tapped your office line. Knowing those scoundrels, they may even have had your line bugged from the day you started working for AMA years ago. With the kinds of major league scams they are running, I would imagine they would like to know what the VP of Internal Audit is working on at all times."

Nodding his head, Eric added, "You know, I think you are right. I bet those sorry dogs have been watching my every move since I started."

Suddenly, Brad's calmness was replaced by panic. "Oh, no!" he blurted out.

"What?"

"I forgot about getting across the border. Victor and his cronies are probably going to pay off the Mexican immigration and customs officials to be on the look out for us! Somehow, we are going to have to get across that border. Normally, they don't check much on the Mexican side when people are crossing into the U.S., but every once in a blue moon they do a car-by-car inspection, especially if they think someone is trying to flee the country."

"Do you mean to say that there is a bounty on your booty?" Eric asked.

Brad grinned. "I am afraid that there probably is, and there is most likely a bounty on your booty, too."

"Well, look on the bright side, Bradley," said Eric with a smile. "This is probably the most attention our booties have received in twenty years."

Brad chuckled. Eric's humor was good medicine. Unfortunately for the two accountants, Brad's instincts were correct. At that moment Carmen Silva, the HR Director and one of Victor Reyes' lieutenants in his dark world, was e-mailing pictures of Brad and Eric to her contact at the Mexican immigration office in Nuevo Laredo, Mexico. Once the immigration official in Nuevo Laredo received the digital photos, he forwarded them on to other officials at immigration offices in the border towns of Tijuana, Mexicali, Juárez, Reynosa, and Matamoros.

They were all told that Brad and Eric had brutally assaulted and attempted to kill several Monterrey police officers. The notice claimed that the two accountants were "armed and dangerous." They were to be brought into custody, dead or alive. There was a reward for their capture of $100,000 U.S. dollars each offered by an undisclosed group which was, in reality, *the compadres*—Rick, Harry, and Victor. CFO Bryan Taylor was not aware of this diabolic plot.

The notice to Mexican Customs generated a lot of interest along the U.S.-Mexican border that afternoon. Every Mexican customs and immigration agent up and down the border wanted to be the one to catch the two American fugitives and collect the $200,000 American dollars. They would be waiting for the Controller and his companion when they arrived at the border.

* * * * * * * * *

Early that evening Brad and Eric arrived at the central bus station in Reynosa, Tamaulipas, which was just across the border from McAllen, Texas. They then took a taxi to the home of Sofía's Aunt Vera. *Tía* Vera lived in a modest house located in a middle-class neighborhood on the west side of Reynosa.

"Bradley! *¿Cómo estás, hijo?* What a pleasant surprise!" she said as she greeted him with a kiss on the cheeks.

"*Muy bien, Tía. Gracias. ¿Cómo está usted?*" he replied.

"*Bien, hijo.* Just getting older every day!" she said as she walked back to the dining room table. "*Siéntate, por favor.* It is so good to see you!"

"*Tía*, this is a colleague of mine, Eric Johnson," Brad said, stretching his arm toward Eric.

"*Mucho gusto, Señor Johnson.*"

Brad looked at Eric. "That means 'Pleased to meet you.'"

"Oh, OK. *Mucho…gusto,*" Eric replied cordially.

Brad chatted with *Tía* Vera for about 20 minutes in Spanish, focusing on what was happening with the family members, both his and *Tía* Vera's. He did not want to get into the details of what was happening with AMA. While they talked they drank hot *té de canela*, or cinnamon tea, sweetened with honey.

After their conversation, *Tía* Vera went into the kitchen and prepared a delicious meal consisting of chicken *enchiladas* covered in melted Swiss cheese, fried rice, and a light salad of green vegetables, carrots, and tomatoes. As *Tía* Vera labored over a hot stove, the rich aroma from the kitchen began to make its way into the living room where the two accountants were resting. The smell of the spicy food was mouth-watering. Besides the cookies on the bus, they had not eaten since breakfast.

Finally, *Tía* Vera brought the food to the dining room table. Brad and Eric stared at the food before them like ravenous wolves. *Tía* Vera gave thanks for the food and then began to pass the plates to her two guests. To drink she served a delicious orange beverage called a *naranjada* made out of freshly-squeezed orange juice, mineral water, and sugar. Both men ate until they were stuffed.

Eric sat back, rubbing his stomach. "Oh-h-h-h-h, man. I can't believe I ate the whole *enchilada!*" he said, smiling at Brad.

Brad looked at him and chuckled. "That was lame, Eric."

"Sorry, Bradley, but I had to say it," Eric said grinning from ear to ear.

Shortly thereafter Brad and Eric said good-bye to *Tía* Vera, hopped into a taxi, and headed for the international bridge that would take them back to their beloved United States of America. The taxi driver was a relative of *Tía*

Vera's next-door neighbor. He could be trusted, she assured Brad.

It was dark by now, but the bright illumination of public lighting allowed Brad to see several hundred yards ahead. After a while their taxi reached the tail of the long slow-moving line at the U.S.-Mexican border. Since the devastating September 11th, 2001 terrorist attacks, the U.S. Department of Homeland Security had stepped up inspection efforts at the border. The additional security resulted in even slower-moving lines to cross the border. However, before they made it across the bridge to the U.S. side, they first had to get through Mexican customs.

As they advanced in the long line and came closer to the bridge, Brad saw a group of men on the Mexican side of the border in green uniforms standing over a car, taking great care to see who was in the car. All of the Mexican customs officials had large, industrial-use flashlights, the kind with the long handles that can also serve as weapons to strike someone on the head. A whack on the head by one of those flashlights, and it would be lights out for the poor victim on the receiving end.

The Mexican customs officials were shining the flashlights into the cars very methodically, scanning for something. *What are they doing?* Brad wondered. *Something is amiss. This is not normal on the Mexican side. There shouldn't be anybody checking anything.* Then, the Customs agents asked the driver of a vehicle about twenty cars in front of their taxi to open the trunk. They repeated the same procedure with the next car.

They know! Brad was sure of it. *Victor has alerted them to the fact that he would be there. The Mexican officials never check this thoroughly when cars are departing the country.*

"*¡Alto!   ¡Alto, por favor!*" Brad shouted with authority to the taxi driver as soon as he realized the predicament which he now faced. Eric looked ahead to see what had alarmed Brad.

"*But, Señor, don't you want me to take you to McAllen? We are almost there,*" asked the taxi driver with a puzzled look on his face. "We are at the international bridge!"

"*No, gracias.* We changed our mind. Would you take us back to downtown Reynosa? Don't worry. I will pay the same fare as if we had gone to McAllen."

"OK, *señor. El que paga manda.* The customer is the boss, I always say," replied the taxi driver with a confused look on his face. Slowly, a smile replaced the confused look on the kind-looking gentleman. "Oh, *ya entiendo.* You *caballeros* want a little nocturnal entertainment before you go back to *Gringolandia.* Well, I know just the place. The girls are pretty and they are clean. They are not like the normal *chicas de la calle.* You will really like these ladies. Trust me! I always get good tips when I take the *americanos* to this place."

"*No, señor,*" Brad said adamantly. "We are not interested in that sort of thing. I'll tell you where to go once we get closer to town."

"OK, *señor.* Like I always say, e*l que paga manda,*" repeated the taxi driver, now more perplexed than ever. He began to maneuver his cab to get out of the line without hitting any of the other cars. It was not an easy task, but he made it look easy. He was a well-seasoned taxi driver, and his years of experience were apparent.

By now, Eric had seen the immigration officials. He was thinking the same thing Brad was thinking. As requested, the taxi driver turned around and drove back toward downtown Reynosa. When they entered the downtown area, Brad motioned to the taxi driver to pull over next to a telephone booth. Brad and Eric stepped out of the car, and Brad paid the driver a generous amount for the fare which included a nice tip. The taxi driver drove off as happy as a lark.

"What do we do now, Brad?" Eric asked with a tone of desperation in his voice.

"We have to get into McAllen tonight. Victor and his goons will do everything they can to catch us before we get across, so every minute counts."

"That's right," agreed Eric, "time is of the essence."

"I think I know just the person to call," Brad said as he put a Mexican coin into the pay phone.

Chapter 22

The Perfect Cover

After he dialed the number, Brad turned to Eric and said, "I am going to call Sofía's Aunt Vera again and get the telephone number of Sofía's cousin, Beto. He could be the only one who can help us get out of this mess right now."

Brad dialed *Tía* Vera's number and waited for her to answer. The phone rang and rang. *Come on, Tía. Please, answer the phone! I need this information.* Finally, a sweet voice answered on the other end.

"*Bueno.*"

"*Tía, habla Brad.*"

"*Hola, hijo, ¿qué pasó?*"

With an urgent tone of voice, Brad asked her for Beto's telephone number.

"Beto? Bradley, why on earth would you want to talk with Beto? He is a man of such ill repute. It pains me to say that about a member of my own family, but it is the truth. He is an embarrassment to our family."

"There is a matter of some importance that I wish to discuss with him, *Tía*. Trust me on this. I know what I am doing."

Against her better judgment, she complied with Brad's request. Poor *Tía* Vera was now worried. Brad did not want to get her involved, but he had no choice. He immediately called Sofía's cousin Beto.

"*Bue-no-o-o-o,*" answered a smooth-talking man with a playboy voice.

"*Beto, hola*, this is Brad, Sofía's husband. *¿Cómo estás?*"

"Brad. *¡Qué onda, güey!*"

"Beto, I am in trouble and I need your help. Can we meet now? This is an extremely urgent matter."

"*Espérate.* Bradley, you are in trouble? You? Mr. Clean? You gotta be kidding me!" said Beto as he erupted in laughter. "Bradley, you are the straightest *vato* I know. What did you do, *güey*, forget to tip the waiter? Get a traffic ticket? Or, worse yet, did Sofía catch you looking at another *chica*? I know how jealous she and all her sisters are, Brad."

"No, Beto, it is nothing of the sort. This is serious. A friend of mine and I are in dire straits."

"Dire straits? I never heard of that place, *güey.* Where is it?"

Brad shook his head. "No, Beto, I mean to say that we are in trouble, big trouble. I need your help, please."

"OK, Bradley, tell me, where are you?"

"I am standing outside of Rosita's Restaurant on the corner of *16 de Septiembre* and *Loma Verde.* I'll be inside Rosita's waiting for you."

"Yeah, I know the joint. *Mira, Brad,* let me give you a health tip. Don't eat any of the food there. Rosita's is just a front for some *narcos*, and the food is terrible. It will make you sick."

"OK, I'll just have a diet soda. I'll be with a friend from my company."

"*Cerveza*, Bradley. Drink a *cerveza!* You and your diet drinks, *güey.* You crack me up. OK. Sit tight and I'll be there in about fifteen minutes."

Brad hung the phone up and walked inside Rosita's Restaurant with Eric. Brad ordered his Diet Coke. "What would you like to drink, Eric?"

"Are you kidding me? After what we went through today? Give me a bottle of tequila!"

As they sat there in their corner booth sipping on their drinks, Eric broke the silence. "What makes you so sure that this Beto guy is going to help you, Brad? Can you trust him?"

"He'll help," Brad said with a confident look.

"How can you be so sure? I ask because, well, we have no time for mistakes."

Brad did not want to get into the details, but he felt that the situation warranted it. The day had been very difficult, and the night promised more of the same. It was important that Eric trust Beto. "All right, Eric, I am going to tell you a little bit about Beto, but please keep this between us. OK?"

"Sure, no problem."

"Well, Beto is my wife's cousin. They were very close when they were growing up, almost like brother and sister. Over the years Beto has made a few bad decisions which have gotten him into a lot of trouble, and I have helped him out a few times."

"Oh, yeah. How did you help him?"

"It's not important. He was family, and he needed help. Everybody else had given up on him. I don't ever give up on family."

Just when Eric was about to follow up on that statement, Beto walked into the restaurant. The modern-day rebel was dressed in a black leather jacket and blue jeans and had not shaved for a couple of days to accentuate the shadow of his dark beard line. He greeted Brad with a manly hug and then a handshake.

Beto was a handsome man, but a rough life had taken its toll on him. A thin, long scar across the right side of his face, just under his cheekbone, bore witness to the fact that he did not move quickly enough to completely avoid a knife slash several years ago in a bar-room brawl. He had an assortment of other scars scattered over his body from similar encounters with the wrong crowd. In his right ear he had a small, diamond ear ring.

Brad pointed to his partner. "This is Eric."

"Hey Eric. Are you an accountant, too?"

"Yes, I am. It's a pleasure to meet you, Beto."

"*¡Ah, caray!* Being seen here with two accountants could ruin my reputation," Beto said as he sat down.

Before they could begin, a waitress walked up to Beto. "*Algo de tomar?*"

"*Sí, una Corona, preciosa,*" Beto said with the most charming smile he could muster. Then, Beto turned toward Brad. "OK, Brad. How can I help you, *primo?*"

Brad looked around to make sure he would not be overheard. He then lowered his head and moved closer to Beto's face. With a muffled voice, he began: "I have some information on some corrupt people in my company that I need to get to the FBI and the SEC. The people after me are trying to stop me from doing that. This afternoon they tried to kill us."

The smile disappeared from Beto's face. "Kill you? Nobody is going to kill my *primo*! Well, you really aren't my *primo,* but you have treated me better than my real *primos.* I'll help you, Bradley, but I ain't gonna have nothing to do with no Feds, *güey.*"

"Your help will not involve you with the Feds, Beto. I just need to get across the border tonight, but the guys that are after me have apparently paid some Mexican immigration and customs officials off to stop me at the border. For all I know, they probably have a warrant out for my arrest for fighting off these four dirty cops that came to arrest me today at my house."

"Arrest you? For what?"

"Yeah, that's exactly what I said to them. We haven't done anything wrong, Beto. You have to believe that."

"I know that, Bradley. You are the cleanest *vato* I have ever known."

Brad continued. "Anyway, it's a long story. Can you help us find another way across the border besides the bridge?"

"That's it? That's all you need?"

Brad looked a little puzzled. "Yes...that is it. Can you help us?"

"Of course I can! I have a friend who runs a barber shop on the other side of town. Well, he runs a barber shop and he moonlights as a *coyote*. You know what that is, don't you Brad?"

"Yes. It's a guy who smuggles people across the border illegally."

"Well, my friend likes to think of it as providing transportation solutions for the immigrationally-challenged. He can get you across through one of his tunnels. He normally charges $1,000 a piece, but I think I can get him down to about $500."

"Dollars or pesos?"

"*¡Dólares, güey!* For $500 pesos all he would do is point to the north and say 'good luck.'"

Brad pulled out his wallet to check how much cash he had. "Whoa!" warned Beto as he put his hand over Brad's wallet and pushed it gently toward the table. "Be careful with that in here, Bradley. You can get whacked for $50 in a place like this. Keep it on the low-low, *primo*."

Brad pulled the wallet close to his chest and counted the contents. "I still have about $2,000 dollars in cash on me. Can you call him now, Beto?"

"Now? Sure. Let me check my little black book. Here it is...José Manuel Bolio."

Beto dialed the number. *"Manny-boy. Habla Beto. ¡¿Qué onda, güey?! Oye, necesito un favorsote. Mi primo y su amigo necesitan pasar al otro lado, pero ya. Son norteamericanos. Sí, sí güey, no estoy bromeando. Claro que sí. Tienen la lana, pero necesito que me des un descuento ya que se trata de mi familia. OK. Ya me arranco para tu casa. Nos vemos."*

After he had finished the call, Beto looked at Brad. "It's all set. I will take you to Manny-boy's house. I am going to personally go with you through the tunnel to make sure you don't have any problems. I trust Manny-boy, but I don't know who else you could run into there, so you're going to need someone with some pull to watch your back."

Brad breathed a long sigh of relief. He was tired, scared, and just wanted to be with his family. "Thank you, Beto. I don't have the words to…"

"Bradley! What are you talking about, *primo?* You have been there for me when my own flesh and blood turned their backs on me. You're like my brother, man. Whenever you need help, you just call me. I got your back. You know that, *primo.*"

"I know you do," Brad said as he patted Beto on the shoulder. "Thanks, *primo.*"

* * * * * * * * *

Brad and Eric climbed into Beto's shiny, black Firehawk. Beto was already in the car and strapped in. The Firehawk was a Pontíac TransAm which had been modified to give it more performance. In the year 2000, the year in which this car was manufactured, the Firehawk came off the line with 327 roaring horsepower. The muscle car was equipped with an after-market supercharger, which added another 100 horsepower for sudden bursts of speed when the situation presented itself.

The front of the hood of the Firehawk had a smooth-looking ram air intake which was more subtle than the normal ram-air Trans Am. There were also two heat extraction ports on the hood close to the windshield. It was a beautiful machine.

To help even the odds in street intelligence gathering, Beto had also wired a police band scanner and a radar detector. Eric looked at the equipment but did not say anything. He wanted to stay on the good side of Beto. His life depended on it.

Beto cranked up the powerful V-8 engine. The high-performance after-market muffler system allowed more of the air to flow though the exhaust system quicker and gave the Firehawk extra growl. *Man, that sounds so cool,* Brad thought to himself. He loved the roar of these powerful muscle cars.

Noticing the smile on Brad's face, Beto decided to show Brad what his Firehawk could do. He slammed his foot down on the gas pedal, causing the big, 19-inch wheels to spin quickly, generating a loud, squealing sound. The spinning tires caused so much smoke that it looked like the haze of cigarette smoke lingering over a pool table in a pool hall. Eventually, the traction of the tires managed to seize the pavement and thrust the black car forward like a road rocket.

Traveling in that Firehawk, it did not take them long to reach the run-down neighborhood in a bad section of Reynosa where Manny-boy the *coyote* lived. It was the kind of place you did not want to be in during the daytime, much less at night. By now it was 9:00 p.m. on that fateful Wednesday. As a precaution and a sign of respect, Beto drove slowly through the neighborhood, allowing the residents to recognize him. Brad and Eric received threatening stares from young gang bangers hanging out on the street corners, protecting their turf from any unwelcome visitors. It was their neighborhood, and nobody was going to just waltz right into it.

They all seemed to know Beto and his black, super-charged *carrazo*. It had an unmistakable sound to it as it cruised through the streets. As he drove by young gangsters, they greeted him with respect and admiration in their own unique manner characteristic of the gang world, a world that had been foreign to Brad and Eric— until this night. Tonight it would be the members of this world, not the members of The Establishment, who would keep them alive and bring them to safety.

Manny-boy was waiting outside his house when Beto pulled up. He quickly jumped into Beto's road rocket. Together the four drove outside of town for about thirty minutes until they reached a deserted area filled with brush. It was a relatively quick drive due to the lack of traffic in the street and the horsepower under the hood of that Firehawk. There was very little small talk except to confirm that Brad and Eric had their $1,000 fee on them. Beto drove slowly down a dusty dirt road.

When Beto drove up to the entrance of the secret tunnel, he was greeted by two large, muscular Mexican men bearing MP5 submachine guns with delayed blowback action. The selector lever was set to "F" for fully automatic firing to empty the .9mm, 30-round magazine faster than one could blink an eye. These weapons were perfect for the type of close-quarter battle skirmishes in which Manny-boy's soldiers frequently engaged. Once they realized that Manny-boy was in the car, they returned to their posts.

Before they got out of the car, Brad handed Manny-boy ten one-hundred dollar bills. "I appreciate your help, Manny-boy," Brad said with gratitude.

"No problem, Brad. *Mi carnal* Beto has told me a lot about you. I met you a long time ago when you and Sofía were dating. I was just *un escuincle*, so you probably don't remember it. Beto says you are the most honest *vato* he has ever met. That doesn't surprise me when I look at the kind of people he hangs out with," he said with a laugh. "You ain't got much competition in that department. Just one thing, though," Manny-boy said as he held up his hand, pointing his index finger at Brad. Manny-boy's facial expression turned firm and serious. "Once you pass through this tunnel, forget you ever saw it. *¿De acuerdo?*" Manny-boy held out his hand to shake Brad's hand gangster style.

"*De acuerdo,* Manny-boy," Brad replied as he shook Manny-boy's hand. Brad surmised that a violation of his pact with Manny-boy would certainly result in a painful death. He intended to abide by his part of the agreement.

Manny-boy was very protective of his commercial enterprise. He knew that the U.S. government would quickly put a halt to his business, and perhaps lock him behind prison bars again, if his tunnel were discovered. The Human Smuggling and Trafficking Center as well as other inter-agency groups worked with the U.S. intelligence community to rout out and stop these kinds of operations. Although Manny-boy could not articulate the names of these groups, he knew they were out there, and he was always very cautious.

After the friendly warning and the handshake, Manny-boy began to walk his latest customers through the underground tunnel. Brad was shocked. He had heard stories from his friends in the military about the small, narrow tunnels which made up the extensive underground network of the Viet Cong back in the 1960s and 1970s in Vietnam. Tonight he was expecting to go through this tunnel crawling on all fours.

This tunnel, however, was much better than what he had prepared himself for mentally. There was enough room to walk through the tunnel standing up with plenty of headroom to spare. The tunnel had a concrete floor, and there were thick, wooden supports made out of oak about every ten feet along the way. *Wow, this is much more than a place to cross undocumented aliens into the U.S.*, Brad thought.

The walk through the secret tunnel was a long, silent one and provided Brad with ample time to reflect upon what he was seeing. *I wonder how many thousands of people have entered the U.S illegally through this tunnel*, Brad wondered. The tunnel was also the perfect vehicle for channeling weapons and terrorists into the U.S. If any MANPADS, or man-portable air defense systems, made it through this tunnel, terrorists could shoot down a U.S. civilian air craft from the sky. That would wreak havoc on the American economy—again.

However, that was not a very probable scenario. The *narcotraficantes*, or drug lords, had no incentive to share their business or their profits with anybody else, especially terrorist groups. It would be counterproductive to their interests.

In addition to their greed as a disincentive to working with the terrorists, the last thing the *narcos* wanted was another horrendous terrorist attack such as that which occurred on September 11, 2001. Such an attack would most likely result in the U.S. closing her border with Mexico. If there were concerns that the terrorists had entered through Mexico, the Office of Homeland Security would seal the border even tighter.

Shutting down the border would cut off the supply chain of drugs into the U.S for these *narcos*, thereby slamming shut the doorway to their biggest market in the world: the United States of America. The U.S.- Mexico border was the principal place of entry into the U.S. for cocaine shipments. Mexico was also a principal supplier of heroin, methamphetamines and marijuana. The interruption of the cash flows of these powerful drug lords would bring catastrophic results. The *narcotraficantes* depended on that daily cash flow to feed the greed in the illegal drug supply chain.

At that moment, however, Brad was not concerned about the other implications of the existence of this tunnel. His sole mission was to return to his family safely, and nothing was going to stop him. Nothing.

* * * * * * * * *

It took them about an hour to go through the tunnel and reach the surface on the U.S. side. The point of exit on the U.S. side was well-disguised. The tunnel ended with some steps made out of cement. There was an electrical light at the foot of the stairs. Brad, Eric and Beto followed Manny-boy up the stairs. He opened a door which led into the basement of an old ranch house. The basement was dark and full of spider webs and old junk including a bicycle without a wheel and an old washer and dryer in disrepair off to the side. They proceeded through the basement and walked up some wooden stairs to another door which led to the ground floor. The modest, stucco-covered house blended in well with the terrain. The house was nowhere near the U.S.-Mexican border, which explained the long walk. *We*

must have been walking for a long time under U.S. soil,
Brad deduced.

As Brad and Eric walked out onto the porch of the
ranch house, they saw an elderly couple sitting
innocently in a swing on the porch enjoying the cool,
night-time breeze. Both of them were sipping a glass of
lemonade. *No one would ever guess that below this
house was a busy link into the U.S. - Mexican
underworld,* he thought. *It was the perfect cover.*

Manny-boy, whose strength obviously did not lie in
his interpersonal skills, looked at Brad and said, "The
only reason you made it through that tunnel is because
Beto is my *carnal* and I trust him. Most people that pass
through my tunnel have to walk blindfolded the whole
way through the tunnel, so you are lucky you didn't have
no blindfold on. Remember: forget you ever saw this
place. *¿Me entiendes?*"

Brad nodded humbly in agreement. Then, a van
drove around the side of the house. Beto approached
Brad. "*Primo,* now they *are* going to have to blindfold
you, but don't worry. Just sit back in the van and relax
until you get into McAllen. That will take about an hour
and a half. Don't worry, nothing will happen to you.
They know they have to answer to me. These *pelados*
are my *compadres.* "

"Thank you, Beto," Brad said as he hugged Beto. His
eyes were watery. All the stress was beginning to tell on
his emotions. Beto would never know how grateful Brad
was for his help. Brad then walked toward the van with
Eric.

Everything proceeded exactly as Beto had described.
They arrived in McAllen around midnight, and the men
in the van left them at a cheap hotel called the Cozy
Border Inn. They did not want to leave any electronic
trails, so Eric paid for the hotel room in cash under an

assumed name. Both Brad and Eric were exhausted from the long day. They walked into the room and collapsed onto their twin beds.

* * * * * * * * *

At 2 a.m. Victor's home phone rang, waking him from a deep sleep. "Victor, this is Harry. Bring me up-to-date on the situation."

"Harry, it is 2 o'clock in the morning. Is this really necessary?"

"Victor, we have discussed the gravity of this situation several times. You botched things yesterday. Now, please, tell me the situation has been resolved."

Victor sat up in his bed, and wiped the sleep from his eyes. Montserrat was stirring, but she was still more asleep than awake. "I haven't heard anything from my contacts at the border," Victor said, the agitation obvious in his voice, "so they have not attempted to cross the border yet."

"Do you know that for a fact? Maybe they got past your guys."

"That is impossible, Harry." Victor looked over at Montserrat, now beginning to cross over into the world of the conscious. "Wait a minute." He got up from his bed, uttered a few of his favorite vulgarities in Spanish, and walked down the hall into an empty bedroom out of hearing distance from Montserrat. He softly closed the door for added privacy.

"Harry, those greedy customs officials are checking every car that goes through the border," he said confidently in a muffled voice. "My contact tells me that each time a car comes up they jump on it like piranhas feeding on a fresh piece of meat. With $200,000 American dollars up for grabs, Harry, believe me, those

Mexican customs officials want to find Brad and Eric more than we do. Hey, are you sure those two didn't travel by air?"

"I am positive. Buzz Blakely has his people monitoring all the airline databases and he has people at all major airports with service from Monterrey in case Jenkins and Johnson fly under a different name. He also has people all along the U.S. border as well."

"Well, maybe Brad is waiting it out somewhere until things cool over, Harry. He is a smart guy."

Harry was quite vexed by the situation. He had hoped that the Mexican customs officials would nab the two accountants at the border that night. "I'll tell you what he is: he is a risk to us, and we need to eliminate that risk, *pronto*. Keep me posted, and I mean that, Victor. We have to stay in close contact until this problem has been handled. I'll let you know if we hear anything on our end."

"*Adiós.*" Victor hung up the phone. He was aggravated by Harry's phone call in the wee hours of the morning. With all his tomcatting, Victor did not get much sleep. He had been sleeping well that night until the rude awakening by the King of Cool.

Victor complained to himself silently about Harry's audacity. "*A veces me cae gordo* Harry. *¿Quién se cree* I need to make a note to myself to call *him* at 2 a.m. next week." Victor commented to himself as he walked back to his bedroom. He looked over at Montserrat, who was still asleep. He then lay back down and soon afterward returned to the wonderful, deep sleep he had been enjoying before the phone call.

Chapter 23

A Morning Gone Awry

The next morning the sound of car doors closing and engines starting outside woke Brad and Eric around 7:00 a.m. After he had fully acclimated himself to the world of the conscious, Brad called Sofía on the hotel phone and told her he was on his way to Austin. His beautiful wife of fifteen years was elated to hear his voice. She said the children were fine, but they missed their daddy.

"Sofía, it is imperative that you not use any credit cards," Brad warned. "Do not leave a trail of any kind which could indicate where you are." She agreed, and then he asked her for the cellular telephone number of his good friend in the FBI, field agent Jim Dove. After pulling her little address and telephone book out of her purse, she found the "D" section and located the telephone number.

Brad did not want to get into the details of what had happened yesterday. There would be time enough for that once he made it safely to Austin. For the time being, he simply told her that he loved her and that everything was going to be fine. As always, their last words on the phone were *"te amo."*

As soon as Brad hung up with Sofía, he called Jim at his San Diego office, again opting to use the hotel phone rather than his cellular phone. "Hey, dude!" answered Jim when he realized it was Brad. "What have you been up to since I saw you in Monterrey?"

"Jim, I am in a bad situation, so I will get right to the point." Brad gave Jim a quick synopsis of what had transpired over the last few months.

Jim, whose military career and years as a field agent in the FBI had exposed him to many terrible things that most people never have to confront, took the news in stride. "Look, Brad, I think I can help you on this. I am going to talk to a good friend of mine at the SEC. Her name is Lety Cuellar. She is the Assistant Director for the Enforcement Division at the SEC in Washington, DC. Lety is a GS-15. That is a lot of juice, my boy! She is a really nice lady and is the equivalent of an ASAC, which is an Assistant Special Agent in Charge in the FBI. Stay where you are and I will call you back within two hours. Give me a number where you can be reached."

Brad wanted to give him the hotel number, but he was not sure if they would still be at the hotel after two hours. Accordingly, he gave him his cellular number.

Following that brief phone call, Brad and Eric shaved and showered, and then decided to put an end to the grumbling in their stomachs. They had seen a restaurant across the street last night as they were walking to their rooms, so they decided to give it a try. Brad put on his sunglasses and a blue baseball cap he found in the room left over from a previous hotel guest.

Eric looked over at him and exploded in laughter. "Where did you get that goofy-looking blue hat?" he cried out. "Is it your new look?"

Brad smiled. "Yes, as a matter of fact it is. I call it the 'I don't care how I look' look. It is all the rage among accountants running for their lives."

Eric laughed. Last night's rest had served him well.

"Seriously, though," Brad said, "I found it behind the door in the bathroom. It smells a little funky, but it will help me to keep a low profile. I suggest that you try to keep a low profile as well."

Eric cleared his throat. "Uh…Brad…I don't know if you have noticed yet, but there are not many African-Americans walking around here on the border. I'll do my best to blend in, but don't expect me to put on a goofy hat, too," he said with big grin.

They walked across the street to the Rio Restaurant. It was a simple building painted light pink on the outside and off-color white on the inside. When they walked inside, Brad was relieved to see that it was clean. They took a seat in a corner booth which would allow Brad to monitor the entire restaurant.

Brad found himself checking where the exit signs were in case they needed to make a quick escape. His eyes, refreshed after a good night's sleep, surveyed the room like a roaming camera. There was an elderly couple of Mexican descent on the other side drinking coffee and reading the newspaper. They seemed to know the waitress well and exchanged pleasantries in Spanish. Brad also carefully observed an Anglo-American man with a crew-cut, cowboy hat, short-sleeved shirt and jeans sitting in a booth close to the door. *Probably a trucker or local rancher*, Brad thought to himself. Everything seemed safe for the moment.

Eric said he wanted the number nine on the menu, which he called "the cholesterol special": cheese eggs with greasy hash browns, bacon, and buttered toast. "I think a group of cardiologists owns this place," he said jokingly.

Brad looked at Eric with a bewildered look on his face. "How do you gather that?"

Eric continued his analysis. "It's sort of like a strategic investment for them. Their customers come in and eat this greasy stuff, day in and day out, year after year. Then, one day years down the road, they 'suddenly' develop clogged arteries and, what do you know, they are now patients of the cardiologists. But the food tastes so good, nobody cares."

Brad smiled and then sipped his hot coffee. He was beginning to see more and more of this jocose side of Eric unknown to him prior to their journey. Eric's humor succeeded admirably in lifting Brad's spirits at a time when he really needed it.

* * * * * * * * *

After they had clogged their arteries at the Rio Restaurant, they walked back to the hotel room and waited on Jim Dove's call. They waited and waited. Eric watched the morning news while Brad stretched. If there were ever a time when he needed the stress-relieving effects of his exercise routine, it was now. Finally, Brad was unwilling to wait anymore.

"We need to check out and get out of here," he said anxiously. As they were about to open the door to go to the lobby, Brad's cellular phone finally rang. It was Jim.

"Brad, I briefed Lety on your situation and gave her your cellular number. She was really busy when I talked to her. She said she was up to her ears in work because this year the SEC is going to bring over 500 civil enforcement actions against individuals and companies. Lety told me very frankly that although she could not make any promises, your situation sounded very serious, and she would do her best to look into it immediately."

Brad sighed with relief. "That's good news, I guess."

"That's right, Brad, it is. Let me tell you that if Lety and I had not worked on some cases in the past, I would not have access to her like this. The SEC's enforcement division has the same problems most governmental agencies have: a heavy workload and not enough staff. So, the SEC cannot pursue every case. They have to prioritize them, just like we do at the FBI, just like the DEA does, and just like local law enforcement agencies have to do."

"Jim, they *have* to take this case, or else a lot of people are going to lose a lot of money. If those scumbags stay in charge of AMA, they will bleed it dry, and then the company will go under for sure, leaving the stockholders with worthless stock and the employees with no pension. Could you give me Lety's address in Washington so that I can send this information to her this morning?"

"Yeah, that's a good idea."

Brad wrote down the Washington, DC address. "Great. I'll be back in touch with you."

"All right, man. Look, you watch your six and make sure to keep Sofía and the kids in a safe place. Another thing: don't use that cellular phone anymore. I doubt that they would, but it is conceivable that these scumbags could track you down with electronic surveillance if they have someone who knows what they're doing. I doubt very seriously, though, that a manufacturing company would have that kind of sophisticated technology."

"Uh, oh. I have bad news, Jim. AMA has this old security guy named Buzz Blakely who used to work for the National Security Agency at Fort Meade, Maryland. When I first came aboard with AMA and was going through the orientation for new hires in Atlanta, by chance I sat down with him at the company cafeteria, and he struck up a conversation. As I recall, he was a very well-mannered person. To make a long story short, as we chatted he found out that I spoke Spanish and some Mandarin, and he told me about his experience at the NSA. I remember him saying there were lots of linguists working at the NSA. Buzz also told me that he specialized in electronic surveillance in…what did he call it….signals… something."

"Signals Intelligence, or SIGINT. Buddy, if he is ex-NSA then we could have some problems here. Technically, SIGINT intel is limited to foreign organizations and international terrorists. But if this guy worked for SIGINT at the NSA, then he could be exploiting his expertise domestically to private enterprise and making a tidy profit—in this case from good ole AMA Electric International. What concerns me in your case is that he could be an expert in demodulating and unraveling the internal structure of electronic signals. I bet he is good in 'DF-ing.'"

"What is that?" Brad asked.

"DF-ing is short for Direct Finding. Your cellular phone sends a unique electronic serial number out to other towers, or antennas, within a close area in addition to emitting a signal to the primary tower. These electronic signals can then be triangulated within that multi-antenna region. It's called the tower triangulation method. Your cell phone emits these signals whenever your phone is on, even if you are not using it at the time. Shoot, you may even have a GPS tracking system built right into your cell phone. Brad, we probably should get off this phone now. Turn your cell phone off and leave it off. I suggest that you and your friend get out of there now — double time. When you get a chance, call me back on the following telephone number. It is a secure line.   Code in with…um…the name of the barbeque restaurant you and I used to go to on Saturdays. Don't say it over this unsecure line, and turn that cell phone off!"

"I understand, Jim. Thanks for your help, and I'll call you later."

Jim gave him the telephone number to the FBI secure line and then Brad hung up the phone and turned it off. He looked at Eric. "Eric, I fear that I may have committed a grave mistake. You know who Buzz Blakely is, don't you?"

"Yeah, he is the old guy who is head of corporate security for AMA. I never could warm up to him. I can't put my finger on it, but there was something about him that made me uneasy. Perhaps it was that he was too stand-offish or cold—like a robot."

"Well, I hit it off real well with him. It just so happens that Buzz was bragging to me during my orientation in Atlanta that he used to be an electronic surveillance expert for the NSA, the National Security Agency. Those guys can track down anything that has an electronic signal, like this." Brad held up his cellular phone. "We have had our cell phones on all morning. Make sure your cell phone is turned off and stays off. They can track us anytime our cell phones are on."

Eric reached over and turned off his cellular phone.

"Good," Brad said. "Now, we need to get a move on. Before we depart McAllen, though, I need to send the documentation in your audit bag via overnight mail to my contact at the SEC in Washington, D.C."

"Right. But what if this is lost or never makes it to the SEC?"

"Don't worry. Jorge del Valle, one of the plant managers in Monterrey and a good friend, has a full copy of the documentation. Also, my mother in Columbia, South Carolina, has another copy locked away in a safety deposit box at her bank."

Eric nodded at Brad. "OK. Let's hit the road."

* * * * * * * * *

Brad and Eric hurriedly made their way to the lobby area. At the front desk a pot-bellied man in his mid-twenties with a tooth pick in his mouth was sitting back lazily watching an old movie on his 13-inch television set on the counter top. The Cozy Border Inn TV did not include cable TV among its limited amenities, and so the TV reception was poor. In an effort to improve the reception, the clerk whacked the side of the TV a couple of times, but it was to no avail.

"Excuse me, sir, we are checking out," Eric said politely.

"Yeah, OK, hold your horses," said the clerk. He stood up and begrudgingly attended to Eric, glancing back at the TV every chance he could. Eric paid for the rooms and the phone calls.

Brad walked up to the counter and addressed the clerk. "Would you be kind enough to call a cab for us?"

The clerk looked arrogantly over at Brad. Using his tongue he rolled the tooth pick from the right side of his mouth over to the left and then back to the right several times very quickly. Then, he reached up and grabbed the toothpick with his right hand and pointed it at Brad. "Are you sure you don't want to use the hotel limousine?" he said sarcastically.

Brad did not react to the clerk's impoliteness. The clerk, who had "Butch, Jr." written on his name tag, reluctantly leaned over, grabbed the phone, and called one of the local cab companies. When he hung up, he looked over at Brad and said, "Your taxi should be here in about five minutes."

"Thank you," Brad said with a smile.

Within a few minutes a yellow taxi pulled up. Eric held his audit bag with all the documentation of Brad's investigation close to his body. The two accountants walked outside and got into the cab. The cab driver was a friendly, 55-year-old Mexican-American who introduced himself as Guillermo Cruz.

"Nice to meet you, Mr. Cruz," Brad replied tactfully. "Would you please take us to the nearest post office as quickly as possible?"

"Sure thing. There is one about three miles from here." Mr. Cruz cranked up the engine of his sedan. Brad could hear the V-8 power in the engine when it started. Mr. Cruz looked back at Brad and said cheerfully, "She's getting up in years, but she can still shake a leg when she has to!" He then patted the top of the dashboard as if he were petting his dog, and off they went to the post office.

Neither one of the two accountants noticed a dark blue SUV with heavily-tinted windows parked across the street. As their taxi pulled out of the Cozy Border Inn parking lot onto the street, the dark SUV slowly moved away from the curb and onto the street, just like an alligator easing quietly into the water after spotting its prey.

Mr. Cruz made his way down one of the main boulevards. Brad said something to him in Spanish, and the two switched over to *español*. It was obvious to Brad that Mr. Cruz was in the right profession, because he quickly opened up a lively conversation with the Controller. The taxi driver indicated that he had emigrated to the U.S. over twenty years ago and had been driving a taxi that entire time. He had been married to his wife for 34 years. They had four children and three grandchildren.

Mr. Cruz came to a halt at a traffic light. The dark SUV stayed one car back at all times. At the next stop light, the taxi took a right turn onto an isolated side road. "I'm taking a short cut to the post office," informed Mr. Cruz.

The dark SUV followed the old yellow taxi onto the side road and gradually pulled up next to it in the left lane. The right rear tinted window of the SUV slowly lowered.

Brad was listening to Mr. Cruz talk about how his granddaughter did not like to keep her diapers on. "She takes them off and runs around the house with nothing on but her little pink bracelet," he said cheerfully.

Brad commented that his son Michael used to do the same. Then, he looked over at the dark SUV that he thought was trying to pass them. He saw a man with long, blonde hair and a thick scar above his right eyebrow sitting by the window. Then, the barrel of a .45 caliber pistol with a sound suppressor edged its way out of the window, pointing directly at Eric. "Eric, look out!" Brad yelled as he ducked his head down.

Four muffled rounds were fired through the taxi window and into Eric's head and neck. Mr. Cruz looked back and saw blood beginning to pour out of Eric's left temple. He froze with fear.

"Floor it!" Brad screamed at the top of his lungs, keeping his head beneath the window. Two more shots were fired and barely missed him, passing over his head and through the other window. Brad pulled Eric's left arm so that his friend fell across the back seat. Then, he put his left hand on Eric's neck. There was no pulse.

"Eric!" he said with desperation in his voice as he closed his eyes and shook his head in disbelief. He opened his eyes and looked at his friend who was now dead because Brad had pulled him into this nightmare with one phone call. "I'm sorry, my friend, for ever getting you into this," he said, as tears collected in his eyes.

Brad quickly pulled himself together, wiped his eyes on his right sleeve, and looked up. Mr. Cruz was pushing his old taxi to the limit, swerving back and forth, and doing everything in his power to shake the assassins in the dark SUV. The gunmen fired several more shots, so Brad dropped his head down again and stayed out of sight. Unknown to Brad, one of the bullets had struck Mr. Cruz in the side of the head, killing him instantly. He collapsed onto the steering wheel. The weight of his foot pressed down on the accelerator pedal, causing the taxi to accelerate even faster. Brad felt the speed of the well-worn taxi engine increase.

"*Señor Cruz,* are you all right?"

No answer. Brad repeated his question. *No answer again. Something is terribly wrong. Maybe he has been shot.* Brad poked his head up to take a peak and saw the 55-year-old gentleman draped across the steering wheel. His face was covered in blood.

Brad looked out the windshield and then back at the speedometer and realized that the taxi was advancing toward an old, brick warehouse at about 60 m.p.h., and the speed was increasing with each second. He was bound for a head-on collision with the building and needed to act quickly.

The dark SUV was forced to pull behind the taxi due to oncoming traffic. *What a lucky break!* Brad reached over the front seat, pushed the taxi driver's lifeless body to the right on the seat, and grabbed the steering wheel. He glanced up and looked out the front windshield at the big, brick building getting closer with each second. He was almost there!

Brad swerved the vehicle to the left just in the nick of time, barely missing the warehouse. *Thank God,* he thought. *That was a close shave.* That gave him enough time to climb over the front seat and slide into the driver's seat as he pushed Mr. Cruz's feet out of the way.

Poor Mr. Cruz, Brad lamented. *If he had not picked us up a few minutes ago, he would still be alive.*

Another shot was fired from the SUV and came close to hitting Brad's right shoulder before it shot out through the glass above the dashboard. By now the traffic had cleared on the left side and the SUV was coming up on his left side again for another pass at Brad. With sweat pouring down his face and his hands trembling, Brad tried to think of a defensive action. He looked into the side rear-view mirror and saw that the SUV was almost upon him. *Do something or you're dead!* Suddenly he slammed on the brakes. *Screech!* The SUV went speeding by the taxi firing several shots at the Controller that missed and hit the front of the taxi.

Brad shifted the taxi in reverse and sped backwards about 50 yards, burning rubber on the pavement and revving the engine to 7,000 RPM on the tachometer. With all the finesse of a trained secret service agent trying to protect the President, he slammed on the brakes again and turned the wheel of the taxi to the left. This quick thinking caused the car to swing around 180 degrees and continue forward due to the weight of the vehicle and the speed of the turn. With lightning reflexes he moved the gear from reverse to drive and slammed his foot down on the gas pedal again. The old taxi took off on all eight-cylinders, pushing itself to the limit as it roared off down the street, sputtering a little every once and a while.

Meanwhile the sinister, dark SUV reacted much slower than Brad. It tried to turn around and pursue its fleeing prey, but its driver proved to be much less adept than Brad at handling the turn. Obviously, his core competency was murder, not driving. Brad's adroit maneuvering had given him a lead of about three blocks.

He continued speeding through the streets of the west side of McAllen, Texas hoping to attract the attention of a police patrol unit. Sweat was streaming down his face profusely. Some sweat had entered his eyes and the salt was stinging them. He wiped his face off in a micro-second, not daring to take his eyes off the road. His life depended on his actions over the next few minutes. Brad had to stay cool and think logically, but it was hard. "I must stay focused! Don't lose it, Brad," he said out loud to himself, just as a trainer would say to his boxer sitting in the corner between rounds, struggling to win a tough match.

"Unit 15, unit 15, please advise of your 20. We need a pick-up of two passengers on Texas Boulevard." Brad looked down to the right and saw the taxi's CB radio. He grabbed the handle. "Hello! Hello!" he screamed desperately.

"Go ahead unit 15."

"This is Brad Jenkins. I am a passenger of this taxi. Somebody in a dark blue SUV is following us. They killed your driver, Guillermo Cruz. They are still after me…."

"Calm down," replied the middle-aged, female voice on the other end, apparently not hearing Brad nor realizing the gravity of the situation. "Who is this?"

"This is Brad Jenkins!" Brad cried out in desperation, his anguish almost overcoming him. "Brad Jenkins! I am a passenger in this taxi. People are after us. They killed your driver and my friend! They are in a dark blue SUV!" he screamed. "Notify the police now!"

"Where are you now, sir?"

"I don't know! I am moving too fast to see any street signs. I am somewhere on the west side of McAllen."

"Why are you driving the vehicle?"

"Because your driver is dead! He's dead! Do you hear me? I have been trying to tell you that there are some killers chasing after me at this instant in a dark blue SUV! They are right behind me!" Brad screamed, almost out of patience with the cab company dispatcher. He glanced into his rear-view mirror and saw the big SUV quickly advancing on him. The Controller shouted at the top of his lungs: "CALL THE POLICE!"

"Oh, my word!" the lady said with a terrified voice. It finally dawned on her that Brad was probably telling the truth and that this was no joke. "Sir, I will let the police…"

Brad turned off the CB radio so that he could concentrate on the task at hand. The SUV had gained ground on him while he was talking on the CB radio. He needed to put some space between him and the dark SUV quickly, or his life would end. He wiped his face again and exhaled heavily.

As he pulled his sweat-drenched arm away, he caught sight of a police squad car parked at a stop sign at the oncoming intersection. *Thank you, Lord,* he thought as he contemplated how to best handle the situation. *Do I stop next to the cop? Do I slow down? Should I keep going and let him follow me?* Brad's mind raced through the alternatives. He had to decide quickly because he was fast approaching the intersection.

He decided that the best thing to do would be to race through the intersection blowing his horn all the way with the SUV behind him. That would definitely draw the attention of the police officers without giving those murderers behind him a chance to get him in their line of sight. If he stopped, the assassins could take him and the cops out before the cops knew what was happening.

Brad punched the accelerator with his foot and sped through the intersection at 80 m.p.h., 35 m.p.h. above the limit. He was beeping the horn with a pulsating rhythm. *Beep! Beep! Beep! Beep!* The SUV stayed right on his tail. The police squad car took immediate notice of the chase and sped off after them, its siren blasting and lights flashing. Brad now had the murderers in the SUV right where he wanted them: between him and the police.

The police cruiser's big, super-charged V-8 engine quickly pulled up behind the dark SUV. "This is the police! Pull over!" the officer ordered through his PA system. "Pull your vehicle over now!" Unbelievably, the gunman in the SUV opened fire on Brad again. Brad began to swerve his vehicle to avoid the bullets.

The police cruiser roared and pulled along side the SUV. Another gunman on the left side of the SUV sprayed the police cruiser with a 9 mm Uzi machine gun. In less than four seconds, the hitman emptied the 32-round magazine of the Uzi into the police car, filling both police officers with holes. The patrol car veered off to the left, running off the road and crashing into a telephone pole at high speed. *KA-BOOM!* The car exploded into a ball of fire as Brad sped down the road. He looked into his rear-view mirror and saw the dark SUV still following closely behind him.

"No!" Brad screamed out. "I can't believe this!" Brad panted frantically for a few seconds. He yelled in anger: "*¡Desgraciados!*" The old taxi was now traveling at over 100 miles per hour. Brad swerved left and right to prevent the dark SUV, with its heavy-duty V-8 engine roaring behind him, from passing him. The old taxi he was driving was doing its best to respond to Brad's demands, but he did not know how much longer the aging car could hold out. If the SUV got close to him, it would be over.

Chapter 24

My Friends Call Me Skunk

Brad continued to push the old taxi to its limit as the old V-8 engine roared down the road. Suddenly, appearing like an oasis in the desert, he saw a fire station coming up on the right side of the road. One of the fire engines was parked out front, and there were several firemen outside engaged in some activity, but Brad could not take his eyes off the road long enough to determine what exactly it was that they were doing. The large, aluminum door to the inside of the fire station was open.

Brad abruptly slowed down from 105 m.p.h. to about 50 m.p.h. and swerved into the parking lot, slamming on the brakes and coming to a screeching halt inside the fire station building itself. His notorious entrance was clearly evidenced by the long, black tire marks and almost gave the firemen cardiac arrest. He had barely missed hitting two firemen in the process, but their quick reflexes enabled them to jump to safety before the taxi cab reached them. The commotion brought several firemen sliding down the poles to see what had happened.

Anger and profanity filled the air as the big, tough firemen, who were nearly trampled by Brad's entrance, made it to their feet. One tall, blonde-haired fireman picked himself up from the ground and scraped the dust off his arm as blood began to flow out of the deep scrapes he had received when he leaped out of Brad's way. The Controller felt bad about the disturbance he had caused, but there was no time for remorse. His very life and the well-being of his family depended on his staying focused and making it back to them safely. He urgently needed to get them into protective custody.

The dark, sinister SUV had followed him a few feet into the parking lot of the fire station but had stopped short of going into the building. The ominous vehicle remained there with its big engine rumbling, staring at the firemen as they stared back at it and talked among themselves. Luckily for Brad, the dark SUV was a perfect distraction which drew attention away from him. The darkly-tinted windows provided an opaque barrier which gave the occupants of the SUV time to re-evaluate their strategy without being recognized.

These cold-blooded killers could take life without compunction, but there were too many witnesses here. It could get very messy with even more collateral damage. Two cops had already been killed. That in itself may lead to further problems shortly. Did they want to complicate their mission even further by taking out all of these guys?

Fifteen seconds passed, and finally several firemen began to approach the SUV. The large, dark vehicle slowly backed out of the parking lot as the firemen continued their careful approach. Suddenly, with a load roar the sinister SUV sped off down the highway.

"Hey, Aaron, did you get the license plate number?" asked one of the firemen.

"He didn't have one," said Aaron. "I can't believe it, but he didn't have a license plate."

* * * * * * * * *

Under the cover of all the commotion, Brad grabbed the audit bag, jumped out of the cab, and ran straight through the fire station. One husky fireman managed to grab Brad's shoulder from behind as he was running, but the Controller spun around in a circular motion while knocking the fireman's grip loose with his hand, sending the fireman tumbling across the slick, well-waxed fire station floor.

The backside of the fire station was also open to let air flow through. When Brad came out on the other side, he found a barbed-wire fence leading to an open field. He hastily climbed over the fence, cutting his hands on the barbed wire in the process. As if he were racing to some imaginary goal line to win the game, he then took off running at full speed through the field with the audit bag tucked under his arm like a football.

On the other side of the field was a gas station. Brad slowed down to a brisk walk, but his heart was still beating hard as it worked vigorously to pump oxygen and nutrients back to his thoroughly exhausted limbs. He came around the corner of the gas station and, lo and behold, there sat an 18-wheeler tractor trailer parked at the diesel pump. He looked around for the driver and then spotted him. A heavy-set man in jeans and a bright, red-checkered, flannel shirt who appeared to be in his mid to late 60s was walking toward the truck. The old truck driver had just paid for his fuel and was about to get into his rig when Brad approached him. Brad's face was flushed red from running, and his clothes were soaked with sweat.

"Excuse me, sir. I desperately need to get to Austin as soon as possible. Would you be going that way?"

The old truck driver took a long look at him. He was not accustomed to picking up hitch hikers. *This boy looks like a clean cut feller*, the old gent thought to himself, *but he is sweaty and looks a little spooked. Somethin' ain't right.* Having sized up Brad, he said,

"Matter of fact I am gonna pass through Austin, son, but I don't need no company."

Brad pulled out his wallet. He still had $1,000 left. He pulled out two one-hundred dollar bills and showed them to the driver. "I can pay for gas," he said meekly, throwing himself at the mercy of the unwilling truck driver. "Please, sir. I urgently need to get back to my family."

The truck driver thought to himself for a minute, then nodded his head in acceptance of the proposal. "I reckon it'll be all right. Go on, hop in, young feller."

Trying to hide a sigh of relief, Brad quickly climbed up into the roomy cab of the tractor-trailer. He had no words to express the gratitude he felt at that moment, but the truck driver saw it in his eyes. The old-timer was about to start the big, diesel engine, and then he stopped and looked over at his passenger. Brad's heart almost came to a stop. He looked at the driver, expecting the worst. Had the old gent changed his mind?

Then the silence was broken. "But I choose the music. You ain't got no problem with country music, do ya, boy?"

"No, sir. No problem."

Brad looked over at the aged truck driver. He had a full head of white hair, a thick white beard, and a pot belly. He looked a lot like Santa Claus. *Looks like Santa decided to leave his reindeer at the North Pole this year and make his deliveries in an 18-wheeler,* Brad thought to himself jokingly.

"Where ya from?" said the old timer, trying to make conversation.

Brad cleared his throat and tried to swallow, but his throat just locked up. It was as dry as the desert. His mind was focused on getting something to quench his thirst. "Well, I have lived all over the place, but I grew up in Columbus, Georgia."

"Well, now, ain't that a coincidence," said the old trucker, now really beginning to warm up to Brad. "I'm from Valdosta, Georgia. That's just a hop and a skip from Columbus. Pretty country. Yes, sir."

The two just sat there and listened to country music for a while as the 18-wheeler made its way up to the ramp and onto US 281 North.

"I never got your name, son," the old timer said, trying to recover his manners.

"I'm sorry, my name is Brad Jenkins."

The old timer held out his sun-beaten, calloused hands and shook hands with Brad. "My name is Benjamin Carter, but my friends call me Skunk. You can call me Skunk, too, if ya like," he said trying to make Brad feel at ease.

"It is a pleasure to meet you, Mr. Car...uhhh... Skunk," Brad said in his gentlemanly manner.

"Pleasure's all mine," said Skunk as he took off his black baseball cap and scratched his head. Then he looked in the mirror at his full head of white hair. "You know, my hair went grey when I wuz still in my 20s. By the time I hit my early 30s, it was solid white. I got really worried, cuz I still hadn't gotten married. I 'member one day sittin' out on the porch of my pappy's house, takin' a dip of snuff, well, I was takin' a dip. Pappy ain't never used that stuff. He was smokin' one of his big ole cee-gars. Anyhows, I says to my pappy that I'm worried about my hair goin' grey on me so young. You know what he says to me, Brad?" Skunk looked over at Brad with a smile.

"No, sir, what did he say?"

"He says, 'Benji,' that's what Pappy called me, 'same thing happened to me when I wuz a young buck 'bout your age, but I didn't never give it no thought. I really didn't care what color my hair turned, just as long as it didn't turn loose!'" With that the old timer burst into laughter. He laughed and laughed, and his big pot belly jiggled and jiggled. The more Skunk laughed, the more Brad laughed. It felt good to Brad to laugh again.

Skunk looked over at Brad and smiled, pleased to have Brad as a traveling companion that day. Skunk kept the conversation lively with his anecdotes and pearls of wisdom. Brad enjoyed listening to Skunk. There was another benefit to their conversation: it had given Brad a welcome respite from his own problems.

The old trucker explained that he had done a two-year stint in the Vietnam War back in the mid-1960s. The first year he volunteered to be one of the "tunnel rats." Brad commented that he was somewhat familiar with the tunnel rats due to stories passed on to him by his friends who had served in the military.

Skunk explained to Brad that he and his tunnel rat buddy Jessup would enter the extensive underground tunnel system of the Viet Cong and crawl through the dark tunnels with a flashlight in one hand and a pistol in the other. Sometimes they would find supplies, maps and weapons in the tunnels. After they finished their journey through the tunnel and had returned to the surface, they would have to go back down in the tunnel and plant some C-4 plastic explosives. Once they had come back out of the tunnel again, they would "blow that dern tunnel to kingdom come. But them VC's, that's wut we called them Viet Cong boys, they was crafty and would build them tunnels back within a few weeks. It was like wut we done didn't amount to a hill o' beans over there."

The old trucker mentioned that one time, on about his tenth or eleventh trip into a tunnel, he and his tunnel rat buddy Jessup encountered two Viet Cong also crawling through the tunnel coming from the opposite direction. "Them VCs didn't use no flashlights like us, so you couldn't see when they was a comin' up on ya in them tunnels. We came up to them and my buddy Jessup shined the flashlight right square in the eyes of one of them VC boys. It liked to scared us to death. Funny thing, though, somehow a skunk crawled down into the hole, and the skunk came up behind me. My buddy Jessup opened fire on them VCs lickety-split, and they returned fire, and that dadburned skunk opened fire on me. That varmint soaked me good."

Brad smiled. In his mind's eye he could picture the gunfire and the skunk spraying the old timer.

"My buddy didn't make it outta there alive, but he took them two VCs out before he died. After the gunfire stopped, I pulled Jessup out of the tunnel and radioed for help. When the other fellers in my outfit got there, I was stankin' like that ole skunk. It was a sad day for me, losin' my tunnel rat buddy like I did. That Jessup was a good boy, and he gave his life for his country, God bless him. Anyhows, so we went back to the camp and everybody starts telling me that I was a stankin' like a skunk. After that the name just kinda stuck: 'Skunk.' I didn't like it at first, but then I got used to it. My wife Rosemary says it fits me cuz I'm a real stinker, but she's just foolin'. After that experience, I didn't wanna go down in them tunnels no more, so I transferred to logistics and started driving first aid trucks, supply trucks, whatever they needed. After I did my tour in 'Nam, I got back to the States and guess what I did?"

Brad looked at him, and with a warm smile said, "You started driving 18-wheelers."

"Nope, then I started drivin' a snow cone truck, which I really liked. I used to have this little sales pitch when the kids would ask me what flavors I had. Went somethin' like this: We got raspberry red, good ole grape, cherry berry, blueberry blue, tutti-frutti and bubble gum."

Brad really liked the way Skunk had rattled off those snow cone flavors. He did not just recite the flavors, he sang them with passion.

"Weren't no money in it, though," the old timer continued. "So that's when I started operatin' 18-wheelers. I've been drivin' this humdinger of a rig for the last eight years. She's a beaut, ain't she?"

"Yes, she is, Skunk. This is a nice rig," Brad said admiringly.

"Hey, I got a hankerin' for somethin' to drank, Brad. I'm gonna stop in here and git me a Co-Cola at Earl's."

* * * * * * * * *

They pulled into a small, old country gas station whose architecture resembled that of the 1960s. The outside of the building had peeling, white paint, and there were two old-fashioned gas pumps in front of the store. A mechanic was working in the garage to the left of the store. "This is ole Earl's place. There's his boy Josh workin' over in that there pit. I'll just step in and say hey to 'em right quick-like. Can I git ya somethin?" Skunk asked with his country-boy smile.

Brad was relieved to hear the news. By now his throat was so parched dry that he could barely swallow. "Thanks, Skunk. I would appreciate it. I am very thirsty. Would you get me a Diet Coke? Here, they're on me." He gave the old truck driver two dollars as he got down from the cab of the truck to stretch his legs.

"I'll be back in two shakes of a lamb's tail," Skunk said as he walked over toward the store. Brad interpreted that to mean that Skunk would return soon. He was quickly growing fond of the old timer. Skunk seemed to have a love of life just like his Mexican friends. Within a few minutes the old truck driver had re-appeared with the drinks. Brad gulped down his Diet Coke like lightning. The cold, carbonated beverage was absolutely delicious and hit the spot.

"Tarnation, boy! You wuz thirsty! I thank that's the fastest I ever seen somebody drank a Co-Cola. Want another one?"

"No, thank you, Skunk. I really need to get to my family in Austin as soon as we can. Oh, by the way, here's the $200 for gas we agreed to back in McAllen."

Skunk took the two one hundred dollar bills, folded them, and put them neatly away into his red-checkered flannel shirt pocket. "Much obliged, Brad."

"On the contrary, Skunk, I am much obliged to you for the ride. You will never know how much it means to me. Perhaps one day I shall be able to repay the favor."

"Shucks, you already did with this here $200, Brad."

"Skunk, before we get out of here, I need to visit the restroom. Would you give me a couple of minutes?"

"Sure thang, Brad. I already went, so I'm good to go. I'll wait fer ya here in my rig."

Brad made his way to the restroom at a brisk pace, ever respectful of Skunk's time. After he had washed his hands in the old, run-down bathroom, he heard the sound of a heavy engine pull into the gas station. The old windows in the bathroom were thick and did not allow for him to see through them. He reached over to the side and began cranking the handle to open the window panes, which looked like shutters, just enough to allow him to see who it was outside. His heart began to pound! It was the dark blue SUV with heavily-tinted windows! Three of the doors opened to reveal the men who had taken the life of his friend Eric Johnson and that of the taxi driver Mr. Guillermo Cruz. Brad noticed their holstered side arms as their jackets moved when they were getting out of the SUV. Now he was sure: it was that group of villainous murderers!

Two of them began walking toward the bathroom while the other one conversed with the gas attendant. All three looked to be in their early to mid-30s. The two coming toward the bathroom were of medium height and of Anglo-Saxon ancestry. They were coming straight toward Brad.

As they walked closer, Brad recognized one of them. He had long, blonde hair and a thick scar above his right eyebrow. *That is the same cold-blooded murderer that killed Eric and Mr. Cruz*, he thought. *Their mission is to kill me, and they are not going to stop until they do—unless I stop them first.* He had to think quickly. The small bathroom did not afford much room to maneuver. Outside the bathroom he could hear footsteps which were becoming louder by the second!

The entrance door to the bathroom opened and the long-haired blonde killer walked inside. With the speed of a bullet, Brad shot a front snap kick into the abdominal area of the blonde killer, knocking the wind out of him. The man bent over, putting his arms over his stomach and gasping for breath. Brad grabbed the killer by the back of his hair with his left hand and by the jaw with his right hand. Stepping back with his left leg, the Controller violently twisted the neck of the blonde killer, snapping it instantly and sending him to meet his Maker. This assassin would kill no more.

Frightened by what he had just seen, his accomplice reached into his holster with his right hand in an attempt to remove his black .45-caliber pistol. Brad moved in quickly by stepping sideways a couple of steps and then launching a side kick solidly into the right rib area of the second hitman. The killer was heavy set, so Brad's kick did not do the damage he hoped it would, but it still rocked the big guy. As the murderer pulled his pistol out of his holster, Brad grabbed his wrist with both his hands and moved in right in front of the hitman with his back to him as if he were going to do a judo throw. The inside of the killer's arm was facing upward and his elbow was resting on Brad's shoulder. Brad quickly squatted down and then thrust himself upward like a rocket while holding the hitman's arm over his shoulder. His upward movement caused the killer's arm to bend unnaturally against the joint, snapping the killer's elbow and causing him to drop his pistol.

Before the murderer could shriek with pain, Brad elbowed him in the stomach with the back of his left elbow and then turned and kneed him in the stomach, knocking the wind completely out of his lungs. The murderer gasped for breath. Brad then stepped in with a left jab which grazed the left side of his assailant's face and set up a right reverse punch which struck the killer square in the nose. Brad followed with a left hook, which connected solidly with his assailant's jaw, and then threw a right uppercut to the chin. The force of the final punch knocked the assassin's head back against the cement wall, dazing him momentarily. Brad followed with a ferocious downward elbow strike to the murderer's face, knocking him to the ground, and then stomped his head against the cement floor. It was KO number two for the Controller.

Brad reached down and removed both the side-arm and the back-up weapon from each of his attackers. After he took the driver's licenses from their wallets, he patted them down for anything else they might be carrying. He found an 8½ x 11-inch piece of paper with his picture on it as well as some notes scribbled at the bottom.   He managed to make out one word: "Neutralize." Brad leaned his head back and closed his eyes for a brief moment.   His worst nightmare was confirmed. This death squad was in his honor. He put the piece of paper in his pocket along with the driver's licenses.

Brad stood up quickly to see if anyone else were coming into the bathroom. The other hitman had walked into the store, and was still chatting with Earl the gas attendant. Earl had his radio blasting a country music tune inside the store and outside in the garage area. Fortunately for Brad, the music was loud enough to drown out the commotion in the bathroom. All was clear. He did not know if there were anyone still in the SUV, but he doubted it because this looked to be a pit stop for all of them. *I am surprised that they have not ditched that SUV already*, he remarked to himself. *There has to be an APB out on it. I know the firemen got a good look at it. These guys must be desperate.*

Realizing that Skunk would soon begin to wonder what was going on, Brad checked the window once more. No sign of the third assassin. Consequently, he decided to sneak out of the bathroom, which was located to the right of the store, and make his way around the back of the store, hoping to surprise the third assassin. He took the .45 and stuck it behind him between the small of his back and his belt. Then he moved cautiously out of the bathroom and around the back of the store. Easing into the side entrance to the garage, Brad slipped by Josh the mechanic who was underneath a car working on the transmission of a 1987 Ford Taurus, and made his way to the side of the entrance of the store.

Skunk, who was growing impatient in his 18-wheeler, spotted Brad in the garage. "Hurry up, Brad, we gotta git on the road, boy!" Brad closed his eyes in despair. *Oh, no! Skunk has blown it!*

The tall, lanky assassin was still in the store eating a hot dog. When he heard Skunk say "Brad," he paused for a moment. He had the same look in his eyes that a bird dog does when it hears a strange sound and its ears go straight up. The assassin slowly stepped outside and looked around. Brad remained hidden, plastering himself against the garage wall which separated the garage from the store. The tall assassin walked out in front of the garage entrance and looked around, focusing on Skunk's rig.

Instinctively, Brad stepped out from against the wall and kicked the tall assassin from behind in the bend of his right leg with a right stepping side kick, buckling his knee and causing him to drop to the ground on his right knee. The assassin tossed his hot dog with onions and chili beans on the pavement and went for his holstered gun. Brad pulled out the .45-caliber pistol he had taken from one of the thugs in the bathroom and pointed it directly at the assassin. "Get your hands on your head, NOW!"

The assassin, who was a slick fellow, smiled at Brad and remained calm. "Take it easy, sir. You must have me confused with someone else," he said, still on his right knee with his hands raised. Brad chambered a bullet in his pistol in an effort to warn the killer that he was no novice and would not hesitate to use the firearm. While keeping about ten feet from the killer at all times, Brad slowly walked around in front of him.

In the interim, Skunk had gotten out of his rig and was walking toward Brad with his sawed-off, double-barreled shotgun. At the same time, Earl, the middle-aged owner of the gas station, walked out with his .38 Special pistol. Josh the mechanic, who was still lying on a dolly under the Ford, scooted away from the four men in fearful anticipation of gunfire erupting. The cowardly mechanic was not about to get caught up in the crossfire.

"What in tarnation is goin' on, Brad? What 'cha doin', boy?" Skunk asked in an uncomfortably high pitch.

"I am looking into the face of evil," Brad said as he remained focused on the murderer in front of him.

"Skunk, do you know this man?" asked Earl.

Brad kept his gun aimed directly at the assassin's head. Brad and the assassin continued to stare directly at each other. The assassin had a confident, sinister smirk on his face, as if he were the one who held the upper hand in the stand-off even though the gun was aimed at him.

"I just picked him up a couple of hours ago, Earl. Seems like a nice enough feller. Brad, what's this all about, son?"

"Skunk, it is a long story, but this guy and two others in the bathroom are paid assassins and have been sent to kill me because I have some information that could put some rich people behind bars," Brad shouted. The anxiety was notable in his voice.

Earl had a skeptical look of disbelief on his face. He looked over at Skunk. "What has this fella been smokin', Skunk? What kind of far-fetched nonsense is he spoutin' off?"

Brad dared not look away from the man in front of him and maintained his target within his gun sight. Without ever turning to look at his truck-driving friend, Brad continued to explain to Skunk what was transpiring. "This morning this murderer and his two accomplices killed my colleague Eric Johnson right before my eyes. They also killed the taxi driver, Guillermo Cruz. Then, they shot two police officers who pulled up along side them while these murderers were chasing me, causing the police patrol unit to run into a light post and explode The two cops in that car are probably dead…"

The assassin interrupted. "Look, Brad, or whatever your name is," he said calmly and politely. "I am a salesman for the National MicroChip Computer Company. South Texas is my sales territory. You obviously have me mixed up with somebody else. Please stop pointing that gun at me! You are making me nervous. Here, let me give you my business card." The killer's story sounded very convincing. He started to reach his hand into the inside of his coat, supposedly to retrieve his card.

"Get your hands up or I'll put a bullet in you!" Brad shouted.

Earl, the gas station owner, began to lose his patience with Brad. "Now you look here, sir, you need to put your pistol down so we can all talk this out." Earl looked over at his son the mechanic hiding cowardly in the corner. "Josh, quit bein' so dadburned yellow-bellied and go call 911."

"Yes, Josh, do that," Brad said approvingly. "I'm sure this scumbag would love that." Brad kept staring directly into the eerie eyes of the assassin. They were dark eyes that had no soul. "If you are a computer salesman, then why are you carrying a .45 caliber pistol under your coat?" Brad asked accusingly.

Both Skunk and Earl looked at the assassin, still on his right knee. Brad continued to point the .45 caliber pistol at the assassin. The fight in the bathroom had caused his body temperature to rise, and sweat began to trickle down his face. Both Earl and Skunk kept their firearms ready for action, but they were not pointing at either Brad or the stranger still on his right knee. They leaned over and were able to catch a glimpse of the pistol neatly tucked away in a brown, leather shoulder holster.

The assassin knew that the popular vote was swaying to Brad. "There's no need to get the law involved, Mr. Earl," he advised calmly, still trying to appear like the reasonable computer salesman he was holding himself out to be. "Let's just all calm down, I'll show you who I am, and then I can be on my merry way, and we can just forget about this little mix-up. I still have two more sales calls to make today." He resumed his movement toward the inside of his jacket.

"Don't move!" Brad warned, but the assassin continued reaching into his jacket.

Skunk looked at Brad. "Brad, you just calm down. Maybe this feller's tellin' the truth. Give him a chance to…."

Suddenly, the assassin reached for his .45-caliber pistol. Before the assassin could get a shot off, Brad fired his gun into the assassin's right shoulder, forcing him to drop his pistol and yelp like a dog. Brad kicked the pistol toward Skunk and pounced on the assassin like a leopard. He rolled him over on his stomach, and then put his left knee into the assassin's back while keeping his gun anchored at the back of the assassin's head.

"Ah-h-h!" screamed the assassin in pain as Brad drove his knee into the murderer's spinal column. Brad pulled the assassin's right arm back into an arm bar, anchored it with his right knee, and then he did the same with his left arm.

Brad looked up at Earl, his face still sweating. "Do you have any rope, Earl?" he inquired.

"Uh…yeah, we got some heavy-duty cord, if that will work. We use it to strap things down in the pick-up truck."

"Yes, Earl, that should suffice. Please bring it to me quickly so that I can tie this murderer up."

"Josh, go get this gentlemen the cord in the back of the store."

Josh nodded his head and sprinted toward the store. The assassin tried to move, and Brad tightened the grip on the left arm lock so hard that he almost dislocated the assassin's shoulder. Within seconds Josh returned. Brad thanked him and, taking the rope, tied the assassin's hands together behind his back.

Next, Brad tied the assassin's feet together. Finally, he pulled the feet up toward the back, and tied his feet to his hands. The assassin looked like a skydiver who had jumped out of a plane and was in a freefall. "This piece of trash is not going anywhere," said Brad confidently. As he stood up, he pressed his knee into the assassin one more time for good measure.

Brad rolled the assassin over and shook him down, discovering a back-up weapon strapped to his left ankle. He removed that as well and gave the gun to Earl. The assassin's shoulder was still bleeding, but Brad was not inclined to spend any more time there. His mission was to get back to his wife and family and get them into protective custody. Everything else was secondary. *The package!* Brad recalled. *I need to send the package to the SEC. Well, that will have to wait.*

Brad glanced at Earl. "Earl, please go check your bathroom, but take your gun. I left two more of these hired killers lying on the floor. Take Josh in there with you. If you talk with the McAllen police department, you will be able to confirm what I said about the murders in the taxi and the two cops. Many people saw that SUV."

Nobody said anything, not even the talkative Skunk. Brad resumed his dialogue. "I need to get back to my family. These killers have been contracted by some executives at AMA Electric International. I don't have time to explain this any further, Earl."

"Well," Earl said, "you are going to have to wait here until the cops get here."

"No!" Brad said emphatically. "Don't you understand? These murderers are going to go after my family. I have to get them in protective custody. Just tell the police to call Jim Dove, a field agent for the FBI. Here is his telephone number." Brad turned back to Skunk. "Skunk, could we get on the road?"

Skunk looked into Brad's eyes. "I believe ya, Brad, so I'm gonna help ya. Git in." Then the old timer looked over at his pal. "Earl, why don't cha do just as the young feller says. I'll call ya later. I need to git this load to Chicago by tomorrow night anyhows."

Brad reached down and removed the wallet from the immobilized assassin's coat pocket. He took out his license and read it aloud: "Nicky Wells." Brad then put the license in his pocket along with the other two licenses he had taken from the two hitmen in the bathroom. Patting the assassin down, he found a cellular phone, which he removed. He hit re-dial.

"Hello," said an older, scratchy voice on the other end. *I know that voice!* Brad thought to himself. "Nicky, is that you?"

Finally, Brad placed the name with the voice. It was Buzz Blakely, head of security for AMA. Brad remained quiet. He hadn't the slightest intention of gratifying Buzz's curiosity.

"Nicky? Hello?" Buzz asked.

Brad hung up the phone and turned it off to prevent an electronic trace, and handed it to Earl. "When the police get here, please give them this. It will come in handy as evidence. Tell them I have the driver's licenses of these three, which I intend to turn over to the FBI."

"OK," Earl said in an unsure voice, still uncomfortable with what was happening.

"All right Skunk, I'm ready if you are."

"Let's git goin, boy," he replied to Brad. Then he turned to his old friend Earl whom he had known on this route for many years. "Earl, call the po-lice and have them attend to this. I'll talk to ya later, buddy."

Skunk continued on his way to Austin, taking U.S. 59 to Highway 37 North, then Loop 410 around San Antonio, and finally I-35 North to Austin. Along the way, Brad explained to Skunk the entire story of what had happened.

"That don't surprise me none, Brad," Skunk admitted. "Those presidents of them big companies are like them robber barons of 100 years ago. Can't trust 'em. You just make sure you git these varmints at your company. People's a dependin' on ya, boy."

"I'll get'em, Skunk," Brad said with a determined look on his face. "Believe me, I will get them."

* * * * * * * * *

Finally, they arrived in Austin. Skunk drove into a Quick and Easy convenience store in the northern part of the city. Brad hopped down from the big 18-wheeler's cab. Before he closed the door, he looked up at the old timer. "I shall not forget your kindness, Skunk," he said. "I am in your debt."

"Don't thank nothin' of it, boy," Skunk said modestly. "Jest git back to that wife and yer young 'uns. That'll be thanks enough for me."

Brad was taken aback by the goodness of this man. Up until this morning, he had not even known of Benjamin "Skunk" Carter. However, if it had not been or Skunk's help, Brad might not have made it through he day. He was indeed indebted to this kind soul.

The18-wheeler pulled onto the main drag, and the diesel engine moved the mammoth carcass of steel northward. *Honk! Honk!* Skunk sounded his horn to say his good-bye, trucker style, to his new friend as he continued on the road to his Chicago drop-off point.

Although he was still quite anxious, Brad was relieved to be in Austin. Now all he wanted to do was to hear Sofía's voice and see her beautiful smile. He put two coins in the pay phone outside of the convenience store and dialed his sister-in-law's house. The phone rang several times. *Please, pick up, please! I need to now that you are all OK.*

"Hello," answered a friendly voice.

"Fritz! Hey, this is Brad. How is everyone?"

"We're all fine, Brad," Fritz said serenely. "Are you OK?"

"Yes, Fritz. May I speak with Sofía, please?"

"Certainly, just one moment and I'll put her on."

After a brief silence, Sofía answered. *"Mi amor?"*

Never had Brad needed to hear her voice so much. He closed his eyes and smiled. *"Hola, mi vida.* It is so good to hear your sweet voice."

"You are all right! *¡Gracias a Dios!*" Sofía said, relieved to hear Brad's voice as well, although she had no idea of the tribulations which Brad had suffered during the last 24 hours.

"I am fine. Look, right now I am at a convenience store on the corner of Chetwood and Caborca. Would you please ask Fritz to come pick me up? You stay there with Liliana and little Michael, please."

"Está bien, mi amor. I know where that is. You are very close to us. Fritz will be there shortly. I can't wait to see you! *Te amo mucho.*"

Chapter 25

Drop-Dead Gorgeous

Within 10 minutes Fritz Leibig appeared in his minivan. He had a bright smile on his face when he drove up to the area where Brad was standing at the Quick and Easy convenience store. A pleasant and upbeat fellow, Fritz was of German descent but had grown up in Rio de Janeiro, Brazil. He spoke fluent German, English, Portuguese, Spanish and some French. The conservative and soft-spoken manufacturing engineer worked as a manager for a large manufacturing company.

After exchanging pleasantries, they returned to Fritz's house. Everyone in the family knew that this house was Fritz's pride and joy. It was a relatively new, spacious, two-story dwelling in an upper middle-class neighborhood in a northern suburb of Austin. He had worked hand-in-hand with the architect to develop the custom plans for the builders. Later, during construction of the house, he had visited the site almost every day to inspect the quality of the work. When it came to his house, he was indeed a stickler for detail.

Once they had moved in, Fritz began working on the landscaping of the property. This labor of love consumed his nights and week-ends to get the soil ready, plant the grass, trees, and flowers, and then nurture the growth of all that he had planted. The mild-mannered engineer had done a splendid job developing the landscape. Working outdoors and being close to Nature, a sharp contrast to his long, monotonous days in front of a computer, was something that Fritz truly relished.

Sofía's sister Isabel had graduated with honors from the Monterrey Institute of Technology with a degree in business administration years ago and then moved to Austin to study English. Later she discovered an interest in teaching, and began teaching in the bilingual program in Austin. It was there that she met Fritz. Within two years, they were married. When she began having children, she opted to take time off and be a full-time mother to give her own children the formative education she felt they deserved.

Once Brad and Fritz had walked inside the house, Sofía and Liliana came running to greet Brad. Brad was overcome with emotion. He had made it! The long, horrid journey fraught with peril had mercifully ended. *Thank you, Lord, for bringing me back safely to my family*, he prayed silently as he hugged his family.

Brad picked Liliana up, and she gave her father a big hug. "Hey, funky face," he said with tears in his eyes. Suddenly, she pushed against Brad's rock hard chest and moved her head as far backward as she could. "Ooh-ooh-ooh, Daddy, you stink!" said Liliana with a sour face and a playful smile. She waved her thin, dainty little hand back and forth to try and dispel the stench emanating from her exhausted father. "You need to take a shower with lots and lots and lots of soap! Maybe you need to take two showers!" She said with playful admonition, giggling.

Brad smiled and put her down on the floor. His odor was the last thing on his mind right now. Nevertheless, Liliana was right. He did have a bad odor about him.

"Hey, where is little Michael?" Brad asked, looking around for his son.

Liliana motioned to her father for him to lean his head down to her face so that she could tell him something discreetly, which Brad did. She pinched her nose with her left hand to protect herself from her father's malodorous condition. Then she edged her head over to Brad's right ear and whispered, "He is doing pooh-pooh behind the couch. He doesn't want anyone to know what he is doing."

"He's wearing a diaper? I thought he was in training pants now."

"Sometimes Mommy puts a diaper on him, like at night. But most of the time he wears his training pants."

"OK, Sweetie. Well, he does like his privacy. I'll go say hey to him in a minute when he has finished with his business, but we need to get him completely off diapers as soon as possible." They smiled at each other. Liliana's eyes sparkled with the magical felicity that a wonderful childhood bestows upon children.

"*Quieres un café, mi amor?*" Sofía inquired with the sweet voice that Brad so loved to hear.

"*Sí, mi vida, por favor.*" Brad walked upstairs and into the bathroom. After quickly disrobing, he turned on the water and eased into the shower stall. The calming effect of the heat and steam coupled with the emotional comfort of being back with his family were deeply relaxing. He emerged from the shower a rejuvenated man. After the shower he changed into some clothes that Sofía had packed for him. *Without my even asking her she packed some clothes for me*, he thought to himself. *She always thinks about me. That is, indeed, true love. need to make sure every day that I am worthy of her love*

Sofía walked upstairs and brought Brad his coffee. Standing there quietly, he just smiled and kept his eye on her as he slowly drank the delicious cup of freshly brewed coffee. He studied every facet of the subtle lines and curves that made up her beautiful face.

"*¿Qué?*" Sofía said as innocently and flirtatiously as a teen-age school girl.

Brad simply said, "*Te amo.*" That was all that his wife needed to hear.

* * * * * * * * *

Shortly thereafter Brad called his good friend in the FBI, field agent Jim Dove. He called in over the secure line that Jim had given him.

"Code in," said the voice on the other line. Brad recognized the voice. It was Jim.

"Wilson's Barbeque," said Brad, using the name of the restaurant where he and Jim used to eat on Saturdays.

"Bradley, my boy, where are you? Don't worry, this is a secure line."

"I am at my sister-in-law's house in Austin, Texas, but things are really hot right now."

"Well, did you send that package of information via express mail to Lety Cuellar at the SEC?"

Oh, man! With all that had happened, I have completely forgotten about sending the information to the SEC! "No, Jim, it just dawned on me that I haven't done that yet. Let me tell you what has happened since we spoke this morning." Brad proceeded to inform Jim of all that had happened, including the murder of his friend and fellow accountant, Eric Johnson, as well as Guillermo Cruz, right before Brad's eyes. He then explained the face-off he had with the three assassins in that country gas station outside of McAllen.

Jim, who had seen this in his work with the FBI, was undaunted by what he heard. "I'm sorry about your friend, Brad, but I can tell you one thing: you are lucky to be alive."

"You're right, Jim. I am very fortunate to have made it through that ordeal alive and unharmed. I'm grateful, very grateful, for that, but I feel terrible for Eric's family."

"Don't beat yourself up about that, Bradley. It's not your fault. We'll get the guys who did this to your friend. Another thing, you big lug: I'll never tease you about that Hapkido stuff again. I might even start to study that myself. I am really impressed. Hey, have you thought about moving out of accounting and into something a little more exciting, like coming to work for us here in the FBI? We could surely use you in the Bureau's Mexico City office working with the money laundering task force down there. You wouldn't have to do any field work. You would sit in an office all day. Hey, we also just sent a guy to Beijing. How is your command of Mandarin Chinese holding up after all this time?"

"*Wo de Zhong Wen bu tai hao*," Brad admitted. "Jim, let me tell you something. If accounting gets any more exciting than this, I think I will have to consider changing to a career as a librarian."

Jim chuckled. "You are one of a kind, Bradley, my boy. Well, keep that possibility open. I'd love to see you come aboard with us. Anyway, we need to get you and your family into protective custody ASAP." Jim looked down at his Omega watch, a gift from his wife last year for their seventh anniversary. "Let's see, right now it is 4:30 p.m. my time, 6:30 p.m. where you are. I'm in my office just outside San Diego right now, but I can catch a late flight on a commercial airliner out of San Diego and be at your sister-in-law's house by midnight your time. I'll bring a couple of local agents with me—people I can trust. From there, we can get you set up for he longer term under the Bureau witness protection until he trial is over. The SEC and FBI will need your estimony in this case, and those accounting *bandidos* vill definitely want to have you out of the picture, so we leed to get to work quickly. I'll see you later on tonight. Keep a low profile until we get there."

"Thanks, Jim. I really appreciate your help."

"Anytime, Brad. Besides, you're making me look good. I'll probably get a promotion if we can get these scumbags behind bars. This is a big case!"

"We will, Jim," Brad said with conviction as he remembered the Johnson family that would never see their father Eric again.

* * * * * * * * *

It was just after midnight. The others had already gone to bed because tomorrow was Friday, which was a workday and a school day. Brad was sitting quietly in an antique wooden bench located in the entrance hall waiting for his friend Jim Dove. The lights were off so that no one could see inside.

In his mind's eye he kept seeing Eric sitting in the back of the taxi with him, smiling and chatting, and then the terrible sound of glass cracking and bullets whizzing through the air, and then Eric, slumped over and covered in blood. Eric Johnson, the first person in his family to graduate from college, who had gone on to earn an MBA from an Ivy League school, the youngest person to make partner in his accounting firm, a corporate officer with AMA Electric International, a devoted husband and father, an esteemed colleague of Brad's, a man who had lived his life summa cum laude, was dead.

Brad was seldom given to rage, but at that moment it ran through his body like of jolt of electricity. He clenched his fists so tightly that you could hear it. The Controller knew who was responsible for this, and he was going to make sure that they were punished for their crimes. First and foremost, however, was the safety of his family. In an hour or two he would have them in protective custody, and he would be able to breathe easier.

After a while Brad began to battle sleep. It had been a long, terrible day, the worst one of his life, and he was absolutely exhausted. He found himself dozing off and then coming back to consciousness. Finally, he heard a car drive up alongside the curb in front of the house. Lifting his heavy eyelids, he leaned forward and moved the front window curtain back slightly so that he could peek out of the window. Jim Dove emerged from the vehicle, accompanied by another man and a woman. They walked to the door and, before they could knock, Brad quietly opened the door.

"Hey, Bradley!" Jim said in a muffled voice as he gave Brad a manly pat on the back.

Brad invited them inside. Jim had one suitcase filled with personal items and another, special suitcase containing weapons and communication equipment. They moved to the kitchen table and sat down so that they could talk without waking the others.

Jim pointed to the man on his right. "Brad, this is FBI field agent Tom Vincent." Tom was a tall, middle-aged Anglo-American man with thinning, red hair and a pleasant smile. Then, Jim introduced the woman. "This is Lisa Benedetti, also an agent with the Bureau. Both Tom and Lisa are based out of the local Austin office and were hand-picked by me for this assignment. I met them back when I was in Special Forces. Don't worry. I trust them with my life, because they saved it a couple of times."

Lisa smiled and shook hands with Brad. She looked to be in her late 30s but in excellent shape. She had long, dark hair and olive-complexioned skin.

"Oh, by the way, Brad—Lisa is a lethal weapon. She holds a black belt in Kenpo and earned a silver medal in marksmanship in the Olympic Games in Atlanta in '96. I thought you two would hit it off together."

Lisa added: "Jim was telling us all about you on the drive over. I understand that you study Hapkido?"

Brad was a little embarrassed to talk about his martial arts prowess. He generally liked to hold that card close to his chest. "That's right," he replied succinctly. "May I offer you something to drink?"

"No, we're fine right now, Brad," Jim spoke for the group. "We will need a strong pot of coffee for the night, however. Tom and Lisa will be staked out here all night, but they have been working day shifts, so caffeine will be important. We will get reinforcements in the morning."

"That sounds good, Jim."

"I am sure that you must be worn out, buddy, but don't worry. You're in good hands, now." Jim glanced around the room and then looked back at Brad. "Well, I didn't come all this way to sit around and scratch fleas. Why don't you show us the layout of the premises?"

Brad gave them a brief tour of the first floor, which included a spacious guest room, two bathrooms, a den, a living room, and a large kitchen. Once he had put a pot of coffee on to brew, he said goodnight and made his way upstairs to retire for the night. He curled into bed with his wife and kissed her gently on the cheek. She smiled, still half-asleep. Life was good again.

* * * * * * * * *

That Friday March morning, Brad arose at 6:00 a.m. He and his friend, field agent Jim Dove of the FBI, left the house at 7:20 a.m. to take the audit information to the express mail office for same day delivery to the SEC in Washington, D.C. Once the package had been safely sent, Jim called Lety Cuellar at the SEC and gave her the tracking number of the package. The events which had occurred yesterday in McAllen and at that sleepy little gas station along U.S. Highway 59 North had made national headlines. As a result, Lety was very interested to know if there were a connection of those tragic events to the AMA case. Her interest in the case was substantially heightened once Jim confirmed that indeed those events were directly related.

Brad and Jim then went to the local FBI office so that Brad could give a statement about what had transpired. On the way over, Brad advised Jim that there were two more copies of the accounting fraud documentation. He had given one copy to plant manager Jorge del Valle for safe-keeping. He had given the other copy to his mother in Columbia, South Carolina, where it was locked away in a safety deposit box at her bank.

They arrived at the FBI office and met several top-ranking people. Brad gave them the driver's licenses that he had removed from his attackers after the fight at the gas station outside McAllen. Of particular interest to the federal agents was the piece of paper containing Brad's picture and the word "neutralize." He gave a statement describing the murderous acts of the hitmen, including his own struggle with them in the bathroom at the gas station. The Controller still had the driver's licenses of the Monterrey police, but he had decided earlier that he would keep those items for himself as insurance just in case there was trouble down the line. Although Sofía's parents were visiting her sister in South Carolina, they would have to return to Monterrey eventually.

The FBI indicated that the two local McAllen policemen involved in the high-speed chase unfortunately did die in the crash. As a result, these assassins in the SUV were now cop killers. Local McAllen police had rushed to the fire station where Brad had abandoned the taxi cab. They recovered the bodies of Eric Johnson and of the taxi driver Guillermo Cruz.

State police had arrived at the scene of the gas station on U.S. 59 shortly after Brad and his trucker buddy Skunk had departed. Two of the men with whom Brad had fought were arrested and taken to an undisclosed San Antonio hospital were they remained in stable condition. The blonde-haired assassin with the scar over his right eye was pronounced dead at the scene. No charges were going to be pressed against Brad in that death. It was obviously self-defense. The hitmen had long criminal records and were known assassins. They were all on the FBI's "Most Wanted List."

The two assassins recovering in the San Antonio hospital were being questioned by FBI officials there in the deaths of the McAllen police officers, Eric Johnson, and the McAllen taxi driver. They were also being interrogated for murders in other non-related cases.

Police forensics had determined that the 9 mm bullets found in the autopsy of the McAllen police officers matched the Uzi machine gun found in the dark SUV. In addition, there was one spent 32-round, 9 mm cartridge on the floor of the SUV. The autopsy further revealed that the .45-caliber bullets that killed Eric Johnson and the McAllen taxi driver matched the guns found on the assassins, and the fingerprints lifted off the casings matched the prints from the assassins.

It was an open and shut case. However, law enforcement officials were aware that these little fish were, literally, just the trigger men. The FBI wanted the big fish, and for that they needed Brad's help to identify them and bring them to justice.

The FBI asked Brad for his help to nail the people who hired the killers. Brad assured them that they would have his full cooperation. Jim Dove had filled them in on the bigger picture, and the FBI said they wanted to work in conjunction with the SEC. The government was putting its team in place to go after Rick Less and his villainous *compadres*.

* * * * * * * * *

"WHERE IS HE?" screamed Rick Less into the speaker phone in his office. Harry Allen was seated to the left of Rick, dressed in his usual designer long-sleeved shirt with the cuffs rolled up, khaki pants, and penny loafers. He was sipping a Jack Daniels straight up

"I don't know, Rick!" barked Victor Reyes, seated in his plush Monterrey office. "I did everything I could to keep that *canijo* from getting out of Mexico. I had the borders sealed up tighter than Fort Knox."

"Victor, this question was addressed more to Buzz," commented Rick in a condescending tone. "We know that Brad is in the U.S. Buzz, where are you right now?"

"I am in El Paso, Texas, with one of my men, Mr. Less. We are staking out Mr. Jenkins' house here in the northeast section of town. There is no sign of him here."

"What about his family in Columbus, Georgia, and Columbia, South Carolina?" Rick inquired.

"I have men staked out there as well, sir," said the ever-steady Buzz. "No sign of Mr. Jenkins. I also have men in Atlanta and all over the state of Texas. In total, I have 15 men deployed in strategic locations."

A firm voice interjected: "Buzz, this is Harry. Look, that fiasco in McAllen yesterday and then the mess at that country bumpkin gas station have brought the authorities into this. It was on the national news. You are letting Brad Jenkins embarrass you and your men. Let's just stay focused and get this guy. Now, what do we know? Do we have any leads from our contacts at the FBI or the NSA?"

"No, sir, we don't. We pinpointed Mr. Jenkins in McAllen by 'DF-ing' him off his cellular, but we have not been able to trace him electronically or through any other means since."

"What? How could that be possible?" Harry challenged him in disbelief.

"I admit that it is...disappointing, sir. I am in touch with our people in the Bureau and the NSA every few hours. If I hear anything, you'll know about it immediately. Mr. Jenkins is a very adept individual and has proven himself to be a worthy adversary."

"Buzz, he's just an accountant, not a Special Forces commando. Don't make this out to be more than it is," Harry said disparagingly.

"With all due respect, Mr. Allen, he is not just an accountant. No ordinary accountant could have made it through what he has. I checked his background out thoroughly. He has no formal military experience; however, he is an expert in Hapkido. When I was attached to a Black Ops unit in Vietnam in the early 1970s, a Hapkido Grandmaster and his demonstration team from Texas flew over to 'Nam. They trained our unit along with some South Vietnamese on Hapkido techniques. A lot of what they showed us was mortal. That is a deadly art, sir."

"Buzz, I don't care what kind of martial art he is into," Harry griped disrespectfully. The COO obviously had never studied the martial arts and had no appreciation for them whatsoever. "This guy is not bullet-proof, so put a bullet in him! It's that simple."

Rick jumped back into the conversation. "Keep the pressure on all our resources, Buzz," he instructed in his usual commanding tone of voice. "We need this problem resolved *pronto*. Just make it clean. I don't want any loose ends."

"I understand, Mr. Less. We are working around the clock on this."

"The worst part is that two of those three men you assigned to this job have been taken into custody by the FBI at some hospital in south Texas," Harry added emphatically. "That represents serious exposure to us. How do you intend on handling it?"

"I'm…not sure I understand you, Mr. Allen."

"We cannot permit those clowns that were negligent in carrying out their duties to have a chance to chat with the Feds, Buzz."

This comment caught Buzz off guard. He felt torn between wanting to please his employer who compensated him quite handsomely and wanting to protect his team. "Sir, I recruited those men. I have known one of them, Nicky Wells, for over 20 years. I have the utmost in confidence in their loyalty. They won't talk."

"That is a risk that I am not prepared to take, Buzz. They failed at a simple task, and now they represent a significant liability to all of us, especially to you, Buzz. You're the guy that they will finger if they squeal to the Feds. Aren't you worried about that?"

"No, sir, I am not. As I said before, they won't give up anything to the Feds."

Harry looked over at Rick and made an expression that would have shaken Buzz's confidence in who his true allies were had he seen that dastardly look. "All right, Buzz. We'll take it from here."

Buzz sighed grimly. There was an uncomfortable silence for a few seconds. Finally, he spoke: "One more thing, sir: yesterday morning Brad Jenkins made two calls from the Cozy Border Inn Hotel in McAllen, Texas. One was to a number in Austin that was unregistered, but we have been able to determine that it belongs to a Fritz Leibig. I don't see what the connection could be, but we have the address, and I have some men traveling to Austin to check it out. The other call was to the FBI office in San Diego."

"Great," remarked Harry sarcastically. "Jenkins has already made contact with the Feds."

"Buzz," Rick said, "that phone call to the FBI highlights the need to get this problem resolved today."

"I will, sir." When he hung up the phone, for the first time in many years Buzz had mixed emotions about what he was doing. He had always complied with security tasks before, no questions asked, but nothing had approached what they were asking him to do now. Even he had his code of honor. How could Harry expect him to kill his own team members? It was one thing to take out the enemies of his employer, such as Brad Jenkins. It was another thing to turn on his own men. That would never happen.

* * * * * * * * *

Around 2 o'clock that afternoon, Victor walked out of his office. "I have a luncheon date with a customer, Lupita," he said to his executive assistant as he darted out the door. The smell of Victor's freshly applied cologne told her otherwise.

Since Lolita Loya had discovered Victor in a very compromising situation with Zulema Palma, the flamboyant 53-year-old executive had made an exhaustive effort to get in touch with the Latin beauty. To Victor's dismay, there was no sign of Lolita anywhere. Although he was rather dejected over the loss of his most prized possession, he still was not about to give up his old tomcat ways.

Chato, Victor's number one man of confidence, had spotted a gorgeous young woman named Estrella who supposedly could give Lolita a run for her money. Estrella fit the profile that Victor liked. However, before he embarked on that conquest, he had a rendezvous with his youngest *muchacha*, Jackie Villalobos. That afternoon they would meet in the beautiful mountains of *Las Montañas Azules* just outside of Monterrey for what promised to be a wonderfully romantic interlude.

The highway to *Las Montañas Azules* was somewhat dangerous due to the ominous cliff which had a drop-off of two hundred feet. However, Victor had made the trip dozens of times over the years and, consequently, he had become quite comfortable with the drive. For Victor the trip was always an agreeable experience, and that afternoon was no different. The weather was pleasant. There was not a cloud in the sky.

As Victor casually made the journey up the mountain, listening to a lively Spanish tune on his ten-speaker car stereo, he looked over to the left and, out of the blue, he saw a sensationally attractive lady in white shorts and a tight, pink blouse walking out to the parking lot from one of the stores. She was drop-dead gorgeous. The long-legged brunette held Victor's undivided attention and smiled flirtatiously at him when he drove by her. *I need to make a quick detour and check her out more closely,* Victor thought with a devilish smile on his face.

Before Victor could roll down the window to ask her to wait, he heard the frightening sound of a loud, deep truck horn and quickly turned his head to check the traffic. To his horror, he realized that he had inadvertently drifted over into the lane of on-coming traffic. To make matters worse, there was a huge Mack truck coming down the mountain right at him. A head-on collision was imminent. Victor panicked and swerved wildly to the right to avoid the gargantuan truck, but he lost control of his car and went rolling over the side of the cliff.

The result was nothing short of catastrophic. His car went into a free fall for about 50 feet, and then the front of the car struck the dirt on the side of the mountain. From that point it began to tumble, flip, and bang itself all the way down the rest of the mountain, leaving a trail of shattered glass and broken car parts.

Finally, the horrific fall came to a loud halt when the car smashed against a huge rock at the foot of the mountains and landed upside down. The mangled car looked like an aluminum can that had been crushed from all sides. Its wheels continued turning slowly, and steam leaked out of the radiator. Victor was no where to be seen.

Chapter 26

The Package is Delivered

Brad Jenkins and Jim Dove returned to Isabel and Fritz Liebig's beautiful house that afternoon. Brad was greeted at the front door by the one of the two new FBI agents who had relieved Lisa Benedetti and Tom Vincent. Lisa and Tom would return at 8:00 p.m. that night. Brad walked into the family room where Little Michael and Liliana were watching cartoons. "Daddy!" they shouted gleefully in unison and ran up to give their father a big hug.

Walking over to Sofía, Brad gave her a kiss on the forehead and sat down with her. "*Mi vida*," he said, "Do you have a minute? I need to bring you up-to-date on the day's events." Brad proceeded to explain everything that had happened at the FBI office. Once Sofía was up to speed, they all sat down and had a nice, hot dinner.

Around 7:30 p.m. that evening, Jim Dove received a call from Lety Cuellar of the SEC. Lety was a 47-year-old Mexican-American who had begun her career as an auditor at a large, national accounting firm and then moved over to the government sector. She had been with the SEC for the last twenty years and was well-respected by her peers and subordinates as well as the top brass at the SEC. In fact, she was being groomed to take over as Director for the Enforcement Division within the next twelve months.

Lety spoke briefly with Jim, and then asked to speak with Brad. Jim passed the phone over to his friend.

"Hello," answered Brad.

"Well, it is an honor to finally talk to the famous Controller Brad Jenkins," Lety said in a cordial attempt to break the ice. "This is Lety Cuellar, Assistant Director for the Enforcement Division of the SEC, in Washington, D.C. How are your doing?"

"Fine, thank you, Ms. Cuellar."

"Please, call me Lety. I received your package this afternoon. Jim Dove had asked me to review it personally, which I have done. I must say, Brad, it looks like you have done your homework. This information is very well documented. Congratulations on the fine work."

"Thank you, Lety. So what happens from here?"

"Well, Brad, in general, we look at how serious the reported issue appears to be and what message we would send to business and to the American public if we took a case. In the case of AMA Electric International, thanks to your efforts I think that we have enough evidence here to open an investigation and bypass the 'matter under inquiry' stage."

Brad sighed with relief.

"My enforcement staff will review this information further. In the morning I am going to instruct a couple of my people to arrange for an on-site review of AMA's accounting records and then follow back up with you for your testimony and any other relevant information."

"Will there be any subpoenas issued at the investigation stage?" Brad asked.

"Perhaps. Sometimes it is formal with no subpoena authority, but sometimes we do issue subpoenas. Remember, at this stage it is still a non-public investigation."

"OK. I'm with you so far."

"From the intelligence discovered in this non-public investigation, I will determine whether to recommend that the SEC authorize a civil or an administrative enforcement action, or both. The SEC does not have any 1811 agents. My team conducts its investigations principally with lawyers. Although we have subpoena powers, they are limited subpoena powers. Another thing—we do not have access to investigative tools such as wire taps like they do in the DEA or FBI. Therefore, I may team up with the FBI on this. From that point the Commission will authorize the Enforcement staff to initiate civil actions or administrative proceedings. My instincts tell me it is likely that we will initiate civil action concurrent with the FBI's pursuit of criminal charges."

"Good. Rick Less and the accounting *bandidos* need to be stopped."

Lety was intrigued by Brad's comment. "The what?"

"The accounting *bandidos*. It's just a code name that we gave this group."

"I like it. It has a nice ring to it."

"Lety, there is one thing I wanted to mention to you in the hope that you, given your visibility within the SEC, can help to change."

"Certainly, Brad. What is it?"

"In the case of AMA as well as with other American companies, I feel that there is an unhealthy focus on short-term earnings by CEOs. This is a *big* problem. Companies are so caught up in the trap of trying to please Wall Street's expectations for the quarter that they find ways to justify inappropriate accounting treatment. I believe that it is imperative for the future of financial reporting and American capital markets that CEOs move away from their obsession of meeting short-term earnings and look at the long-term health of their businesses. This critical issue has not received enough attention in the past, and I think the SEC could be an effective agent to move this more to the forefront of American business."

"I totally agree with you, Brad," the SEC veteran replied. "The focus on short-term earnings by American companies is perhaps the biggest issue we face today in terms of threats to good financial reporting. It has received considerable attention within the SEC, but I hear what you are saying. The SEC is indeed in an excellent position to make this problem more visible and work with the business community at large to attack it. I will address this at our next staff meeting." Lety was impressed with Brad's insights and shifted gears for a minute. "Look, Brad, now that you are no longer working for AMA, would you be interested in coming to work for us at the SEC?"

"I am flattered by your offer, Lety, but my calling is working abroad for subsidiaries of U.S. companies. The challenge of working in a foreign country and in a foreign language is very meaningful to me."

"I understand, Brad," Lety replied, the disappointment evident in her voice. "Well, if you change your mind, please look me up. There will be a job waiting for you here if you are interested. We need accountants with your talent, integrity, and courage."

"Thank you for your kind words, Lety."

"In the meantime, I am going to send in a team to push ahead on the investigation. We'll be in touch."

* * * * * * * * *

At a county hospital in San Antonio, TX, the FBI coordinated with local police to have a team of two of

San Antonio's finest guard the two assassins whom Brad had given a thorough thrashing at the country gas station on U.S. Highway 59. The injured assassins were recovering in the same room. One police officer was seated in a comfortable chair just outside the room reading the sports section of the San Antonio newspaper, and the other officer was standing at the entrance to the room. They rotated every hour so that each stood for an hour and sat for an hour. They checked in with an FBI field agent at the beginning of each 12-hour shift to advise of the status.

Up to this point, the FBI had learned a sum total of nothing from these two murderers. Just as Buzz had indicated, they were not talking. Curiously, a prestigious New York law firm was representing them. It was improbable that these two hitmen would have the economic means with which to pay for such high-priced legal services. The FBI strongly suspected that the true head honchos behind the killings were footing the legal bill. However, that secret was protected by attorney-client privilege and would never be revealed.

Earlier that day, Dr. Raymundo Pacheco had been making rounds on the same floor where the two assassins were staying. Dr. Pacheco was a young, Mexican-American doctor in the second year of his residency to practice as a general physician. He walked up to the door of his second patient of the day, Nicky Wells, the assassin whom Brad had shot in the shoulder. The cop at the door checked Dr. Pacheco's I.D. badge and confirmed that it was a name on the list of approved doctors. Dr. Pacheco went into the room, accompanied by the police officer.

"Is this really necessary, Officer?" protested the young doctor.

"I'm sorry, Doc. Strict orders from the FBI. No one is to be alone in the room with these two. They are professional assassins, and they are both on the FBI's 'Most Wanted List.' You should be glad that I am in here watching your back."

"Very well," Dr. Pacheco remarked, his irritation being held in check by his overriding concern for his patient. He proceeded to examine the two patients and then exited the room. The two assassins were heavily medicated due to the pain from their injuries, and they drifted in and out of consciousness.

At 7:00 p.m. there was a shift change for both the police officers. The second group of officers assigned to guard the assassins read the same sports section from the same paper that their fellow officers on the day shift had left for them. For the two officers assigned to guard the assassins that night, the hours seemed to drag on forever.

Around 3:30 a.m. Darrell, a young Afro-American police officer who was seated, indicated that he was going downstairs to get a cup of coffee. His partner Jake, a young Anglo-American, was also beginning to succumb to the comforting temptation of sleep. Jake indicated that he could use some coffee right about then as well. "Make it a large, Darrell. My body has still not adjusted to the night shift."

"Sure, partner. I'll be back in a few minutes."

Darrell's legs and back had stiffened somewhat from so much time sitting down. He slowly lifted himself from the chair and made his way toward the elevator. An attractive blonde nurse seated at the nurse's station saw Darrell take the elevator down to the cafeteria floor where the coffee machines were. She grabbed her cellular phone and hastily dialed a number to a paging service which was scribbled on a small piece of paper in blue ink. She then typed in "1221", which was the code to move in. That one little phone call had cost the *compadres* $10,000. The blonde nurse then stood up and conveniently went into the women's bathroom.

Just like clock work, three men dressed in green hospital gowns came out of the elevator. As they approached the room where the two assassins were, they pulled out their weapons. Police officer Jake immediately went for his service revolver. However, before he could manage to pull it out, he had been shot by a stun gun with 100,000 volts of electricity shooting through his body. Jake's body convulsed briefly, and then he fell to the floor.

This assignment had strict orders: no dead cops. One of the men in the green hospital outfits pulled out a syringe and injected its tranquilizing contents into Officer Jake. With that dosage, he would remain unconscious for at least four hours. He was quickly dragged into the men's room and placed in one of the stalls.

One of the intruders remained posted at the door while the other two made an entry by stealth into the room where the two assassins were recovering. Their victims lay sound asleep and never saw the end coming. The intruders emptied five rounds into the chest and head of each assassin, ensuring that these murderers would forever hold their peace. The sound suppressors, or silencers, on the 9 mm pistols reduced the sounds of the gun shots to mere thumps on a pillow. The three intruders slipped down the stairs and out the building just as imperceptibly as they had come in. Their mission had been executed more precisely than any other operation performed that day in that San Antonio hospital.

* * * * * * * * *

When weather permitted on Saturday mornings, Harry Allen loved to sit out on the backyard porch of his Norcross, Georgia, home with his wife Irene, sip coffee and read the newspaper. On this particular Saturday morning, Harry's three-year old Irish Setter Sean was lying by his side when Harry's private cellular phone rang.

"Yes?" Harry answered with his usual even temperament. He glanced at his wife who had learned long ago to tune out such conversations.

"We have effectively neutralized the targets, sir," reported an unfamiliar voice on the other end. "No cops were killed."

"Very good," the white-haired COO commented without emotion as he took another sip of coffee. He hung up his phone, reached down to pat Sean on the head, and then turned the page of his newspaper.

* * * * * * * * *

That same Saturday morning in Austin, Texas, FBI field agent Jim Dove addressed the same issue with the Controller. "Brad, could you step outside for a minute," Jim said to his long-time friend. "I need to discuss something with you."

"Sure," Brad said as he grabbed his coffee and walked out to the beautifully landscaped backyard of Isabel and Fritz's home. The big back yard was almost a half-acre in size. The grass was the greenest of greens and looked as picturesque as a golf course. The yard was highlighted by a long flower bed which ran along the perimeter of the eight-foot wooden fence which Fritz himself had built. Planted within this long flower bed was a wonderful variety of colorful flowers whose natural perfume filled the air and pleased the senses of all those who were fortunate enough to be in their presence.

"Brad, my boy, I'm afraid that I have some bad news to report." Jim said with a heavy face. Brad was not used to seeing the FBI agent worried. "Look, the hired guns that were being treated in that hospital in San Antonio have been killed."

"What? Both of them?"

"Yes," Jim said with an uncomfortable sigh as he scratched the stubble under his unshaven chin. "It was a professional hit. Clean as a whistle. We've got diddly squat to go on. Whoever was behind this has got a lot of money. Hired guns that good do not come cheap."

"What about the cops assigned to guard those two assassins? Why didn't they do their job?"

"Brad, the people who made that hit were pros. Even if San Antonio police had posted five cops, the same thing would have happened, except that they would all be lying in body bags. Fortunately, in this case, the cops were not injured. One was downstairs in the cafeteria and the other was hit with a stun gun and then drugged. That hit was executed to perfection. Now I am nervous. If they can breach security and pop two people like that right under the noses of local law enforcement, then maybe we are not safe here anymore. I think we need to move you and your family to another location as soon as possible."

Brad sat there reflecting upon what he had just heard. He took a few seconds to respond.

"Are you OK, buddy?" Jim asked.

"Yeah, Jim, I'm all right." Brad took a deep breath and looked out at the beautiful lawn. "It's just that I thought that this whole nightmare was over, but it is beginning to look like that's not the case. I think that whoever took those guys out, and I have a good idea of who it was, did so because they represented a potential risk that information would be divulged." Brad looked Jim squarely in the eyes. "Well, I am in the same situation. My testimony, coupled with what I have turned over to the SEC, will be devastating to Rick Less and the accounting *bandidos* once this thing goes to court. What do you suggest?"

Before Jim could respond, a heart-stopping sound came from inside the house. *KA-POW! KA-POW!* Brad and Jim dropped to the ground. Jim pulled his model 22 Glock .40 caliber pistol out of his shoulder holster and chambered the first bullet.

"Stay down!" he told his friend as he crawled across the wooden deck which Fritz had constructed. Jim approached the back door entrance and quickly stood up, keeping his back to the wall. He reached over and quietly opened the door, still keeping himself out of harm's way. With his weapon drawn Jim inched into the house, scanning the rooms robotically. Suddenly, a strange odor grabbed his attention. He sniffed several times, like a rabbit might do, but was still unable to identify what the smell was. It smelled somewhat like the sulfur from gunfire, but it had a funky kink to it. He continued his cautious approach through the den. There was no one in sight. Once again Jim smelled the air, but this time he inhaled deeply. *Something is burning,* he surmised.

FBI agent Lisa Benedetti appeared silently in front of him. Jim motioned to her to make her way into the kitchen. She entered through the hallway and Jim through the den. They eased into the kitchen, and there before them was a horrendous sight.

"Oh, no!" remarked Lisa.

Jim stood there shaking his head.

The two FBI agents bore witness to the charred remains of two eggs which had exploded and were strewn all over the kitchen.

"Yuk!" Jim complained as he looked at the stinky mess. He turned toward the back window. "Brad, we have a situation in here," he yelled.

Brad came charging into the kitchen. "Not good," he said. The three went about cleaning up the eggs. As they were performing this unenviable task, Liliana walked into the kitchen. "Ooohhh, what stinks?"

Jim, Lisa, and Brad turned around all at once and looked at her. Suddenly, Liliana covered her mouth. "Oh, no! My eggs! I left two eggs boiling while I went upstairs to watch cartoons," she said.

"Indeed you did, young lady," Brad scolded gently. "The water must have completely evaporated, and then the eggs were heated so much that they exploded."

Liliana giggled. "Cool!" she exclaimed with fascination.

"Not cool, Liliana," Brad said. "You could have caused a fire. In the future, if you are cooking something in the kitchen, stay close to what you are doing."

"OK, Daddy. I'm sorry."

"That's all right, Love. I just want you to learn from this. Now, help us clean up this egg-traordinary mess."

"Oh, Daddy," Liliana said grinning, "that is pretty lame."

"Egg-xactly. That joke stinks as badly as these eggs," Jim added.

Lisa smiled and shook her head while everyone joined in the laughter.

After they all had cleaned up the kitchen and opened the windows to draw out the stench of the exploded eggs, Jim and Brad returned to the backyard deck to finish their conversation.

"Like I was saying, Brad, the thing that worries me is that I don't know whom I can trust right now. Someone on the inside—either at the Bureau or the local police, is feeding the bad guys intel. That hit in San Antonio was evidence that we have a leak. I am going to wait until Lisa Benedetti and Tom Vincent come back tonight, and then we are going to move you, Sofía, and the kids somewhere safer than this house early tomorrow morning. Talk to Sofía and make sure she is ready to move at the break of dawn tomorrow. Oh, and Brad...," there was a moment of silence.

"Yeah?"

"Tell Sofía not to say a word to anyone about this, not even to her sister. Remember, we leave at dawn's first light."

"OK, Jim," Brad said uneasily. *It is not over,* he thought. *Not yet.*

Chapter 27

House Calls

Later that Saturday evening, Liliana was looking for her brother everywhere. Little Michael had wandered off without telling anyone. She ran into her Aunt Isabel's master bedroom, where Sofía and Isabel were chatting on the sofa. "Mommy, have you seen little Michael?" she asked.

"Uh…no, *mi amor*, I thought he was playing with you in Claudia's room."

"No, Mommy, he isn't," Liliana replied. Then it dawned on her. "I know where he is!" she said with a proud smile. The young sleuth had solved her mystery. "He is doing pooh-pooh somewhere. He always hides because he doesn't like for anyone to see him. I'll go find him!"

Sofía chuckled light-heartedly. "OK, *mi amor*."

The petite 8-year-old went from room to room upstairs searching for her brother. She opened the door to the upstairs hall bathroom. *No, he's not in here,* she thought. Then she opened another bedroom door. *Not here, either. Hmmm…Where could he be?* She then walked into her cousin Claudia's room. No sign of her little brother. She peeked in the closet. *Nope. He is not here, either.* She even looked under the bed—no little Michael. She put her palms on the floor and began to stand up, and all of a sudden she saw a tall figure dressed in a black bodysuit and black ski mask crawling through the window in Claudia's bedroom. She was terrified and took off like a jack rabbit running out of the room.

The intruder jumped at Liliana and managed to grab her leg, causing her to trip and fall on the floor. She landed just like she had landed hundreds of times in her Saturday morning Hapkido grappling class: on her forearms with her head turned to the right to prevent her from banging her head on the floor. As the intruder came toward her, she braced herself on her forearms and left knee and kicked backward with her right leg with everything she had in her 60-pound frame. The heel of her foot landed squarely on the nose of the intruder who was caught completely off guard by the kick.

Never in a million years would he have expected this little girl to hit him with something like that kick, but it just so happened that this particular little girl was a red belt with four years of martial arts training. She had been prepared for this moment by investing hundreds of hours practicing "strike and flee" techniques. Although she was very frightened, her training took over without her consciously thinking about it.

The intense pain inflicted by the kick dazed the 180-pound intruder briefly. It had broken his nose, and blood began to pour out. His eyes were watery. *I can't believe that little girl caught me with that lucky kick*, he thought in anger. Fortunately for Liliana, that brief lapse had given her enough time to stand up and run out of the room. She ran down the hall to Aunt Isabel's bedroom screaming "Mommy! Mommy! There's a bad guy in the house! Get Daddy!"

Downstairs in the kitchen Brad was listening to a fitness channel on the small, 13-inch TV sitting on the granite countertop as he sliced the choice cuts of meat into strips for grilling. Fritz had taken his mini-van to the grocery store to pick up some steak sauce, flour *tortillas*, chips, soda and other assorted goodies for the cook-out. He would be back in a few minutes. Then, the two of them would charbroil the meat for *fajitas* on the grill outside. *Umm-mmm, delicious!* Brad's mouth watered as he thought about the tasty *fajitas* he would soon be eating.

He could faintly hear the screams of Liliana, but he shrugged them off thinking that she was playing chase or some similar game with little Michael and Claudia and that those screams were playful sounds of glee. While he was making the last cut on the meat, he glanced into the window above the sink and saw the reflection of a tall individual dressed in a black outfit tiptoeing through the den. He thought to himself: *Am I imagining things?* Brad turned around to see that the image was real. The intruder had Brad in his pistol sight ready to pull the trigger.

KA-POW! sounded the gun shot which was followed by a thud as the body fell to the floor. Just then Jim Dove emerged from behind the entrance hall, his model 22 Glock .40 caliber pistol smoking at the barrel. He looked to the left at Brad and nodded his head stoically, as if to say "you owe me one, buddy." There was no need to utter a word; Brad knew he would have been history had it not been for Jim's expert marksmanship. Jim pulled out his model 27 baby Glock back-up, which had been strapped to his ankle, and showed it to Brad. "Do you still remember what I taught you back in Atlanta?"

"Yes," Brad replied. "Toss it over."

Jim threw the pistol over to Brad in an underhand motion. Brad chambered the first shot. Lisa Benedetti and Tom Vincent came running into the entrance hall, each from different points of the house. "There's been a security breach!" Jim said firmly. "Tom, go upstairs and watch the family. Lisa, you stay down here with me. Take the back entrance."

"Roger that," Lisa said coolly as she dashed toward the back door.

On his way up the stairs, Tom saw the intruder whom Liliana had kicked in the nose making his way down the hall. The intruder was still feeling the pulsating pain of his bleeding, broken nose. The dark upstairs hall lit up in a blaze of gunfire as they both fired several times at each other simultaneously. When the shooting had stopped, Tom looked down at the pain in his left shoulder. He had taken a bullet! Fortunately, however, Tom's gunfire had forced the intruder to seek cover in one of the bedrooms, preventing him from reaching the master bedroom where Sofía, Isabel, and the children were.

At precisely that moment three more intruders dressed in black came exploding into the house through two different points of entry on the ground floor. Two used a shield to break through a window, and the third kicked in the back door. FBI field agent Lisa Benedetti was walking down the hall when she saw the intruder at the back door. Lisa put two rounds in his chest and one in his forehead. The intruder fired a couple of rounds from his M-16 rifle which struck the wall next to Lisa's face, sending splinters into her cheek. However, her gunfire was the last thing the intruder heard in this world. He was dead before he hit the floor.

Lisa peered outside to see if there were any more of them lying in wait. She saw a shadow which looked like it could have been another attacker about 100 feet away and fired at him. He was in the middle of the yard and had no cover except for the darkness, which proved to be enough even for the expert marksmanship of the former Olympic medal winner. He turned around and ran toward the wooden fence, disappearing completely into the darkness.

"I'm going after one of them!" she yelled as she jumped off the steps and sprinted after the would-be assassin.

* * * * * * * * *

Back in the house, the two intruders that entered through the window together came in guns a-blazing. They pinned Jim down behind a wall. Jim immediately dropped to the floor to give his adversaries little to shoot at through the wall. Brad was still in the kitchen. *I must help Jim out of this jam and get upstairs with Sofía and the kids. I need to create a distraction.* Brad looked around and found one of Isabel's glass vases next to the kitchen counter. Keeping his head down, he carefully reached over to grab it while gunfire continued in the den.

The kitchen had an open counter area with a full view into the den. Brad launched the vase like a grenade over the counter and in the general direction of the two intruders near the window. It would have hit one of the intruders in the head if he had not caught a glimpse of it in the corner of his eye and moved to the right, which is exactly what Brad needed. Brad stood up and fired the baby Glock pistol thrice directly at the other intruder. The first two shots missed, but the last shot hit the intruder in the upper right chest. He screamed in pain and Brad ducked behind the counter again.

The gunfire stopped for a few seconds. Brad yelled out, "Jim, I hit one of them." Jim stuck his head out from behind the wall and fired two rounds into the same intruder Brad had hit, sending him staggering backwards and then to the ground. Upon hearing Brad's voice, the other intruder began making his way toward the kitchen. Brad was the mark, the primary target. That is where the attention needed to be focused. Anything else was a distraction. The intruder advanced cautiously.

There were two entrances to the kitchen: one from the den and one from the entrance hall. Logic dictated that Brad exit through the entrance hall. Access to the kitchen from the den was quicker and more direct, so Brad thought the intruder would be coming from there. Still crouched over, Brad walked briskly over to the entrance hall, clutching his weapon tightly in his right hand. By the time he reached the entrance, the intruder was standing there in front of him. *Wrong choice!* Brad never slowed down and hit the intruder at full force in the mid-section, tackling him to the ground. The fall knocked the wind out of Brad's attacker, but it also caused both men's guns to go sliding across the marble floor, into the dining room, and under the sofa.

Brad looked at his attacker, completely covered in his tight, black outfit. Only his eyes were visible. His eyes were the cold, heartless eyes of a man who could kill you just as easily as he could look at you. For an instant, both men were frozen, each one thinking about what he should do. That instant seemed like an eternity. Brad's heart was pounding. He looked at the attacker. The attacker looked back.

Suddenly, the intruder launched himself at Brad and they began grappling. Jim Dove came running in, but the two men were so entangled that Jim could not fire at the intruder without risking shooting Brad. The intruder grabbed Brad in a headlock and squeezed hard. Brad would not be able to break the force of that hold, so he went for the weakest point of the grip: the pinky finger. He grabbed the right pinky finger of his attacker and pulled it back all the way, snapping it like a twig. The intruder screamed violently in pain.

Brad then moved behind his attacker and, with his right arm, secured a choke hold around his attacker's neck. Then he reinforced the choke hold by grabbing his own right arm tightly and pulling back. At the same time, he slipped his legs around the waist of the intruder, maneuvering into a leg scissors hold on him. Brad squeezed like a python against his attacker's waist and his neck. Within a few seconds, Brad had squeezed the life out of the assassin.

"Thanks for the help!" Brad said to Jim with playful sarcasm as he kicked the deceased murderer off him and came to his feet.

"Well, you looked like you had things under control. Besides, you guys were moving around so much, I couldn't get a shot off!"

Brad reached under the sofa and grabbed the baby Glock pistol. "I'm going upstairs with Sofía and the kids," he said.

"Go! I'll stay down here with Lisa and cover the ground floor."

On the stairs leading up to the second floor, FBI field agent Tom Vincent was still exchanging gunfire with the bloody-nosed intruder whom he held at bay in one of the upstairs bedrooms. However, he was running out of ammo and did not have a spare clip on him.

Sofía, Isabel, and the children had sought refuge in the bathroom of the master bedroom. The children were lying down on the floor of the tub. Isabel and Sofía were lying down on the bathroom floor. At that moment Sofía realized that she had forgotten all about her son. "¡Dios mío!" She looked into the bathtub at Liliana. "Where is little Michael?"

Liliana reported the bad news: "I don't know, Mommy. I looked all over for him, but I couldn't find him."

Sofía looked her sister right in the eyes and said she was going after her son: "*¡Mi hijo! ¡Voy por mi hijo!*" She stood up and ran to the bedroom door.

Isabel told her to stay there with them. "*No, Sofía, no te vayas. ¡Quédate aquí!*"

Sofía stopped at the door and looked back at Isabel. In her eyes was an anger and determination that only a mother could feel at a moment like this. She opened the door and started down the upstairs hall.

"Sofía, get back!" yelled Tom Vincent. "I have one of them pinned down in the bedroom in front of the stairs." Sofía froze at the door. Now she began to fear for her daughter who was back in the bathtub. She was torn between running through the storm of gunfire to look for her son or staying there to protect her daughter.

By that time Brad had made it to the place where Tom was positioned on the stairs. He looked at Tom's shoulder and saw that his white cotton shirt was soaked with blood. Tom saw the concern in Brad's face. "Don't worry about it, Brad. The bullet went in and out cleanly. I'm OK." Tom noticed that Brad was carrying a pistol. "I need some cover to get closer to that guy. How many rounds do you have in the mag?"

Brad released the pistol magazine and saw that he had six bullets left. "I have six in the mag and one in the chamber."

"Good," Tom said. "On my mark, start firing." The bloody-nosed intruder apparently had taken advantage of that time to change the 10-round clip in his 9 mm pistol. He shot one bullet that glanced off the wall right next to Brad's head, causing Brad to duck his head quickly. Tom fired back. Then he looked at Brad: "Now!"

Brad opened fire on the bedroom entrance, forcing the intruder to back up a few steps deeper into the bedroom. Meanwhile, Tom charged up the steps and took a better position against the wall right next to the bedroom door where the attacker was. He looked over at Sofía still standing in the doorway to the master bedroom, put his index finger over his lips to indicate for her not to make a sound, and then motioned with his hand for her to move away from the door. She did as instructed. Brad lowered his head and crawled up the stairs one stair at a time, just like a leopard inching across a heavy tree branch just before it springs on its prey.

The gunfire had stopped, and now all was quiet. The smell of gun smoke permeated the air. The intruder realized that there was no escape through the bedroom door and that the good guys' guns outnumbered him by at least two-to-one. He looked back at the bedroom window and decided to make a run for it.

Tom was within a foot of the entrance to the bedroom door. He looked over at Brad, pointed at himself and then pointed into the room. The message was unequivocal. Tom was going in.

By now Brad had gained a vantage point on the stairs from which he could fire at the intruder in the bedroom. Ever so carefully, the bloody-nosed intruder eased the window upward. Tom moved inside the dark room and dropped to one knee, ready to fire at will. He saw the shadow of the intruder trying to escape through the window. "Freeze! FBI!" He said. The intruder continued out the window, so Tom fired a round directly into his posterior. The intruder yelped like a dog, rolled down the roof and then fell on the ground. When he landed, he heard his elbow crack. The injured intruder slowly got up and hobbled off into the darkness, angrily cursing his broken nose, the bullet in his rear end, and his broken elbow.

Brad entered the bedroom and ran right up to Tom.

"He went out through the window," Tom announced with frustration. "I'm going after him."

"OK. I'm going to stay with my family. I think that they are all in the master bedroom."

"All right."

Tom ran down the stairs and saw Jim patrolling the area. "Jim, one got out the back. I'm going after him."

"Go! I'll stay here and make sure there are none left."

Outside in the back, FBI field agent Lisa Benedetti was running at full speed after the intruder she had seen from her vantage point at the door. He was now trying to scale the eight-foot wooden fence in the back. Lisa grabbed him by the seat of the pants and pulled him off the fence. He hit the ground and rolled over a couple of times. When he looked up, he was staring at the barrel of a .45 caliber pistol ready to fire. "FBI! You are under arrest! Don't move!" The defeated, six-foot tall man stayed on his knees and put his hands over his head. He knew the drill.

Lisa grabbed her handcuffs and threw them over to her prisoner while she kept him in her gun sight. Her arms were fully extended and locked, and she was clutching her pistol firmly with both hands. "Cuff yourself! Do it now!" The man slowly began to put the handcuffs around his left hand. He was moving at a snail's pace, trying to buy as much time as possible. All of a sudden Lisa heard a sound over to her right. It was Tom Vincent, who had run down and tackled the intruder who had escaped out of the upstairs bedroom window.

When Lisa turned back to her prisoner, she saw that he was coming straight at her. She did not have enough time to react. The weight of his 200-pound body collided against Lisa's athletic, 130-pound frame, dislodging her weapon and sending her flying back several feet and onto the ground. The attacker bent over to pick up the weapon, and Lisa swept his feet out from under him with a low circle kick. She made an attempt to get the gun, but the attacker stood up and faced her, blocking the path to the gun. He glanced downward to get a visual on the gun, and Lisa launched a round-house kick to his face which connected solidly, knocking a couple of teeth loose. The Kenpo black belt followed with a stepping side kick to the stomach, which doubled the big fellow over. Then, before he realized what was happening, she did a jumping front kick, landing the kick squarely under the attacker's jaw. The speed of the kick generated so much force that it had the impact of an uppercut by a heavyweight boxer. The attacker went stumbling backward and landed flat on his back.

Lisa quickly recovered her service firearm and put the big man back in her sights. She picked up the handcuffs and again threw them at the man, who was very groggy from Lisa's potent kicks. "Now," she said with determined anger, "like I was saying, put the cuffs on! Or perhaps you would like to play some more with Lisa." The attacker shook his head and groaned. He then cuffed himself and lay down on the ground. He wanted no more of FBI field agent Lisa Benedetti.

Lisa looked at Tom, who was also cuffing his attacker. "Are you OK?"

"Yeah, I took one in the shoulder from this scumbag, but I'm all right. How 'bout you?"

"I'm fine. Let's take these two back into the house."

* * * * * * * * *

Tom and Lisa led their handcuffed prisoners into the house where Jim Dove was waiting for them. Sofía and Brad were looking frantically everywhere for little Michael.

"Son, where are you?" Brad yelled, terrified that something had happened to his son.

"They have kidnapped him!" Sofía said, bursting into tears. "Those *desgraciados.*"

"*Tranquila, mi vida.* Let's keep looking," Brad said, trying to calm his wife. "Son, where are you Big Guy?"

After all the commotion had come to a halt, the door to the small closet in the laundry room opened slowly. Jim and Lisa drew their firearms and pointed them in the direction of the door, ready to fill the intruder with bullets. Once the door had swung wide open, little Michael stepped out. Poor little Michael's eyes were puffy and red, sure signs that he had been crying profusely all through the noise and gunfire. Brad ran over to little Michael, picked him up, and held him tightly. "Son! Thank God you are all right!"

Sofía showered the small child with motherly kisses. Her tears of desperation changed to tears of joy. "*¡Mi amor, mi amor, qué bueno que estés bien! ¡Bendito sea Dios!*"

Brad could see that his son was still suffering from the trauma of the harrowing experience. *It must have been terrifying for him*, Brad thought to himself. "Let's walk, son," he gently told little Michael as he began walking around the house with his son in his arms, caressing his back gently. Sofía walked along with both of them, stroking little Michael's hair affectionately.

Brad interjected: "Son, were you in that closet all the time?"

"Yes, sir."

"What were you doing in there?"

"I had to go pooh-pooh, Daddy, so I went in dere," he said timidly, still visibly shaken. "I couldn't go pooh-pooh, so I stayed in dere. Den I heard de *pow pow pow pow* from de guns. I got scared and so I did lots of pooh-pooh. You wah see?"

Brad smiled and patted his son on the back. "No thanks, son. I'll take your word for it. I must admit that a couple of times during all the *pow pow* I almost went pooh-pooh myself."

"Are de bad guys dead, Dad-dy?"

"No more bad guys, son. Now I am going to take you upstairs and change your diapers, and then you and your sister are going to bed.

"OK. I love you, Dad-dy."

"I love you, too, son, more than life itself."

FBI field agent Jim Dove was on the phone with Austin's finest. "Send a couple of black and whites out here immediately. We need ambulances as well. We have an officer injured." He then called his supervising officer back at the FBI in San Diego. Lisa Benedetti was on her cellular phone briefing her boss who was working late at the Austin FBI office.

When Jim had finished apprising his boss of the situation, he walked casually over to Brad with a smile on his face as if nothing had happened. Brad, who could not believe how calm and collected his friend was, said, "How did they know we were here?"

"I don't know. Did you call this house when you were on the run?"

Brad thought intensely for a minute. "Yes, I called here from the Cozy Border Inn in McAllen, but I did not use my cell phone. I used the hotel phone."

"That ex-NSA guy probably discovered the call by breaching the phone company's database. Those guys are unbelievably resourceful."

The Controller, still holding his son in his arms, nodded silently, realizing that he had made a serious error in judgment by calling Isabel and Fritz's house. "Jim, how can you be so relaxed after something like what just happened here? I'm still trembling. It all happened so fast! Look, Fritz has not even returned from the store yet."

Jim patted Brad on the back so hard it made Brad stumble a little. Little Michael smiled, thinking his daddy was playing a game with him. "It was just a house call, Bradley, my boy. The bad guys make house calls, too. Didn't you know that?"

Brad smiled. "Oh, yeah. I received a house call in Monterrey. Those Mexican police got off easier than these guys, though. What was the final body count?"

"Four are dead and two are being taken into custody."

"Hey, Jim, I appreciate your taking that guy out when he was about to pop me."

"All in a day's work, Bradley," Jim said nonchalantly. "No thanks necessary. I'll tell you one thing. These assassins were not expecting to find us here. I believe that they thought that they were going to waltz right in here, take you out, and then disappear into the night just like what happened at the hospital in San Antonio. These are probably the same guys that made that hit."

"I imagine that they were quite surprised to find the FBI here," Brad said with a smile.

"The element of surprise can be lethal, Brad," Jim said confidently. "They thought they had the advantage when they came in, but then they realized they had walked into a den of lions."

"Jim, how did you learn to shoot like that? You did not miss tonight. Weren't you in the Special Forces?"

Jim chuckled. "Yeah, I was attached to them, but I was an intel weenie."

"Well, how did you develop your marksmanship?"

"Brad, I'm from Georgia, my boy, just like you. Our state motto is 'pack heat.' Didn't you know that?" Jim said with a wink of his eye. They both laughed.

* * * * * * * * *

Shortly afterward Fritz walked in the front door holding two large paper bags of groceries. He proceeded through the entrance hall and into the kitchen. "I'm ba-a-a-a-a-ack," he said merrily as if he were singing. "I have the steak sauce, the chips….the…*tortillas*…" Fritz froze and looked around him. His lower jaw dropped, and his bags of groceries fell to the floor with a crash.

There was complete silence. Sofía looked at Brad and had an expression as if to say, "Uh-oh!" Jim Dove, Tom Vincent and Lisa Bennedetti looked down at the floor, trying to fight back their smiles. Everyone knew how much Fritz adored his house.

Fritz surveyed the broken glass, the bullet holes in the wall, the blood on the floor, and the general disarray of his most treasured possession. He was struck with horror. "MY HOU-OU-OU-OU-OUSE!" he screamed at the top of his lungs. There was a pause, and his voice became very feeble: "What… happened… to… my…house?" Poor Fritz was dumbfounded. His dream house, the object of hundreds of hours of his loving labor, was a wreck. He looked again at the bullet holes in the walls and the blood on the floor and very weakly said, "Somebody killed my house."

Jim, Lisa, and Tom could not contain themselves any more and erupted in laughter. Brad bit his tongue to keep himself from laughing, but it was a futile effort. After the terror of tonight's events, he needed a good laugh and joined in with the others.

Fritz stood there paralyzed from the shock. Fortunately, at that moment Isabel walked over to Fritz and put her arm around his waist. "Breathe, *bebé*, breathe and walk." They started walking to the doorway leading to the backyard porch. Fritz stepped over the bashed in door and heard the glass crunching and crackling beneath him. "Keep walking, *bebé*," she coached. "*Muy bien*, just keep breathing and walking."

Once they were outside, Isabel sat Fritz down and explained to him in detail what had happened. She knew her husband, and she knew how to quell his anxiety. That conversation changed Fritz's whole perspective on the situation. After the shock of seeing his house shot to pieces had subsided, Fritz realized how fortunate he was that none of his family members had been hurt or, worse yet, killed. He thanked Jim, Lisa, and Tom for their heroic defense of his family.

"That's my job, Fritz," Lisa said. "By the way, you do have homeowner's insurance, don't you?"

* * * * * * * * *

Around 11 p.m. Jim Dove was sitting at the table with Brad, Sofía, and Lisa Benedetti. Together with Fritz, they had just finished repairing the back door and windows with make-shift materials that would have to do for the night. Tom Vincent had been taken to the emergency center of a local Austin hospital to have his shoulder treated. Although he had lost some blood, his prognosis was very good. Fritz and Isabel sat down in the den to watch late night TV. The children were asleep upstairs, oblivious to anything outside of their wonderful world of deep slumber. All their stomachs were full of delicious, char-broiled *fajitas*.

Jim shifted the subject from harmless chit-chat to serious business. "Brad, right now we have two units of Austin police assigned to the area: one right outside this house and another unit a few houses down. They will be on duty all night with relief coming at 7:00 a.m. tomorrow. I have requested a 'G-ride' to get us out of here tomorrow at the first light of dawn. Once we get on the road, I'll fill you in on where we are going."

Brad interrupted, "What is a 'G-ride'? That sounds sort of kinky." He looked at his wife and winked. Sofía looked back at Brad and flirtatiously elbowed him in the side.

Jim replied, "It's a 'Bureau ride,' you know, a 'G-sled,' an 'OGV.'"

Brad, now more confused than ever, looked at Jim with a funny expression. "Thanks, that certainly clears it up for me," he teased.

Lisa jumped into the conversation: "An 'OGV' is an 'Official Government Vehicle.' We will use a governmental car to transport you tomorrow."

Jim shook his head and smiled. "You civilians really crack me up. What would you do without us watching your backs?"

Brad lifted his coffee mug and declared: "Speaking for these civilians here tonight, we would be in bad shape without you watching over us." He toasted Jim's tea glass, and they both said "¡Salud!" simultaneously and smiled.

Jim continued, "With these lowlifes we took in tonight, at least the two that are still breathing, we should be able to get some good information about their operation."

"How are you going to protect these guys so that they are not executed like those two in San Antonio?"

"Are you bonkers, Bradley? These baboons tried to whack federal officers. They are going to spend some serious time in jail. We'll do everything we can to make sure that they don't make bail due to the nature of their crime and the other events surrounding this case. So," he concluded, "in the meantime we are going to be extracting information from them. We might even get them to cut a deal with us by fingering the head honchos behind this."

"We know who those head honchos are," Brad said with great certainty.

"Proof, Bradley, we gotta have proof. With these baboons, we are in good shape in that department."

Brad turned back to the two federal agents. "I am eternally grateful to you for what you did for us tonight. I shall not forget your heroism."

"Just seeing your goofy face in one piece is enough for me," Jim said jokingly. "Go get your beauty sleep. Unlike me, you need all you can get."

Chapter 28

Lying in the Darkness

"My manhood has been taken from me!" Victor cried out to the doctor as he lay in his hospital bed at Monterrey's Santa Cruz Hospital wallowing in self-pity. Dr. Emilio Velázquez had just broken the news to him that he would be paralyzed from the waist down for the rest of his life. "Look at me! I am pathetic!"

"*Señor* Reyes, you are lucky to be alive," Dr. Velázquez said in an effort to lift Victor's spirits.

"Alive?" Victor challenged the doctor. "You call this being alive? I'm only half alive! I can't play sports anymore, I can't go dancing…I can't even do something as simple as walk. *¡Caray!* I am not even in control of my own bodily functions. Worst of all, never again will I be able to make love to a woman!" He looked up at Montserrat apologetically. "I mean, make love to my wife."

Montserrat stroked her husband's face gently, trying to show her empathy. "Victor, I still love you. The physical part does not matter. We can still be very happy. You will see, *querido*."

Victor looked up at his wife. At this point in time he was so utterly miserable that he could not stand it, but he nevertheless had to recognize that he was exceedingly fortunate to have such a grand woman as Montserrat by his side. The womanizing 53-year-old knew very well that he was totally undeserving of such a woman. His eyes became teary as he grabbed her hand and kissed it. She leaned over and kissed him gently on his smooth, bald head.

Unfortunately, it was not long before the hot-headed Victor returned to his ranting and raving. He cursed the ineptitude of the medical staff for not having done better work during his operation in spite of the fact that Dr. Velázquez was one of the finest neurosurgeons in all of Mexico and had assembled a team of specialists that would have been fit for a king. When it became apparent that Victor was not going to calm down, Dr. Velázquez directed the nurse to administer a sedative. The calming effect of the medication pulled Victor back into the peaceful world of sleep.

Around 11 p.m. that night Victor was awakened by the sound of a nurse moving things in his room. By the time he had fully regained consciousness, he saw her walking out the door and closing it quietly. Then it occurred to Victor that this night was Saturday night. Normally, on a Saturday Victor would have invented some fabrication to tell Montserrat so that he could go out on the town, either with one of his *muchachas* on the side or with the *compadres*.

Those days were gone forever. The *Don Juan de México* had been dealt a cruel blow which was almost too great to bear. He leaned over and saw Montserrat asleep in a chair close to his bed with her arm stretched out and touching him. Such a simple act of this noble woman shamed him and caused him to shake his head in disapproval of his life so foolishly squandered. While he had held himself out to the community to be an honest businessman and a loving family man, in reality he was a miserable wretch who had hurt so many people and engaged in so many acts of corruption that the bridge between the two worlds was immeasurable. Everything he had ever done was for self-gratification. Lolita was right: he was indeed a sanctimonious old hypocrite.

Overcome with despair, he began to entertain thoughts of ending it all that night. Perhaps the only factor that prevented him from departing this world was fear. Victor had lived such a wicked life that he had no doubt about where he was headed when he passed on, and he was in no hurry to get there.

Now, lying in the darkness, Victor had to come to terms with his own depravity. He had always been a corrupt, greedy man. The only difference was that before he had never had to slow down long enough to face reality. His life had been a dark string of events in which he went from one self-gratifying moment to another one. In his present condition, however, he would no longer be able to drown out the man he really was with alcohol and women. Now, he would have the rest of his life to reflect on the sins of his morally impoverished past. Justice had been served.

* * * * * * * * *

"Give me a status report, Buzz," COOL Harry Allen said in a voice which hinted of concern. He knew that all had not gone as planned because he was just now hearing from Buzz Blakely. It was before 7:00 a.m. on Sunday. Harry, still in his burgundy silk bathrobe, was walking in his back yard with his Irish setter Sean tagging along at his side. In one hand the silver-haired executive held his cell phone and in the other hand he carefully held a steaming hot cup of coffee.

"I'm afraid that I do not know, Mr. Allen," Buzz said with a considerable degree of embarrassment in his voice. "The team has not checked in yet." Buzz was obviously frustrated by his inability to deliver results.

"Nobody has checked in? We know nothing?"

"I'm sorry, sir. I have been trying to call them at the designated rendezvous point, but there has been no answer."

"What about Jenkins?"

"We are in the dark on that as well, sir. Local officials and the Feds are keeping a lid on this. Our sources can't get any intel."

"Brad Jenkins," said Harry with dismay. "Never would I have thought that it would come to this. He was our shining star in Monterrey; the man with the golden glow." Harry laughed weakly and shook his head. "Now, however, he is nothing but a pesky fly that keeps getting into the milk, the butter, the potatoes, in everything, and we can't seem to swat him. No matter how big our fly swatter is, he manages to avoid it. If we don't swat him soon, he is going to ruin the whole dinner."

"Your message is perfectly clear, sir," the very proper Buzz affirmed.

Harry took a deep breath and exhaled slowly. "Well, Buzz, I guess you were right about Brad Jenkins. He is not just an accountant."

There was a moment of silence as Harry reflected on the situation. Not only was the silver-haired executive exasperated, but now he was quite worried. "Keep me apprised of the situation, Buzz," he said with a sad calmness. "We cannot take action until we know what the status is. Let me know something no later than 9 o'clock tonight."

"Yes, sir. I'll do just that."

"Good-bye."

"Good-bye, sir."

I need to bring Rick up to speed on this, Harry thought to himself. *This has gotten way out of control.*

What should have ended quickly in a Monterrey jail has grown into a problem of enormous proportions and is threatening the entire plan.

* * * * * * * * *

That same Sunday morning was a sleepy one in Austin, Texas. It was hard for Brad to get out of bed while it was still dark, but he knew that they had to be on the road at the crack of dawn. The last few days had pushed him to the limit and drained him almost to the core. He desperately needed to rest. Brad could smell bacon and eggs cooking downstairs. Jim Dove, a man of many talents, was acting chef that morning. The inviting smell was enough to charge his batteries and get him moving.

After a delicious breakfast, it was time for the Jenkins family to move to a safer place. They said their good-byes to Isabel, Fritz, and their kids, who were surprised to see their kinfolk leaving so early in the morning. "The next family gathering we have will be at *your* house, Brad," Fritz said jocosely. "I'll bring the dynamite."

Shortly thereafter, Jim Dove, Brad, Sofía and the children took off in a "G-ride" toward a destination to be determined en route. The G-ride was an unmarked 2004 Chevy Suburban with government plates. Following closely behind in an unmarked 2003 Ford sedan were FBI agents Lisa Benedetti and Patrick McGillis, a replacement for Tom Vincent. Jim indicated that Tom was continuing to recover nicely in an Austin hospital.

As they rode along the highway, Brad's mind drifted back to his road trip with Benjamin "Skunk" Carter. He recalled what a jolly fellow Skunk was and remembered the lively conversations they had on that trip. *I will not forget his kindness*, Brad vowed to himself.

Just after they had merged on to I-10 about 80 miles outside of Houston, Jim's cellular phone rang. He had modified the default tone and chosen one that sounded like those big, black, old-fashioned phones from the 1940s. It was a brief conversation; however, by the expression on Jim's face, Brad knew that it was good news. When Jim hung up, he turned to Brad. "Do you remember the guy last night that Liliana kicked in the nose?"

"Yes, and if memory serves me correctly, he also took a shot in his greater gluteus and broke his elbow," Brad added.

"Yeah, that's the one. Well, we just got a big break. His name is Greg Ferguson, and last night he copped a plea. He sang like a choir boy in exchange for leniency by the U.S. Attorney's office for his cooperation. Ferguson named Buzz Blakely as the one who orchestrated last night's foiled executions. The Austin police have just picked Blakely up at the Austin airport. He was coming from El Paso. They turned him over to our people in Austin who are questioning him as we speak."

"That is great!"

Brad and Jim continued to chat about the events that had unfolded within the last 12 hours. By the time they arrived in Houston, it was around 11:30 a.m. and they were hungry. Jim asked Liliana and little Michael what they wanted to eat, and the response was a loud and resounding "hamburgers!" They ordered through the drive-through window of a local burger place and then continued on to an undisclosed hotel on the west side of Houston. There they would remain incognito until further notice.

* * * * * * * *

By now the FBI knew that it was on to something big. Brad's incriminating research on AMA Electric International coupled with the murders had elevated this case to a top priority. Accordingly, the Bureau flew in one of its most talented and persuasive interrogators, Bobby Sebastian, to go to work on Buzz Blakely at the FBI office in Austin. Bobby was a folksy fellow with a natural talent for communicating, even in the most stressful of situations such as this one. His objective was clear: squeeze Buzz Blakely until he divulged the names of the top brass behind this operation.

"Buzz, we know you are not the one calling the shots on this," Bobby said sympathetically. "I must warn you, though, that Greg Ferguson, one of the pros sent to take out Brad Jenkins last night, has rolled over on you. He named you as the contractor, Buzz. We now have you on conspiracy to murder. You can get life for that. Are you prepared to do life in prison for the people you are protecting?"

Buzz remained silent.

"Your men fired on federal agents, Buzz. One of the agents was hit and has been hospitalized," he continued in his down-to-earth manner. "Listen to reason. You are in a bad position. Your cell phone records link you to the killers and to executives at AMA on the days of the murders."

Oh, no! Buzz thought to himself. *I cannot believe that I did not erase the electronic trails of my telephone calls. Now they know about all those calls I made to Harry Allen. I was going to clean that up as soon as Brad Jenkins was out of the picture! Brad Jenkins. We just never were able to get our hands on the ever elusive Brad Jenkins. Trying to catch him was like trying to catch a shadow.*   Now Buzz was worried, but he continued to feign a stoic indifference.

FBI interrogator Bobby Sebastian kept the pressure on Buzz. "Two cops were killed last week, Buzz, by your men. Last night more of your team tried to kill federal officers. Look, if you keep up this tough guy act, I know that the attorney general will go after the maximum penalty. Think about it. Harry Allen was the one directing you, wasn't he Buzz? Everything points to him."

Buzz just looked straight ahead at the wall.

The FBI interrogator decided to approach the issue from a different angle. "Think about your wife, Buzz. She is 64 years old. Don't you think that she is going to need you as the years go by? You two have been married for 45 years. In today's society, that is quite an accomplishment, which I personally admire. My own parents have been married 41 years. That takes commitment and love. If you are sent to prison for twenty years, what will happen to her? It does not have to be that way, Buzz. If you work with us, I can guarantee you that you won't do time. The U.S. Attorney's office has given me the authority to offer that to you."

In an amazing show of control under pressure, Buzz continued to sit there quietly in the cramped, hot, stuffy interrogation room, staring into oblivion. Streams of sweat were rolling down his temples, a detail that did not escape the trained eye of Bobby Sebastian. The skilled interrogator stuck his head out the door. "Larry, would you bring us two sodas, please." He turned toward Buzz. "What kind of soda can I get you, Buzz? Would you like a Coke?"

Buzz simply shook his head.

"We know that you were just passing along those orders, Buzz. You're just the messenger. We don't want to crucify you. We want the people orchestrating this. I urge you to think about this logically. Some of your boys were caught and then murdered in San Antonio. What do you think is going to happen to you? Do you think that whoever is calling the shots is thinking about your welfare? Of course not! They could care less. They are thinking about this conversation that you and I are having right now. Even if you tell us nothing, they won't believe you. They are probably planning when and where they are going to put a bullet in your head, Buzz, just like those guys we caught and held in San Antonio. No, I'm sorry, not one bullet—five bullets. They shot each of your boys five times. If we let you walk out of here, you won't last 24 hours on the street. I can't help you, though, if you don't help me. Do the smart thing for yourself and your wife. We need your cooperation to go after the people pulling your strings."

There was no response from Buzz. Bobby was quickly realizing that Buzz was going to be a tough nut to crack. Buzz did, however, have a level head on his shoulders. He knew that he had let the $350,000-a-year salary Rick Less was paying him cloud his judgment, but it was more than that. Rick had given the aging ex-NSA agent an opportunity when others would not even take his calls. For Buzz, that counted for a lot and had ingrained in him a fierce sense of loyalty to Rick.

However, that allegiance would only go so far. He was quietly digesting every word that this Fed was telling him, and he fathomed that perhaps Bobby was right. The Fed had struck a painful note when he talked about the potential impact on Buzz's wife if he were to go to prison. Yes, he also conceded the fact that Harry might send some more professionals to execute him, or even to kidnap his wife and hold her as leverage. Both Harry and Rick were ruthless. Buzz had seen how they turned on Brad, a man with a sterling reputation who was beyond reproach.

While on the surface Buzz presented a strong front, it was just an illusion. Beneath that cold, hard surface was a molten mass of red-hot turmoil and indecision. How long could he continue this façade?

* * * * * * * * *

The next morning was a Monday. When Harry arrived at work, he marched into the office of Rick Less and shut the door.

"What's the problem?" Rick said as he looked up from his desk where he was reviewing some paperwork which the legal department had left on Friday for him to sign.

"Buzz Blakely was supposed to have called me no later than 9 p.m. last night, but he never called. That is not like him. The guy is so dependable I can set my watch by him."

"That is unusual," Rick concurred. "Maybe he became ill or was involved in an auto accident. Something could have come up. Give him a call."

"I tried. There was no answer on his cell phone. It was turned off."

Rick sat back in his burgundy leather chair and put his hands behind his head to stretch a bit.

"Another thing," Harry added, "when I talked to him yesterday morning, he had not heard from the team he sent to Austin to take out Brad Jenkins. Now, I am really worried."

"Don't worry, Harry. Remember, even in the worst case scenario, they have nothing on us. All we have to do is stay calm and play the innocent victim."

"Look, Rick. You and I have known each other for 20 years. I'm not one given to worry. I plan well and execute to plan on everything I do so that I don't have to worry. We have not been executing well on this Jenkins problem. In fact, it's a disaster. He should have been taken care of by Victor's crew in Monterrey. I cannot believe that it has reached this point."

Just then, Rick's executive assistant Alice Starnes interrupted them on the intercom.

"Rick, Bryan Taylor is on the phone. He says it's urgent."

"Thank you, Alice. Put him through."

"Yes, Bryan, what may I do for you?"

"Rick, there are five people from the SEC waiting at the reception desk to see me! What's going on?"

"The SEC?"

"That's right."

"Well, handle it, Bryan. Whatever it is, you can handle it. That's your department. Just stay calm and collected. You remember our conversation at the cook-out, don't you?"

"Yeah, sure, I remember," Bryan said, notably worried. "OK. I'll see what they want and follow back up with you."

"You do that."

Rick hung up the phone and looked at Harry. "Bryan worries me. Sometimes he is so weak. He told me that the SEC has just shown up at our doorsteps."

"What? The SEC is here?"

"Yes," Rick said with concern. "Look, make sure he gets Sarah out of here now."

The silver-haired King of Cool nodded his head, stood up, and headed back to his office at a brisk pace.

* * * * * * * * *

Bryan soon learned that the SEC team was there to review the books of AMA Electric International. The SEC accountants and lawyers set up camp in one of the conference rooms and spent the next three weeks pouring over the accounting records. They were joined by FBI agents on their third day.

At the end of the three weeks, their review corroborated the information that Brad submitted concerning the $400 million overstatement of sales plus other accounting irregularities. The interagency task force had sufficient evidence to indict several mid-level managers on financial fraud charges. Nevertheless, they needed more evidence to get Rick, Harry, and Bryan—the accounting *bandidos* actually responsible for this lie to the American public. They had incriminating testimony from some of the frightened managers, but they needed written evidence as well to ensure that they would prevail in court. Accordingly, they delayed some of the indictments. All the interviews indicated that superstar CEO Rick Less was the one driving the deceit.

The FBI paid a surprise visit one Sunday afternoon to Bryan Taylor's house. When Bryan realized who his visitors were, he nearly fainted. The FBI agents explained to him what they had discovered with respect to Brad Jenkins' investigation and testimony as well as what their own people had confirmed working in conjunction with the SEC during the three-week field work they had just completed on-site at AMA. They also talked about the attempts on Brad Jenkins' life and the murder of Eric Johnson.

At first Bryan dismissed their murder allegations as absurd. It was incomprehensible to him that Rick and Harry would go to such lengths as trying to murder Eric or Brad. In the back of his mind, he knew that the two unscrupulous executives were guilty of "cooking the books," but murder? That was out of the question.

However, after a telephone call that they arranged over a secure line with Brad, who was still hiding out in Houston, Bryan realized that their allegations were true. The wavering CFO did not trust the Feds, but there was one thing of which he was certain: Brad Jenkins did not lie. From one accountant to another, Brad attempted to convince Bryan to come clean and cooperate with the Feds. Bryan put up a good front during the visit by the FBI, never admitting to anything, but once they left, he fell into despair and became frantic.

That night Bryan sat alone by an antique lamp in his living room until the wee hours of the morning, contemplating his fate. The CFO felt betrayed. He had never been privy to any of the information about killing Eric Johnson and trying to assassinate Brad. Now he was beginning to worry about being linked with all the violence and murders. He was not a violent man, just a greedy, spineless accountant.

Yes, he thought, *I have made a mistake by falsifying the accounting records and lying to the American public about AMA, but I thought the situation would be temporary. I thought we would be able to cover it up when the market demand came back—exactly as we planned it—replacing the fictitious sales with legitimate sales as the economy improved. That just has not happened, unfortunately, and now the fraud itself has grown out of control.*

Rick's master plan never included killing people. Murder? No! That was crazy! If they killed Eric

Johnson and tried to kill Brad Jenkins, what would they try to do to me? Certainly, I know more than Brad. I don't trust either Rick or Harry. I never have, really. They are so manipulative. At least I have Sarah. Without her help, I would not be able to keep order in this fraud. As long as she is with me, she will protect me.

He finished his third glass of Scotch and rubbed his eyebrows. *What about my people? The Department of Justice has already indicted three of them! They will go to jail while Rick and Harry go free! They are good people. All they did was follow instructions, and now they may take the fall.*

Turning on the antique lamp sitting on the wooden table next to his chair, his eyes were drawn to a picture of his wife of 17 years, Lee Anne. She had no idea what was going on at AMA. Just the mere thought of her finding out about his deplorable crimes brought him great shame and sorrow. How would he be able to face her? How would that impact her career?

Then, he pulled out the business cards of the FBI officials that had visited him that very day. Brad Jenkins had given them enough information to indict his people. What were his people saying to the Feds? How much more did the FBI and SEC know than what they revealed today? He stared at those business cards for a long, long time.

* * * * * * * * *

On Monday morning Bryan retained a lawyer. After a lengthy three-hour counseling session, upon advice by his attorney they decided to approach the FBI officers that had visited Bryan yesterday. During a meeting that afternoon, Bryan's attorney had skillfully negotiated an attractive deal for his client given the circumstances.

Bryan was to plead guilty to conspiracy to commit fraud and would agree to help prosecutors pursue other cases in exchange for extreme leniency in his sentencing. In addition, he would be absolved of any connection to the murders. Bryan owed much of his change of fortune to his good friend Sarah.

Bryan explained to the FBI and the SEC that in order to keep things straight between actual sales and falsified sales, the CFO kept his own set of books to account for all the falsified sales. These detailed records were written in a small, thick notebook with a black binder he fondly referred to as "Sarah." It was the only written document linking him to the crimes and abounded in contemporaneous references to instructions from CEO Rick Less. Without this book, he would not have been able to maintain the necessary order over what was real and what was falsified in the fraudulent web of deceit.

Throughout the entire period in which he and the accounting *bandidos* were perpetrating the financial fraud, Bryan kept Sarah locked securely in his office in a secret safe. Only Rick Less and Bryan had access to this safe. No one else knew of the safe except for Harry Allen and Buzz Blakely. On the first day that the SEC arrived at AMA's corporate headquarters, Bryan had taken Sarah with him and locked her in his bank safety deposit box.

The federal agents were elated to have this piece of evidence and the testimony of the CFO. Now, they had everything they needed to go after superstar CEO Rick Less and the King of Cool, Harry Allen.

Chapter 29

A Universal Truth

From his suite at an undisclosed Houston hotel, Brad turned on the TV to catch up on the latest news.

"*AMA Electric International CEO Rick Less surrendered to the FBI Thursday morning. Less faces criminal charges stemming from a $600 million accounting fraud that has engulfed the electrical products manufacturer. According to sources within the FBI, Less pressured employees at AMA to overstate sales by $400 million and to reduce expenses by another $200 million using what the Securities and Exchange Commission calls 'accounting hocus-pocus.' The high-profile CEO was also charged with civil fraud charges by the SEC, including conspiracy to commit securities fraud and filing misleading information with the US Securities and Exchange Commission.*

"*The investigation also claimed that Less misled Wall Street by giving investors expectations of double-digit growth during a weak market in which other electrical product makers were posting poor results. During his administration, the celebrity CEO allegedly demanded that subordinates meet his unrealistic profit expectations by doing 'whatever it takes.'*

"*Less was led away in handcuffs from his plush corporate office in Atlanta to a federal courthouse to face criminal charges related to the company's accounting scandal. Through his lawyer, Less declared* *adamantly that he knew nothing of any accounting misrepresentations. Instead, he alleges that he was misled by his subordinates. He said that he always trusted that the numbers were prepared properly. As CEO he claimed that he did not keep track of the details but instead operated 25,000 feet above the trenches managing the company. Shareholder lawsuits allege Rick Less gained more than $38 million from selling a large amount of his AMA stock, about 40 percent of his holdings, over the last 12 months, indicating that further charges related to insider trading could be forthcoming.*

"An arrest warrant has been issued for AMA's Chief Operating Officer, Harry Allen, who has been given 48 hours to surrender to the U.S. Marshals Service, according to the Justice Department. In addition to civil and criminal charges related to the accounting fraud, Allen has also been indicted on conspiracy charges related to the deaths of five individuals, including the former AMA Vice-President of Internal Audit Eric Johnson and two McAllen, Texas, police officers.

"According to reliable sources, the head of AMA's corporate security, Buzz Blakely, has agreed to testify against Allen and Less in exchange for immunity from prosecution.

"Former AMA Chief Financial Officer Bryan Taylor has pleaded guilty to two counts of conspiracy to commit fraud and agreed to help prosecutors pursue other cases.

"A federal court official, speaking on condition of anonymity, said the grand jury heard evidence last week from witnesses, including some of the former AMA mid-level managers who have pleaded guilty..."

Brad turned off the TV and sat there on the couch with his wife. None of that was news to him. The Controller had been privy to all the ramifications in the case in which he would be a key witness. He looked over at Sofía and said, "There is one universal truth that has been true since the beginning of time: You reap what you sow."

"*Sí, mi amor,*" Sofía said with her beautiful smile. "Sooner or later, your sins of the past have a way of catching up to you. That is an undeniable reality in life."

* * * * * * * * *

In Ciudad Juárez the first shift was ending at one of the hundreds of maquiladora plants operating in that amazing industrial city. While most of the workers were getting on the buses to return to their homes after a tiring day, one of the newest and most dedicated workers was making her way to the training room to attend her company-sponsored *preparatoria* class to finish her high school education. The lovely Lolita Loya was the first one in class. She had faithfully completed her assignment and was eager to learn more.

Two weeks earlier, from an undisclosed hotel in Houston, Brad had contacted María de Jesús Ponce, the Manager of Human Resources for a large and growing *maquiladora* plant in Juárez. María had worked with Brad before and held him in high esteem. As a result of her conversation with Brad in which he explained Lolita's situation, María had contacted the Latin beauty in Monterrey and offered her employment as an HR assistant working for her in Juárez.

Not only did María secure gainful employment for Lolita, but with her extensive social capital in this "city of maquiladoras," María also managed to secure employment for her father and brothers in Juárez. Upon Brad's recommendation, María had also introduced Lolita's mother, *la Señora Aurora Loya*, to the director of one of Juarez's orphanages so that *Señora Loya* could

continue with her good work in making this world a
better place. Honoring Brad's request, María never told
Lolita who had interceded on her behalf.

Within time María would sign Lolita with a local
modeling agency so that she could embark on a part-time
modeling career as well. With such a full plate, Lolita
had very little time for a social life. That was fine with
her, though. After her heart-wrenching break-up with
Victor Reyes, she had merely endured life. She vowed to
herself that she would never again make the mistake of
falling for a married man. Now, Lolita was beginning to
live life once again.

* * * * * * * * *

"Stop yelling at me," the saucy Paco Delgado
jokingly said to his stomach as he patted his round belly.
"Help is on the way." Paco grabbed his car keys and left
the office to go get a quick bite to eat.

The pudgy Paco got in his car and took off down
Romero Highway. *Today I guess I will go to Heriberto's
Hamburgers in honor of Brad Jenkins*, he thought.
*Things have not been the same without Bradley. I miss
toying with him. He was always such a good sport about
it. Come to think of it, Bradley was the only person
around here with enough self-confidence and humility to
allow me to poke fun at him. Everybody else is so touchy.
As much as I needled ole Bradley, I could have become a
master tailor. Hah! Hah! Hah! Paco, you are too funny.
You need to get an agent and move to Las Vegas. Think
about it: fame...fortune...wild women...no more
deadlines...all the booze I can drink...wild women..
going to bed at 4 a.m. and waking up whenever I wanted
to...no more Sarbanes-Oxley documentation...wild
women...*

Within ten minutes Paco was walking into Heriberto's Hamburgers. He walked up to the counter, and the cashier turned away from the fountain drink machine to greet him. Paco's jaw dropped to the counter and his eyes almost popped out of his head. Standing before him was a vision of loveliness that he had never seen before at this restaurant.

"Welcome to Heriberto's," said the gorgeous cashier. "Would you like to try our new 'Big Beef Burger' made with a pound of ground beef?"

Paco just stood there drooling over this beautiful girl.

"Sir? Would you like to place an order?"

The irreverent *chaparrito* shook his head. *Get a hold of yourself, Paco*, he thought to himself. *Come on, lay the ole Paco charm on her.* "Yes, I would like to order, uh..." he looked at her name tag. "Zulema. My, what a pretty name that is. Yes, I'll take the Big Beef Burger. Give it to me hot and juicy with lots of sizzle!"

"Would you like fries and a drink to go with that, sir?" the blonde bombshell asked.

"Sure, give me a Coke. No, make it a Diet Coke. I'm in training right now."

"*Muy bien, señor.* What event are you training for?"

"You."

The blonde vixen just gave him a look which indicated that she was not impressed with him and continued to gather his food.

"Wait a minute. Zulema, what is a beautiful girl like you doing flipping burgers in a joint like this? You should be a model or a movie star."

Zulema smiled, revealing her bright, picture-perfect teeth. She liked the sound of that. *Maybe this goofball is an agent or has some contacts that could help me*, she thought.

"Whoa! Hang on a minute!" Paco reached into his shirt pocket, pulled out his sun glasses, and then put them on. "You just about blinded me with that beautiful smile!"

The blonde vixen laughed. "Are you a talent agent?"

"No," Paco replied. "I am a business executive."

"Oh really," she replied, intrigued by the possibility of Paco's being wealthy. "Do you have your own business?"

"No, but I will soon," the feisty Paco lied nonchalantly.

"Are you rich?"

"Well, let's just say that I'm not poor," Paco said as he blew on his knuckles and then rubbed them against his chest trying to be suave and debonair.

"Are you rich?" Zulema asked again with her sultry voice.

"Not exactly…"

"That'll be 45 pesos," she said abruptly.

Paco handed her the 45 pesos. "Hey, when you get off, why don't you and I get together so that we can pursue this discussion further?"

"Next!" shouted Zulema.

"Hey, take it easy there, gorgeous. I just think we need to hook up and get to know each other…"

Zulema leaned toward Paco and said softly and discreetly, "Look, sir. I'm a realist. You are neither rich nor famous, and you certainly are not good looking. Therefore, I have no use for you. If you think that I am going to spend the rest of my life flipping burgers, dropping fries and waiting on fat little jerks like you, then you are a fool. This job is only temporary until I meet the right person. Come back and see me when you are a multi-millionaire." Then, she pulled her head back and stood up straight. "Next!"

"Ouch! Who let you out of the cage this morning?" Paco said as he grabbed his Big Beef Burger, fries, and drink and headed toward a booth to sit down and sulk.

Chapter 30

¡Qué Hermosa Vista!

Brad awoke to the rhythmic sound of the ocean waves and the smell of salt water. The Jenkins family had rented a villa at a Cancún resort nestled on the shore of the alluring Mexican Caribbean Sea. Brad opened the sliding glass door and walked out to the patio, which was about 20 yards from the ocean. The turquoise blue of the crystal water had a hypnotic effect on Brad, and the irresistible appeal of the waves beckoned him to come immerse himself in the natural beauty before him.

Brad felt Sofía's arm slip around his waist and her chin come to rest on his right shoulder. She was equally awestruck by the view. "*¡Qué hermosa vista!*" she said slowly in a wonderfully relaxed voice. "The view is absolutely glorious. There is no other place more enchanting on earth than the crystal blue waters and white sand of the Caribbean."

Brad turned around to face her. It was the first time he had seen her so tranquil in quite a while. Sofía then opened up her oversized, white beach robe to reveal a brand new, white bikini. It was a striking contrast to her beautiful, *morena* skin. She looked like a dream. "Yes, I agree with you. *¡Qué hermosa vista!*" Brad said approvingly as he cast his eyes upon his wife. The two of them snuggled closely out on the patio of the villa for several minutes, lost in the moment of the magical Mexican Caribbean.

Sofía looked up at her husband, flashed that beautiful smile, and said, "You're so cuddly, like a big Teddy bear."

Brad stroked her back and shoulders gently for several minutes as they listened to the sound of the waves caressing the shore tenderly. Their fifteen-year marriage grew stronger with each day.

Inside the villa, Liliana reached into her little pink suitcase and put on her pink bikini bathing suit. She ran into the bedroom where little Michael was slowly waking up. Liliana gave him several nudges until he was fully awake. "Come on, Michael, we are at the beach! Let's go outside and play!"

A smile overtook the toddler's sleepy face, and he lifted himself up from the bed. They were greeted by their parents, who had just walked back inside from their refreshing gaze over the wondrous Mexican Caribbean Sea. They left the door open to the patio to be able to hear the soothing sound of the ocean waves and to allow the warm, humid tropical air of the Caribbean to accompany them inside their villa.

"Look, my signature color!" said Liliana as she proudly walked around the room in her pink bathing suit, posing as if she were a supermodel prancing on the catwalk. "I have on my bikini. It's my favorite!"

Brad looked at his petite daughter. "Sweetie, you are only eight years old. Why do you want to wear a bikini? They are generally for girls much older than you."

"Because, Daddy," Liliana said with a big grin, "if I have my bikini on and I get bored, I can play with my belly button like this. Look!" She pulled her skin around her navel so that it looked like a volcano. "A volcano!" Then she stretched her skin on each side with her two hands. "Now look! It's the evil eye!" She burst out laughing, as did the rest of the family.

"Kids," Sofía said. "Where do they come up with this stuff?"

Little Michael got up from the floor, grabbed his water pistol which Brad had filled, and then walked up to Liliana and starting squirting "the evil eye" with water.

"Whoa," Brad said trying to prevent an indoor water fight. "Let's wait until we get outside before we start playing with the squirt gun."

After a quick continental breakfast of *pan de dulce*, coffee, and tropical fruit juices, the Jenkinses covered themselves with sun screen and walked out to the white sands of the beach. Little Michael began blasting everyone with his water pistol as Liliana and Sofía screamed and ran for cover.

Brad eased into the waves. The warmth of the sun was soothing to his back and had the effect of a radiating, solar massage. The coolness of the water splashing against him and the gentle pull of the undercurrent at his feet increased the relaxing effect of the sun. He had his back to the open sea as he watched his family running around in the sand. Soon, they waded out to join him in the waves.

Liliana and Michael shouted with joy as they jumped up and down in the water. Sofía looked over at her husband and smiled. *What a captivating smile she has*, Brad thought and smiled back at her.

All of a sudden someone cried out: "Brad! Over here!"

Brad recognized the voice, but he could not determine from whence it came.

An elderly couple made their way through the waves over to Brad and his family.

"Tarnation, boy! This here water is the perdiest I ever seen! Thanks for the invite!"

Brad smiled and shook hands with his friend Skunk, welcoming him to the beautiful Caribbean. He turned to his wife. "Sofía, I would like for you to meet Benjamin Carter, the gentleman whose roadside assistance saved my life that fateful day."

"Pleased to make your acquaintance, ma'am. The name's Benjamin Carter, but my friends call me Skunk. This here's my wife Rosemary."

"It's nice to meet you both. I have heard so many wonderful things about you, Skunk," Sofía said with all the grace and charm of a diplomat.

"Mrs. Carter, it is nice to finally meet you," Brad said as he introduced himself.

Skunk looked at Liliana and little Michael, who were riding the waves. "Them there critters must be your young'uns," Skunk said. "They take after you both." He looked at little Michael. "Yeah, this' un is the spittin' image of ya, Brad. Fine lookin' boy."

"Thank you, Skunk."

After the introductions, Skunk and his wife retired from the water and took refuge from the tropical sun under a large umbrella. Sofía looked at Brad with her big, beautiful eyes. She smiled at Brad but did not say anything.

"*¿Qué pasa?*" Brad inquired innocently.

"What did Skunk mean about 'the invite'?" she asked. She knew the benevolence of her husband quite well.

"Well, I wanted to show my gratitude to him for helping me out of such a perilous situation, so I sent him and his wife plane tickets to come here to Cancún, meet the family, and…"

"*Mi amor, te amo mucho,*" Sofía said as she hugged her husband.

For the rest of the afternoon Brad, Sofía and the children continued to romp and frolic in the waves. They played on the beach and in the water until their energies were depleted. Then, they returned to their villa to rejuvenate their tired bodies.

That evening the Jenkins family met Skunk and Rosemary for dinner at the hotel restaurant. The menu included many Mexican culinary delights as well as a generous assortment of fresh seafood. Of course, the hit of the evening was Skunk, who kept everyone laughing with his side-splitting stories of the things he had seen in his forty years on the road as a truck driver. It was a wonderful evening.

* * * * * * * * *

The next morning Brad received a call from Jorge del Valle. "Bradley, please forgive the intrusion on your vacation, but I wanted to share something with you."

"Jorge, it is always a pleasure to hear from you. How are things in Monterrey?"

"Well, now that Victor Reyes has been terminated, the new COO has named me the *Director General* of AMA Monterrey. Can you believe it?"

"Congratulations, Jorge, and yes, I certainly can believe it. As a matter of fact, I cannot think of a more qualified and honorable person to lead the Monterrey organization."

"Thank you, Bradley," Jorge said modestly. "Well, my first order of business was to fire that malevolent snake Carmen Silva. She was out the door within five minutes of my first day."

"Good move, Jorge. Carmen was poisoning that entire organization."

"Well, she's history. I plan on gradually making some more changes in my staff, but I want to do so in a manner which will not be disruptive to our business.

That brings me to the nature of my call, Brad. How would you like your old job back as Controller of AMA Monterrey."

Brad smiled and thought for a few seconds before he responded.

"Would you be interested?" Jorge asked, knowing that it was a long shot, given what Brad had gone through.

"There is no one for whom I would rather work, Jorge, than you," Brad said graciously. "However, I have to think about my family, and I just do not think that it would be prudent for them to be in Monterrey right now while things are still hot. I want to allow ample time for things to simmer down before I think about returning to Monterrey."

"I understand, Bradley," Jorge said with disappointment in his voice. "Oh, by the way, I guess you heard about Rick Less getting the book thrown at him."

"Yes, I did. The only numbers he will be working with for the next few years will be the ones on the back of his government-issued orange uniform," Brad remarked triumphantly. "He got his due punishment for trying to swindle honest, hard-working Americans out of their pensions and savings."

"That's right, and the SEC also hit Rick with disgorgement. That crook will have to repay all of the $38 million dollars of illegal gains he made on his stock sales. You know that has to hurt someone as greedy as Rick Less."

"No doubt about it, Jorge," Brad said with deep satisfaction. "Unfortunately, however, the FBI has still not been able to locate Harry Allen. They feel certain that Harry and his wife fled the country as soon as Rick was arrested. The FBI has frozen his bank accounts and other assets, so the only money he has to live on is what he took with him. There is a lot of effort being invested by U.S. and international law enforcement agencies to bring him to justice. He will be apprehended in due time."

"Yes. His luck will run out one day, and then they will nab him," Jorge said confidently. "Well, I will let you get back to your fun in the sun. Please give our best to Sofía and the kids."

"I will, Jorge. *Saludos* to Zayra."

* * * * * * * * *

The rest of that week Brad spent enjoying time with his family and appreciating the moment to its fullest. From time to time, the memory of the horrible nightmare at AMA Electric International tried to seize his thoughts and rob him of the joy of that wonderful week. However, he only had to gaze upon his wife and children, and all the trauma of the past few months became something to be charitably forgotten.

Brad had always believed that there were a few brief moments in an individual's life that defined the essence of that person, trials that tested the very fabric of one's character. His experience as the Controller of the Monterrey operations of AMA had left an indelible mark on him. It had tested his belief in his duty to the American public as an accountant.

Along the way in this journey, his faith in the goodness and nobility of people was reaffirmed by the brave and exemplary conduct of individuals such as José Luis Serrano, Jim Dove, and Eric Johnson.

It was certain that there had always been and would always be dishonest, greedy people attempting to commit treacherous acts in the world of business. At the same time, that dark force of evil would be countered by the honest decency of American business people who placed living an honorable life above all else. These true patriots, guided by an unwavering sense of moral clarity, would work tirelessly to strengthen the public trust in capital markets so that our great nation would continue to grow and create jobs for Americans.

That force of honor would always be there to help protect and fortify the foundation upon which America was built: honesty, freedom of speech, freedom of religion, adherence to the rule of law, equal opportunity for all, and concern for others. Those who attacked that foundation would do so to their misfortune.

As for Brad Jenkins, the door to Monterrey had been closed. Now, a new door was about to open. Soon, in some foreign subsidiary of an American company, there would be a man of honor diligently working away in the accounting department, championing the cause of truth in financial reporting, and protecting the American public from the darkness of human depravity. The Controller would be on the job.

The End